I0749670

About the Author

Norman diPenna is a writer currently living in the Central Texas hill country. His interests include physics, metaphysics, existentialism, philosophy, history, spirituality, and the dynamics of personal relations. He seeks to write fiction which is based on these themes.

For more information please visit www.dipenna.com

In the Purple Twilight

A novel
by
Norman diPenna

In The Purple Twilight

First Edition

Legal Disclaimer: *In the Purple Twilight* is a work of fiction. All perceived similarities to actual persons, either living or dead, are purely coincidental and unintended by the author.

ISBN: 0615605095
ISBN-13: 978-0615605098 (PMI Publishing)

- to all who are seeking -

When the sun rises, and the hot dust flies,
And the creatures of the earth resume their great strife,
You, with your striving, what shall you each seek?

Bo Juyi, 810 AD

1.

At the time, I was looking for an adventure. What other young men will do to alleviate boredom, or to forget, I can only imagine, but for me this seemed to be the cure. And so, as I watched the last golf ball arch across the green expanse of the driving range, I began to think of the items that I would be packing for my trip. Not a trip really, but more of a full fledged relocation. By this time next week, I would be three thousand miles and a full three time zones westward. Good bye to the oak and the maple. Hello to the palm and the eucalyptus. Good bye to the steamy Atlantic. Hello to the cool Pacific. Good bye to dark dreary winters. Hello to never ending summers. At the western edge of the continent, where so many journeys had ended, I was hoping that mine would there now begin.

As I boarded the westward bound airplane, I could not help but invoke God's name and ask that his hand, through Bernoulli's principle, keep the plane aloft. I wanted to make a new beginning. I imagined stepping off the plane into a dazzling sunshine, and there, in the cleansing light of a new day, imagined myself awaking refreshed as from a long dream. It is always possible to begin anew, to forget one's past mistakes, and to believe that they would not be repeated. On the West Coast, I would breathe deeply the new air. What I was seeking was out there, somewhere. I would be in the City of Angels, and there perhaps benevolent seraphim might grace me with their smiles.

In Los Angeles, my practical friend Laura Goodwin, an old college acquaintance, had secured me a small apartment on the west side of town. I bought a used bicycle for transportation, and during the few free weeks before the start of classes I would ride it to the beach. The Pacific Ocean was cool, too cool for swimming, and instead I would lay on the sand listening to the waves, letting the sun darken my color to better match that of the locals. Each evening, as the sun dropped near the horizon, I marveled at its farewell display of colors, fascinated by the lingering purple hues, savoring their delicacy as another day tactfully transitioned itself into night.

I spent most of those days reading at the beach in preparation for the classes soon to commence. I had been accepted into law school at the University of the City of Angels, a radical change from my previous career in the sciences. But the thought of studying law now seemed to be the correct next step in my life. Compared to the vagaries of my former scientific pursuits, the steadier promises of a legal career offered a safe and practical alternative.

I had always been one whom people had felt comfortable to approach for advice. So why not make a profession of it? A trusted adviser, this would now be my future role in life, a trusted, and well paid adviser to other men steeped in industry and ambition. The legal profession of course is quite varied in its specializations, and I had not yet decided on the exact focus of my new pursuit. But I was certain that over the course of the ensuing year a specific niche would probably endear itself to me.

"Why not study *torte* law?" Laura had joked. "That sounds delicious."

Laura's suggestion had made me smile. But I knew that the years ahead of me would be anything but delicious. There would be many late nights and many early mornings. I suspected that I was now embarking on a journey which would have no true end, a journey of diligent service undertaken solely with the hope that, eventually, it might arrive at a life well spent.

But all of that lay in the future. For the present, practical Laura suggested that we might undertake a quick excursion before the start of classes. There was a remote old mansion further up the coast, which was now in public hands and open to tourists. Friends had told her that it would be well worth the three hours' drive to reach it, and they had piqued her curiosity to visit it. I needed a change from my beach going routine, so I agreed to join her.

She arrived early one Sunday morning in her second hand car, second hand many times over, unexpectedly accompanied by her friend, Jenn Devaine. Like Laura, Jenn was also enrolled in the Russian studies program at the university, and, like me, Jenn also seemed eager for a quick diversion before the start of classes. I was still drowsy as we made our way out of town and northward up the coast highway. There was little traffic and I absorbed myself into admiring the California coastline, the soft rounded contours of its many golden hills, and the blue seductive waves of the Pacific, thrusting unrelentingly onto the shore.

Laura and Jenn began discussing vague nuances of the Russian language. In particular, the mysterious case of the Cyrillic letter '*R*' that had suddenly and strangely mutated, roughly four hundred years ago for no apparent reason. The cause of this was a hotly contested research topic in the Russian language studies community. There had been some unforeseen influence that had induced this disruption, but the specifics of it remained unknown.

"Paul, do you think the Cossacks may have had something to do with it?" Jenn asked me from out of the blue.

In response, I could only smile. I knew nothing of the Cossacks, nor of the particular linguistic problem in question.

"*Nyet,*" I replied shaking my head, and pushing my fluency in Russian to its absolute limit.

"Paul knows nothing about Cossacks," added Laura. "But you can ask him anything about the stars or the universe. And in a few years he'll even be an expert in yummy torte law."

I appreciated Laura's confidence in my abilities. But, in that particular moment, I cared to discuss nothing even remotely connected with science or with the law. For that moment I was content to merely find myself in the back seat of Laura's car as it sped north through the bright California sunshine. I noticed that this sunlight had a particular affinity for Jenn. Her pale golden hair seemed to naturally absorb it, and then send it back out, amplified to warmer more radiant hues. Her skin, deeply tanned, was made even more golden by it. I found myself fascinated by the lilting sound of her voice as we chatted, until, as she turned round in conversation, the gaze of her pale green eyes catching me full on, it suddenly occurred to me what an exceptionally beautiful creature she truly was.

****

We were still two miles away when, rounding a last bend in the coastline road, our mansion jumped prominently into view. Even from such a distance it was an imposing sight. Set atop its own private hill, it hovered almost a quarter mile above the coastline road. The full mass of the structure, complete with countless vaults and two soaring towers, then leapt an additional hundred feet higher into the California sky. Protected by pampered green lawns and concentric rings of precisely planted palms, the building stood boldly apart from the surrounding brown hills, shining barefaced in the bright Pacific sun.

"That's not a mansion," I remarked, "that's a castle!"

"That's *San Simeon*!" announced Laura.

"Sans Simian?" I ventured. "It has no monkeys?"

"No," she countered. "San Simeon. That's French for Saint Simon!"

To have considered Saint Simon, with monkeys or not, as a mansion was clearly an understatement. Mansions are cozy, compact displays of a bit of excess wealth. As an added flourish, a mansion could perhaps include a guesthouse, some gardens, and might be situated on a unique parcel of decorated land. The particular mansion we were about to visit was like this, but on an unfathomably grander scale.

"Well somebody certainly wanted to be noticed," observed Laura.

"A newspaper mogul, supposedly," added Jenn.

The tour guide confirmed Jenn's supposition. The fellow responsible for this castle, William Randolph Hearst, had indeed made his fortune from newsprint, during a time when America's appetite for the printed news, whether true or otherwise, had been insatiable. From this fortune had then come this castle, built to a scale which reputedly was surpassed only by that of Hearst's own ego.

Our tour guide volunteered additional mind boggling information. For example, the sheer number of rooms, nearly two hundred, was a staggering figure. There were more than fifty bedrooms alone, all spacious, and complete with private baths. There were vast halls for dining and entertaining, porticos and loggias for strolling and loitering.

There were rooms dedicated to the minutest of activities, such as waiting, or reading, or sipping tea. We passed through countless smaller rooms, unfurnished and seemingly without a purpose, all offering prominent ocean views and easy access to fresh Pacific air. Were these rooms dedicated to simply staring and breathing, I wondered?

"Everyone needs a little breathing room," I observed to no one in particular.

This remark, although not intended as a joke, managed to elicit a slight smile from Jenn, who, for the most part, had remained stoically silent throughout the entire tour. She was a cool one, not as outgoing and chatty as Laura. But, then again, Jenn did not have to be, as her irrepressible beauty spoke for her instead.

In any part of the castle I almost expected to encounter its original inhabitants, and find them, depending on the particular room, either sitting, reading, sipping tea, or breathing. But it was not to be. The castle had been deserted for most of the century now. Supposedly there had been a mistress, and a divorce, and the newspaper baron, subsequently confronted by the oppressive solitude of his remote Xanadu, had removed himself to less lofty confines.

We eventually wound our way to the summit of one of the castle's impressive towers. The tour concluded there, apparently unable to surpass the magnificent views of the castle grounds as they spilled headlong into the Pacific nearly one thousand feet below us.

"So it's true!" remarked Laura. "Life really is best viewed from the top!"

Laura then had the novel idea to snap a photo of Jenn and myself, at these lofty heights, from down below. She went back down, leaving Jenn and I to continue our vigilant watch of the blue Pacific. For a brief moment I allowed myself to feel as though the newspaper baron might have, decades ago, imagining how here, perched in solitude at the edge of the continent, he had reached the pinnacle of his own journey's end. It was in such a wistful mood that I turned to Jenn, hoping to say something profound. But as I looked into her green eyes, I was shocked to find them filled with tears.

"Are you all right?" I asked, suddenly concerned.

"Oh, it's nothing," she intoned.

"Sure, but aren't you crying?" I asked. "Why are you sad?"

"Well, it's silly really," she said shaking her head and forcing a slight smile, "but haven't you ever dreamt of living in a castle?"

This particular desire had never come over me really. Even in children's fairy tales there were always only a select few individuals who might have listed a castle as their mailing address, and I'd never imagined myself to be one of them.

"As a little girl, I dreamed of living in a castle," she offered.

"It's strange what children can imagine," I said.

"Yes, it is," added Jenn. "And sad too, don't you think?"

Jenn's tears attested to the sadness of such futile thoughts. It had been her little girl's desire to live in a castle, and, for the moment, Jenn had transformed again into that helpless little girl. But the sight of her lovely eyes, now swelled with tears, filled me with such compassion that I longed desperately to conjure a castle for her to live in. From down below, Laura signaled us to pose for her photo. We waved and smiled for the camera, and, although Jenn's eyes still gushed their tears, from such a height, it hardly mattered.

****

We reunited on the immense westward pavilion after Laura had snapped her photographs. There were still swimming pools, guest cottages, and even the remains of a hobby zoo waiting to be toured. But with the bright sun now almost at midday, we made instead for the shaded cover of the adjacent gardens. The gardens were a cool refuge, and, like the castle itself, were still meticulously maintained. Perhaps every leaf lay exactly as it might have when the newspaper baron and his entourage had strolled past them nearly a century before. I imagined those lucky few as they might have frolicked, happy in their belief that perfection could be coveted, attained, and then sheltered from an all too imperfect world.

We lingered among the garden paths for almost another hour. I immersed myself in the variety of plantings, a few of which reminded me of my own parent's smaller garden back East, but most of which were of this other world. I found myself absorbed into the garden's green womb. Only occasionally, at the garden's fringe, might one spy a glimpse of the surrounding brown hills, still coveting their lost terrain.

The green oasis produced a healing effect on Jenn, whose face then showed no trace of her prior tears. I thought of the countless innuendos of the human heart that must transpire each day, and how most are relegated into discreet oblivion. But every so often the veil does tear, and our true natures are revealed, leaving these chance aberrations to forever haunt our memories. I could not ever again look upon Jenn without thinking of the teary little girl who desperately wanted a castle.

"I'm tired of topiary," Laura finally announced. "How about a quick lunch? And then we need to start back."

We again followed her lead, but this time with noticeable haste. Our time was limited. Collectively, we absorbed the soft afternoon air, savoring it as a token memory of our last day of freedom. By this time tomorrow I would be staring at chalkboards, desktops, and reading lists half a mile long.

There was a roadside restaurant on the coast highway just south of our castle. Coincidentally, the restaurant was named *The Castle Café*. But, with its simple fare, I doubted that Bill Hearst would have ever cared to dine there. We were seated onto an outdoor patio, and, while waiting for our food, I watched the ocean breeze weave itself through Jenn's lilting blonde hair. The breeze completely exposed her face as she turned into it, and I noticed that she bore a strong resemblance to a particular actress of our day. Seemingly our waiter had also noticed, as he bestowed Jenn with appreciably more attention than on either Laura or myself. Eventually he ventured to speak.

"Say, but aren't you….*her*?" he asked Jenn with some trepidation.

Jenn shook her head and smiled. No, she was not *her*. But as the waiter retreated, the supposed resemblance to *her* did not. Other diners had followed our waiter's lead, and were now staring unabashedly in our direction. But in response, Jenn only turned her gaze to the open water, and, like Venus on the half shell, braced her composure against the wind, and sun, and pestering waiters.

"You must get that quite a lot," I remarked, "the attention, I mean."

"I do, yes," said Jenn nodding. "Unfortunately it's never from anyone that matters."

"Ever think of becoming an actress yourself?" I continued, trying for conversation.

"No. Well, yes of course," she replied.

"Jenn's mother was an actress," added Laura.

"She was," confirmed Jenn. "But it never really worked out for her…."

I sensed Jenn's reticence to speak any further on this matter and so I did not press her for details. Our conversation then moved on to concerns of the ensuing semester, continuing so even while we drove back. During that drive I lapsed into a gentle sleep, nestled comfortably in the rear seat of Laura's car. When I awoke, the day was swiftly coming to its end. To my right lay the pastel horizon, now painted in violet hues as one more day of life slipped irrevocably into our past. My thoughts were already being drawn to the next day, and the cycle of lectures, and assignments, and studying that would once again begin. As doctoral students, both Laura and Jenn had the luxury to pursue a more independent course of study. But for me, as a first year law student, I faced only a grim regimen of rote assignments, and formalized toil.

"Well, it's been great fun" I said, as my apartment came into view. "We should visit another castle sometime."

As we said our hasty goodbyes, Jenn flashed me a magnificent smile, one that left me almost speechless. It was only through forced effort that I then recovered my senses.

"Oh, and good luck with that letter '*R*' problem," I blurted out as Laura's car pulled away.

I was left standing on the now silent street, with the vision of Jenn's smile still hovering before me. I thought of the thread of my life, and of how there had almost seemed to have been none. There is indeed a standard recipe for living that we can all choose to follow. I wondered how much outside of that recipe is beyond our control, and guided by nothing more than mere chance. But then again, I had not planned to have met Jenn on this particular day, and, if not for mere chance, I would not have.

I recalled reading of a man who, since his teen years, had decided his life's choices by the indifferent toss of a coin. Which college should I attend? What profession should I pursue? Which dessert should I eat? Even, which woman should I marry? These questions had all been decided by mere chance, and, by all outward appearances, this man had apparently seemed to have lived a perfectly normal life. I wondered if my own life would have fared better had I too merely tossed a coin to decide it. Then, at least, my failures might be blamed on a coin, rather than on my own foolishness.

But I was now tired, and decided to put such thoughts aside. I drew a deep breath and let the cold evening air brace my senses. God's hidden hand had taken me this far, and surely, I hoped, it would continue guiding me a bit further. But I did indeed feel a sense of how alone, how truly alone, I now was. I listened as all around me lonely crickets chirped out their evening songs. But these were songs of hope, hoping to attract others, hoping that loneliness could be dispelled.

****

The next day engulfed me like a whirlwind. One of my reoccurring dreams had manifested itself in the night, and, as a result, I did not have the good fortune of a sound night's sleep. I suspect that most students have experienced a similar dream. But in my version of it I am at a school, usually the college preparatory school of my youth, wherein I find myself hopelessly lost and searching for my scheduled classes. I have no agenda to guide me, but arrive haphazardly at any given classroom, where the professor, distraught over my situation, sends me packing. This dream usually continues until I force myself awake, after which I do not usually fall asleep again.

And so I had again dreamed at the start of this school year. As a result, I found myself stumbling through my next day's classes, barely noting all of the fresh faces, most of which seemed significantly fresher than my own. At the end of that day, I found myself burdened with a daunting reading list on topics ranging from the history of law, to the foundations of law, to the procedures of law. Ahead of me also lay classes in constitutional law, contracts, and trial procedure. These three topics alone represented a significant workload, and I began to suspect that the primary purpose of this first semester's curricula was merely to weed out all of the undedicated players.

By that evening, my head swam with newly acquired obligations. After a hasty dinner at the student union, I embarked to a lonely carrel in the law school library. Approaching the library, I couldn't help but think of the other students I had encountered on this first day, all seemingly determined, as myself, to have the title of *Esquire* eventually affixed to their name. But the study of law is no easy undertaking. In the final analysis, the legal codes, as they are written, are a tedious homologation of contorted phrasing which, one would hope, is fundamentally rooted in a sound logic. There is little enjoyment to be found in the reading of the countless statutes and rulings that comprise the basis of our modern legal system. As such, it is hard to imagine that the study of this discipline is a matter of love. If there are lawyers who truly love the study of law, they are undoubtedly a small minority. Rather, I suspected that most of my fellow classmates, like myself, perceived the law as a means to professional respectability and a prosperous livelihood.

But the law library was a lonely enclave on that first evening, and by eleven o'clock I could no longer bear studying. I decided to declare victory for that first day, and, in the morrow, when the load of my classes would be lighter, I would recommence the chase. My thoughts then strayed to a pub outside of campus that had seemed inviting, and so I went there for a celebratory drink. I had much to celebrate after all, having now successfully completed the first day of study in my newly chosen profession.

The atmosphere in the pub was undoubtedly more festive than in the law library, but I was surprised by the large crowd. Apparently, with the entire semester, less one day, still ahead, plenty other students had opted to revel rather than to read. I squeezed myself into a remote corner with my drink, next to a loud group of students who appeared to be enjoying themselves quite well by collectively ignoring their studies.

"We're here every Monday night," one of them told me, "to celebrate the beginning of each week. We're the *Monday Night Club.*"

"Sure, but why not celebrate the *end* of each week?" I asked. "Wouldn't that be more appropriate?"

"Oh, we do that too," he said. "But that's our *Friday Night Club.*"

They welcomed me as an impromptu member of their club, and offered to buy my next drink. They seemed a harmless bunch, and, out of courtesy, or perhaps out of loneliness, I accepted their offer. I learned that they were undergraduates, now in their final year. I identified myself as a first year law student.

"Law school is fine," said one. "But all of the real money is made in finance."

"Yep, Wall Street finance," added another.

Unfortunately they were right. At that time, the great financial boom of the Nineties was in its full swing, and the Wall Street gold rush was attracting all able minds into its mines. Once there, one could make as much money as one's conscience would allow.

"We're all going there," said the first. "Make a quick killing, and then get out."

"I've heard that it's easy money," I said, "like robbing a bank."

"Yes, except perfectly legal," he corrected me.

We continued conversing, but after the first few drinks, our speech blurred into one continuous cadence of bantered epigrams. It wasn't until we found ourselves back outside, at closing time, that the cold night air began to restore my senses. I loitered about with my newly found friends, who had now promoted me to an official member of their club.

"We're going to the Asian Arts Museum," said a fellow club member. "Would you care to come along?"

I knew of the museum, and of its prized collection of Han Dynasty pieces.

"Wha's there?" I asked, somewhat bewildered. "An' besides, isn't it closed?"

"It is closed," another member said. "But we know a way in. We're going to play a joke on them. Doesn't that sound like a hoot?"

Actually, it did sound like a hoot, if but a dangerous one at that. Perhaps a younger me would have quickly agreed to go along.

"I've got some important classes tomorrow," said an older me instead. "How about I catch up with you again some other Monday night?"

As I then watched my new friends disappear into the deepening nighttime mist, I realized that much of my youth was also disappearing with them. Suddenly I felt very old, even though I was actually not much older than they. There must be a certain threshold over which one crosses in their mid twenties, after which one is no longer young. I had crossed over it several years ago, and I knew that there was no going back, especially for one, like myself, who cared not to repeat his past mistakes.

I missed the last scheduled bus for that night, and had no choice but to walk the long two miles back to my apartment. There I fell into a deep and weary sleep. The next morning I overslept and missed the first of my important classes, and I wondered if a truly dedicated future attorney would have ever allowed such a careless thing to happen.

2.

Of the long ritual hours spent in lonely library crevices, only a true student can feel a melancholy satisfaction. There is always the yearning that those hours might be more pleasurably spent in the laughing company of lighthearted friends. But, while in the company of those friends, there is always the doubt that those hours could be more productively spent in the solemn pursuit of some scholarly ideal. And so it was for me over the ensuing weeks, in the many hours past midnight, in the solace of a tomblike carrel, with the library long deserted.

But for me there were no lighthearted friends to forsake. I was indeed, truly and utterly, alone. Of course that had been my plan all along. For by traveling nearly three thousand miles to the western end of the continent, to attend this one law school, I now had no choice but to focus on this one single minded goal. But, unlike my undergraduate studies in physics, I found it more difficult to focus on the study of law. Whereas the brilliant concepts of astrophysics had freed my mind to wander recklessly through the vastness of the universe, the study of law, with its confined focus on the human condition, only left me longing for the sympathetic company of other humans.

I thought of the people that I had known throughout the years, and how so many of them were now scattered, like myself, on their own private quests for apparent self fulfillment, a symptom of our society. But then again, what else might be expected of a nation of immigrants, of descendants of peoples blessed with vivid imaginations and an over abundance of optimism? Every day we are tempted by the masking horizon, a cruel joke played on us by God in making the world a globe. He could just as easily have made it as flat as a communion host. Then, with the horizon so vanquished, we would see that in the distance there were only restless others like ourselves, staring back at us.

But of the many acquaintances from my undergraduate years, I knew of a few who had also ventured westward to the City of Angels. There was Laura Goodwin of course, but in addition, there was Jonathan Schwarzchild, pursuing his doctorate degree in physics at a university across town. And there was Dave Richards, pursuing, I surmised, the further glorification of Dave Richards.

I thought to contact either Jonathan or Dave. But it would have been at the expense of my studies, or so I rationalized. Instead it was all too easy to simply delve into yet another law book, and to forget about past acquaintances. Rather, it seemed more promising to think about the possibilities of new acquaintances, and, in particular, I found myself now optimistically thinking more and more about Jenn Devaine.

What I thought about Jenn is not easy to describe. She was beautiful of course. But it was not the type of raw exotic beauty that leaves one breathless. Instead, hers was the simple calming beauty of a lush summer night. Her eyes were clear and still, and in their easy glance I felt all the unspoken promise of that summer eve. Her lips were full and inviting, and capable of producing that awe inspiring smile. I thought of that smile quite often, and of the overwhelming promise that it ever seemed to convey. Someday, some fortunate fellow would be blessed to see that smile in each passing day. I wondered who this fellow might eventually be, and, in the late night confines of a lonely library carrel, I almost deluded myself into thinking how that fellow should eventually be me.

"*Be good. Be serious,*" I thought stoically. "*All things will of themselves become.*"

I resolved to let God's guiding hand do its work, and let my days pass in their sated ritual of lectures, and study, and sleep. I came to know more of my fellow classmates, but for the most part I only anticipated their company during the scheduled lectures. In the evenings they would transform themselves, like me, into solitary, single minded sponges, dedicated to absorbing as much legal knowledge as possible before the start of the next day's classes. So, in the pressured frenzy of that first year's studies, I resigned myself to the tacit understanding that any attention to both intimacy and solidarity was to be summarily sacrificed for academic success.

By the middle of that first semester however, I desperately longed for some familiar company. So I arranged to meet Laura for dinner one evening. When she mentioned that Jenn too might have interest, my heart leapt at the thought, and I anxiously counted the minutes until that night. But, when I arrived at the restaurant for our prearranged evening, I found only Laura, alone and without Jenn.

"Jenn's decided not to join us," Laura informed me.

I drew a deep sigh inward, feeling very much the fool for letting my thoughts run astray as they had, for letting my emotions run over my intellect. Jenn and I had spent but that one day together. What possible reason could she have for wanting to see me again? I doubted that over the last few months she had spent even a trifling thought on my account.

"She went to visit her father," added Laura. "He hasn't been feeling well lately."

"What's wrong with him?" I asked.

"Not sure. He's just old, I think."

I thought it unlikely that Jenn's father was actually ill. But I consoled myself with the notion that she had excused herself in such a considerate manner. Here was a Saturday eve, and undoubtedly a girl of Jenn's caliber would not be lacking in viable options. But still, I struggled hard to overcome my disappointment, and to refocus myself onto the evening ahead with Laura. By chance, the university's homecoming parade was scheduled for that evening, and after dinner it would provide a suitable distraction, I reasoned, to Jenn's absence.

"Oh, by the way," said Laura, "Happy Birthday!"

I smiled. It was indeed my birthday, or at least it would be tomorrow. And, while I had completely forgotten, or had not wished to remember, somehow Laura had. I strained to think of any other friend that might have also remembered. But, for the life of me, no other name came to mind.

****

Our chosen restaurant was decorated, for whatever reason, with a casual rain forest motif. Laura and I were seated next to a large potted plant, which, for the remainder of our dinner, seemed to be attacking us with one of its large overhanging fronds. I scanned the menu to see if, in keeping with the entire theme, there was not perchance an endangered species of some type being offered as the evening's entrée.

"What a disappointment," I said, "there's no spotted owl soup on the menu tonight."

"Too bad," smiled Laura in agreement. "We'll have to order the bald eagle pâté instead."

We both laughed. Laura was good company. She had a light spirit and an easy smile, and, like the old acquaintances that we were, we quickly lapsed into talking excitedly about absolutely nothing in particular. We had known each other since our undergraduate days in that stuffy old alma mater of ours back East, now seemingly so distant and so far removed. We had met there, finding ourselves enrolled in the same American literature study group one year.

Laura had quickly endeared herself to me. Throughout that particular class, she was fond of innocently critiquing our various assigned readings not as being good, nor bad, but more often than not as simply being *delightful.* Reading Mark Twain had been *delightful. The Great Gatsby* had been *delightful.* And, even while Ahab chased his whale, Laura had found immediate *delight* in the entire ordeal.

I eventually discovered that Laura approached almost all situations with such a lighthearted simplicity. In our very self important university, where most everyone else seemed to be overly fixated on complications, Laura's attitude became a comfort. There was nothing pretentious about her. I marveled many times at her unfaltering self confidence and optimism, and I often wished that some of her nature would possibly find its way into my own.

"You complicate your life too much," she would tell me.

"But life *is* complicated," I would remind her, in response to which she would only sigh.

From an early age, Laura had displayed proficiency for languages. In college she chose to specialize in Slavic languages, Russian in particular, only because of the inherent challenge that these languages presented.

As her fluency in Russian increased, she became fond of quoting ancient, supposedly wise, Russian colloquialisms, one of which she offered me that night.

"My Russian is a little rusty," I said. "What does it mean?"

"It means - *those who love you will follow you,*" she said.

This was a very interesting old saying, interesting enough that it caused me to give it a moment's thought.

"Well then," I mused at length, "it seems that no one has ever bothered to follow me."

With this remark I also offered her a smile, a half hearted one at that, which I hoped might possibly have summed up the last few years of my life.

"Jonathan told me that you were engaged after college. Is that true?" she asked.

"Well, he ought to know," I volunteered. "He was almost the best man."

But obviously I was no longer engaged. I could not refuse Laura her curiosity, but I was saddened to be drawn back to thoughts of my previous life. I was now no longer safely removed by my newly found distance of three thousand miles. I was no longer enshrouded by the cool evening mists of the Pacific. I was no longer cleansed by the scouring antiseptic rays of the west coast sun. I was now suddenly naked, exposed, and again feeling the old pains.

"But that's all in the past," I finally said with a deep breath. "You know, maybe some things just weren't meant to be."

I heard those words ring inside my ears, and immediately felt how ambiguously hollow they had sounded. There was more, much more that I might have said. But already my voice was turning distant, and I did not have the heart to provide any more details. I did not have the heart to face up to my own lack of character, to my own shortcomings as a human being. And in the final analysis, I did not have the courage to admit of my failure to give love, of my selfishness, and of my own misguided motives.

I looked at Laura. She seemed to sense my unease. She was a good friend, if not my only friend, but I felt no obligation to confide in her. In my heart I knew she was seeking answers from me, but in my own heart, so was I. From my former studies in physics, I knew of the natural order of things, of the natural tendency of the universe to fly apart. There was a dark energy driving the entire fabric of creation ever further apart from itself, and no amount of confiding could ever dissuade it from doing so.

"It's strange," said Laura as we stepped outside after dinner, "how we lost track of each other, as though neither of us had ever existed."

"Yes, it's strange how that happened," I agreed.

But I knew that, in truth, it was not so strange after all. In fact, the laws of the universe almost demanded it.

"You know, I've even lost track of Jonathan," I said.

"I can give you his number," Laura volunteered. "But what were you up to all these past years?"

"I wish I knew," was all that I could reply.

****

We stepped out of the restaurant to find the nightlife already in full swing. Over the years, Westwood Village, adjacent to the university as it was, had become popular with street performers of all types. On any given night one might easily find a magician, or a juggler, or a street clown. There were also musicians, typically at least a half dozen or so strewn along the pavement, who, along with the many stand up comedians and the occasional mime, transformed the village streets into an outdoor variety show.

Because of the homecoming parade that evening, the village streets were swelled with an abnormally large crowd. Along the parade route on Westwood Boulevard bodies had already lined up nearly five deep.

Laura and I shuffled along until we chanced across a thin spot to look through.

"I heard there's going to be a bonfire after the parade," I told Laura.

"Yes. And maybe even fireworks," she added.

"I hadn't heard that," I said. "Well, then this is going to be some night!"

We had much to look forward to, but still my thoughts strayed to Jenn. I seemingly recognized her blonde hair and slender figure at the far end of the block. She appeared attached to an especially athletic looking fellow as they both swam through the crowd. But at such a distance, and with the fading light, it was difficult to gauge if this were indeed her, or just my lonely mind imagining her. I gave my eyes a firm squint to be sure. But, by the time that I had refocused them in that direction, the vision of her was gone.

"Don't you love parades?" asked Laura.

I did love parades, and, surrounded by so many eager undergraduates, I too began to feel their excitement. Tomorrow, eleven men wearing a certain uniform would play, for honor and glory, against a different eleven men wearing a different uniform. The victors would be treated as heroes, revered as alumni, and would probably receive more adulation than any of the university's attorneys, or even physicists for that matter, ever might.

We milled about restlessly until, right on time, a loud blast from the university's marching band signaled the start of the parade. The crowd then shifted its collective gaze towards the far end of Westwood Boulevard, where the band was assembled, and where the parade floats had been staged into their correct order behind it. The marching mass of the parade then began making its way along Westwood Boulevard, en route to the university campus.

Laura and I strained for a better view as the music drew closer. When at last the band had reached us, the sound of it was deafening. The sheer size of this band testified to the prominence of the university. This was no thin motley arrangement of haphazard student musicians. Rather it was a synchronized army of marching maestros all playing with the full exuberance of their youth. I estimated at least four dozen heads in the brass section alone, playing every possible instrument, from tubas to piccolos. In the drum corps, there were cymbals, and snares, and bass drums galore. And with these also came other instruments such as xylophones and woodwinds, all marching in precision, and all flanked by a squadron of baton twirling, smiling ingénues spinning about like marionettes on a string.

Behind the band there then glided three open air automobiles carrying the entourage of required dignitaries. I recognized the university's chancellor in the first car, and the university's illustrious football coach in the second. But it was the third car, carrying the parade's Grand Marshall, which audibly caught the attention of everyone in crowd.

"Isn't that Bruce Robinson?" I murmured to Laura.

"It is," she affirmed. "And, my, but he *is* handsome!"

With Hollywood removed by only a few miles from Westwood Village, it was not unusual to see the occasional film celebrity along the village streets. But the one celebrity now floating before us had transcended far beyond mere movie star status. If anything, Bruce Robinson, over the course of a fabled career, was now revered in deific proportions.

I was a bit of a sports fan, and was well familiar with Robinson's career. He had been a star running back for the university, consistently making the All American team. During his senior year he had carried the team, almost single handedly, to a national championship. He naturally went on to a professional career, and established numerous rushing records, some of which still stood unchallenged. After professional sports he garnered roles in feature films, action movies mostly, where his larger than life presence on the big screen continued setting records, this time for theater attendance.

All eyes were now fixed on his towering figure, here in real life. He appeared to thrive, instinctively, on the generous adulation offered him. Fitted in a silk suit and a smooth tan, he rose above the crowd, and cast a confident smile into it. I was immediately struck by his physical conditioning, obvious even through the shroud of his suit, and seemingly little diminished since his former athletic years.

Robinson was not alone. Beside him sat a woman almost my age, whom I presumed to be his wife, also smiling and waving to the crowd. She was a voluptuous creature made up of curves and cheeks and curls, all packed into a pink taffeta dress, perhaps a half size too small, which struggled to adhere itself onto the contours of her form. She had the type of body which in a few years would struggle with its own weight, but, for now, imbued her with the aura of an alluring fertile goddess. My own wide eyes gravitated naturally towards her, the sight of her instilling me with the sudden urge to start a large family.

"You know, but that's not his wife," Laura confided as Robinson's car drove by.

"Is his wife ill?" I asked.

"No, she's not. She's divorcing him."

Laura, who followed the tabloids, knew of such matters.

"Then who is that with him?" I asked.

"Oh probably just some eye candy," she said with a shrug.

Robinson's companion was indeed sweet on the eyes. However, with a divorce in progress, and probably with a substantial portion of his personal wealth at risk, I wondered why he did not maintain a more discrete profile. But I suspected that for a man such as Robinson, there could be no recourse to mere discretion. He was *the* Bruce Robinson, and he simply had too much life to live. How could such a luminous star cease to shine? Even the celestial stars did not dim themselves so meekly, but only did so with one final magnificent farewell display.

****

Once Robinson's car had passed, another corps of smiling, baton twirling majorettes followed. They spun about in the ever cooling night air, launching on perfect cue two dozen glistening batons into the evening sky. The airborne batons hovered momentarily, and, as they fell back to earth, the crowd held its collective breath, dreading that one might be fumbled and dropped. But none were, and, as they returned safely into nimble hands, the crowd cheered, celebrating that, for this one moment at least, the perfection of God's universe had remained undiminished.

A battalion of spectacular parade floats then followed. Each had been meticulously assembled by gangs of undergraduates dedicated, if not overly so, towards their extracurricular activities. The parade's theme, *Great Moments in History*, had a clear academic foundation. And what better way for students to learn of history, really, than to have them construct paper mache floats depicting historic events?

I peered down the boulevard, curious for a view of the first history lesson. From my limited vantage point I discerned the outline of a large plumed hat. The hat hovered above the crowd, and as it drew closer I saw that it rested atop a somewhat portly man clothed in a cape, waistcoat, and knickerbockers. His belt and shoes were festooned with large yellow buckles. The entire figure was almost fifteen feet tall from buckled shoes up to his plumed hat.

As this particular float drew near, I also discerned a large outstretched paper mache hand, clutching a large paper mache Bible, both bouncing rhythmically as the float moved along. The Bible was being offered to a second figure, this one of a Native American, roughly twelve feet tall. In exchange, the Native American offered an ear of corn, which similarly bounced in his darker hand. The figures were both smiling, seemingly satisfied with the trade they were about to transact.

"Columbus?" I guessed.

"No, it's Plymouth Rock," said Laura. "See the corn?"

She was correct of course. The ear of corn made it obvious.

"But Columbus also had a Bible," I suggested. "And he probably ate corn."

"Well, if you insist," Laura obliged. "But that's not Columbus up there!"

We agreed to disagree. But regarding the identity of the second float, we both concurred. Standing at the prow of a rowboat, with his three cornered hat, his powdered wig, and his gaze sternly fixed towards the Hessians that awaited him on the far shore, it could have been none other than George Washington, crossing the paper mache Delaware. Behind him were eight living undergraduates, dressed in period costumes, casually rowing a paper mache boat. They occasionally smiled and waved to the crowd, leaving the boat to glide along without their assistance. I glanced at Washington, hoping that perhaps he too might smile, but, preoccupied by thoughts of the ensuing battle, he did not.

It was becoming apparent that the undergraduates had interpreted the parade's theme as "Great Moments in *American* History". As such there would be no depictions of Moses leading the Exodus, of Siddhartha suffering under the Bodhi tree, of Alexander entering Egypt, of Scipio triumphant at Zama, of Jesus on the mount, of Caesar crossing the Rubicon, of Charlemagne governing the Franks, of Mohammed summoning the faithful, of the Normans invading Britain, of Shih Huang Ti uniting China, of Guttenberg printing his Bible, of Martin Luther at the church door, of Magellan circumventing the globe, of Wellington victorious at Waterloo, of Newton devising the calculus, or of Einstein conjuring the general theory. These events were studied in American schools of course, but here on our private, self contained secular continent, still ripe with the promise of a new world, the happenings of the ancient world were casually regarded as those of a distant, lost civilization. No, this parade dealt with American history, and, as we would eventually see, with the history of California, where, on its far shore, America had come to its thrilling end.

And so, as the remaining floats passed by, we were treated to depictions of Abraham Lincoln granting keys of freedom to a grateful slave, of Lewis and Clarke happily surveying the Pacific, of the completion of the Transcontinental Railroad, and of the discovery of gold at Sutter's Mill. Until at last came the final and most extravagant float, which, traditionally, also carried the homecoming queen and her entourage into the university grounds.

At first sight, the queen's float seemed to depict a surreal vision of an imaginary world. It did not appear to be any great historic moment that I was aware of. The queen herself, fitted in flowing robes, blonde curls, and smiling teeth, stood at the helm of it on the crest of a cloud enshrouded paper mache hillock. From beneath her emerged a foaming gush of actual water, which tumbled down the hillock, through the paper mache cloud line, and into the confines of a paper mache city. The city was surrounded by the queen's entourage, each dressed as smiling nymphs. At the back of the float an enormous figure of a man, dressed coincidentally in the university's colors, stood proudly with outstretched arms. I strained to think of which great moment in history I was now witnessing.

"What is that?" I asked to no one in particular.

"That's the Mulholland float," answered Laura.

Of course, the figure towering above the parched paper mache city could have been none other than the great William Mulholland himself. Through his tireless efforts at the turn of the century, the City of Angels had secured the crucial water supplies which had allowed it to bloom in the southern California desert. Were it not for him, neither the homecoming queen, nor her nymphs, nor myself and Laura, nor the crowd around us, would have been present in this very place. Or perchance we were, then we would certainly all have been here unwashed, and very, very thirsty.

The entire production was an engineering triumph. I marveled at the intricate design of this culminating float. Some in the crowd were even moved to applause. Under the star strewn sky, the bejeweled homecoming queen lovingly smiled from atop her cloud covered hillock, while Mulholland gazed approvingly at his nascent city, now bursting with life giving water. Everything seemed perfect, until a chance gust of wind, hoping perhaps to hasten the float along its way, suddenly appeared and set off a chain of events which I will always clearly remember.

The entire crowd must have heard the shriek, even above the loud din of the university band. When the wind hit, it was of sufficient force to throw the homecoming queen only slightly, but sufficiently, off balance. The poor startled girl then tumbled down the paper mache hill, following the self same path as the gushing water. It was not such an extreme height to fall from, most likely only a dozen feet, but sufficient for her to gather enough momentum to complete raze Mulholland's paper mache city as she slid into it. The stream of water that she fell into must have been icy cold, for as it splashed onto her nymphs, they too let out a series of startled shrieks.

After the initial confusion, the queen's nymphs rushed to extract her from the ravaged city, as Mulholland looked on, mortified. At length the queen arose, drenched and dripping, but unharmed thanks to the cushioning effect of the paper mache city, now leveled and destroyed. It was pointless for the queen to resume her previous perch. So she and her nymphs continued waving, and smiling, until the float passed, undaunted, through the university gates.

****

After the parade, most of the crowd flowed into campus and towards the bonfire site. But Laura knew of another place from which to view the upcoming festivities. This other place, it turned out, was from atop the Linguistic Studies building.

"I have a key," she confided. "And the roof is always open."

As usual, Laura was right. For as we stepped onto the flat, gravel covered roof, an unobstructed view of the bonfire site opened before us. Atop the roof, a cool breeze seeped into us, and Laura drew close to me for warmth, close enough that she pressed against me. Overhead, a clear sky was bursting with the constellations of late autumn.

"It's a beautiful night for fireworks, don't you think?" she asked.

"It is. But are you sure? I thought there was just the bonfire tonight."

"There might also be fireworks," she said. "You never know."

The band played fight songs as the bonfire was lit, and the assembled students sang to the music. The fire grew, fueled, as was tradition, by the remnants of the paper mache floats that were cast into it. In future years the university's need for additional building space, and its fear of a liability lawsuit, would end this ritual. But for now, tradition held sway. The crowd cheered as the great figures of history met their demise. Into the flames went Washington, Lincoln, Lewis and Clark, and all the rest. Even Mulholland, still drenched, was unable to escape his fiery fate.

As the flames reached high into the night air, I became aware of how physically close Laura and I had become. She had rested her head against me, and, without thinking, I had begun running my fingers softly through her brown hair. She looked up, her lips slightly parted, wanting to be kissed. The bonfire below us blazed intensely. I leaned towards her, pulled her closer, and kissed her gently.

"Perhaps there'll even be a virgin sacrifice tonight," I joked.

"Yes," she said, "let's hope so."

A podium had been set up overlooking the crowd, and the university's chancellor offered a few opening remarks. He then introduced the evening's main speaker. When Bruce Robinson rose to the podium he was met with unbridled applause. Even from my rooftop view, Robinson appeared larger than life. The bonfire's light illuminated him like an ancient shaman, and, wrapped in its mystical glow, he basked in the chanting of his worshipping tribe. He raised his arms to silence the noise, but to no effect.

But eventually the cheers did subside, and Robinson addressed the crowd. I could not hear every word of his speech, but I gathered the general tone of it. He began with a story, from his years as a college athlete, and of the doubts he himself had faced prior to a particular homecoming game nearly twenty years ago.

"But I believed in myself," he announced. "I believed myself more capable than any other player on the field that day."

And Robinson's self confidence had proved correct. He set a new rushing record that day. Later that year, in a close game against what proved to be an exceptional team from Ohio, he carried his team to a national title. Robinson's on field exploits that season had elevated him to legendary status, and as the very legend now spoke, everyone seemed to absorb his every word.

Robinson kept his followers enthralled for nearly an hour. After recounting his struggles as a star athlete, he went on to tell of his experiences as a different star, a film star. Even in that arena, few believed that he could have become so successful. But again, he had believed in himself, and through sheer strength of will had in the end triumphed. In closing his speech, Robinson sought to imbue his audience with the extra worldly aura of his own success, and with his belief that victory in tomorrow's game, as in life, could be undoubtedly assured.

"And remember," he said finally, "anything is possible, if you just make it happen."

He withdrew from the podium, engulfed by the confident auspices of enthusiastic cheers. The crowd then began to disperse as the glowing embers of the spent bonfire signaled that the festivities were at an end. I wondered if it was now time for the supposed fireworks. The night air had become noticeably cooler and thinner on our rooftop, so much so that, beside me, I could feel Laura shivering.

"It's getting late," she said. "Why not spend the night at my place? It's nearby."

"In your tiny apartment?" I asked.

"Sure," she said. "Why not?"

I looked at Laura and thought of all of the years that I had known her, as a friend. Now she was suggesting another possibility, a new and uncertain one. I thought of the joyous times that we had shared over the years, and of how pure and unspoiled our friendship had been. It would have been a misfortune to lose this.

"You know, I was hoping to give you a birthday present tonight," she said.

I thought of how it might be between Laura and myself, knowing that, regardless of our intentions, there would then be no going back to our original friendship. Our current relationship, as the pure diamond which we had created, could only become flawed and diminished. I thought of Laura and of her wonderfully uncomplicated and giving nature. How could she then remain uncomplicated to me? And I thought of myself, and, if pressed to admit it, of how unworthy of Laura I truly was. In this world, there certainly existed another pure and gentle heart that she was destined to meet, and I could not presume to believe that it was my own.

"You're too kind," I said at length. "But we really do make good friends, don't we?"

"Just friends?" she asked.

"Sure, friends are good," I said. "And I need a friend."

Laura looked at me and smiled. As though on cue we held each other in a desperate comforting embrace. I supposed that she, like myself, was victim to the same longings and desires that leave one awake and anxious through the quite night. Below us the embers of the bonfire were being doused with water, and the crowd had thinned. Probably there would be no subsequent fireworks on this particular night.

On our way down from the rooftop, we stopped by Laura's desk in the Slavic language department. She wanted to retrieve Jonathan's contact information for me from her files. Laura shared her office with Jenn, and across from Laura's jumbled and overburdened desk, I noticed the somewhat pristine and uncluttered one of her officemate. Jenn's desk seemed sparse and aloof in comparison. There was a writing tablet, a book of poems by Pushkin, a few journal articles, and a photograph of a brilliantly smiling young man on horseback. The sight of this tall fellow was enough to make my heart sink. As I sought to gather a closer look, Laura appeared beside me with Jonathan's phone number scratched onto a slip of paper.

"That's Jenn's father," she volunteered, "in his younger days."

I examined the photo more closely. The young man's captivating smile especially, was the same as Jenn's smile.

"Yes, I see the resemblance," I said, greatly relieved.

I unburdened Laura of the phone number, and thanked her for it. It had been a long evening, and I was starting to feel it. Standing outside in the chilling mist, an awkward silence fell between us as we each fumbled for a pleasant way to say good night. But there was really not much more to say. I reached out to Laura and gave her a farewell embrace, kissing her on the top of her head.

"You know, I'll be studying in Moscow next semester," she said.

"All semester?" I asked. "What for?"

"For my dissertation. And yes, all semester."

She looked at me, her grey eyes asking me the same question they had asked up on the rooftop. But as I gazed into them, I could not think of Laura. My only thoughts then were of Jenn.

"I'm going to miss you," she said at length.

"Me too. But you'll be fine. You'll see," I predicted.

We departed, and as I walked towards my bus stop, the remnants of the evening's festivities were still apparent, the parade's lingering debris being tossed about by the evening winds. By the morrow, cleaning crews would have restored the village to its regular pristine state. But where were the cleaning crews that would tidy up the lingering debris of my own life, I wondered? Through the evening mist, the lights of the night's last bus appeared. I climbed on board, its only passenger, and let it carry me back to my apartment.

That night I slept soundly, but still had the strangest dream. In it I found myself wandering through windswept city streets, apparently lost and alone. Everywhere was empty, with not a friend, nor any human being for that matter, to be found. I became cold, confused, and disheartened. Eventually I came to a poorly maintained shack of a bungalow. As I approached, the door opened to reveal that the home's occupant was someone I had once known. It was Jonathan Schwarzchild, and, as I drew closer, he invited me inside, where it was well lit and warm.

3.

The next morning, still drowsy with lingering thoughts of my dream, I awoke to a phone call from my parents. They had called to wish me a happy birthday. But, being three hours behind them in the time zones, I was barely coherent enough to acknowledge their greeting.

"Twenty seven years old," my father reminded me. "When I was your age, your mother and I already had your brother and sister."

It is futile to compare one generation to another, and I was not about to try, especially on so little sleep. But in deference to my father, I sought to conjure a coherent response, hopefully something intelligent and agreeable.

"I guess those were different times," was all I could think of saying.

And indeed those must have been different times, as all times are. Perhaps they were simpler times, when existence was allowed to unfold based on an accepted preset schedule. Marry by a certain age, bear children by a certain age, do all things to a proven time line which guaranteed success. Probably, so many of my own generation wished that life could again be so simple, and perhaps life was indeed so simple, but we had simply refused to acknowledge this. There were more lifestyle choices available now as never before, or perhaps these choices had always existed, and we were now simply freer to choose them. But, at that early hour, it was pointless to engage my parents into a philosophical debate. Instead, I simply assured them that the clockworks of my life were indeed still ticking correctly.

"Don't worry," I said. "Be patient, and you'll soon have an attorney in the family."

I couldn't return to sleep after the call. Outside, a glorious day awaited me. I had planned to spend my birthday at the beach. And so, packing a light lunch, I bicycled westward the four miles or so through Santa Monica towards the Pacific. Upon reaching the coast I was greeted by a calm ocean still shrouded in morning mist, with the towering bluffs of the Pacific Palisades ever keeping their watch over the western shore.

The beach path ran for a full twenty miles in either direction. To the south, it flowed past lazy beach communities in flat, gentle curves. Eventually it led to the fabled Marina del Rey, where the yachts of the rich resided. To the north, the path coiled its way into the more rugged areas of the coastline, and eventually climbed into the Malibu hills. Straddling my bicycle, I glanced towards the ocean. I stood where so many countless others had most likely stood before me, here at the continent's end. From this point, there could be no more wanderings. There was no further allure of a farther horizon. But here at land's end, so firmly delineated on any given map, neither was there any going back.

I looked to the north, and the climb into the hills. This route would have made for a spectacular day of cycling. But I checked my legs, and they felt weak. Whether this was due to my lack of sleep, or to my lack of conditioning from the many hours spent poring over law books, I wasn't sure. But I was sure that on this day I lacked the resolve for a hill climb. Instead, I looked to the south, where the path was level and steady, and required little resolve.

This southern path bustled with people, and dogs, on their morning walks. I maneuvered my bicycle through them, sporadically, until eventually I was stalled by a man sporting a mobile telephone, still an expensive oddity in those days, and walking two large leashed Dobermans. He blocked my way, and, from my place behind him, it was almost impossible not to overhear his conversation.

"It's not about the money," he barked into his phone. "You're my lawyer, and I want you to teach those bastards a lesson."

It occurred to me that someone like this fellow might possibly be a client of mine someday. As his attorney, it would then be my responsibility, through proper legal channels of course, to teach a different lesson to a different set of bastards. Whether this lesson was deserved or not was irrelevant. Rather, I would be obligated to satisfy my client's wishes, and, for this duty, I would be highly compensated. So when I finally broke past this prospective client, I flashed him a friendly smile, to which he only responded with a quizzed look.

I eventually made my way through the crowd of walkers, and the beach path opened clear and bright before me. I was soon lost in that unique trance induced by wind, motion, and endorphins. The world streamed by as my bicycle and I became one, both of us balanced by the mystical workings of angular momentum. I streamed past the various beach communities, and with each fresh gulp of ocean air my mind cleared itself of all random thoughts until only one persistent thought, of Jenn, remained. How I wished that she might have been bicycling beside me on that particular day, with the two of us speeding forward to absolutely no place in particular.

I reached Marina del Rey just before noon, as the marina's restaurant bustled with the lunchtime rush of the leisure class. For my own meal, which I'd brought, I located a shaded area close to the docks. Along with my sandwich I savored the boats, or yachts rather, as they bobbed in their moorings, their halyards clamoring noisily against swaying masts. A steady breeze blew from the ocean, and I gauged it to be about four knots, ideal for an unhurried afternoon sail.

I dreamed of being on a sailboat again. But in this corner of the universe, where shoreline space was valued at head spinning premiums, sailing would be a luxury that I could never afford, and all of my daydreaming was bound to be just that. Still, I thought that there might be a way to sail, albeit not on my own boat. With many of these larger boats there was always a call for deckhands, especially experienced ones. I could easily man the jib sheets, or hoist a spinnaker, a small price to pay for being out on the water once again.

I walked to the marina and made my way to the management office. A man there informed me to leave my information, and he would append it onto a list they maintained for volunteer crews. But he alerted me not to expect many calls, as most of the boat owners were very particular about their deck hands.

"Do you know anyone who is a member of the yacht club?" he asked.

No, I did not. Without a referral of this type, he informed me, being chosen for deck duty might prove especially difficult, if not impossible. I stepped back outside, somewhat dejected, blaming myself for having been so overly optimistic. But, at this point in my life, optimism was the only thing afforded me, and it was too easy to indulge myself with its hopeful promise. All things were possible, I knew. But whether my dreams of sailing, or of Jenn, or of anything else, would ever come true, I did not know. The hands of the angels were ever busily at work, but whether they were working for me, who might say?

****

After lunch, I satisfied myself with a last long look at all of the lovely unattainable boats in the marina. The benign nature of the West Coast climate, and the diligent care of their owners, had bestowed these boats with eternal youth. All were unblemished and flawlessly trimmed in oiled teak and polished nickel. The boats had me again entranced, and I had embarked on yet another daydream involving sailing, Jenn, and myself, when a firm hand landing squarely on my shoulder snapped me out of it.

"Why Paul, is it you?" someone remarked.

Startled, I turned to examine the hand, and then the person attached to it.

"Yes, it is me," I said, recognizing the face. "And this is a small world indeed!"

Both the hand and the face belonged to Dave Richards. We remarked how good it was to again see each other. And we lied that, aside from our tanned complexions, we had not changed in the least since our old college days.

"I'd heard you were out here, somewhere," I said.

For a moment I was almost transported back to my undergraduate days. I hadn't seen Dave since then, and there were now five years for us to catch up on. He suggested that I join him for drinks. He had just brought his boat in from a morning sail, and he and his deck hand were about to take a late lunch on board. He led me to his boat where his deck hand, clad in a string bikini, was prodigiously exercising on the aft trampoline.

"This is Meghan Cleary," Dave said, introducing his deck hand.

Without missing a step, Meghan flashed me a broad smile.

"My name is Meghan," she said between breaths. "But everyone calls me Crystal."

While Crystal bounced up and down I was quick to notice her healthy frame, her sun blushed cheeks, and her shock of scarlet hair, now windblown and seemingly ablaze atop her head like a raging campfire. Between bounces she threw sweeping, interspersed kicks high into the air.

"This is a new routine I'm developing," Crystal informed me.

I did my best to feign interest in this new routine, but unfortunately all I could think of was her scant swimsuit, and whether it would endure the furious strains to which it was currently being subjected.

"She has lots of energy," I remarked to Dave.

"She does," agreed Dave, "and I'm going to capture it in a series of exercise videos."

He informed me that he was in the video business these days, and that his next project would be a series of exercise videos featuring Crystal herself. I nodded, wondering how he would possibly subsume all of Crystal's exuberance into a simple video cassette.

Crystal continued bouncing until the marina staff eventually delivered a light lunch, forcing her to temporarily contain her energy. I declined the lunch, but helped myself to a drink. Between sips I looked at Dave. He had come a long way since our college days, when I had known him to run the undergraduate betting pools. Since then he had apparently gambled for even higher stakes, and, from the looks of his yacht, he had seemingly won. But he gave no appearance of suffering from the depressing '*sudden wealth syndrome*' which had become so common with the current young and suddenly successful set. By all appearances he seemed extremely happy in spite of being suddenly and, without a doubt, exceptionally wealthy.

"Business is merely the art of pleasing yourself," Dave had once advised me.

And certainly, on seeing him again, now tanned and affluent, he had done just that. Over lunch we caught up on the years gone by. Whereas, for myself, there was little that I wished to recount, for Dave the past five years had been a whirlwind of activity. After college he had made straight for the City of Angels, where he began, innocently enough, with an investment in a single health club. In such an image obsessed city, this one club quickly grew into a chain of clubs, which Dave eventually sold for what I gathered to be a respectable amount.

"The smartest thing I did was to sell those clubs," Dave said.

For this sale had then launched the beginnings of his next empire. Flush with funds, he expanded his business activities. Like so many, he had at first dabbled in real estate. But, like a savvy few, he then discovered the amazing fortunes to be made from selling celluloid.

"What films have you produced?" I asked.

"Oh, health films mostly, lifestyle films, that type," he indicated, as though I were an expert on this particular genre.

"That's right, lifestyle films," confirmed Crystal, who until then hadn't uttered much.

But I was not familiar with these types of films, and so I simply nodded with the silent hope that my ignorance would not be further tested. I learned that Dave and Crystal had met as a result of these films. Crystal had appeared in several of them before going on to serve as Dave's deckhand. The next step was to feature Crystal in exercise videos. These would then spawn customized exercise equipment, meal plans, or even a clothing line, all endorsed by Crystal's ensuing star status. The key to success, Dave reasoned, was to enlist a known celebrity to also appear in these videos.

"Have you ever heard of Bruce Robinson?" Dave asked.

"Of course," I replied, shrugging my shoulders, "everyone has."

"Exactly!" whispered Dave, apparently entrusting me with his secret strategy for success.

"Sure," I replied. "But easier said than done."

However I had learned not to underestimate Dave. After his college betting pools had been discovered, his expulsion had seemed certain. But if he could have persuaded our crusty old dean of undergraduates to drop all charges, as he had, then I did not doubt that he could also persuade Bruce Robinson to appear in a trifling exercise video. There was no better testament to Dave's determination than the boat which now floated beneath us, twin hulled and boasting a full fifty foot span.

The day then drifted into late afternoon, and the ocean breeze turned noticeably cooler. Crystal, in her scant swimsuit, complained of being chilled and motioned that we should be going. Probably all of our sitting had finally caught up with her. I could only imagine the tremendous stores of energy now pent up inside her, clamoring for release. I went with Dave and Crystal as far as the marina parking lot, where we then said our goodbyes.

"We'll have to play squash again. Do you still play?" Dave asked me.

I did still play. In fact, I had even brought my racquet from back East with that exact hope.

"But I can't find a court anywhere," I complained. "No one here knows the game!"

"No problem," Dave assured me. "My house has a squash court."

I watched Dave's convertible speed off, leaving a flurry of dust and noise behind it. As the open top car drove away, the sun and wind intermingled with Crystal's scarlet mane, fanning the flames of it even further. Once the car was out of sight, I drew a deep breath and mounted my bicycle for the three hour ride to my apartment. On the way back my mind wandered. Among other things I thought of Dave's house, and that it was large enough to contain, of all things, its own squash court. It was impossible not to admire Dave, and the apparent mastery that he wielded over fickle fate. With relative ease he had shaken the tree of life, and had dislodged it of its fruits, a talent which I desperately envied.

****

After my chance encounter with Dave Richards, I focused my time solely onto my studies. The month which followed brought my first semester of law school, in a final flurry of reading assignments, to a frenzied conclusion. Afterwards, the holidays then loomed ahead and I had made no plans to spend them back East. Jonathan's phone number, written in Laura's scrawl, still called for my attention, but all the while I had found myself avoiding it. So when classes ended I instead called Laura to wish her a good trip. She would be spending Christmas in chilly Moscow, and I would not see her again until after the Soviet snows had melted.

"I've asked Jenn to look after you while I'm gone," she warned.

That was kind of her. But as the holidays passed I never did receive any calls from Jenn. Instead I found myself spending the ensuing weeks alone. I did finally get around to calling Jonathan Schwarzchild, only to be greeted by his answering machine each time. I was beginning to feel like the loneliest person on the planet when, after the New Year, another human being actually reached out to me. Suddenly, at the other end of the phone line. It was Jenn, looking after me just as Laura had asked her to. She was about to leave town, and was wondering if might wish to spend a few days before the start of classes at her father's ranch.

"Yes," I replied, containing my heart, "I'd love to see more of California."

The next day I woke up singing, anxiously anticipating Jenn's arrival. The sun suddenly seemed to be shining a bit brighter, and for once I felt that it was now shining directly onto me. But it was pointless becoming overly optimistic about my prospects with Jenn. While shaving that morning, I examined myself in the mirror - my body a bit too slight, my shoulders a bit too stooped, my chin a bit too weak, my nose slightly off center. Perhaps one could make a case that I possessed a certain eccentric appeal, but I would be a fool to assume this. It was much more realistic, depressingly realistic, to simply imagine Jenn with a more appropriate partner.

I actually breathed a sigh of relief to think that Jenn could not possibly have any attraction towards me. Her invitation was merely a sympathetic gesture, extended from purely friendly motivations. It was easier for me to think of our relationship in this light. But still, when the doorbell rang, my heart leapt up into my throat. With trepidation I opened the door, and there was Jenn, sporting her trademark radiant smile. Outside it was a glorious day and instantly all of my fears vanished, replaced instead with a calming sense of well being brought on by the sight of her.

4.

The greater part of southern California is formed of semi arid desert. Along the coast, the cool Pacific waters maintain daily temperatures within completely agreeable limits. But the interior regions are not so fortunate. Temperatures there often soar to extremes which are above any sane comfort zone. As Jenn and I made our way to her father's ranch, this inland heat became quite apparent.

Her father's ranch was situated in one of the inner valleys southeast of the city. We had driven down the coast for more than an hour before Jenn had then pointed her old car eastward to cross over the San Gabriel range. We moved into the hills and the car sputtered and choked, and billowed out gray smoke as it attempted the increasingly steeper grades. By then, the manicured suburban communities had given way to a noticeably sparser terrain. We passed through a large swath of barren land which, according to the posted signs, was designated as the Cleveland National Forest. I glanced about, wondering where all of the trees in this particular forest might be possibly hiding.

"We used to hike here when I was younger," Jenn told me. "There were still trees here back then."

Over the ensuing years, unsparing wildfires had apparently decimated most of the original stands of ponderosa pines. These fires, combined with ongoing years of drought in an already arid climate, had permanently hindered the forest's resurgence. It had already been another dry winter. And should it also prove a dry spring, the slightest malicious spark would suffice to again set the hillsides ablaze.

At the crest of the forest's main ridge stood a lone ranger's outpost, flanked by what seemed to be the last remaining stand of still living pines. Jenn brought the car to a stop there so as to give the old engine a rest. I got out and looked around. To the west was the clear boundless horizon of the Pacific, while to the east there now emerged the vast yellowed visage of an inland valley, its horizon shrouded by the undulating cover of a seemingly hot and dusty curtain.

"The town where I grew up is over there," said Jenn, pointing towards a brownish blotch in the southeast stretch of the valley.

I examined the blotch and tried to imagine Jenn as a young girl in that particular place. I am not one who is inspired by barren stretches of desert landscape, and the only inspiration which I could conjure at this point were from thoughts of Jenn growing up in that remote setting. She must have been like a desert flower in bloom, and as to how many young men there must have caught their breath at the sight of her, I could only wonder.

"What was it like growing up there?" I asked.

"Oh, quiet, lonely," she said. "Mostly I just dreamed of other places."

Jenn had spent so much of her time dreaming, and reading, that her dreams of other places eventually led her to read the works of the various romantic writers. From Eyre, to Balzac, to Stendhal, she had read them all. But there was something about the Russian romantics, and their tales of colder, wilder places, which had left her addicted to that genre of literature, and had eventually attracted her to the native language of its prose.

"Is that how you came to study Russian?" I asked.

"Yes," she intoned, almost sadly. "Blame it on Pushkin, I guess."

Her father had wanted her to pursue a business career like himself. But Jenn, like Laura, had displayed such a natural affinity for assimilating languages, that her fate was practically sealed. She had never thought of how to actually enable a living with this talent, but lately, she confessed, this had become a particular concern. Jenn seemed to lack the all encompassing intellectual drive that Laura possessed. Unfortunately, only this level of commitment would propel a long arduous career through the halls of academia. I tried to imagine Jenn as a future university professor. Certainly her lectures were bound to be well attended, especially by the many young men who had suddenly found themselves also interested in studying Pushkin.

We drove off again, and back in the car I turned towards Jenn. Her gaze was fixed onto the twists and turns of the hillside road, and, as the car maneuvered them, the warm afternoon sun scanned across the soft features of her lovely face. I could not help but view Jenn with a different perspective now. She suddenly seemed more vulnerable, more in need of kind support. Perhaps this was the unspoken bond which was developing between us. Her outer shell was lovely indeed. But inside her I suspected a heart beating a rhythm similar to my own. I felt that, like mine, hers too was another lost and searching soul.

When we finally descended from atop the last ridge, the outside temperature began to climb precipitously. The sweltering heat from the valley below seemed to overflow out of it, and spill itself over the rim of encircling hills. Down in the valley itself, the air was like a blast furnace. It only turned cooler once we had begun our ascent on the far side. The car eagerly wound its way up a series of switchbacks, it too seemingly grateful to be gulping at the cooler air.

We eventually reached the top of the eastern ridgeline, where a steady breeze blew, its temperature noticeably cooler. We then proceeded for a short distance along the ridge until Jenn suddenly veered the car onto an unpaved road which hastily plunged into a stand of towering eucalyptus trees. A stenciled wooden sign along the way proclaimed that we had entered the confines of the *Eden Ranch,* with *James Devaine,* as its *Proprietor.*

"Don't you love the smell of 'calyptus?" remarked Jenn, as it engulfed us.

We followed the eucalyptus trees deeper into the property. Their leaves rustled softly as we drove by them, tainting the air with an antiseptic essence. We moved along a downward incline until the car finally emerged out of the trees and into a wide open rift nestled into the folds of the ridge. Open terrain now stretched before us like an inviting lover. Ahead of us were the nearly two hundred acres of the Eden Ranch, gilded in the metallic hues of the winter season. Our road formed a slithery snake through a sea of silvery grass, eventually leading to a solitary house at its far end.

The property immediately impressed me as spectacular. Its sea of grass nestled into the folds of this miniature valley, the rim of it bound by proud green pines set against a lapis blue sky, made for an inspiring sight. How far away the city with its heated struggling, and the rest of the world with its countless worries, now seemed! Here was a place of serene beauty, where nothing but beauty could exist. I glanced at Jenn, and saw how she and this place were the same.

"*You will know a tree by its fruit*," I thought, waxing suddenly Biblical.

Near the house, I noticed the white outline of a horse. And beside the horse there appeared the image of a man, apparently expecting us. The horse seemed old, and, as we drew near, I noticed its drooping eyelids, sagging back line, and matted coat, all giving clear indication of advanced age.

"That's my father," Jenn pointed out. "And that's Ariel, my old Andalusian."

Ariel nudged up to our car as it came to a stop, and I suddenly found myself face to face with the inquisitive muzzle of this new acquaintance. Meanwhile Mr. Devaine peered into our car from the driver's side window. He greeted his daughter and extended a hand across to me. I reached to shake it, while at the same time trying to fend off Ariel's persistent nuzzling with my other hand.

"Nice to meet you," drawled Mr. Devaine. "I'll get that horse out of your way."

He shook my hand firmly and flashed me a radiant smile. Again I saw that Jenn's smile was his smile, and, given his long lanky build, that his daughter's lithe slender form was also his form. As I extracted myself from the car, Ariel gave me a parting prod before Mr. Devaine tied her to a nearby fence. I examined the property, absorbing the healthful air.

"Well," I announced, "this is quite a place!"

****

Jenn's father had prepared a light dinner for us. But food was inconsequential to me at this point. I felt no hunger. Rather, I was filled with the calming essence of a quiet contentment, and gratitude for the moments I was experiencing. Since arriving, a wave of warmth and well being had seeped through my body, and I was completely overwhelmed by it. After my twenty seven years of life I had found myself in this divine place in the presence of a beautiful young woman, a kind old man, and an extroverted white horse. In this place, as inconceivably incredulous for me to imagine, I no longer felt any desires, as if all my desires had been suddenly fulfilled.

Sufficient daylight remained after dinner that Mr. Devaine suggested a short hike to view the sunset. Behind the home a well worn trail meandered upwards to the northern ridge, and we filed onto it. After the long sweaty drive, it felt good to be walking again in the open air. Jenn and I quickly took the lead. Our youth gave us an advantage on this hike, but surprisingly, given his age, Mr. Devaine did not lapse far behind.

Jenn and I reached the ridgeline after an easy twenty minute hike, with Mr. Devaine probably only a few minutes behind us. From atop the ridge I looked down onto the Eden Ranch and its sprawling sea of burnished grass. From this height it seemed that I could simply dive into the lush folds of its grassy womb, and that it would gladly receive me, and lovingly nurture me for eternity.

"Look, you can see the city from here," said Jenn, pointing north.

In the approaching twilight, the distant electric glow of the City of Angels was becoming apparent. Of the countless strivings and weary struggles currently ongoing there, I could only imagine. But for that moment I put any thoughts of them aside, and contented myself solely with the divine feeling of serenity which had overtaken my own being. I looked at Jenn, knowing that any man would now gladly wish to be in my place. God has smiled upon me to have brought me here, and I almost wished that He would suddenly appear, so that I might thank him personally for this kind gesture.

It was at that point that Mr. Devaine arrived atop the ridge. I marveled that a man of his years could still manage such a steep hike. But as the rays of the setting sun diffused a warming glow onto him, he did, for a brief moment, indeed appear to be ageless. Standing beside us, he surveyed the surrounding countryside. I pointed northward toward the City of Angels, now glowing magnificently in the deepening twilight.

"Quite a sight, isn't it?" I remarked.

"Yes, the City of Angels. Fallen angels," he said shaking his head. "I haven't been there in years."

"Not even to visit Jenn?" I asked.

"No, not even for that," he confirmed.

The sky was soon drenched in the rich crimson hues of the unstoppable sunset. Various pockets of electric light beneath us began to ignite, as, one by one, the numerous communities scattered beyond the city began to glow, their lights firmly entrenched into what was once a barren desert, but now offering shining testament to the miraculous energy of unceasing humanity.

Mr. Devaine began naming the many scattered communities. He had lived at the Eden Ranch for almost fifteen years and, over that time, had watched these outpost settlements sprout and grow. Always the city had spilled its excess population into the surrounding terrain, with real estate developers ever eager to accommodate this expansion. In the bang of a hammer, they had transformed immense tracts of dry desert scrub into lush neighborhoods of manicured lawns and backyard savannahs. The nearest development seemed now but a scant five miles from the Devaine property.

"They'll be wanting my ranch soon," predicted Mr. Devaine.

"And you should sell it to them," added Jenn. "This place is too big for you."

"This place is my home," he responded. "You can sell it to them after I'm gone."

I didn't know what to make of this proclamation. But I also didn't know what to make of Mr. Devaine. There was much to admire in this old man. His stoic demeanor had endeared itself to me. He had the simple, self cultivated wisdom of a strong independent nature. Through him I sensed what the West must have been in years past, when it was still proud, peaceful, and unfenced.

As the sky above us then bled into the darker hues of the impending evening, we started our descent. By the time we'd returned, our path was lit only by the fragile rays of a silvery moon. The hidden indents of the ranch had been transported into night, and the moonlit sea of shimmering grass was imbued with a gleaming ghostlike essence. For myself, I had never seen a more surreal landscape, or one whose lush, mystic beauty felt so overwhelming.

Ariel had remained tied to the paddock fence, and while Mr. Devaine led her towards the stable Jenn and I fetched our bags from the car. I followed Jenn into the house.

"You'll be staying in the spare room downstairs." she told me.

The house was arranged as a typical bungalow, with two small bedrooms on the second floor. The spare room, tucked in the back of the first floor, seemingly functioned as both a sitting room and a third bedroom. A futon there had been splayed out and arranged into a bed. I placed my one bag onto it and looked about. The walls were hung with framed photos of a younger Jenn riding atop, or standing beside, an even younger Ariel. I scanned the photos. Even as a child, Jenn had been beautiful. But, unlike so many other beautiful children, she had grown to fulfill the early promise of that beauty.

A display case in the spare room held a collection of at least a dozen dressage trophies. There were also awards for ballet, swimming, and, of all things, ballroom dancing.

"The dancing was my mother's idea," Jenn informed me. "Do you dance?"

"No, not really," I said. "Where I grew up, it just wasn't done."

Jenn nodded, and with a parting smile she then wished me a good night. But after she'd made her way upstairs, I was still unready for sleep. Outside, there rested a soft and gentle evening, and I longed to see how the stars might shine here, so far removed from the city lights. The early winter constellations would be out in their full glory, and I longed to gaze upon my old friend Orion, floating atop the clear country air. The house had a small porch for sitting, and I made my way to it. From there I gazed towards the heavens, not even noticing Mr. Devaine, who was already seated into an old wicker chair.

"Can I offer you a drink?" he asked.

Startled, I turned around to find him, his drink already in hand.

"Care for a drink?" he asked again. "It's a good seven year old scotch."

I was a brandy man myself, but the offer of a good scotch still had its appeal. I quipped that one serving of a seven year old scotch was probably better than seven servings of a one year old one. With a laugh Mr. Devaine agreed, and he poured me a dram of it. The liquor went down smooth and easy, inviting me to drink another seven years' worth. As the whiskey's warmth seeped through me, I glanced up to locate Orion and his faithful dog, Sirius. I pointed them out to Mr. Devaine.

"Are you familiar with the stars?" I asked him.

He was, and together we ran through the prominent denizens of the winter sky. Mr. Devaine had learned of the various constellations from his father, as a form of simple entertainment in those days before television. I became more curious about my drinking companion. Over the course of several more drinks, I asked him about his father, and of his youth, for I still had no inclination to sleep, and the scotch was indeed very good. But beyond that, I wanted to know more of this tall quiet fellow, of where he had come from, of how he had come to be here, and of how he had come to father such a beautiful daughter.

****

That night I learned that James Devaine was born in the desolate wastes of southern Nevada, the son of a rancher, in a terrain not much suited for ranching. His grandfather had been a prospector who had come to Nevada during the great silver rush of the previous century. This grandfather had indeed found some silver, but after twelve years of prospecting, the jackpot lode had ever eluded him. And of the silver that he had found, it was sufficient to purchase but a few hundred acres of sparse desert scrub that afterwards provided only a meager living at best. This property eventually passed on to Mr. Devaine's father, who had no better luck with.

"My father struggled on that ranch his entire life," recalled Mr. Devaine, "for nothing."

So, when James Devaine left that patch, he knew for certain that no future could be had in it, or in the supposed underground silver stores of Nevada. In his heart he longed for a place which was not desolate, but overflowed with abundant life. He made his way to the City of Angels, which, like the rest of the country at that time, was in the full strides of the post war boom. He first managed with a few odd jobs. But eventually he found his way to a career in sales, where his tall presence, his good natured disposition, and his radiant smile served him well.

Early on Mr. Devaine was forever looking for a budding opportunity, and he found one in the then nascent, and unlikely, area of cosmetic dentistry. After the war America began to reevaluate itself, and soon discovered that it was aesthetically deficient in this particular area. The war had ended, and people wanted to smile. They wanted to smile while being photographed. They wanted to smile while greeting others. They wanted to smile while making love. They wanted the same perfect smiles which beamed out to them every weekend from the movie theater screens. They wanted to show the world that, after coping with a crippling economic depression and a horrific world war, they had finally triumphed to smile again in the victorious light of a new day.

As more and more Americans strove to achieve that perfect smile, Mr. Devaine, for his part, strove to meet their needs. He found that he had a natural talent for sales. In his case, his own naturally radiant smile became of itself an unspoken endorsement for the very products which he sold. In only a few quick years he had become the top salesman in the country's leading dental products supply company. From his main office in the City of Angels, his territory stretched throughout most of the state, from San Diego all the way up to Sacramento.

Business expanded, and he became the regional sales manager for the entire Southwest. A week after this significant promotion, Mr. Devaine rewarded himself with a large convertible touring car, a photo of which still hung on his living room wall. As a further reward, he drove the car to Nevada to visit his parents, and to vacation in the Las Vegas casinos. To his parents, their son had seemingly achieved so much in so little time, that they could only wonder about the wellspring of his business skills. Certainly, there must have been something in the Southern California air which had awakened such formidable talents in their unassuming young son.

"Business is merely the art of pleasing other people," Mr. Devaine had told them.

But once in Las Vegas, for a few brief bacchanalian days, Mr. Devaine only sought to please himself. There he became attached to a group of other young unmarried vacationers like himself. In this group was a much younger, well built woman whom he could not keep from noticing. When she too seemed interested in noticing Mr. Devaine, it was but a matter of time until Nature did the rest.

"When you first fall in love, those are the best days," Mr. Devaine told me.

Hence, the same hope that had brought Mr. Devaine to the City of Angels, eventually also caused him to marry, and to father a child. Jennifer Evelyn Devaine was born on a glorious sunlit day in the City of Angels. She was a beautiful child, and to her father, she represented the just consummation of all of his lifelong struggles.

But of the ensuing years, Mr. Devaine would not share so much. I knew full well the desperate turns that a romantic relationship could take, and so I did not encourage him to do so. We had by now drunk so much that, with but only a few sad misspoken words, the mood might easily turn maudlin. And so, I let that particular matter rest.

Only eventually, from Jenn, did I learn of her mother. She had been a film starlet, of sorts. But her movie career had never progressed into any significant roles, and, when it became clear that none were forthcoming, Mr. Devaine had opted to move his wife and young daughter to a more peaceful life on the Eden Ranch. But the serene confines of this new lifestyle proved too overwhelming for his spirited wife, and, eventually, for their spiritless marriage. Mrs. Devaine returned to the City of Angels, where she then spent the remaining years of her life pursuing her movie career, searching for it at the bottom of every gin bottle that chanced her way.

While listening to Mr. Devaine, the tranquility of the night and the melody of his voice overcame me. The many hours of the long day finally became overwhelming, and the lure of sleep began to distract me. I motioned to my drinking companion how the hour was turning late, and how I would not last much longer. So I helped him out of his chair and we both made our way into the house. In passing, I glanced at our bottle of scotch, noticing how little of it remained. Mostly likely, we had each consumed at least forty years' worth of it.

5.

In spite of the previous night's drinking, the next morning I awoke refreshed. I pushed back my hair and faced the early morning light. After making my way to the kitchen I soon surmised that I was the first one awake. So I busied myself with fixing a little breakfast, mostly for me, but also a bit extra for whoever might next arrive. My rustlings must have awoken Jenn, for she soon appeared in the kitchen doorway staring at the small feast of eggs, toast, and coffee that I had prepared.

"You made breakfast?" she asked.

"No problem," I said. "Tomorrow, you can make it."

"Oh you don't want that," she offered. "I'm a terrible cook!"

But Jenn did not have to be a good cook. Gazing at her from across the kitchen table I savored the delicate outlines of her face. With her tussled hair and sleep filled eyes, she radiated the thrilling promise of a windswept dawn. It was difficult to imagine her stooped over a glowing stove standing watch over a skillet, or of the type of man who might ask her to do so. No, Jenn did not need to be fluent in cooking, for any man would gladly speak to her regardless.

We talked between sips and bites, and, like most students, we commiserated about our studies. Jenn, in particular, was stuck. Her interest in the Russian romantics had led her beyond the Eden Ranch, but no further. Unlike Laura, she had not yet found any pressing linguistics problem to excite and drive her studies.

"Why not study law instead?" I offered. "There's always a need for attorneys."

And, in truth, as long as humans interacted, there was bound to be friction, a friction which the greasy hands of attorneys would have to lubricate. But at this suggestion Jenn only shook her head, as though her own situation was well beyond any hope. Again I saw the helpless little girl, and instinctively I reached out to her.

"Don't worry," I said, touching her hand, "I'll take care of you."

This last remark caught even me unawares. I have often been accused of having a soft heart, and I've long fought to contain it. But in that particular moment it had broken through all the ramparts I'd built around it. Suddenly embarrassed, I struggled to conjure a quick apology for my forthright imposition. But Jenn was quick to offer me a reassuring smile.

"You're too sweet," she said, "too kind."

And with that, I knew that all was well. Over the remaining eggs, toast, and more coffee I told her of the seven year old scotch which I had shared with her father, and of the even older stories which her father had shared with me. She seemed genuinely pleased that her father had found a companion, if for at least one night.

"He's so alone these days," she said. "I worry about him."

He was alone, and overwhelmed, I gathered. For after the breakfast dishes had been put away, I learned that Mr. Devaine had made a list of chores for us to do. There was work to be done, and Jenn and I had been volunteered to do it. Outside, the sea of silver grass basked in the early morning sunshine. To me the grounds of the Eden Ranch seemed perfect in their current state. However there lurked an overgrown patch out back which, according to the list, desperately needed clearing.

"I'll do the inside chores, and you handle that one," suggested Jenn.

I went out to the porch to survey the task at hand. The growth seemed mostly composed of thorny vines, firmly entrenched into an area behind the house. It seemed a straightforward matter to simply tug at the vines to pull them out by their roots - probably only half a day's work.

"Here, you'll need these," said Jenn, handing me a pair of leather work gloves.

I donned the gloves and set to work. I gritted my teeth and I tugged at my fist vine. It gave way rather easily. But I quickly noticed that this particular vine had been dead for at least a season, and had no living root to have offered much resistance. It was only when I attacked an actual living vine that the immensity of the task became apparent. I discovered that one could not simply tug at a vine to remove it. Doing so was but wasted effort as the vine would, at best, snap off in my hand or, at worst, prove unrelenting and leave me holding only a glove full of dislodge thorns.

Through trial and error I arrived at a method which consistently yielded the desired result. The best approach involved grasping a vine at its base, as close to the interred root as possible. I could then apply a sharp yank, using all of arms and legs and back to dislodge the vine and much of its root structure along with it. With this approach, the vines conceded to my determined yanking, and I furiously attacked them, as if they were the devil himself.

After a half hour of diligent effort, I paused. I was breathing heavily, and already my arms and back had begun to ache. About me there now lay the remains of almost a hundred disinterred vines, thorns and all, and I took consolation at the sight of them. But it was a small consolation, as probably another two thousand interred vines still awaited my efforts.

The remainder of the morning progressed as a constant litany of bending and pulling. At midday I paused briefly for a quick meal outside. By this time Jenn and her father had come to take note of my progress. Every joint in my body ached, and I tried to obliterate all thoughts of the remaining work with a half hearted joke.

"Seems like the remaining vines should be left in as landscaping," I suggested to Mr. Devaine.

This remark elicited a small chuckle from Jenn, but no similar response from Mr. Devaine.

"No, they all have to go," he ordered, "or they'll just grow back."

Normally I might have been offended by the directness of such a remark. But in Mr. Devaine's case such an unabashed utterance completely agreed with his character. I had come to respect his unfettered honesty, and I knew that a man of his age was at long last allowed to speak plainly, with indifference to the opinions of others.

"They've grown unchecked too long," he declared. "Do your best to get rid of them."

And with his intentions made clear, Mr. Devaine said nothing more.

"Don't mind him," said Jenn. "He loves this place too much, and he wants it to be perfect."

I agreed, but found little consolation knowing that I was now the appointed means through which this perfection would be achieved.

"But there is no perfection on earth," I reminded Jenn.

"None?" she asked.

"Well, maybe just you," I said.

Jenn smiled. It was a smile that pushed my fatigue aside, and, with a renewed spirit, I returned to work. But all too soon my entire body had turned dull with pain, so dull that I almost no longer felt it. My mind then became detached from the task at hand, which had now automated itself into a robotic sequence of bending and tugging, seemingly under the control of an unconscious reflex. Towards evening, with my work nearly complete and every ounce of determination within me spent, Mr. Devaine emerged to help. Little by little he collected all of the vines which I had pulled, and piled them into a heap. He started a small fire and worked the vines into it.

As the day then faded, only the glow from Mr. Devaine's thorny fire gave us light. By the time that I brought my last handful of vines to him, his fire was burning brightly. The green vines crackled and hissed out random spurts of orange flame. I edged closer to the fire to gain some small comfort from its warmth. After my long day of ceaseless toil, the numbing ache that I had felt at midday had returned. But it had now transformed itself into unabashed agonizing pain.

"This is the only way to be rid of them," said Mr. Devaine as he prodded the glowing embers.

Once all the vines had been burned, I had not even enough strength for supper. My only thought was of retiring to a vine-free, thorn-free bed. I left Mr. Devaine to tend the dying embers and dragged myself to my room. It was a painful struggle to merely undress and insert myself between the bed sheets, and, as I settled into the contours of the mattress, my joints and muscles let out a grateful sigh. But my hands and forearms experienced no similar relief. They throbbed not only from fatigue, but also from the painful onslaught of scrapes and punctures inflicted on them by an army of unrelenting thorns. But sleep soon drew near. And I had almost drifted off, when Jenn appeared unexpectedly by my bed.

"Here," she offered, "this might help."

Like a healing angel, she sat beside me and applied a bit of lotion to my scarred skin. The lotion was cool, but in reality it offered little relief. It was instead the gentle touch of Jenn's hands which filled me with exciting surges of soothing electricity.

****

The next morning I awoke feeling stiff and sore. I sat up and stretched every aching muscle that would let me. I had slept long past the soft light of the new dawn, and from the kitchen I could hear the sounds of Jenn already puttering about. At the table, large helpings of bacon, eggs, and toast stood ready, and, as I sat down, Jenn placed a welcomed cup of coffee before me. I savored every bite of that simple breakfast, even though, as Jenn had warned, she had no talent for cooking. Between bites I wondered what new chores loomed ahead on this particular day.

"No work today," announced Jenn. "I have a surprise for you."

After breakfast, Jenn walked me out to the stable, where, next to Ariel I saw another horse. I learned that he was Mr. Devaine's horse, a sturdy Haflinger named Duke. Both horses were already groomed and bridled, and they eagerly snorted in anticipation of a possible day's outing. We hoisted and cinched the saddles onto them, while Jenn questioned me about my riding skills. I tried to assure her that, after the many Adirondack summer camps of my youth, I was indeed a capable rider.

"How do you counter if the horse unexpectedly rears up?" she asked.

"You stand and lean forward," I answered.

"Which is faster, a canter or a trot?" she asked.

"A trot," I replied. "Next fastest is gallop."

And so it went until we had at last mounted the horses. Jenn had already packed a light lunch, and so we made straight for the ridge trail. My horse, Duke, needed very little guidance. He seemed already familiar with every nuance of that particular trail. My hands were still swollen and sore from the prior day's work, and so I lessened my grip on the reins and let Duke carry me as he would.

We paused atop the ridge to rest the horses and admire the view. We then continued along the rim trail until nearly midday. We came to a branch in the trail which ran downward into an adjacent valley. Jenn led us into it. Eventually we came to a large stand of Ponderosa pines, which engulfed us with their cool shady essence. Beneath us stretched a soft and spongy cushion of eternally accumulated pines needles. Not far beyond the trees, I noticed faint sparkles of shimmering light.

"Is that water?" I asked, somewhat surprised.

We soon broke through the pines and found ourselves by the edge of a sunlit lake. I gazed about, admiring this small bit of God's handiwork. It was a miraculous place, made more so by the fact that it had eluded the unquenchable thirst of the city to the north. I looked for an access road but saw none. The lake was only accessible by trails, and by all appearances Jenn and I were the only souls to have ventured there that day. After the long ride it felt good to dismount. The horses snorted gratefully, in anticipation of the cool water and green shoots which awaited them.

"What a jewel this is," I remarked, gazing at the blue water.

"It's a spring fed lake," said Jenn. "You'll see, it's crystal clear."

I stood enthralled by the exceptional sight before me. Like the Eden Ranch, this lake was also nestled into the soft basin of its own little valley. Around it, the surrounding hills rose up like mounds of brown sugar, carefully heaped there by the hands of a benevolent baker. Jenn spread a blanket beneath the shade of the pine canopy and set out the cheese, apples, and dry crackers she had packed. I reached for a nearby apple and stretched out onto the blanket, letting the underlying cushion of pine needles caress itself into the stiff contours of my back.

"Let's go for a swim," suggested Jenn.

"But I didn't bring a suit," I said slightly bemused.

"Don't be silly," she said smiling. "You don't need a swimsuit here."

I marveled to think of what was about to happen. As though in a dream, I watched as Jenn undressed, without shame, before me until she stood there beckoning me to do the same.

"Are you embarrassed?" she asked.

"No," I said, but then reconsidered. "Well, yes, just a little I suppose."

I hesitated, but only for a moment more. Finally, wearing only freckles, we ran into the water and swam out to the center of the lake. Jenn was the better swimmer, and I struggled to keep up. We reached the center of the lake and paused there, treading water and reaching out tentatively to caress the submerged curves of each other's body.

Back on shore, we dried ourselves in the soft afternoon air, and, lying down again on the blanket, we warmed ourselves again with gentle touches. Jenn stroked her fingers through my still damp hair. There were no words which could have possibly enhanced the mood, and so I simply lay there in blissful silence, smiling. Eventually Jenn drew close, and, as she placed her parted lips onto mine, uncontrollable electricity once again surged through me.

Briefly I wondered how many other times Jenn had played this particular scene throughout her years, with other acquaintances, all thinking themselves as fortunate as myself for such an unexpected encounter with the divine. Certainly there had been others. But they did not matter, and I did not care. For, in that moment, Jenn had chosen me, and I was the fortunate one. In that one moment, Jenn had given herself to me, and she was mine.

It was late afternoon when we again mounted our horses. I gazed wistfully at our picnic site before leaving. A warm breeze lapped across the lake's shimmering surface, turning each ripple into a spoonful of tawny afternoon sunlight. Where our blanket had been spread, the bed of pine needles still traced the contours of our bodies. I let my gaze linger there for as long as it might, knowing this to be a scene that I would never forget.

Back at the top of the ridge, we paused again to rest the horses. As the setting sun painted an orange pallor onto the western horizon I again discerned the outlines of the City of Angels, shrouded as always in the haze of too much civilization. Jenn and I would return there tomorrow, back again to our self imposed bevy of artificial cares. I was already missing the Eden Ranch.

We finally returned by twilight, with barely enough light to stable the horses. As we walked back to the house, the lush grass of the Eden Ranch whispered in the breeze, consoling me with one last night of healing retreat. Inside the house we found that Mr. Devaine had already gone to bed, but had left us a note on the kitchen table.

"There is more scotch if you'd like. Feel free to help yourself," read the note.

But after that day I felt no need for liquor, aged or otherwise, to invigorate me. The silvery rays of a smiling moon danced jubilantly across the sea of whispering grass, and the evening air was redolent with the rejuvenating scent of eucalyptus. From any direction, a trilling army of crickets could be heard, all synchronized so that they sounded as one. The horses gave out satisfied snorts from the confines of their stable, and, as I nestled into the creases of an old wicker chair on the porch, I let out a grateful sound of my own.

"What a lovely evening this is," I said.

Overhead the stars shone brightly yet again, and, as Jenn sat down beside me for company, I pointed out the locations of Orion and of the many other stars that kept him company. Sirius, Rigel, Betelgeuse were all on prominent display, and I lovingly described the nuances of each, seeking to convey the supreme majesty and mystery of these seemingly insignificant points of light. Jenn drew closer as I spoke, until at last her lips brushed against mine.

"Come inside," she whispered, "and let's forget about those stars."

****

Jenn and I found ourselves awaking late the next morning, so late that Mr. Devaine had already risen. This was our day to return to campus, and quickly so, as the spring semester was set to begin the next day. We packed after a hurried breakfast, and I said my goodbyes to Mr. Devaine and to the Eden Ranch.

"Thank you for the scotch," was all I could think to say as I shook Mr. Devaine's hand.

I felt a sense of loss as Jenn's car wound its way through the warm fields of grass and the cool stands of eucalyptus. We quickly passed beyond the confines of the Eden Ranch, and all too soon we again found ourselves driving through the scorched valley below. Still, it had been a miraculous few days, and thinking of them I was moved to reach out and caress Jenn's shoulder. She tilted her head towards me, resting her cheek against my outstretched hand. By now I had come to accept Jenn's quiet nature. Hers was more a persona of presence than of politics. But with any one gesture, she could say more to me than a book full of words.

We drove along in contented silence. I found it difficult to initiate any type of conversation. Anything I thought to say would have sounded trite or artificial. So, in an effort to fill the silence, I reached to the car's radio and switched it on.

"Let's see what we've been missing," I said, searching for a news channel.

For me the broadcast news had always seemed to recount the happenings of a distant world. Of wars, I had never personally experienced one. Of economic events, none had so far directly affected me. Of politics, I had little interest. But these were the topics that most news broadcasts usually dealt with, all of them distinctly removed from the concerns of my own particular life. But not so on that day.

On that day, the lead story at the top of the hour did indeed spark my attention. It involved Bruce Robinson, someone whom I had actually seen in real life. There seemed to be some unfortunate news, not concerning Robinson, but concerning his estranged wife. As the details unfolded, Jenn and I learned that Nicole Robinson had been found murdered, and viciously so, in her Hollywood town home early that morning.

"Who would want to kill her?" mused Jenn.

"Yes," I remarked, "that is strange."

"Imagine that," added Jenn, "and Robinson was Grand Marshall at the homecoming parade!"

"Yes, he was," I confirmed. "Did you see him?"

"No, not so well," said Jenn. "We were too far back in the crowd. Were you there?"

"I was," I said, "with Laura."

The next day, most of the campus, and the law school in particular, seemed abuzz with news of the murder. The news media provided running updates, most of which were not very delicate to hear. According to the reports, Nicole Robinson's lifeless body had been discovered lying in her own entryway by her house cleaner. She had been bludgeoned and shot, and left for dead amidst a pool of blood.

But the police had found no signs of a break-in or of a prior struggle, and, oddly, her neighbors had not even heard any gunshots. By all accounts the murder was starting to appear as yet another senseless crime, in a city full of senseless crimes. But so many ambiguities surrounded the crime that everyone seemed tempted to speculate about it. One of my fellow law students, Bryce Davis, was quick to propose his own theory.

"It was someone she knew," he asserted. "That's why she opened the door."

Over the course of the preceding semester I had come to respect Bryce's opinions. In particular, he seemed especially keen about the inner workings of the City of Angels. I suspected that he probably had access to sources of information which were unavailable to the rest of us plebian law students. It was rumored that he came from an old line California family, and that, somewhere in the remote Sacramento delta, there was even a town which had been founded by a family scion. But I knew him only as Bryce Davis, an aloof but likeable fellow, who, like so many children of the rich, go through life tagged with what appear to be two proper names.

Bryce's opinion was the spark which lit further speculation. Another student went so far to suggest that Robinson himself might have been involved in some gruesome capacity. After all, this student maintained, the California community property laws were mercilessly unforgiving, and so what better way for Robinson to favorably settle his ongoing divorce than by eliminating his pesky wife?

"He would have lost a fortune in that divorce," this student predicted.

"Two fortunes," countered Bryce, "the first to his wife, and the second to his lawyers."

Everyone's speculations, both wild and subdued, continued until the initial flurry of news about the murder subsided. Our attention to it then waned, and most of the law students, myself included, lapsed back into our self imposed monastic routines. But on chance occasions, especially in the midnight stillness of a grim library carrel, I often found my thoughts returning to the murder. I thought not of Bruce Robinson however, but rather of his hapless wife, imagining her in those last forlorn moments, as warm precious life had seeped out of her and onto the cold, sterile tiles of her entryway floor.

6.

The neighborhood which I called home consisted of a motley mixture of student housing, old bungalows, and various small business establishments, most of which seemed to be just barely turning a desperate profit. There was a used furniture store where I had bought my study desk, an art store where I had found a poster of palm trees, and a bedding shop which had sold me a refurbished mattress, supposedly thoroughly sanitized, at the beginning of the school year. There were places to eat, usually populated with a few hurried diners, which catered to the student trade by staying open into the late hours. At the corner where I waited for my morning bus there was also an automobile dealership, long past its prime, which only sold used vehicles, most of them also long past their prime. I would often examine the inventory which lay parked there, weighing the possibility that I might no longer need the bus, if I but had a car.

One morning, in passing by the dealership and its usual collection of needy vehicles, one car in particular called out for my further attention. It was a rakish convertible, more than a decade old, but still carrying its former dignity. The original red paint had faded into a sun bleached powdery taupe. But aside from that, the vehicle appeared to have been well maintained. As I approached the car to inspect it, I felt an immediate bond with it. Perhaps it too was in need of a second chance.

I returned that afternoon to take another look. In the lot's corner office I found a balding man, nurturing a paper cup of coffee. He looked up from his newspaper when I appeared at the door asking about the car.

"Why not take it for a drive?" he suggested. "See if you like it."

He tossed me a pair of worn keys threaded onto a string, and, just that easily, I found myself driving in an open air car towards the Pacific. By the time that I'd reached Santa Monica, I had the radio turned on and was singing along with it. As with any vintage car, there was the smell of oil and smoke. But, as I drew close towards the ocean, the scent of sun laden, salted air overwhelmed it, and I smelled nothing else. The car ran smoothly enough and, as the cool Pacific breeze flowed through my hair, it was easy to imagine myself driving this car, with Jenn seated beside me, over the on-ramp to my new life.

I returned to the dealership already determined to negotiate a price. The dealer, still behind his newspaper, seemed unconcerned that I had actually even returned. He nodded as I expressed interest in the car, and, after I'd inquired about terms, he initiated a phone call.

"There's a kid here int'rested in the convertible," he said into the phone.

There was a brief exchange of words with the other party, after which he asked whether I would take the car as is, or whether I would be requesting any repairs. I told him that the car seemed fine to me, and that I had found nothing wrong with it.

"He'll take it like it is," he told the phone.

After a few more words, he put down the receiver and offered a price. The amount was not exorbitant, but it was certainly enough to impact the balance of my savings. On second thought, I mentioned that there probably were a few repairs that were indeed needed, and so, would he mind reducing the price slightly, as a courtesy to a poor university student? He smiled, probably having been through this routine a thousand times before. Without even bothering to ask about the type of repairs he then proposed, possibly out of sympathy, a price to which I quickly agreed.

"Nice car," he observed as we shook hands. "Now you just need a nice girl to ride in it."

"Oh, I've already got that," I said, smiling.

I wrote out a check for the complete amount and signed the sales contract on the spot. I then spent the remainder of that day obtaining the necessary paperwork for title, insurance, and registration that were required by the state. As a final touch, I also purchased two pairs of black sunglasses, inexpensive of course, for Jenn and myself to wear. The next day, as I returned with my completed paperwork to the dealership, I found the car fully cleaned and waiting for me. All that I then needed was that nice girl.

****

I became less of a social recluse as the months of that second semester unfolded. In addition to Bryce Davis I also made the acquaintance of other students in my class. Of the ones that I remember, there was Ted McCombs, also known as "Red" for his rust colored hair, from Irvine, where his father owned a luxury car dealership. There was Victoria Godfrey, a striking girl from La Jolla, whose parents were not affluent but who had attained their California dream of a carefree, Bohemian lifestyle. There was Bernard Senft, a former football player in college, who, with no possibility of a future in professional sports, had opted to become a professional sports attorney instead. I would often meet with this crowd in a local pub, where we commiserated about the vagaries of our chosen career path over drinks.

But mostly during that second semester, I sought to spend my free time with Jenn. I looked for any opportunity to be with her. Eventually it occurred to me that we might spend a pleasant day together, out of the city, if I were to accept Dave Richard's standing offer to play squash. I called Dave and made all of the arrangements, and then convinced Jenn to come along. Jenn did not play squash, but, at the very least, I thought that she might lounge about with Crystal while Dave and I played our sets. I had made no mention to her of my new vintage car, and so when she arrived that morning she found me seated in my parked convertible waiving to her.

"Whose car are you sitting in?" she asked incredulously.

I explained to her that it was my car, recently bought when an unexpected wave of spontaneity had suddenly crashed over me. Admittedly, I had very much surprised myself with this purchase. But, as Jenn swung open the passenger door and seated herself into the car, nothing could have seemed more perfectly planned.

And so, on a brightly lit Saturday morning, Jenn and I found ourselves, wearing our black sunglasses, driving north along the coast highway towards Malibu. Up there the highway became fringed by the beach bungalows of the very rich on one side, and by the hilltop estates of the even richer on the other. A perceptible explosion of color engulfed us. Pure white sand, each grain seemingly meticulously maintained, carpeted the shoreline. Against it beat the shimmering waves of a cool blue ocean, while off to our right, the former golden hills, now made green by early spring rains, stood pregnant with the abundant promise of new life.

Following Dave's directions I turned the car east onto one of the canyon roads, a narrow two lane affair which clung sheepishly onto the steeply sloped tuff. Our car climbed further and further upward, narrowly skirting the outcroppings of juniper, sage, and lavender which lined the roadside. Signs of human habitation appeared when we neared the top, as private driveways and lush landscapes pushed aside the natural scrub. Occasionally we passed imposing hedges, which teased us with glimpses of the princely homes beyond them. I ventured to imagine myself someday living in such a place with Jenn, atop one of these exclusive hills. There she would be as a radiant jewel, mounted onto a setting of lush green and gold. She deserved no less really, although I knew that to make such a thing happen required a miracle that only Midas himself could perform.

"Do you like Malibu?" I asked as we drove along.

"Sure," she said. "Who wouldn't?"

Squinting forward, I spied what appeared to be our eventual destination. Up ahead, clinging onto the slope of the hill before us, was perched a magnificent wedding cake of a house, a large white structure done up in stucco and glass and heaped into three full stories. Cantilevered onto the house were various decks and verandas which, from their lofty height, must have provided glorious views of the entire coastline. But the home seemed to visibly challenge its surroundings. It wasn't so much built into the hill as it was balanced onto it, vying with both gravity and nature for its very existence. I wondered why Dave would build such a tenuous house. He was calculating to a fault, and here, in a land where homes commonly slid down rain drenched slopes, this house seemed but pure folly.

"What does your friend do?" asked Jenn as we drew closer.

"I'm not sure exactly. But he seems to make plenty of money at it," I observed.

I endeavored to explain Dave's former involvement in health clubs, and of his recent one with health, or rather, lifestyle films, whatever that meant. But still it was difficult for me to convey how these seemingly simple ventures could have enabled such lavish wealth. I did not doubt the existence of worldly individuals such as Dave, who so easily tapped into the secret wellsprings of affluence, the whereabouts of which the rest of us hadn't barely a clue. He was indeed a breed apart, and whereas the old adage maintained that the meek would eventually inherit the Earth, Dave's substantial home, now looming before us, reminded me that, in the meantime, it was the wealthy who would inhabit the hilltops.

We eventually reached Dave's property, and then drove through an imposing gate set squarely between the erect vigilance of two towering cypress trees. Before us stretched the manicured grounds which were the spoils of Dave's alchemistic endeavors. As we neared the house, glimpses of gardens and tennis courts, and of a shimmering swimming pool came into view. I heard splashing sounds coming from the pool, and so, after parking my car in the circular drive, Jenn and I made our way there.

Crystal was swimming laps back and forth in the pool. I called to her, and after our presence had eventually caught her eye she emerged, dripping wet, to greet us. Her striking red hair, previously piled loftily atop her head, now fell flat around the contours of her face, a face which I might have recalled as pretty, but now, in Jenn's immediate presence, seemed only plain. Similarly, Jenn's slender limbs had deprived Crystal's sturdy build of its former athletic appeal, and, in contrast, Crystal's build was quickly transformed into that of a crude and ungainly creature. Jenn extended a supple hand in greeting, and, as she did so, a cool breeze seemed to suddenly well up and chill Crystal down to the bone. She quickly reached for a towel and shrouded herself into it.

"Dave isn't back yet," she said, shivering. "Can I offer you a drink?"

Apparently Dave had gone to meet with Bruce Robinson's agent to discuss the matter of Crystal's exercise video. We easily had time for a drink or two before he returned, and so Crystal produced a pitcher of freshly extracted fruit juice, the pulpy bluish color of which was foreign to me.

"What's this?" asked Jenn.

"It's aloe juice," Crystal informed us. "Try it, it's good for you."

Crystal had discovered this juice on a recent trip to Mexico where, according to her, the aloe plant, still unknown in this country, is revered as a life giving source of vitamins and antioxidants. I had never heard of the aloe plant, nor of antioxidants for that matter, but Crystal assured me that I soon would, as an American nation addicted to sugary soda pop would eventually come to realize the error of its ways.

Intrigued, and being in favor of good health, I sampled the juice. But my first impressions were not positive. It had a strong medicinal taste, like cough syrup, but much worse than any that my mother might have cajoled me into swallowing as a child. In fact, the taste of it made me wonder how I might endeavor to avoid any antioxidants from then on.

"It could use a little sugar," I said.

"Are you serious?" asked Crystal. "Sugar is the absolute worst thing for you!"

Sugar was bad, and aloe was good, and as Crystal continued expounding the benefits of this juice, I felt as though Jenn and I had unwittingly stumbled into an impromptu marketing campaign. With a nod to diplomacy I deferred to Crystal that she had indeed discovered a unique concoction, and that perhaps, with proper positioning, aloe juice might eventually become as popular as cola.

"How about '*Say Hello to Aloe*'?" I suggested as a possible product slogan.

But comedy was never my strong suit, and my weak attempt at humor elicited only a bare smile from Crystal. Jenn on the other hand was not so diplomatic. After her one sip, she made no pretense to liking it.

"I'd rather say *goodbye* to it instead," she said, hardly joking.

I cleared my throat and forced myself to suffer another sip of the drink. A cool breeze had once again passed through us, especially through the air separating the two girls. I was struggling to conjure a warming remark of sorts when, luckily, the heated rumblings of a hungry engine diverted our attention towards the cobbled drive. Dave had arrived, not a moment too soon, and as his bright red sports car came into view I looked to it with relief.

"And who is this starlet?" asked Dave as he approached us.

"This is my friend, Jenn Devaine," I said, as a rudimentary introduction.

Dave offered Jenn a friendly, but polite greeting. Crystal meanwhile offered him a fresh glass of aloe juice.

"Not for me," said Dave. "You know what I think of that stuff."

With this remark, Crystal's marketing research suffered yet another setback. Her mood appeared to darken temporarily. But, with noticeable effort, she regrouped her spirits and looked to change the subject.

"What did Robinson's agent say?" she asked, fishing for some good news.

"It doesn't look good," Dave informed her. "His wife's murder hasn't helped."

Dave told us that because of the murder, Robinson's attorneys had cautioned a low profile. Any new film roles, public appearances, and, certainly, appearances in exercise videos had been put on hold. On hearing this news, Crystal's mood seemed to again turn dark.

"But you promised," she scowled. "You did!"

"Cheer up, babe," Dave consoled her. "I'll make it work out. You'll see."

But Crystal did not cheer up. She remained crestfallen, almost angry. As Dave and I then made our way to play squash, we left the girls to keep suitable company with themselves. I dreaded what might transpire while we were gone. Briefly, I imagined returning poolside to find one of the girls, possibly Jenn, floating face down in the water. But, as I glanced over my shoulder while walking away, I spied Jenn settling herself into a lounge chair which was a sufficient distance removed from both Crystal, and from her dreaded aloe juice.

****

The game of squash originated in the British boarding schools of the eighteen hundreds. There, well off young men discovered that a punctured tennis ball became slow and '*squashy*', and could be used to play a game akin to tennis, but indoors and on a significantly smaller court. With *squash*, as the game became known, these young men could indulge their passion for racquet sport even during the dreariest days of a British winter. This new game eventually evolved so that the ball became smaller, to roughly an inch and one half in diameter, the racquet more slender to accommodate this smaller ball, and the court to one which was completely enclosed.

The game then gravitated across the Atlantic, where well off young American men sought to emulate their British counterparts. In this way the sport flourished within most of the private Eastern boarding schools, and in the old line universities such as the one Dave and I had found ourselves attending. But outside of this limited ecosystem, squash was not well known and did not thrive, certainly not to the extent as did its more vulgar cousin, racquetball.

"I wouldn't be caught dead playing racquetball," Dave had once remarked.

And I had agreed with him. Racquetball is nothing more than a Neanderthal's version of squash, good only for working up a sweat. The proper use of a squash racquet is more akin to working with a surgeon's scalpel, rather than with a woodman's axe. In squash, innuendo counts more than demeanor. For, unlike racquetball, squash is not about merely hitting a ball, squash is about *placing* a ball. Squash is about coaxing the ball, wooing the ball, persuading the ball, to move with just the right trajectory and spin so that your opponent cannot reach it.

Now, I only digress so much about the game of squash to possibly convey how those addicted to it might perceive themselves as a select brotherhood. Finding a good squash partner is no chance affair, and, if there existed a singular entity which bound Dave and myself together through our college years, it was our passion for this game. In those days, Dave and I had been well matched as opponents, so much so that the outcome of any of our games was ever in doubt. But now, in his private subterranean squash court, I found this to no longer be the case.

Our first set, usually a limbering one, was played causally enough that I was able to win it. But during the second set I realized that the caliber of Dave's play had clearly improved since our college days. I began to struggle as my own game, through neglect, had unfortunately only worsened. Dave also played with a greater intensity than I had known him to possess, so that, by the middle of our fourth set, I began to feel that the match was lost for me. And when, after a long volley to break a tie at eight, he returned the ball with such a determined spin that it curved past my wrist in a blur, my spirit broke completely, and well beyond recovery.

By the fifth set, my play had been reduced to a dismal formality. I felt drained of energy and knew that I could not win. Dave also sensed it, and, in response, he showed no mercy. He easily won the last few games, with me desperately helpless to stop him. After the match I felt truly embarrassed about the poor quality of my play.

"Sorry," I bleated out sheepishly. "Looks like I've been spending far too much time studying."

"Perhaps," countered Dave, "or maybe I'm just the better player, that's all."

Back at poolside, I greedily drank two tumblers of aloe juice, hoping that their antioxidant marvels might miraculously lift my fallen spirit. Psychologically, half of me was still shaken from the drubbing I had received. The other half was in shock about what I had assumed would have been a friendly game of squash, but, in the end, had turned so cruel and vicious.

I gazed at the peaceful vistas which stretched out beyond the pool. In the distance, the blue Pacific shimmered undisturbed under a bright noonday sun, enticing me to draw some comfort from it. The girls were still lounging separately, quietly, and apparently completely engrossed by the specific magazine that each stared into.

A light lunch had been set out, but I could not identify any of it. As we sat down to eat, I dreaded having to ingest more aloe, albeit in different forms. But Crystal explained that, now awaiting us as patties, nuggets, and chips, was not aloe, but soy and seitan, ready to infuse us with their own particular health enabling essences. All I really wanted was a sandwich, but Crystal assured me that this type of holistic menu was the cornerstone to her active lifestyle. Strict adherence to this diet, she maintained, would guarantee a long life.

"If not," Dave added dryly, "it will make it *seem* like a long life."

"Don't mind him," Crystal pronounced. "This food is good for you. Eat."

I scanned the unidentifiable selection before me, and, for lack of a better strategy, began choosing items based solely on their color. I drew a deep breath and nudged something beige and rather coarse into my mouth, wondering by how many minutes, or possibly hours, my lifespan had been now increased. And indeed, as the tasteless mass fought its way down my throat, it instantly seemed to produce the desired effect, just as Dave had predicted.

"I think that bite alone was a good half hour's worth," I informed everyone.

"Here's a whole day for me!" said Dave as he took in a large helping.

But all our joking aside, Crystal did indeed appear to be undeniably healthy. For comparison I glanced at Jenn who, since I'd known her, had never concerned herself with her diet in the least. Nor did she exercise. Yet, in spite of this, she gained no apparent weight. It seemed as though any calories she consumed would indifferently pass through her body, leaving her slender figure untouched.

"It's amazing how Jenn stays so trim, without exercising," I casually observed.

"I've heard rumors of women like you," interjected Dave, "but never thought I'd actually meet one."

On hearing Dave's remark Crystal suddenly turned furious, and launched into a heated lecture about the undisputed need for proper exercise and nutrition. Countless studies, in health magazines, had firmly established the boundless benefits of a controlled diet and of a daily regimen of elevated cardiovascular activity. She feverishly argued that deviating from these practices would most certainly endanger the quality of one's life, not to mention the final span of that life! This was but a fundamental choice between life and death, and by ignoring diet and exercise, Crystal explained, Jenn was in fact placing her very life in danger. With this pronouncement, both Dave and I turned towards Jenn, examining her as though she had only scant moments to live.

"I used to ride dressage," offered Jenn, in defense. "Isn't that good exercise?"

"No, it's not!" countered Crystal. "Because the horse is the one who's exercising!"

But Jenn insisted that all of her trials atop a saddle had indeed improved the overall tone of her body. As proof she stood up to give a live demonstration, pointing out the especially supple shape of her upper arms, thighs, and calves. While Jenn spun about, both Dave and I admired the lithe lines of her muscles, mounted as they were onto her straight and slender frame like the tight riggings of a fast yacht.

"Indeed," observed Dave, nodding, "I would say that dressage really is good exercise."

I too nodded in agreement. But Crystal remained unmoved. She knew nothing of dressage, except that it involved the use of a horse, perhaps even an improperly nourished one at that.

"Speaking of dressage, do you still ride?" Dave asked Jenn.

"Not so much now," said Jenn, "only when I'm back at my father's ranch."

"That's too bad," Dave added. "You shouldn't let your skills get rusty."

Dave now recalled an elderly couple further up the canyon road who kept horses, mostly for the use by their grandchildren who, in truth, seldom ever visited them. They had a large stable and the horses were always in need of someone to exercise them.

"I can introduce you to them, if you'd like," he suggested to Jenn.

"Yes, I would love that," remarked Jenn.

On hearing this, I noticed Crystal's completion turn noticeably redder, almost to the point of matching the shade of her hair.

"I've had enough of this horse talk!" she announced.

And with that she arose abruptly, and informed us that it was time for her afternoon exercise routine. The rest of us watched as she stormed away into the house.

"She can be a bit trying at times," said Dave, almost apologetically once Crystal was out of sight.

****

With Crystal gone, we sat in silence for a few moments as a warming breeze drifted onto us from the surrounding canyon. I still felt drained from my drubbing on the squash court, and my legs were starting to turn stiff from sitting. Dave on the other hand seemed fresh and ready for whatever other activity that his hillside compound might facilitate. The shimmering water in his pool still beckoned any eager swimmer to dive in, while his outdoor tennis court awaited anyone who wished to volley a ball with a racket. For simpler recreation, numerous hiking trails wound behind his property and into the many recesses of the surrounding hills. I was about to propose an afternoon hike when Dave summarily spoke up.

"You know," he suggested, "I haven't shown you the house, have I?"

No, he had not. Until then, my own interests had been confined solely to his subterranean squash court. But the expanse of his home ran considerably beyond that. Both Jenn and I agreed to his suggestion, and we followed him towards the house with peaked curiosity. To me the home had initially appeared as a large, sparse, sugar cube stacked onto the hillside, and I had somehow assumed the inside of it to be in the same sterile style. But entering the residence through its proper front entryway, an explosion of color suddenly engulfed us. As the two towering front doors swung open, there appeared a palatial expanse of gleaming marble and brass, precisely polished and pristinely immaculate.

This entry hall itself was of cavernous proportions, almost thirty feet from floor to ceiling, anchored in its center by a pendulous pendant of a chandelier, and framed on either side by wide sweeping stairways racing upwards in marble to a wide gilded balcony. Along the walls an expanse of mirrors enhanced the voluminous feel of this already substantial space. The hall was decorated with little furniture. Instead, an inherent opulence emanated from its prominent marble floor, virginally white but fractured throughout by rich veins of deep blues and indigoes.

"This marble come from only one quarry near Torino," Dave casually informed us.

Apparently Dave had *stumbled* across this marble a few years ago while skiing in the Italian Alps. There a similar stone had graced the halls of the medieval mountainside chalet where he was staying. At that time, his current home, and its squash court, was still under construction, and nearly complete. But the siren song of the indigo marble proved irresistible. So on a whim Dave located the remote quarry, still in operation after several centuries, but now catering only to a select clientele. Undaunted, he convinced the owners of his dire need. Dave did not mention the specific price of the subsequent transaction, but I readily surmised that a small fortune now rested beneath our feet.

Beyond the marble floor, I myself admired the chandelier and mirrors. Dave informed us that these too were similarly rare, the glass in each tracing its pedigree back to eighteenth century Austria. I stared ceremoniously into one of the mirrors, hoping perhaps to see the visage of some long departed Habsburg returning my gaze.

"I feel like royalty," Jenn suddenly announced, gliding across the marble tiles.

"And why not?" Dave confirmed. "You certainly look like royalty!"

Our tour then continued. Adjoining the entry hall were servants quarters, and waiting rooms, and a large dining hall which ran for what seemed to be a city block. We made our way to the rear of the home, where it again abruptly expanded into another cavernous enclave. Here however, the home flowed into a wide, tiered space packed with gleaming chrome, dark green leather couches - each seemingly capable of swallowing a person whole - and almost an entire rain forest's worth of teak flooring. One side of this secondary cavern was commanded by a full bar, stocked with all liquors and liqueurs, and fenced by nearly a dozen bar stools.

"Makes me thirsty to just look at all those bottles," I remarked to Dave.

"Sure, so how about a drink?" asked Dave. "You were a great drinker in college. Do you still drink like that?"

"No, not anymore," I told him. "Well, not as much anyway."

"So, maybe just one drink?" Dave suggested.

But it was far too early for even one drink, and so I declined. I gravitated instead to the opposite side of the room, if the term room could still be applied, to where a casual dining area was set up. Past the table and chairs however, it was impossible not to notice the fish. But not just a few fish, an entire wall of them, swimming behind one substantial plate of continuous glass which spanned the entire side of the room. They were beyond counting, and of all different varieties.

"Look at all the fish!" exclaimed Jenn.

"Do you like them? I captured this one last summer while diving near Catalina," Dave said, while pointing to one in particular.

The creature which Dave singled out was strikingly unique, and imbued with a golden aura which obscured any notice of its lesser fellow fish. Although far removed from its feral foraging through the wild Catalina shoals, the fish seemed comfortable enough in the more docile environs of Dave's aquarium. Jenn and I both admired this fish, who then stared back at us, apparently content with being so admired.

But as amazing as this wall sized aquarium had appeared, the room's true attraction proved to be an even larger aquarium - namely, the Pacific Ocean itself. For the remaining side of the room, its westward side, was not a wall at all, nor a wall with windows. But rather it was simply a single all encompassing expanse of glass, beyond which unfurled the green folds of the canyon below as it tumbled unobstructed towards the shimmering blue ocean. Dave parted what had seemed to be a seamless section of glass, and led us onto an outside terrace. We stepped into the warm sun, the ocean breeze, and the unavoidable majesty of this hilltop outpost. Jenn walked to the edge of the terrace and rested herself onto the railing.

"Wow, the sunsets from here must be truly spectacular," Jenn observed as she peered westward.

She gazed towards the Pacific, as though a spectacular sunset were already in progress. While Jenn watched her imaginary sunset I envisioned Dave and Crystal admiring actual sunsets, with drinks in hand, from this veranda, savoring the enormity of God's creation from their exclusive vantage point.

"Yes, this is a great spot for sunsets," added Dave. "It's too bad that Crystal doesn't care for them."

"Why not?" I asked.

"Oh, she just finds them boring," said Dave.

I nodded understandingly, finding it hard to imagine Crystal containing herself through the torturous slow motion ordeal of an entire sunset. But after the mention of her name I then wondered exactly where, in this vast house, she had disappeared to. It was not until we'd made our way to the second floor that I eventually found her in one of the upstairs rooms. I'd heard music coming from this room as we'd passed it and had opened the door to unexpectedly find her, her flaming hair bobbed back, jumping up and down in time to what I recognized as a selection from Bach's Brandenburg's.

"I call this routine *Jumping to the Classics*," she blurted out between heavy breaths.

"Yes, very nice," I said, with raised eyebrows and a bemused smile. "Sorry to have interrupted."

I nodded apologetically before excusing myself, and after closing the door I sought to catch up with Dave and Jenn. They had gone further along the upstairs landing into what turned out to be a library.

"So many books!" exclaimed Jenn just as I'd rejoined them.

"And they're not a façade," added Dave with some pride. "The books are all real."

Apparently, Dave's decorator had initially suggested a mere façade of aged books to complete the look of the room. But Dave had insisted on the real deal. So he had hired a man to scour for used book, as far north as Seattle, until nearly two thousand unique, and often rare, volumes had been collected. I scanned the titles on the shelves and was amazed by the variety which Dave's man had located. There were works of fiction, history, and biography of course. But there was also a small, but impressive, smattering of law and science books. Of the law books, a very early pressing of Cardozo's treatise on judicial process was a notable standout, while of the science books I was a amazed to find a first edition copy - in the original German! - of Heisenberg's theories of quantum mechanics.

"These books are amazing!" I remarked.

"Yes, and Paul, don't forget that all of them are also.....*delightful*," Dave added with a wink.

I immediately understood his reference to Laura Goodwin, for in that particular college literature class, Dave too had been enrolled.

"Say, whatever happened to that girl, do you know?" he asked.

"Oh, Laura Goodwin, she's around," I informed him. "She's in Moscow, last I heard."

"Yes, and she's now probably freezing.....*delightfully!*" added Jenn, catching on.

Dave laughed at Jenn's remark, but I did not. Knowing Laura as I did, I could not bring myself to laugh at her expense.

"Pretty, *and* with a sense of humor," said Dave. "*Now* I'm impressed."

Dave then escorted Jenn out to an attached balcony. There they continued talking, Dave still apparently enjoying Jenn's sense of humor, one that, since I'd known her, had mostly seemed to have eluded me. But I lingered behind in the library which, in addition to its many volumes, also contained several overstuffed chairs. I sunk into one of them to peruse a few books, the pages of which, delightful or not, Dave had probably never actually parted. The book by Heisenberg, especially, was a rare jewel, and, although I knew not a syllable of German, the bold and lucid equations which pronounced his beautiful initial musings on quantum mechanics were a language which all physicists understood.

I savored those equations deeply, trying to relive the wonder which Heisenberg himself must have felt when he had first put them onto paper. Of the mysteries of the universe, he had but scratched their surface. But he had paved the way for the many other curious souls which had subsequently followed. I had once been one of those souls, in my own small way, and had ventured to think myself capable of similar insights. But in the great void of the cosmos, where my own curiosity had wandered, the mysteries there had proven too unyielding, or at least too unyielding to my own feeble attempts. For a brief moment however, with Heisenberg's book still in hand, I deluded myself into again thinking that I did indeed have such abilities. But eventually I let out a sigh, and returned the book to its shelf before rejoining Jenn and Dave, still chatting on the balcony.

"So what keeps the house from sliding downhill?" Jenn was asking him.

"Well, it's the foundation," explained Dave, "and how I designed it."

And with that he explained how the house was supported by numerous steel pylons, sunk thirty feet into the hillside. The house itself was flexibly affixed to them, and could withstand shocks from most any earthquake, or other acts of nature. Even a severe landslide could not budge it.

"This was a property that no one thought possible to build on," Dave added, "not even my architect."

In the end however, as with his Italian marble, Dave's persistence had prevailed, and he was rewarded with the lofty perch from which he now viewed his sunsets. But that particular day's sunset was still hours away, with both Dave and Jenn seemingly eager to talk until it eventually arrived, when the long absent Crystal finally appeared in the doors behind us. She had finished her exercising, and had come to remind Dave of the evening's upcoming engagement.

"With Siegel, remember?" she added.

"I'm sorry, but some unfinished business," Dave said turning to Jenn and me, but mostly to Jenn. "Perhaps we can enjoy a sunset some other time."

So we followed Dave downstairs and he walked us out through the veranda. As we skirted past the pool, so that I might retrieve my squash racket, he insisted that we should meet again.

"How about we all go for a sail sometime?" he suggested. "The more, the merrier, I always say."

"A sail?" asked Jenn. "On whose boat?"

"Why on my boat of course," said Dave. "Didn't Paul tell you?"

"No, I never mentioned your boat," I said. "I must have forgotten to."

So Dave launched into a description of his boat, from its length to its purchase price. When we at last reached my car, the influence of boats, and rare books, and imported marble had begun to affect me. I was starting to feel a bit affluent myself.

"What do you think of my car?" I asked Dave, pointing to it.

"Cute," said Dave smiling. "Maybe I'll trade mine for fifty of yours."

****

That evening Jenn and I returned to my apartment which, after Dave's estate, suddenly felt as gloomy and miserable as an ancient tenement. The earlier part of the day then seemed as but an exquisite dream from which we had abruptly awoken. Jenn was especially quite that evening. She made little conversation over a sullen dinner which almost verged on moribund.

There was no view of the sunset from my apartment's balcony. In fact, there was no balcony. And so after dinner we retired early, and arose early the next morning. After a hasty cup of coffee, Jenn rushed off to the university library, hoping to make some breakthrough in her long stalled research endeavors. As for myself, I had lecture notes and cases studies to read. I packed a few books, and was almost out the door on my way to the law library when the phone unexpectedly rang.

"So, do you have time today for an old friend?" asked the voice at the other end of the line.

It was Jonathan Schwarzchild, finally returning my call of a few months past. He had just returned from a two month's stay in New York City, and was now finally replying to the many phone messages, including my own, which had been hibernating on his answering machine.

7.

Quite simply, Jonathan Schwarzchild was the most brilliant individual I had ever met. His grasp of advanced scientific concepts was unusually sudden and flawless, and no nuance of any mathematical derivation, no matter how abstract, seemed to be beyond his comprehension. For in present day physics where theoretical concepts have gone beyond the limits of human observation, Jonathan's ability to think in pure abstractions was a prized asset. Especially in the realm of string theory, which was Jonathan's specialization, it was not possible to discern the actual strings themselves, let alone capture them and gather them into some type of magical jar for collective measurements. Rather, these mystical entities were exclusively examined, experimented with, and demystified, only abstractly as mathematical equations on a chalkboard.

The field of physics thrives through contributions from raw unbridled genius. Hence, Jonathan's obvious and ample talents were immediately welcomed by his professors, and eventually by his fellow students. But the study of physics can be a humbling experience. I know of no other academic pursuit wherein the vastness of the universe, or the infinitesimal minuteness of subatomic particles, will so readily lead one to an awareness of one's own insignificance. For Jonathan Schwarzchild however, this was not the case. He clearly believed in his own significance, and in the significance of his own prodigious abilities. This belief imbued a drive within him which at times trespassed into arrogance, and which, needless to say, did not readily endear him into the hearts of his fellow undergraduates.

As for myself, I bore no ill feelings towards him. My own area of study, cosmology, did not conflict with his, and so we would readily share ideas rather than dispute them. But even then, my own talents waned so much in comparison to Jonathan's that I never felt threatened. For my part, I admired him, and gladly came to view him as more of a mentor than an adversary, especially when my own professors seemed to have little inclination towards those students of a lesser caliber, such as myself.

I first met Jonathan during our sophomore year in a thermodynamics class. There he became quickly bored by the easy nuances of endothermic systems. In the next semester's class on electromagnetism he showed more interest. But once he had mastered Maxwell's equations, to a point where he effortlessly applied them to even three dimensional problems, his boredom once again returned. It was not until junior year that he firmly broke free from everyone, and began advancing with his own strides. While the rest of us stumbled through basic quantum mechanics, Jonathan was tilting at problems in relativity and, eventually, relativistic quantum dynamics. By senior year he was already engaged in graduate level research.

Jonathan had spent the last five years in the City of Angels pursuing his doctoral degree at a rival university across town. I had seen him a few times after college, back on the East coast, but had then lost track of him in the subsequent years. But throughout those years I had missed him, as one might miss a part of one's own nature that had been undeservedly set aside.

On that City of Angels Sunday morning when Jonathan had called, I had already planned a cloistered day in the law library. But when he then proposed that we meet later that day to catch up, it was impossible for me to refuse.

"It will be good to see you again," I said. "Where should we meet?"

"Do you know the Page Museum?" Jonathan asked. "It's almost half way between us."

I'd heard of the museum. It was on Wilshire Boulevard, near the so called Miracle Mile. We made plans to meet there in the afternoon. So after a late lunch I jumped on one of the Wilshire line buses, hoping to arrive at the museum by two. The bus dropped me off at the western edge of the Mile, a half block from the museum and in front of that strangest of Los Angeles anomalies, the LaBrea tar pits.

Few tourists, or even locals, are familiar with this prehistoric anomaly, now a fenced enclave adjacent to the grounds of the Page Museum. I walked towards its bubbling pools of tar, which I had long thought to visit, and lingered briefly. Amazingly I spied a hapless plasticized mastodon trapped in the muck as, in a seeming spell of whimsy, someone had seen it fit to adorn the tar pools with life sized replicas of several Pleistocene era creatures. On one edge of the pool, a second mastodon, still on firm terrain, cried out helplessly, while at the opposite edge a saber tooth cat prowled menacingly. As the statues reenacted their life and death struggle from eons past, I wondered if the cat would indeed risk the tar for a good meal. But this question was to remain unanswered, as I had to attend to my rendezvous with Jonathan.

I arrived at the Page Museum precisely at two o'clock. But Jonathan did not. When he eventually did arrive, it was nearly three. He offered a half dozen excuses for being late, none of which held any substance, but taken collectively they possibly comprised a plausible cause. There had been a last minute phone call. Then Monica, his girlfriend I gathered, had detained him. His old car had refused to start. There had been too much traffic. He had guessed the wrong cross street, twice. And, finally, he had found no convenient parking spot and had to settle for one almost four blocks away. But no matter – I easily forgave him, as I was so glad to see him again.

"I've had legal training," I joked on hearing all this, "and none of your excuses would ever stand up in court."

"Yes, but they're all physically valid," Jonathan countered.

My first impression of Jonathan was that had changed considerably since I'd last seen him. The lenses of his eyeglasses had become noticeably thicker. His face now sported a full beard, while the top of his head, as though to compensate, sported far less hair. Whether he knew it or not, he had come to resemble the stereotypical image of the academic scientist which he was. His pale blue eyes still possessed their trademark sparkle, but on this particular day, the boundless enthusiasm that I recalled of him appeared markedly diminished. In all, he seemed to have grown precipitously older than the past few years might have allowed for.

"So, have you figured it all out by now?" I asked him.

"Well, almost," he said with a faint smile.

By his answer I knew that, in all seriousness, he must have been truly close, and that he was searching for that last crucial piece of the great puzzle which had consumed his passion for the past seven years. I had been present when Jonathan's quest had first begun, on a rain drenched day during junior year when we had first heard of a tentative new concept, which, for lack of a better term, was being referred to as '*string*' theory. And in many ways this moniker was accurate. For in its simplest form the theory did indeed describe the behavior of vibrating strings. But in its more exotic derivations, the theory could also describe the unimagined properties of those incredible components of elemental energy which eventually came to be referred to *as* strings.

A new idea in the field of physics is always greeted, as in other fields, with a full dose of skepticism. The existing order is usually wary to veer from a tried course which has been comfortably established. And so it typically becomes the responsibility of an upcoming generation to strike the new path. As such this new theory shook both Jonathan and myself like a thunderbolt as we both came to suspect its far reaching significance. From within its framework, string theory could conceivably describe an entire reweaving of the fabric of time and space, so that onto this new fabric might then be superimposed the unique infinitesimal patterns which defined the exotic properties of quarks, leptons, photons, and even gravity itself.

When string theory first emerged, physics stood atop the culmination of an incredible century of monumental advances. Over the past century, the atom had been demystified, the workings of the celestial cosmos had been charted, and the twin pillars of quantum mechanics and general relativity had been erected. Beyond atoms, quarks had been theorized and discovered, and, in the vastness of galactic space, so had impossible entities such as black holes and universal expansion.

The looming Holy Grail of physics was to now discover that one elusive theory which would bundle all of reality into a single unified framework. Intuitively, both Jonathan and I sensed that string theory would evolve into that framework. And, like a wildfire which might grow to immense proportion, all that was needed was one brilliant spark to set it ablaze.

"I'm going to be the one who solves this," Jonathan had proclaimed that one day long ago.

But that was seven years ago, and he was now late in doing so. Since then, Jonathan's theory had been joined by almost a dozen other string theories. These competing theories, especially one from Edwin Wilson on the East Coast, each held their own unique promise for success. But, like contestants in a beauty contest, each one also had its own peculiar flaw.

All of the theories assumed more than four physical dimensions to describe time and space. With these additional dimensions, up to twenty six in one theory, the so called strings could then be used to model the physical properties of the known universe. Jonathan's theory, true to the uncluttered nature of his own mind, made use of a simple seven dimensional model. He had achieved extraordinary early success with this model, and had published several papers. His approach had proved adept for describing the strong subatomic interactions of quarks and leptons. Unfortunately, Jonathan's version eventually failed once the concepts of mass and gravity were introduced into it.

Correcting this particular flaw had now frustrated Jonathan for more than three years. But, as he described his dilemma, I could only empathize with him. We had often approached difficult problems together. My own talents paled in comparison to his of course, but I had often provided the intuitive guidance which Jonathan seemed to lack. Now, as he struggled for clues, gone were the days when I might provide any meaningful insight. But I sensed that he was close, and I admired him for the distance which he had travelled so far. Unlike me, who had once looked down a similar road, and had instead turned away.

We talked into the late afternoon. Eventually Jonathan suggested that we go to his apartment for dinner, as it would be a simple matter for Monica to set another plate. I thought of my evening's study plan, but quickly abandoned it and opted instead for Jonathan's invitation. There was still so much more that we could discuss, and I did very much want to meet the mysterious Monica. It would be pointless to pore through law books. Jonathan had gotten me thinking of physics once again, and it was doubtful that I would be able to think of anything else for the remainder of that day. So I agreed to his suggestion, with Jonathan even offering to drive us across town in his own car.

****

Jonathan and Monica lived near the other prominent university in the City of Angels, a rival to mine and situated on the opposite, and notoriously less affluent, side of town. As we drove there I recounted a few details of my recent studies in law. All the while Jonathan tried his best to feign a modest degree of interest. But eventually my words began to disinterest even myself. The hollow content of my toils suddenly seemed insignificant compared to the obstacles which Jonathan struggled against. I eventually stopped talking, and simply allowed the many noises from Jonathan's car to fill the silence.

Jonathan's car was a cacophony of every conceivable sound. It coughed, it sputtered, it buzzed, and it rattled. It never missed an opportunity to remind us that it was being employed well beyond the maximum years of its useful tenure. Many times, when we stopped for a red light, the engine would give out a last gasp. Only after considerable coaxing would it again rise to life in a cloud of blue smoke that was heavy with the scents of crankcase oil and engine coolant. The car had no working air conditioning and so I rolled down my window to let in a bit of outside air, only to then find the incoming breeze speeding over me on its way out through gaping holes in the floorboard. I gazed down, and amused myself briefly with this unique view of the road, a moving blur beneath my own feet.

We drove through the old heart of the city, and past the downtown campus of Jonathan's university. His was an old, private college which had continued to thrive even as the area surrounding it had unremittingly decayed. Here, near the city's core, the daily temperatures were noticeably warmer than those of the breezy coast. Over the decades, this part of town had been irrevocably abandoned by the upwardly mobile crowd, and the area surrounding the university was now littered with countless post war bungalows, all hopelessly in need of repair.

Jonathan's own neighborhood was in an especially overlooked section of this forgotten part of town. This was a place where every paycheck mattered. Even grass seemed to be a luxury here, as every small patch of front lawn was either threadbare, or completely brown from lack of water. But Jonathan and Monica did not live so lavishly as in one of these old bungalows. Instead, their income, or lack thereof, only allowed them a small apartment in one of the government sponsored housing blocks. Jonathan's particular building was a nondescript brown brick affair, which lacked even parking for its tenants' cars. We had to circle Jonathan's block several times before I at last spied an available spot.

"No, not there," said Jonathan, nodding towards some grimy youths loitering near it.

He raised his eyebrows at my naivety. I had not lived a sheltered life, but clearly I was unfamiliar with the dangers peculiar to this part of town. And so I entrusted our search to Jonathan. We eventually chanced across an open spot nearly three blocks away, where, sandwiched between two cars in almost equal states of disrepair, Jonathan's own car gave out its latest last dying gasp. We locked its doors, although I could not imagine why, and made our way to Jonathan's apartment.

Once on the sidewalk I immediately felt it, a distinct arrogant gloominess evident even in the full sunlight of the late afternoon. The air here was still, and dense, and oppressively desperate. We walked in silence past vacant lots and abandoned, or nearly abandoned, homes. Occasionally, in passing by a fenced yard, we might startle a group of dogs, who barked out no warm welcome. There were few, if any, birds singing, and, aside from barking dogs, or the occasional passing car, or the faint sound of a police siren, all was silent.

"This part of town is so sad," I remarked.

"I know," said Jonathan. "Monica and I can't wait to get out of here."

But for now, this part of town, as dangerous and depressing as it was, offered them the most convenient and affordable alternative. For Jonathan, there was its proximity to the university. While for Monica, a social worker, it offered immediate access to a seemingly endless supply of vagrants, unwed mothers, drug addicts, broken families, and troubled youths. I wondered what drove a person such as Monica, from what little I knew of her, to reach out to so many lost causes of humanity. Certainly she must have been endowed with a caring nature, and blessed with more than an average allotment of stubborn optimism. But her name was *Monica* - Monica Alvares, to be exact - and it occurred to me that, over the course of my short years, of the few other Monica's that I had chanced across, they all had been, for whatever reason, more than exceptionally kindhearted.

"Jonathan, how did you meet this Monica?" I asked as we walked.

"Oh, we met by chance," he said.

Jonathan told me how they had met in one of the university cafeterias at the height of lunch hour, when the only available seating had placed them across from each other. This was a fortuitous happenstance for Jonathan, who, like so many other students of science, and of physics in particular, led a life inherently limited in social opportunities. Naturally, it was Monica who initiated their first conversation.

"Care to make small talk over lunch?" she had asked him.

As usual, Jonathan was mentally detached into the nuances of his physics research, and had no interest in conversation. But Monica entreated him with such a captivating smile, that he summarily put aside all thoughts of physics, at least for that moment.

"No, I don't mind small talk," said Jonathan. "In fact, the smaller the better."

To Monica's surprise she discovered that Jonathan's concept of *small* extended far beyond that of most anyone else's, down in fact, to the subatomic level. But after speaking with him only briefly, she found him to be polite, witty, and unlike anyone that she had ever met before. Jonathan was similarly charmed. He immediately found Monica to be attentive, and completely interested in his opinions. In many ways they made an ideal match - Monica, who was a caring soul, and Jonathan, who was a soul that needed caring.

That was three years ago. Since then Monica had earned her degree in social work and was now actively applying it. She worked full time in a government welfare office, and also volunteered *pro bono* community service a few evenings each week. Her minimal salary, supplemented with Jonathan's small stipend, brought their combined income up to just below the poverty line.

"You're lucky to have found such a girl," I mentioned after hearing all the details.

"I am," he replied. "But they're a necessary inconvenience, aren't they?"

I had never known Jonathan to be prone to sentiment, but this observation still left me somewhat bemused. I thought briefly of Jenn, and how it would never have occurred to me to consider her in the same way. But then again, I was not Jonathan Schwarzchild.

****

Jonathan's apartment was but a small chink in a much larger complex. As befitting the neighborhood, the surrounding grounds were barren of any living plants. Only a few neglected palms stood out as someone's feeble attempt at landscaping. The palms surrounded a decaying swimming pool, empty of water and having a long, pronounced crack running along its bottom, hinting that the empty pool would most likely remain so for the foreseeable future. We climbed a corner stairway up to a second floor landing. Nearing the apartment, I saw its lights turned on, and heard a woman's voice pleading from inside of it.

"But I can't live without my baby!" exclaimed the voice emphatically.

Two women inside were seated at a small kitchen table. Both were roughly the same age and similarly dressed, but I assumed Monica to be the one who was predominantly listening. The other woman seemed quite agitated, and as Jonathan and I entered the apartment, we sought to become as unobtrusive as possible. From the little information I gathered, the woman's husband had run off with their child, a five year old girl. He had accused this woman of being an unfit mother, and thought it best that he, and his pregnant girlfriend, raise the child instead.

"Dolores, please come back tomorrow, and we'll go to the child custody office," advised Monica in a reassuring tone.

But Dolores could not be calmed. She insisted that something had to be done, immediately. She demanded that the police should be contacted, and that her husband be arrested. Monica then explained how the matter required a resolution from the child custody court before any police involvement was possible. This procedure alone required at least several months. Upon hearing this, Dolores' grief could not be contained, and Monica struggled to console her. I too began sympathizing with Dolores' situation, when I unexpectedly found myself drawn into it.

"That man there is a lawyer," said Monica, pointing a finger towards me. "He can tell you."

I had remained as detached as possible during the entire ordeal, and so I was startled to suddenly find myself a part of it. I was not yet a proper attorney of course, but I sought to play along with Monica's fabrication. Gathering myself, I assumed as much of an authoritative air as seemed appropriate, and proceeded to explain what little I knew of child custody law to Dolores. She could inform the police of her husband's actions, but they were powerless to do anything. Her husband was well within his rights as the little girl's father to be in possession of the child, and only an order from the custody court could resolve this matter. I told the woman nothing which she had not already heard from Monica, but my authoritative demeanor, such as it was, seemed to persuade her.

"But will *you* help me?" she pleaded. "I don't know any lawyers."

I really had no intention of becoming further entangled in the matter, and so I cast my own beseeching glance towards Monica. Like a saving angel she informed Dolores that my involvement would not be necessary. There was sufficient legal counsel available, free of charge, at the social services center, and that, again, Dolores should simply come back tomorrow morning when all the *pro bono* legal counsels were available.

"Yes, that would be the best approach," I too advised. "Otherwise, I would have to charge you, and quite a bit, for my services."

This united stance of both Monica and myself was enough to finally placate Dolores. Convinced that we did indeed have her best interests in mind, she agreed to Monica's plan. After Dolores had left, Monica apologized for having drawn me into this particular affair. But, in the heat of the battle, she had been desperate for help.

"No problem," I said. "I'll see plenty of other messy situations as an attorney, I'm sure."

I suggested to Monica that she and I were both in the same line of work, namely, dealing with troubled people, although Monica's motivations were most likely more altruistically inclined than my own. And there would be no end of work for either of us. For, until a better breed of human could be devised, we would each be quite dutifully employed. Jonathan for his part simply shook his head, regarding us as two unfortunate souls who had unduly burdened themselves with the inane dealings of glum humanity.

"You both have my sympathy," he added.

As for himself, he cared nothing for any of it. His own concerns lay far removed from the misguided struggling of the human race. In the rarefied air of his existence there was no tolerance for frailty, or vanity, or poor judgment. In Jonathan's world, where I too had resided for a brief time, only perfection and truth prevailed. His was a world filled exclusively with highly intoxicating ideas, which were then further distilled into their purest and most ethereal essence.

But I could not disregard Jonathan for being aloof and uncaring. In many ways, the study of physics and mathematics is an opiate which frees one from the cares of inane existence. One can become absolutely lost in the contemplation of mathematical abstractions to the point of feeling completely disjoint from one's body. I myself had many memories, fond memories, of long midnight hours transfixed by these outer worldly concepts, wherein mentally I would journey through the far reaches of the cosmos, exploring galaxies, nebulae, and black holes. How distant the earth becomes on such voyages, just a small speck in space which gives no indication of the countless sorrows encased therein.

But I envied Jonathan's detachment from human affairs. I had set myself onto a course which would fill my days, and likely also my nights, with so much of the human experience, and so little, unfortunately, of the divine. I would find material benefits along my newly chosen path, and these, I surmised, would have to sustain me. Certainly, satisfaction could be had from charitably helping such lost souls as Dolores'. But, in the final analysis, ultimate success in the legal profession involved little charity. Success would depend on entering into the belly of the beast, and therein gorging oneself with everything that the beast had swallowed.

****

After Dolores had left, we started discussing dinner plans, and Monica informed us that there was no dinner to be had. She had been so interrupted that day by the trials of Dolores and others like her, that she'd had little time to prepare anything. We were all starving, so Jonathan conceded that their household budget, for this week at least, could allow for a dinner out. I felt honored.

"How about the little Asian place?" he suggested to Monica. "We can afford that."

Monica agreed. She then disappeared briefly to make herself ready, while Jonathan and I remained waiting in the living room. I looked about the small apartment, even smaller than my own. There were basically three rooms, a living room with an attached tiny alcove of a kitchen, a bedroom, and a small bath. On the living room floor in a far corner, I spied a bowl half filled with what appeared to be cat food. As I stared at it, a furtive brown bug appeared over the lip of it, and, as it did, I could not help but think of how far removed Jonathan and I had become from the cloistered gothic walkways of our undergraduate days.

Outside, the air had cooled considerably, to a point where it no longer felt oppressive. The purple tinge of the evening twilight, so prominent near the coast, was barely perceptible in this part of town. But as the stars began to emerge overhead even here, our surroundings seemed to give thanks that another stifling day had at long last concluded.

Jonathan and Monica walked briskly, almost as though they were being followed. Sensing their urgency, I too scuffled alongside them. We walked through a few blocks of treeless, grassless tract homes, each filled with easily started dogs. The homes eventually gave way to a small enclave of commercial buildings, the shops there providing only the barest of necessities. In addition to our Asian restaurant, there was a self serve laundry, a liquor store, a small grocery store, a used furniture shop, a pawn shop, and another liquor store, all having windows which were either barred or shuttered. In passing them, I peered into every gloomy nook, half expecting to find a fiendish criminal lurking inside.

"I worry so much when Jonathan goes on his late night walks," said Monica.

"Don't worry," Jonathan assured her. "The thieves know that I'm even poorer than they are."

With his rumpled clothes, untrimmed beard, and old canvas shoes, Jonathan clearly possessed nothing of any consequential value, and seemed hardly worth robbing. But still Monica worried, especially of late when Jonathan's midnight ramblings had become more frequent as he sought the conceptual breakthroughs that were still desperately eluding him.

"I hope Jonathan solves this thing," Monica told me. "Then he can finally sleep again, and so can I!"

We entered the restaurant to find ourselves its only customers. The lone waiter seemed overly eager to see us, if not anyone, come in for service. He promptly escorted us into a ruby colored booth directly opposite a gold adorned statue of a plump, smiling Buddha - a visage of Siddhartha in his older days, happy and well fed, and far removed from the leaner, more troubled years of his youth.

"*Come*," this older Buddha entreated. *"Come walk along the path of the eight fold weigh!"*

Our restaurant was brightly lit, even starkly so, and I adjusted my eyes to the glare of its fluorescent lights. Monica sat opposite me, and, as my gaze fell onto her, the faint yellow and orange freckles which dotted her cheeks came into focus. I examined the soft contours of her face, slightly rounded, with strong cheekbones and a prominent chin. She had a broad, sloping nose squarely set between two bright, turtle brown eyes, which were just a shade darker than the color of her hair. It was a nurturing face, and just by staring at it I began to feel warm and secure.

"You should try the Lo Mein," she recommended. "It's excellent here."

I placed my order exactly as Monica had suggested, and then quizzed her about her recent time spent in New York. The restaurants there had been exceptional, she recalled. But as a West Coast girl, she had found the winter dreariness unappealing. Still, their time had been enjoyable, a good break for Jonathan, and she had met everyone in Jonathan's immediate family. Jonathan's father, especially, seemed to have approved of her. Unfortunately, Monica was the only thing which he had approved of.

"All the while, he just shook his head whenever he saw me," said Jonathan.

Apparently, Jonathan's father still found it difficult to reconcile his brilliant son with his son's brilliantly impoverished condition. The chasm between Jonathan's intellectual capacity and his destitute lifestyle was difficult for his father to accept. And so, hoping that Jonathan would abandon his current foolishness, his father had proposed a bargain. If he wished, Jonathan could simply join him and his brother at the family's brokerage firm. There Jonathan would receive substantial pay, and he and Monica would want for nothing. After all, his father had argued, what better way to apply Jonathan's keen analytical skills than to the understanding of the complicated nuances of the securities markets?

In the end however, Mr. Schwarzchild had not won his argument. As a consolation, Jonathan had suggested that, rather than another stockbroker, there might instead be a Nobel laureate in the Schwarzchild family. And wouldn't that be a thing to be proud of? Unfortunately, Jonathan's father held little regard for the bank worthiness of such a vain aspiration. From his perspective, there was little need for such esoteric, and unprofitable, pursuits when so much easy gain might be had from the selling of ornate pieces of paper.

"Brains that can't make money are wasted," he had chided his son.

Jonathan recounted the entire saga of his father's concerns during our meal. But he seemed undaunted by his father's lack of support. I could only surmise that he had come to accept it as just another impediment to struggle against. Still, Jonathan's odds of success seemed to be growing longer. I did not know what breakthroughs awaited him. But he had not published anything in several years, and, in the highly competitive landscape of theoretical physics, such a lapse easily allowed others to secure those insights which Jonathan currently lacked. I looked towards him sympathetically as he reached into his pocket to pay for dinner.

"That broker's salary sounds really good right about now," he remarked while scanning through his thin wallet.

Another group of customers came into the restaurant after we'd paid our bill. They seemed to be students like us, but more boisterous and jovial. Certainly they were not physics students, as they did not appear to be weighed down by any unsolvable mysteries of the universe. They were undergraduates, and I would have guessed that eventually most of them would be bound for the simple chores of law or business school. Their future lives, easier and more profitable, would be burdened with the problems of clients rather than with those of the cosmos. I mentally wished them well, knowing that they would lead lives blissfully unaware of quarks, or strings, or Riemannian manifolds. As we left the restaurant, the Buddha continued radiating his unfettered aura of divine contentment.

"*Life should be carefree*," he seemed to intone. "*Why trouble yourself with unrequited desires?*"

And indeed, it would have been a simple relief for Jonathan to forget all of his concerns, as I had, and was still trying to do. But how could he, without denying his true nature? No, for Jonathan there was only one viable journey, and I almost blamed myself that it had become such a lonely one for him.

"You know, I wish I could help you in some way," I said during our walk back. "I really miss those discussions we used to have."

"Well, I'm sure that discussing the fine points of law must now be equally stimulating," he responded.

I assured him that indeed it was, although, in truth, I knew that there was little comparison. So much of legal study involved only mind numbing memorization of established precedents. It is tempting to romanticize exciting images of attorneys busily dashing through legal escapades. But in reality the practice of law consists mostly of the adherence to a strict code of formal procedures. Even the great issues which confronted the legal establishment, that is, those issues which ventured into the territories of morality and ethics, were typically a playground only for academics. For most working attorneys, as I would be, their daily livelihood consisted of much more mundane pursuits involving deeds, contracts, trials, and tribulations.

I wondered as to how many days there would be in my own future when, hunched over the details of some mind numbing contract, my thoughts would turn to Jonathan and to the seemingly unsolvable problems which he might then be pursuing. Certainly, I would eventually read of Jonathan's successes and of his nomination for some significant award. I would then be left to marvel at the elegance of his results, and at the heroic nature of his pursuits. Time would pass, and I would grow old, and probably wonder of what breakthroughs I too might have been capable of.

"You know," suggested Jonathan, "my department has plenty of openings. Why don't you consider applying?"

I surmised that Jonathan was not yet convinced, or perhaps that I had failed to convince him, of my intended career. With such a casual remark, he had demoted my legal aspirations to only a misguided whimsical detour on my part. But I assured him that I was firmly committed to my chosen path.

"No, I'm determined to become an attorney," I said. "I just need a good internship for the summer, and I'll be all set."

"Why not do some pro bono work with my office?" suggested Monica.

Probably Monica could have provided me with no shortage of nonpaying clients. I considered her suggestion, but declined it.

"No, I can't," I said shaking my head. "The words *'pro bono'* wouldn't look so good on my resume right now."

Monica nodded back her understanding. The night had turned cool, and we again walked briskly. The twilight had past, and the stars shown brightly. I looked up towards them, wondering in which star exactly my faults might lie. Were I an ancient mariner I might have used the stars to reach a destination. But for the journey onto which I was now embarked, the stars above offered no helping guidance.

"What are you looking at?" Monica asked me.

"Oh, just the stars," I said.

"Paul is a retired astrophysicist," Jonathan added.

I pointed out to Monica some of the particular ones which I had observed as an undergraduate, and she started at them with seeming interest.

"Speaking of stars," said Jonathan, "my department is sponsoring a star party next month. I could probably get you in, if you wanted."

I smiled at the thought of a star party again.

"It's going to be at Mount Wilson," he added.

My heart leapt at the thought of Mount Wilson. The observatory there, where the legendary Edwin Hubble himself had made his breakthrough discoveries long ago, was world renowned. The self same telescope which Hubble had once used was still there, and I had long dreamed of someday peering through it. It occurred to me that perhaps Jenn too might find it interesting to do so.

"Can I bring a guest?" I asked.

Jonathan assured me that an extra guest would be trivial. He himself planned to bring Monica. In fact, non physicists were especially welcomed to come and expose themselves to a bit of stargazing. Such lucky souls, I thought, who were completely unfamiliar with the cosmic red shift, or dark energy, or the expanding universe, and who could then innocently admire the stark beauty of a remote spiral galaxy or of distant star clusters suspended onto the void of endless space without any weightier concerns. I wondered how Jenn might react when she peered out towards the wonders of infinity. I could impress her with my knowledge of the cosmos, and she, for the first time, might see a side of me which had remained hidden.

"I'll be there," I affirmed. "Mark me down, with one guest."

Back at the apartment I said my goodbyes to Monica. Jonathan and I then trudged back to his waiting wreck of a car. Again we walked briskly, this time not for the cold, along the dimly lit sidewalks. We arrived at his car to find a group of youths congregated next to it, one of them casually leaning against it. I suddenly felt threatened by this loitering crowd of unpredictability. They approached us as we drew closer.

"Need a push tonight?" one of them asked.

"Don't I always?" countered Jonathan.

The youths arranged themselves behind the car, and as Jonathan and I climbed into it, I offered a silent prayer to the patron saint of overly worn automobiles. The youths pushed the car to a roll. But as Jonathan engaged the clutch, the engine only coughed and sputtered, little coming out of it except a cloud of blue smoke. Jonathan signaled to the waiting gang for another push. They did so with practiced precision, and then gave out a great cheer as the engine arose once again from the dead. We lurched off, and I let out a sigh of relief that that my recent prayer had been answered.

"I wouldn't worry about them," noted Jonathan. "They're harmless."

"Well, they sure didn't look harmless to me," I said.

I asked Jonathan to take me as far as the nearest bus stop on the Wilshire line, but he was adamant to drive me all the way back home. The car continued to chug along in fits and spurts. But as the engine grew warmer, it seemed that we would indeed eventually make our way across town. I now worried more about Jonathan, and whether he would return safely. I had come to understand Monica's concerns, and hoped that once Jonathan's doctoral work was complete, they could exchange their current environs for the nurturing lawns of a quite, and safe, university town.

"I'll be expecting you at the star party," Jonathan reminded me once we'd arrived at my apartment.

I assured him that I would indeed be there - with one guest.

"It will be like old times," I suggested, smiling.

And with that he lurched off, leaving me listening to the sounds of his car as they grew fainter, and fainter still, until I no longer heard them. It was now late in the evening, and, returning home, I gave Jenn a quick call to see how her day had gone and to tell her of the upcoming star party. But after there wasn't a response on her end, I left her no message and simply went to bed.

8.

During the following week I thought seriously about the possibility of doing, as Monica had suggested, pro bono legal work. For I'd received no responses to my various inquiries regarding internships, and so my employment prospects for the looming summer seemed increasingly bleak. I expressed my concerns to Bryce Davis one day over lunch.

"You should be able to find an internship *somewhere*," he assured me. "Look at me, I already have one, with Ashton Tate."

"Lucky you," I despaired enviously. "I sent them a resume last month, and so far I haven't heard a damned thing."

Ashton Tate was the premier firm in the City of Angels. Through the experience garnered from within its well paneled offices, one could easily facilitate a highly successful legal career. The firm specialized in providing counsel to the most select clientele in the entertainment field. Bryce had already familiarized himself with the firm's stable of celebrity clients, and he casually rolled off some of the most prominent names in Hollywood.

"They even have Bruce Robinson," he said.

"Sure, but these days isn't Robinson more *in-famous*, than famous?" I joked.

But my remark was not so untrue. After a month's silence, the media chatter speculated that Bruce Robinson might actually be accused of his wife's murder. Bryce suggested that such reports could not be dismissed lightly, as they sometimes originated with the District Attorney's office itself as a way to manage public image. With a high profile case, as this one was bound to become, the intense media coverage would put the competency and integrity of the public prosecutors under intense scrutiny. Future political careers would be at stake, and so nothing was left to chance.

In spite of the media reports however, no clear case against Robinson was apparent. Robinson had maintained his alibi, namely, that he had passed the night of the murder with an acquaintance, a certain Bambi Farinelli, spending the entire evening in her apartment. There had been no witnesses to the murder, and no murder weapon had ever been found. Only one new piece of evidence had surfaced - a dog walker who had spotted someone '*resembling*' Robinson running though Nicole Robinson's neighborhood that evening.

"They'll need more than that to convict him," Bryce had asserted.

"Yep," I concurred. "It's just circumstantial evidence if that's all they have."

So we left the matter at that. Besides, it was difficult for me to be so concerned with Robinson's plight, when my lack of a summer internship provided me with one of my own. The next day I was almost resigned to calling Monica about possible pro bono work when, between lectures, Bryce Davis pulled me aside.

"Listen," he said, "call this number. Not tonight, but tomorrow morning."

And with that he passed me a phone number, scribbled onto what appeared to be a used paper napkin. He provided no further details, aside from mentioning that Ashton Tate was now in desperate need of at least a half dozen interns. One of their attorneys had asked Bryce to recommend any law students who might be available on short notice. This was potentially great news for me, so I hounded Bryce for more details. In response he leaned closer, almost to my ear.

"It's Robinson," he whispered. "He's going to be arrested."

So the media rumors were now coming true. If Robinson were indeed accused, he would need a cutthroat legal team for his defense. Ashton Tate would assemble this team, garnered certainly from the firm's top stars. But supporting these stars would be a dedicated corps of paralegals, secretaries, and interns. An extra half dozen interns is not a trivial amount, and the sudden need for them implied that Robinson's defense team was already mobilizing itself for a possible trial.

"Promise that you'll call," Bryce said. "I've already put in a good word for you."

"I'll call," I said. "And thanks for your help!"

The next morning I brewed my coffee especially strong. I planned to call first thing to convey my initiative, and wanted to be extra alert. It would be mentally easier for me to assume a professional demeanor were I still not wearing a bathrobe. So before the call I also showered, and shaved, and dressed. Finally, at just past nine o'clock, I drew a deep breath and keyed the number which Bryce had given me. I heard the call ring, and, as it was answered, a sudden wave of anxiety broke over me.

"This is Jackson," said a tired voice at the other end of the line.

The name was such that it might have doubled as a first or as a last name, so I was unsure as to how to address him. Perhaps this was a first test in the interview process. My reaction was to simply introduce myself instead, mentioning that Bryce Davis had asked me to call.

"I'm inquiring about a possible internship position," I added casually.

I then held my breath as Jackson neither confirmed nor denied the existence of any such position. Rather, he instructed me to hold the line. The sound of shuffled paper came through the earpiece. I waited patiently, imagining him surrounded by a whirlwind of loose folios flying about his desk, until at length he again spoke.

"I have an interview opening at five this afternoon," he said. "Can you make it?"

I had no classes scheduled that afternoon, and so I accepted. After putting down the phone, I let out a sigh of relief, and almost hurt myself from jumping up and down. With such a large immediate quota to fill, I suspected that Jackson would do so with the least amount of hardship to himself. And if this brief phone call were any indication, the interview itself would be but a simple, straightforward formality.

Still, it was not an opportunity to take lightly. So, after my morning classes, I resolved to leave nothing to chance. In one of my suitcases, still unpacked since my arrival to the City of Angels, I had a business suit, my only suit, left over from my previous, somewhat professional career as a corporate scientist. The suit had been used sparingly, on only two occasions when presentations of my work had been required. I resurrected the suit from its tomb of a suitcase, immediately noticing how badly wrinkled it had become.

I stared at the disheveled suit in a panic, realizing that I did not have that most outdated of appliances, a clothes iron. But, with a flash of inspiration, I conjectured to remove the wrinkles with an appropriate amount of steam. Turning the shower up to full hot, I soon turned my small bathroom into a sauna. I then hung my tired suit near the shower head, and prayed that, encased by a healing shroud of steam, it would magically rejuvenate itself.

****

The offices of Ashton Tate inhabited one of the more conspicuous buildings along Wilshire Boulevard. Poised like a massive black monolith, this building anchored the western end of the so called Miracle Mile. Oddly enough, Ashton Tate's building was situated not far from the Page Museum and the LaBrea tar pits, where I had recently met Jonathan not more than a just few days past.

I shook my head in dismay to find myself unexpectedly back on the same block. After parking my car, I lingered briefly to once more observe the bubbling pool of tar, still sporting its forlorn mastodons and its menacing feline, until my itchy woolen suit reminded me of the interview which I would soon be late for. So I again left the mastodon to its fate, and walked the short distance to my perspective employer's building.

The building's lobby was a cavernous space, seemingly capable of holding a small movie theater. Rather than ushers however, two security guards therein greeted me. At the mention of Ashton Tate they pointed me across a vast expanse of gray tile floor to the main elevator bays. Ashton Tate leased the top three floors of this building, and as the elevator ascended to the fortieth floor, I made a final adjustment to my attire. Thanks to my steaming strategy, my suit was now mostly wrinkle free, although still slightly damp, and a bit itchy. It was a dark, pinstriped woolen affair which, along with a bright red tie and white buttoned collar shirt, blatantly conveyed the style of the previous decade. Dressed like this, no one could possibly accuse me of being enslaved by fashion, and I hoped that my interviewers would interpret such an attire as indicative of a strongly conservative, and hopefully desirable, twist to my nature.

When the elevator doors opened onto the fortieth floor I immediately had a feeling that, as the saying goes, I had *arrived.* Before me ran an expansive wall of glass, punctuated in the middle by two gold adorned glass doors. Behind the doors lay a receiving area, at the center of which floated a large circular desk commandeered by a young woman who seemingly had just stepped out of the pages of a fashion magazine. With easy effort, the large glass doors swung open, and I approached the fashion model, informing her of my five o'clock interview.

"Yes, with Mr. Jackson," she confirmed, now putting Jackson's name into proper perspective.

I was exactly on time for the interview. But, true to some unspoken protocol, I knew that I would be kept waiting. I chose what appeared to be a comfortable chair, preparing myself for a brief sit in it. It was now the end of the business day, and I suspected that Mr. Jackson would be running somewhat behind in his schedule. However I resolved that, when he finally did arrive, I would treat his tardiness as no significant matter. My demeanor would be pleasant and unflustered, as though the mere waiting for him had been an unexpected treat.

I declined the receptionist's offer of a drink, and drank instead of the atmosphere of the place. Clearly no expense had been spared. The receptionist's desk alone billowed with chrome and cherry wood as it floated atop a sea of spotless Berber carpeting. The walls were strewn with objects of modern art. I examined them, with one piece in particular, directly behind the receiving desk, capturing my attention. I stared at it, hoping to unravel its abstract message, when the receptionist looked up, and caught my gaze full on.

"Don't mind me," I apologized. "I'm just looking at that painting behind you."

"Oh, that one?" she confirmed. "It's one of my favorites. Not sure what it is though."

And, indeed, the painting was a pleasure to admire, but it appeared to be only a jumbled assortment of shapes and colors that were difficult to decipher. So after a few unsuccessful minutes of staring at it I refocused my thoughts onto my looming interview. I reviewed the resume that I'd brought. The years that I had spent working as a corporate scientist stood out awkwardly. Likely I would have to explain the motivations behind the abrupt shift in my career aspirations. I could always maintain that I had found the allure of science to be too dry and uninspiring, which I knew to be untrue, and that I now wished to pursue a career which was fundamentally more humanistic. I mentally rehearsed this explanation to myself numerous times, until it finally seemed believable.

The reception area eventually became antiseptically quite, with only me and the receptionist still loitering there. As the time turned to half past five I reminded myself of how enjoyable it was to still be waiting for Mr. Jackson. By fifty minutes past however, this waiting had turned miserable. My suit, still mostly wrinkle free, had become unbearably stifling, its pinstripes resembling the bars of a jail cell, while the red silk tie, fashioned too tightly, was seemingly strangling my neck like a noose. Perhaps sensing my discomfort, the receptionist attempted to reassure me.

"Mr. Jackson is most likely running late with his current interview," she suggested calmly.

I nodded thankfully to her, as though the thought of this possibility had never occurred to me. I then became concerned that this previous interview had now lingered for such an extravagantly long time. Perhaps the interview process was not as casual as I had assumed. I began imagining the hardships which the current candidate might have been enduring. Most likely he, or she, was being challenged with little known case histories, or being asked to argue, critically and spontaneously, obscure nuances of law. In a vision of my worst fears I imagined the candidate amidst a conference room of interviewers, a wolf pack, all straining for a quick swipe at the jugular. My mind was no longer filled with soothing thoughts of smiles and handshakes. Now, anxiously stifled by the oppressive warmth of my woolen suit, I began to sweat profusely.

Only with a forced effort did I regain my composure. When it was nearly six thirty, I was seated alone. The receptionist had at last left for the day, gone back to the pages of her fashion magazine. I myself began thinking of simply doing the same, when the doors from the coveted inner sanctum finally opened. Two individuals then appeared - a trim, blonde haired fellow, who I assumed to be the late Mr. Jackson, and a petite young brunette, who I assumed to be the other interview candidate.

The brunette wore heels and a tidy business suit, perhaps a bit undersized, and she clutched a polished leather portfolio. Her face sported a resolute smile, indicating perhaps that she had done all she could have, if not a bit more, to have made a favorable impression. As Jackson passed by me, I flashed him a broad smile, beaming how delightful all of my waiting for him had been. But he hardly noticed. For the moment his attention was fixed onto the charms of Miss Portfolio, as, escorting her to the formidable glass doors, he gave her a final, reassuring nod.

"Thank you for coming," he said. "You should be hearing from us, soon."

Miss Portfolio also nodded, and I watched as she then made her way to the elevator. There she waited, with upright head and pursed lips, and let out an obvious sigh of relief. As the elevator doors opened she stepped through them, and it was now my turn to come under Mr. Jackson's scrutiny.

Jackson appeared to be in his late thirties, and I speculated that he was most likely a senior associate with the firm. He had been entrusted with the rushed harvesting of this hasty crop of interns, not the most glamorous of assignments, but certainly a necessary one. He was probably a few years away from junior partner, and until then he had little recourse but to dutifully execute whatever marching orders were handed him.

I stood up as he approached me, and greeted him with an outstretched palm. We shook hands and he introduced himself as *Andrew* Jackson. Obviously his parents were expecting great thing of him to have named him after such an historic figure. Like his namesake, this modern day Andrew Jackson also sported a prominent shock of flowing sandy hair, and I imagined it blown back off his forehead while he led a furious charge into the midst of a heated courtroom battle.

"Thank you for coming," he obliged. "But there was no need to wear a suit. Your interview will be very informal."

Jackson was himself casually dressed in loafers and khaki. The only formality about him seemed to be a notoriously expensive gold wristwatch peeking out from beneath the cuffs of his buttoned down shirt. In contrast, my itchy outdated pinstriped suit suddenly made me feel overwhelmingly self conscious. I thought of telling him of my ordeal to free it of wrinkles, but this story now seemed inconsequential. Instead I gave him a firm handshake and consoled myself with the thought that one could never be too overdressed for a job interview. As a conversation starter, I mentioned how I had been admiring the lobby's artwork.

"Yes, Mr. Tate is quite a collector," said Jackson. "He's on the board of the Page Museum. Which is your favorite piece?"

"That one," I said, pointing past the reception desk. "But it's a mystery to me."

"Oh, that's an abstract of Lady Justice," Jackson told me. "But you need to view it from a certain angle to see her."

For the moment however there wasn't time to find this certain angle, and so I took Jackson at his word. I focused my thoughts onto my upcoming interview, and followed Jackson as he guided me out of the lobby and into the inner confines of the firm.

****

Beyond the reception area loomed a different world. We passed through a short corridor filled with photographs of the firm's founders, Messrs. Ashton and Tate, shown posed with assorted clients, most of whom were instantly recognizable. We even chanced across a photo containing a young Bruce Robinson.

"I know Bruce Robinson very well," Jackson mentioned as an offhand remark. "But you know, he isn't as tall as he seems in his movies."

"Yes I know," I added. "I've seen him in person too."

"You have?" asked Jackson. "Where?"

"At our homecoming parade," I said. "He was the Grand Marshall."

"Of course," nodded Jackson. "Yes, of course."

I too nodded, happy that we had found a small shred of common ground. The photo displays eventually concluded at the end of the corridor, after which I then suddenly found myself staring into a voluminous space drenched with the bright orange glow of the late afternoon sun. An enormous atrium, stacked three stories tall with tiers of glass walled offices, now expanded before us. An imposing glass facade spanned the atrium's far side, more than thirty feet from floor to ceiling. The facade looked westward, and one could almost spy the distant palm lined streets of Santa Monica through it. I had the immediate feeling of having stumbled into an exclusive, grandiose aquarium.

We rode a private elevator to the uppermost tier of offices. From this perch the entire western expanse of the city, clear to the blue Pacific, then appeared through the westward wall. I looked down into the open floor below, which was populated with desks and cubicles, and computers and copying machines. Like a miniature Manhattan, well delineated walkways divided the floor into separate neighborhoods of secretaries, paralegals, clerks, and, I assumed, lowly interns, such as I was hoping to become. Jackson's own office resided along the atrium's uppermost tier, and, once we'd arrived to it, I soon surmised that I had underestimated his position in the firm. A simple inscription on his door - *N. Andrew Jackson, Partner* - immediately discredited my prior assumptions about him.

A partner's office is especially well appointed, and, as I dropped myself into a large leather chair, I admired Jackson's walnut desk, bookcases, and credenza. The credenza held aloft various posed photos of Jackson himself, taken while either skiing or deep sea fishing. No photographs of a Mrs. Jackson or of any little Jacksons, but instead, proudly displayed, were images of a sleek silver sports car, and of a unique panting dog.

"That's an interesting dog," I commented. "What breed is it?"

"It's a Labrabull," Jackson informed me, "part Labrador, and part Pit Bull."

I'd never heard of such a breed, and I pondered as to how one might approach such a hybridized animal. The temptation to befriend it could be met with dire unforeseen consequences. But I had little time to pursue this particular train of thought. Jackson then cleared his throat and immediately launched into the formal phase of our interview.

"Our clients are some of the biggest names in the industry," he began, almost mechanically.

By industry of course he was referring to the entertainment industry, which, in this particular city, was the only industry worth mentioning. He casually listed a bevy of names, each one easily recognizable worldwide. These were some of Ashton Tate's most notable clients, their names mentioned for the obvious purpose of impressing any prospective employee. Jackson then spoke briefly about the history of Ashton Tate, of its modest origins, and of its eventual rise to prominence.

He spoke casually during the entire preamble, as though he expected me to already know these details, and was only stating them again for the sake of protocol. For my part I sought to appease Jackson as best as I could. I expressed admiration when he mentioned that the firm was a leader in the highly specialized area of entertainment law, and I expressed surprise upon hearing that the firm also possessed expertise in litigation, for both civil and criminal cases. When Jackson described the firm's humble beginnings I waxed wistful, and when he described the powerhouse which the firm had become, I too radiated a vicarious pride.

Since graduating from college I had suffered through several job interviews, and had come to understand the true purpose of this process. The interview functioned as a forum for the exchange of ideas of course, and it provided an opportunity for the candidate to show his merit. But when Jackson turned the conversation towards me and towards my qualifications and aspirations, I was well aware of the information which he actually sought. He wanted to hear of my unqualified desire for selfless dedication to the firm and to its clients. He wanted to hear that the firm could request any task of me, and that I would dutifully execute it without any question as to the motives. He wanted to hear that I would work ungodly long hours and would forsake any hope of a personal life for the firm's sake. In short, he wanted to hear that I would ever, and always, place the firm's needs ahead my own.

So, in response to Jackson's questions, I eagerly provided the necessary platitudes. I carefully adjusted my voice to a proper tone, timbered and controlled, such that it conveyed a reassuring aura of trust. With measured phrases and punctuated accents, I established my credibility, and reliability. With tempered zeal and steady conviction, I conveyed my desire to make the firm's success indistinguishable from my own, and that, in short, I was his man.

"Let me now ask you some technical questions," he said. "Do you know the difference between a declaration and a deposition?"

Yes, I did know. A declaration is a written statement entered into the body of a case for the purpose of providing information. A deposition, on the other hand, is a much more formal document, involving sworn oaths, and hence submitted as proper testimony.

"And briefly, what constitutes circumstantial evidence? Can you tell me?" he asked.

Yes, I could tell him. Circumstantial evidence is evidence which cannot be materially corroborated. That is, it is inferred from hearsay, or conjecture, or the odd confluence of events. As such circumstantial evidence can usually be discredited or dismissed – except, I noted, and I cited several cases, when presented by a persuasive attorney adroit enough to influence a teetering jury.

"Very good," he said to my responses. "You know, you remind me a bit of myself, from years ago."

And upon hearing this, I knew that Jackson and I had established our bond of trust. I then smiled at him, and he smiled back at me. From that point on we continued to strengthen our newly formed understanding, and the interview progressed with a more relaxed cadence. Jackson asked me of my person interests, to which I replied squash and sailing. As an added flourish, I mentioned that I loved animals, especially horses and dogs. I even told him that I might wish to have a Labrabull of my own someday.

I was Jackson's final interview for the day, and, with the outside sky transitioning into twilight, our meeting concluded. As Jackson escorted me away, I noticed that the atrium had become filled with the buzzing of late working attorneys. I was impressed by the sheer number of them, and I could not help wondering why these individuals were not already home with their wives and children. Perhaps, like myself, they too had once indicated their own undying allegiance to the firm.

They had emerged like so many cicadas in search of an evening meal, and I learned that the firm graciously provided one for them. On the lowest level, we walked past a common area where an impressively catered buffet had been assembled. Like most students I was always wary for a good meal, and so I stared at it, greedily.

"Why not stay for a quick dinner?" suggested Jackson, apparently sensing my need.

His offer took me by surprise. But I quickly accepted, and soon found myself holding a plate heaped tall from the various meats, salads, and breads strewn along nearly twenty feet of counter space. I then followed Jackson to a large table, where we joined a group of other attorneys already seated there.

"Well, my day's half done," proclaimed one of them, "time now for lunch."

The other attorneys chuckled, in apparent morbid commiseration. But between bites there seemed little inclination among them for discussing work related matters. Instead, their attention shifted to me, the new face at their table. After a casual introduction, one of them, John Corsini, enquired about my own particular interests. In response, I dredged up my ancient ambitions about specializing in tort law.

"Tort law is fine," observed Corsini, "but good tort cases are hard to come by. The real money is in divorce. There's no end to that."

The other attorneys nodded in agreement. It was probably true that while transgressions involving corporate negligence were a rare occurrence, those involving human negligence were most likely occurring on a frequent, if not reliable cadence.

"…..and no end to homicide cases either," suggested Jackson.

"Yes, those too," said Corsini. "Well, my loss is your gain I suppose."

"Are you kidding?" offered Jackson. "You dodged a bullet by losing that case!"

"Yes I did," Corsini conceded. "Too bad that Nicole Robinson didn't."

I inferred from this bit of morbid humor that Corsini had been handling Bruce Robinson's divorce, now an unnecessary matter. Although Robinson's murder defense was bound to be phenomenally more lucrative for Ashton Tate, so no harm done. Still, Corsini seemed miffed by the loss of such a choice case.

"Oh well," he added wistfully, "there'll be plenty more."

And indeed, I suspected that, outside the confines of Ashton Tate, the seeds of new divorces were ever being planted. Nestled in the surrounding hills hearts were ever beating, and filling themselves with those desires which might easily lead their owners astray. And, once lost and astray, these hearts would have no recourse but to bargain with a firm such as Ashton Tate, and beg for desperate absolution.

When dinner had concluded, all the attorneys wished me well, and Jackson escorted me back to the reception area. As with Miss Portfolio, we stopped by the glass doors for a few final formalities. He thanked me for making time for the interview, and for considering Ashton Tate as a potential employer. These were remarks made only in courtesy of course. In truth, it was actually me extending a beggar's cups to solicit the charity of the firm. But I also followed the accepted script and thanked him in kind for his own time.

"We'll be in touch," concluded Jackson. "You should hear from us by next week."

And with those words, a nod, and a last handshake, he left me alone to await the elevator. Like Miss Portfolio, I too let out a sigh of relief as I entered it. Before the elevator arrived however, I caught a final glimpse of the golden reception area. The cryptic abstract painting still hovered therein. But in the dim light, and from my particular angle, the figure of Lady Justice did indeed materialize out of the swirling milieu of what had previously been but a random assortment of colors and shapes. Now she sported her trademark robe, blindfold, and scales which, just as the elevator doors closed, I noticed were tilted precariously off to one side.

9.

The next day I told Bryce how well my interview had gone. We then discussed the possibility of our working together, most likely on what appeared to be the upcoming Robinson case. Bryce confided that Andrew Jackson had been tapped as the managing partner for the case, and he was personally giving a thumbs up or down on all hires for it. If I had favorably impressed him, as it seemed I had, then I was certain to be brought on. Still I fretted.

"Don't worry, and just wait," Bryce advised.

And indeed Bryce was right. Any attempt to now contact the firm could only be perceived as superfluous or trite. There was really nothing left for me to do at this point but focus on my studies, and make a strong finish in the upcoming final exams. My fate for the summer was now in the hands of the mailman. For, if a large manila envelope bearing the Ashton Tate seal were delivered, it would likely contain an offer letter. But if a thin white business envelope appeared instead, then I was doomed.

But in spite of Bryce's reassurance, I did not spend a restful night. I was troubled by dreams of angry manila envelopes chasing me about. Occasionally one of the envelopes would catch me and swallow me whole, while at other times I would ensnare one of them instead, only to see it transform itself into a plain business envelope, of no value, as I held it in my hands.

Were I to receive a rejection letter however, it would not mean the end of the world. My only concern was for Jenn, and how I wished to appear successful in her eyes. I had not heard from her in nearly a week, and I dreaded that she was now losing all interest in me. I had left several messages on her machine, but after receiving no replies, I'd stopped calling. Not until the end of the week did she finally return my calls.

"I'm sorry," she informed me, "but my father has been in the hospital."

She had spent most of her time by his bedside as he sought to recover from a variety of complications. He had become exhausted from working too much about the ranch, and as a result he had contracted flu and a high fever.

"He'll never admit it," said Jenn, "but he's just not as strong as he used to be."

"He needs to slow down," I offered.

But I suspected that Mr. Devaine's was not the type of spirit to obligingly sit still. For him, something would always need tending. The thorny vines and their allies were ever on the march, seeking to overrun the Eden Ranch. But the ranch was vast, and impossible for him to tend alone. There were simply too many vines.

Jenn could not help him, for she had become mired in her own problems. Progress in her linguistics research remained stalled, and she had rushed back to the university to again discuss the matter with her advisor. I longed to see her again, and we made plans to meet Saturday for a late meal at her apartment. We had been apart for nearly two weeks, and, as I climbed the four short steps to her front door that Saturday evening, my heart raced with anticipation. I knocked lightly on her door, and as it opened Jenn motioned me inside. I wanted so much to embrace her, but instead, not knowing if she still cared for me, I simply leaned forward and placed a soft kiss on her cheek.

Dinner that night was a simple affair, just bread, wine and a light salad, but it gave us a chance to reconnect. I recounted my recent interview escapades at Ashton Tate. Beyond this however our conversation struggled to flourish. By all appearances she seemed tired. Dark rings outlined her eyes, which, even in the dim light of her apartment, belied a red tinge, as though stained by earlier tears.

After dinner Jenn disposed of the dinner plates, and I seated myself onto her sole piece of furniture, her futon. Her apartment lacked any table or chairs, and we usually ate dinner crossed legged on the floor. There were two boxes pushed into a far corner, still unopened since Jenn had moved in nearly two years ago. All in all she had made no effort to add the slightest amount of charm, as though doing so might prevent her from leaving on a quick moment's notice. In all honesty, the same might be said of my own sparsely furnished apartment. But at least I had made a feeble attempt at decoration with some wall posters and a few lonely plants.

The last few weeks seemed to have taken their toll on Jenn, as she had struggled to attend to her ailing father, to the Eden Ranch, and to her studies. I wanted to help her in some way so as to revive the carefree spirit I had first known in her. Now I wished for Dave Richard's millions, which, although powerless to restore Mr. Devaine's lost youth, could easily help to make his ill health less of a burden.

"You seem tired," I mentioned after dinner. "I should go, so that you can rest."

I rose from the futon and went to give Jenn a parting hug. But she only drew me closer and rested her head against me. I could hear her breath quickening, and I felt her limbs shudder as a fresh wave of tears began to stream onto my shoulder. She was no longer the light hearted Venus that I had once known, but for that moment had turned into a trembling little waif, frightened by the grim reality of existence. I held her close, stroked her hair, and kissed her on the head, almost cursing myself that I could do nothing else for her, but hold her.

"No, please stay," she said. "Please stay tonight."

And so we spent a confused night together, passionate and cheerless. When I awoke the next morning, Jenn had already dressed. That day she was to meet with her advisor to plead an extension for her long overdue thesis. As she made ready to leave, I wished for the luxury of a lazy morning spent with her. But, sitting upright on the futon, I realized that we'd never had such a luxury. In the few months that I'd known Jenn, so much of our time had been cobbled together piecemeal from brief encounters and stolen moments.

"We should take a trip together," I suggested. "You know, get away for a while."

"We should," agreed Jenn. "How about with your friend, Dave? Didn't he invite us to go sailing with him?"

As much I wanted to sail again, this was not the excursion that I'd had in mind. I wanted to be with Jenn, *only* Jenn, without any interference from Dave, or Crystal, or her gut wrenching aloe juice. But even then, I suspected that Dave's invitation had been offered only as a passing courtesy.

"I know of a star party next weekend," I countered. "That might be fun."

I explained to Jenn exactly what a star party entailed. There would be telescopes and stars, of course. But there would also be brilliant physicists, in particular my friend Jonathan Schwarzchild, and the opportunity to revel in the majesty of the heavens above. I waxed enthusiastically about the party. But as I concluded my sales pitch, Jenn remained silent, still apparently unimpressed.

"That doesn't sound very interesting," she said at last. "But let me think about it."

I wondered how else to entice her. Were it possible, I would have whisked her off to an exotic corner of the globe in luxury and style. She deserved nothing less than to be draped in satin and pearls and displayed in public as living artwork. She deserved to be pampered with jewels, baubles, furs, and trifles of all kinds. But I was in no position to do so, and I could not help but feel her beauty being wasted in my presence. And of the simple things that I could immediately offer Jenn, a keen mind, a sense of humor, an honest heart, I was unsure of the value that any of these actually held for her.

So, when it came time to say our goodbye, I was suddenly overwhelmed by the feeling that I might never see her again, that our time together would become nothing more than a lost dream. But there was nothing to be done. I could not change who I was, although I was indeed trying to do so. I knew that there existed a preordained order to the universe, but how Jenn and I would harmonize with that order, I could not predict.

"I'll miss you," I said as we parted, in response to which she only smiled.

****

By next Friday morning I had not heard anything from Jenn about the star party, and so I readjusted my plans to simply attending it without her. Still, I did feel a bit of remorse. We might have spent a pleasant evening together of course, but beyond this, I'd hoped to expose her to a different side of me, a side which, up to now, had remained hidden. That part of me could have shown her the wonders of the surrounding universe, perhaps lifting her spirits, if but for only one night, above the earthly cares which had so recently overwhelmed her. But on that Saturday, as I pondered this lost opportunity, the phone did ring, and it was Jenn.

"I've decided to come after all," she said.

My spirits then suddenly lifted, and were still riding high that evening when I opened my door to see Jenn with her hair pulled back, and wearing heels and a small cocktail dress.

"Uh, it's not really a formal kind of party," I started to say.

But then I stopped myself short and merely smiled, delighted that she was coming. Glad for her company, I simply combed back my own hair and upgraded my own clothes to a more formal shirt and slacks. I fancied thinking us the perfect couple as we drove, through relentless traffic, to the base of the San Bernardino hills. There we stopped briefly, and I rolled back the car top so that we might drive the last stretch, through the San Angeles forest and up to Mount Wilson, under an open sky. The stars had begun to come out, and, as we steadily rose along a lonely switchback road, the carefree palm trees of the valley below gradually gave way to the statelier conifers of a higher altitude.

We climbed higher, and the air grew cooler around us. Jenn fell silent and began to shiver. The car's old heater provided only puffs of warm air, and, as darkness fell, I noticed that my car also had only one working headlight. But still, everything for me seemed perfect, and with each winding turn my anticipation surged. I had peered through telescopes before of course, but not one as renowned as the one atop Mount Wilson. The observatory's original telescope, with its enormous one hundred inch hand cast Saint-Gobains' mirror, a wonder in its day, was still there. I would now breathe the same air, climb the same stairs, and look through the same eyepiece, as Edwin Hubble himself had almost a century before.

Oddly enough, Hubble had also once trained as an attorney. But it was astronomy which finally proved to be his siren's song. He eventually accepted a position at Mount Wilson to chart *nebulae*, the then curious little clouds in the night sky, which, like God's own dust bunnies, seemed to be littered throughout all of space. But Hubble discovered that these bunnies were not made of dust, but of stars, seemingly billions of them, all huddling together for warmth amidst the cold loneliness of empty space. The little clouds were then renamed galaxies, and, as surprisingly countless more of them were discovered, some at phenomenally incredible distances, the true expanse of God's vast creation finally came to light.

Like Hubble, I too had marveled at the selfsame galaxies. But in my undergraduate years, more had been required of me than simply admiring their beauty. Since Hubble's time General Relativity had been formulated, an expanding universe had been postulated, and the unexplained existence of dark energy had been inferred. The stars were no longer just pretty points of light. To understand them now required the scaling of a daunting wall of mathematics. But as an undergraduate, I had unfortunately found it more preferable to turn away from that wall, rather than to face it.

"Look, there's Orion," I said, pointing overhead.

Jenn glanced upwards, but the sight of him did nothing to warm her mood.

"Are we almost there?" she asked. "I'm freezing."

We had been climbing for nearly an hour when the car finally put the last switchback behind us. As we then mounted the ridgeline road our destination came squarely in sight before us, prominent against the evening sky. I wished to now savor every moment of the evening. Finally, and with Jenn in tow, I would proceed along the same paths walked by so many immortal physicists from decades past. Even Einstein had made a pilgrimage here to view firsthand, through Hubble's telescope, the very fingerprints of God.

Jenn felt unremittingly chilled. So after parking the car we dashed towards the warmth of the observatory. Its main door was open and a narrow, dimly lit corridor loomed beyond it. We rushed along the corridor past small Spartan offices to a spiral stairway at the far end. The viewing floor was above us, and I could discern the murmurings of the ongoing star party. I held my breath as I climbed the stairs. I was about to enter astronomy's Mecca, its most sacred shrine. I closed my eyes, and kept them closed until I'd reached the upper landing. I wanted my first sight of Hubble's sanctum to strike me with its full force, and upon opening my eyes I was not disappointed.

Before me there loomed a vast skeleton of a space, which, like a medieval cathedral, elicited wonder through the sheer magnitude of its confined volume. At the centerpiece of this particular cathedral however was not an altar, but Hubble's fabled telescope. In modern observatories the telescope itself is usually hidden and inaccessible behind a protecting shroud. But here it was un-shrouded, the observatory itself forming its shroud, so that the magnificence of it hovered plainly before us.

The long body of the scope extended upward, at an incline, to an awe inspiring length of nearly eighty feet. A gossamer metal frame, in this case painted a sparkling evening blue, suspended the massive body of the instrument. Through this latticework, one could discern the enormous mirrors, handcrafted in France long ago, which had enabled Hubble to make his monumental discoveries. The entire structure, perhaps a full two tons, was mounted in cantilever fashion onto massive gimbals which, properly balanced and lubricated, enabled this colossal blue elephant of a telescope to dance nimbly across the night sky. I marveled at the sight, speechless, and, turning to Jenn, sought her own reaction.

"What do you think?" I asked, nodding at the scope.

"It looks…..almost erotic!" she joked.

I had never actually considered telescopes from such a unique perspective, so such a comment left me unexpectedly bemused. If Hubble's spirit was haunting the observatory, I dearly hoped that it had not heard Jenn's remark. I attempted no reply – how could I? - but instead motioned Jenn's attention towards a nearby group of mingling physicists.

"By the way," I warned her as we moved forward, "we may be a bit overly dressed for this party….."

A dozen or so physics students were congregated ahead of us. As I would have expected, they were all dressed as casually as polite society permitted. In contrast, Jenn and I, in our formal evening wear, seemed to have emerged from a world apart. I introduced us, with all eyes falling squarely onto Jenn, mentioning that we were friends of Jonathan Schwarzchild, who was apparently nowhere to be seen.

"We've come from a prior engagement," I conjectured, trying to put everyone at ease about our dress.

Everyone seemed to allow this as a plausible explanation, and so we fell in with the group. The conversation at hand was of course about cosmology, and in particular about a problem that was still unsolved since my own undergraduate days. The debate still raged regarding whether the cosmic dark energy had forever existed, even since the very beginnings of the universe.

"Oh, you mean like….since the Big Boom?" Jenn interjected.

I smiled, and nodded in agreement, not wanting to correct her. Indeed, perhaps there had been a big *boom*, instead of a big *bang*. Only God could say with certainty, and He had consistently remained silent on this topic. The other physicists also nodded, possibly deferring to Jenn's other obvious talents, which were clearly not related in the least to cosmology. For in a field where females were a rare species, her presence alone must have been a welcomed sight to the other physicist.

"Yes," one of them affirmed, "perhaps the Big Boom was the original source of dark energy."

"Exactly," another suggested, "it's plausible that the Big Boom itself seeded what we currently perceive as the spatial expansion of the universe!"

The speculations regarding the Big Boom became increasingly interesting, and I eagerly anticipated Jenn's next contribution. Unfortunately, Jenn's engagement then only seemed to wane. And just as I was about to offer my own insights, she pulled me aside.

"This wasn't the type of party I'd had in mind," she mentioned. "Perhaps we should go."

But it was too early to leave. I wanted her to meet Jonathan. And still ahead of us were the actual viewings, which I'd hoped would lift her spirits. I searched for any words which might make her stay.

"Let's stay," I suggested. "I was hoping to have compared your beauty to that of the stars."

Jenn had once warned me of my inept penchant for romantic sentiment, and apparently my abilities had not improved since then. It was a feeble remark I knew, and in response she only rolled her eyes. I was starting to feel somewhat tired and frustrated myself. The evening had not gotten off to a good start, and the ludicrousness of our situation had begun overwhelming me. Our inappropriate attire, the tedious waiting, Jonathan's unexpected absence, the Big Boom, were all conspiring against me. Desperate, I too was about to abandon ship when there came a tap on my shoulder, and I turned around to finally see a familiar face.

"I brought some ice cream," said Monica. "Would you like some?"

Monica had brought a batch of cryogenic ice cream, and she had rushed it inside while Jonathan parked their car. Made with sweet cream, sugar, vanilla, and liquid nitrogen, it was the staple of many a star party. The recipe was deceptively simple, assuming of course that one had access to a supply of liquid nitrogen from a nearby research lab. I offered Jenn a spoonful of the stuff, and watched her expression as the frozen concoction effervesced onto her tongue. This was a rare treat which few people would ever experience, and, with raised eyebrows, Jenn seemed genuinely intrigued by it.

"Interesting," she said. "But right now I'd rather have a stiff drink."

I suggested that we should linger but a bit longer, as Jonathan would soon be arriving. I had made mention of him before, alluding to his brilliant qualities. However when he finally did join us, he appeared more ghoulish than genius. Unshaven and, I hated to think, unwashed, he seemed quite a fright.

"Sorry," said Monica, "but he's hardly slept now for three days."

I learned that Jonathan had dispensed with sleep. Rumors were circling that the fabled Edwin Wilson would soon publish his long awaited paper, one which would solidify his version of the elusive string theory. In response to this threat, Jonathan had been racing against time to finalize his own theory. But as he stood before me, gaunt and hollow, I wondered what traces of supernatural reserves still remained within him to draw from. While Jonathan struggled to even converse with us, another physicist approached him.

"It's almost certain," this fellow pronounced. "Wilson is publishing next month."

"So, let him," declared Jonathan. "Then I'll finally be rid of him!"

Startled by Jonathan's tone, the physicist offered no response, and simply walked away, searching perhaps for more congenial conversation. As Jonathan then stood, silent as a ghost before us, I too began to feel Jenn's impatience.

"Well," she said, "I've met the brilliant Jonathan. Can we go now?"

With Jonathan so unfortunately distant, we were reduced to aimless waiting. But Jenn's was not a spirit that willing did so. Hers needed turbulence and exuberance to feel alive, and all of these were absent from this particular party. Across the room, the telescope operators were busily engaged in making their final adjustments. I pulled Jenn towards them as a distraction, leaving Jonathan and Monica behind.

"We're almost ready," one of the operators announced.

He stood before a sturdy control panel which was cluttered with dials and meters and switches, all seemingly unchanged since Hubble's day. Briefly I envisioned Hubble himself manning these self same controls after charting out his planned observations. This particular telescope predated computers, and so, just as Hubble would have, this behemoth of an instrument was scanned across the evening sky guided only by the subtle nuances of a human hand.

"We're ready!" the other operator finally announced.

Now the overhead lights were dimmed and the red viewing lights were turned on. They saturated the observatory's cavernous interior with a diffuse scarlet glow. As if on cue all conversations ceased, and the vast cathedral of a space became filled with a religious silence. The sound of a mechanical switch then hung itself onto the stillness, heralding a harmonious chorus of whirring gears. Then low muffled rumblings, as though from a distant locomotive, surrounded us as the dome's canopy opened, and the large phallus of a telescope was erected for its intercourse with the night sky.

"This is going to be good," I whispered to Jenn.

The viewing agenda was announced. Starting with luminous Sirius, an easy first target, the scope would then arc westward across the night sky to capture a glimpse of Venus, and then of Andromeda, the closest galaxy to our own. The crowd of attendees milled closer to the telescope. An impromptu queue of observers formed which, because of our proximity to the instrument panel, had Jenn and me standing in front.

"These two well dressed people will go first," the operator informed everyone.

An especially narrow catwalk connected the main floor to the viewing station, and Jenn and I were beckoned onto it. We could only walk over it in single file, and so I let Jenn lead the way, following the supple curves of her figure through the crimson glow. At the viewing station I looked through the eyepiece at Sirius, the Dog Star, which as usual was bright, blue, and beautiful. Sirius appears as a single entity to the naked eye, but through the scope the star revealed its tiny secret.

"Look," I told Jenn, "there's a smaller star next to it."

Through the eyepiece it becomes apparent that the Dog Star has a companion, a small flea of a star which is forever flitting about it. I explained to Jenn how the flea star, Sirius B, glows with the characteristic yellow of an ordinary star, while Sirius A, massive and super hot, glowed with the blue tinge of a supergiant. The larger star's life would be brief as it burned its fuel at a prodigious rate. As a result it would eventually explode into a super nova over the next ten million years, obliterating its flea star in the process. Possibly it might have already exploded, with the light from this event not having even yet reached us.

"See, the stars are more than just pretty points of light," I suggested.

Jenn seemed to concede me a tinge of interest, perhaps as she might to a unique flower arrangement. In further hushed tones I sought to convey the wonderment of viewing distant stars. The light which they send has made a long, lonely journey through the empty confines of space before finally impressing itself onto our eyes. So Sirius, as every other star, reaches out to us, assuring us that we were not alone, instructing us, with such clear example, of the greater creation beyond ourselves. Perhaps these particular notions rang too philosophical for that current mood. But with tilted head Jenn offered them a brief consideration.

"Sure, if you say so," she at last concluded.

With a smirk and a nod, she acknowledged my right to harbor such wild speculations. However, as we went back along the catwalk, a warm sense of satisfaction spread through me to think that I'd had the nerve to voice such outlandish ideas. We returned into the mill of the main floor, and waited for Jonathan and Monica to join us after their own viewing.

"What did you think?" I asked Monica.

"That was lovely," she said, content with her simple assessment. "Very pretty."

"Oh, but there's more to it than that, much more," added Jenn. "Just ask Paul."

Yes, as I had already explained, there was indeed much more. I almost went for Jenn's bait, but then caught myself short.

"Listen," I told her, nearly exasperated, "maybe you shouldn't have come after all."

I had now set the stage for a long uncomfortable silence, which hung there between us until helpful Monica attempted to brighten the mood.

"Would you care for my ice cream recipe?" she asked Jenn.

"No, I don't," replied Jenn. "I don't cook."

"But making ice cream isn't cooking," explained Monica. "It's just mixing things together. That's all."

Undaunted, Monica rummaged through her bag for a loose pen, and, finding also an old envelope, she began scribbling the prized recipe. But before she could finish, Jenn turned away.

"I need some air," she announced. "So, if you'll excuse me, I'm going outside."

Monica eventually entrusted her recipe to me, and I tucked it into a pocket. If I cared at all for my well being, I would never ever show it to Jenn.

"Thanks," I said. "I'm sure that Jenn will love it."

"Is your friend feeling alright?" asked Jonathan. "She seems a bit tense."

There was no hiding Jenn's bad mood of course, so I confided all of the stresses, from her father's ill health to the academic challenges that she had been struggling against. I'd hoped for this evening's viewings to have lifted her sights, albeit temporarily, above these problems. But perhaps this had been only a foolish hope on my part.

When it came time for the second viewing, Jenn had not yet returned, and so I proceed down the catwalk alone. I gazed at the glimmering evening star which is Venus. I marveled at her radiance. But I knew that the cool, blue light of Venus is but an illusion, only a byproduct of her hot, seething, toxic atmosphere.

****

After the last viewing I bid my friends good night, and I went to find Jenn. Eventually I made my way to the outside grounds. To the left of the observatory was a small patio bounded by a waist high rail, where now a lone, lithe figure leaned onto it. Jenn gazed westward, towards the dark outlines of the San Gabriel hills and the glowing mass of the San Gabriel valley below. The valley lights sparkled like a vast carpet of stars, resembling a small galaxy of their own.

The high night air had now turned exceptionally cold, and as I approached Jenn I noticed that she was not only shivering again, but also crying. I reached out to her, imagining that the toil of the day had finally overwhelmed her.

"I'm tired," she said wiping a tear. "Can we go now?"

"Sure," I said, nodding sympathetically. "I think we're done here."

I held her, trying to calm her shivering. We walked back to my car with a bright canopy of stars still hovering above us, and I wondered if, around any of those stars, other beings, perhaps more enlightened, had succeeded in living happier, less difficult lives than our own.

I snapped the car's top back into place, and we made our way down the winding unlit road. Beside me Jenn had curled herself into a compact bundle, trying to create a warm space, while I, with my one good headlight lighting the way, focused on returning our tired selves safely back home. A two hour drive lay ahead of us, and as the car swung around the sharp hairpins I saw the gas needle dipping further below empty with each subsequent turn. I had planned to fill the tank during this return trip. But as the engine sputtered to a halt halfway down the mountain road, I suspected that this plan would need to be altered. Beside me, Jenn had quietly fallen asleep.

With gravity as my ally, I was able to maneuver the car completely downhill without any engine power. But at the bottom I had no such ally. As the car coasted to a stop, I considered my options. In this remote part of the foothills, at this late hour, I was doubtful that any fellow traveler, especially one possessing a friendly disposition, would miraculously come to our aid before the morning light. But the thought of spending the night shivering on a cold car seat did not seem appealing either. I glanced towards the electric glow hovering in the distance, and mentally gravitated towards what appeared to be the best plan.

"Seize the moment," I said on exiting the car, with Jenn still asleep inside.

The lights of the San Gabriel valley seemed no more than a half mile's walk away. I would certainly find a service station along one of the main streets, and there purchase some gasoline. I dared not disturb Jenn, and simply left her, for now, blissfully asleep. I walked for half an hour, making my way through empty, dimly lit streets until finally arriving at a main boulevard. There, the anticipated service station soon came into view.

I explained my situation to the station attendant, and he listened sympathetically to my ramblings. But eventually I surmised that he did not understand at all a word of English. I sought to convey my need for a few gallons of gasoline with a more universal language. I pulled some bills from my front pocket, and gesturing to the distant site of the mishap, I offered a more simplified description of the situation.

"Car. Stopped," I gestured. "Gaso-*lina*? *Comprende?*"

Luckily he did *comprende*. Reaching under the counter, he produced a two gallon can reserved for such a particular emergency. As I reached for the can however, the attendant flashed out ten fingers to indicate the amount of deposit money required. I showed him my few dollars, and cast a pleading look towards him. But, with open palms and raised eyebrows, he indicated that he could offer no exception.

I was now desperate. The thought of Jenn left sleeping on a lonely hillside road was starting to weigh on my conscience. But needing only a container I fished through the station's trash bins and found two empty plastic milk jugs. Most likely, transporting gasoline in these containers constituted a violation of some local ordinance. But the attendant made no note of this, and I suspected that in his home country this was a perfectly acceptable means of carrying dangerous fuel.

Gasoline splashed onto my hands and clothes as I filled the jugs, so much so that I then reeked of it. As I rushed back through the empty neighborhood streets, I must have made for a queer, if not disconcerting, sight. What might anyone conclude of seeing a hurried, petrol scented figure scurrying through the dark hours with two jugs of gasoline, except to think of him as an arsonist? I mumbled a silent prayer that such a suspicious sight would not incline anyone to call the police. But as no such call was made, I eventually returned to my car un-arrested, to find Jenn still there, except now fully awake.

"You're back," she said. "Why did you leave me here, alone?"

"Well, we ran out of gas," I started to explain, "and this seemed like the best plan."

As proof I held up the two jugs. But Jenn remained visibly upset to have been so casually abandoned on such a lonely dark road. The subsequent drive home was hardly pleasant. My clothes reeked of gasoline, the smell of which no amount of open air was able to dilute. Jenn too was fuming, and I suspected that if she could have, she would have gladly set me ablaze with a lighted match. We were both exhausted, and luckily Jenn once again fell asleep, leaving me to drive the remaining way in relieved silence.

When we finally reached my apartment, I helped her out of the car, and trudged her inside. I poured her limp body into bed. I myself collapsed onto the couch, and, in spite of the overwhelming smell of gasoline, fell asleep in the self same clothes. I slept until noon, when, on awaking, I found that Jenn had already gone. Out of concern I called her, but got a response only from her answering machine.

"Are you alright?" was all that I could think of saying into the machine. "Please call me when you get a chance."

But she did not call, and I spent the rest of that day feeling exhausted and doing nothing in particular. I tried unsuccessfully to study for my upcoming exams, and to remove the smell of gasoline from my clothes.

But mostly, I tried to fathom how the events of the previous evening could have gone so dismally awry.

10.

Throughout the entire next week I devoted myself to my studies. Final exams were fast approaching, and, deep in the confines of the law library, I sought to make one last push. But the recent star party had gotten me thinking of physics once again, and more often than not, while reviewing some obscure statute, I found myself jotting down equations still remembered from my undergraduate years. Like lost friends, the equations stared back at me, curious as to why I had abandoned them.

But a year's worth of poring through legal case studies was now exacting its wearisome toll. Only through superhuman effort did I manage to keep my thoughts focused, hoping to pack enough relevant details between my ears to avoid disaster in the year end exams. But my future beyond these exams was still uncertain as I had not heard from either Jackson, or Ashton, or Tate. Only Bryce Davis sought to diminish my worries.

"Well, it's a good thing that you *haven't* heard anything," he noted.

His reasoning was simple. If a rejection, then I probably would have received it by now. An actual offer of employment, which required more time to compile, might be easily delayed by at least a week. But I had little time to lose. The summer was fast approaching and I had made no other plans. Gone now were the carefree summers of my youth when I could spend the long lazy days simply reading or thinking, and count these as worthwhile activities. At this point in my life, only demonstrated progress towards life fulfilling goals was now expected of me.

But Bryce's prescience proved to be correct. Arriving home one evening I found an envelope from both Ashton and Tate, swollen and dense, awaiting me. Inside it, a letter detailed the terms of my employment, a brochure described the positive attributes of joining with such a distinguished firm, and a hiring contract awaited my conferring signature. Finally holding this envelope I allowed myself, briefly, to feel overjoyed. I longed to tell someone, especially Jenn, the good news. But that evening I could not reach her by phone. Only on the next day, when I again saw Bryce Davis, did I share my excitement.

"Remember, I put in a good word for you," Bryce observed. "You owe me one."

I allowed him some credit for his help, but also suggested that perhaps Ashton Tate had spotted a few worthwhile qualities in me that might have influenced their decision.

"Well, perhaps," he offered, with a slight nod.

Over coffee we discussed the prospect of our working together. Probably we were slated for Jackson's team. With Robinson's case going to trial, there would be a tremendous need for an agonizingly painful amount of detailed legal research. Foot soldiers like Bryce and me would be assigned to do it, not the most glamorous of duties, but, as part of such a noteworthy case, still an exciting prospect.

"It's sad to think," Bryce admitted, "but criminal law does have its thrills."

And in this respect he was most likely correct. Although one could make a very comfortable living from the mastery of real estate, tort, or patent law, these specializations could in no way compete with the visceral passion derived from interacting with people who had deviated from proper patterns of social behavior. A sensational murder case especially, such as this one, offered an invigorating prospect for any attorney.

I did eventually convey my news to Jenn, albeit through her answering machine. I was overjoyed when she called back.

"I hope you'll do well," she offered.

"Don't worry," I said. "I will."

My summer plans were now finally in place, but as for Jenn's, no such luck. She still lacked a viable research topic, and after final exams she'd only planned to return to the Eden Ranch to care for her father. My heart sank to hear this. I had hoped that Jenn and I might have found ourselves in closer proximity through the summer.

"But we'll see each other again?" I almost pleaded.

"Sure," she conceded, "but just not at another star party. Please."

And, with such casual ease, Jenn left our possibilities for the ensuing summer so ill defined. Deep inside me I braced myself to spend the coming months completely alone. Seemingly, I had been given the chance to play a role in Jenn's ongoing drama, but through no fault of my own I had somehow failed the auditions.

****

When the week of final exams did at last arrive I felt a sense of long awaited relief. There could be no more dread or anxiety, only a sense of resignation to a looming fate. One could no longer study or review the obscure case or statute with the hope of gaining a final edge. Time for last minute heroics no longer remained, but only enough time to gird oneself for the unavoidable ordeal.

Unnervingly, the grades for an entire year's worth of curricula now hinged solely on these exams, and on the responses to the three questions which typically comprised each one. Conceivably one could miss all of the year's lectures, but, by answering a mere handful of question correctly, still achieve stellar grades. I found the system strange, but this is the normal practice in almost all of the law schools. Of course a student might also seek to influence his grades by building a familiarity with his professors. But I had not been one of these students, and my consistent reticence and obscurity during lecture hours now guaranteed me no advantage.

Throughout that exam week I sat in tense, crowded lecture halls, struggling along with my fellow students to provide my best responses. To convey a sense of this I could list, tediously and painfully, all of the questions posed by these exams. But instead, consider this one particular example from my contracts exam.

Hank has decided to sell his home to Martha. But he is called out of the country for a few months before a formal contract can be signed. He accepts a nominal goodwill deposit from Martha and allows her to move into the home while he is abroad.

So far so good for Hank and Martha, but then the trouble starts.

Thinking that she will eventually own the home, Martha initiates renovations while Hank is away. However, when Hank subsequently returns, he realizes how fondly attached he is to his home, and he no longer wishes to sell it. He offers to compensate Martha for the costs of her renovations, plus ten percent for any inconvenience. But Martha refuses, claiming that Hank should sell her the home as they had agreed.

Hank and Martha are at an impasse, and the exam question is now posed.

What contract exists between Hank and Martha, and who has legal right to the home?

To me the answer seemed obvious – both Hank and Martha were fools. Of course, I made no mention of this in my response. I simply provided a succinct and correct answer. Namely, that the original verbal agreement between Hank and Martha was not legally binding, and that, sorry Martha, Hank was still the legal owner of the home. Hank, however, did have to refund the deposit money. But he did not have to compensate Martha for the renovations that she'd made to what was not legally her home.

The remaining questions posed in the contracts exam were of the same bent. I found the questions in my other two exams, criminal law and judiciary procedure, all similarly straightforward, if not actually trivial. So much so, that I completed each exam in almost half of the allotted time. It felt strange to sit there idle while, all about me, my fellow classmates still scribbled furiously. Each time, more than half of my exam book was left empty, and so, with time to spare, I amused myself by filling the remaining pages with physics equations. Maxwell's equations, Schrodinger's, even the dreaded one from Hubble, they all came effortlessly back to me. And while everyone about me perspired, I calmly admired these equations, as the infallible truths they were, until the allotted exam times had passed.

Once my exams were behind me I felt relieved of course, but also surprisingly disappointed. Unlike my undergraduate years spent studying physics, I now felt no sense of real accomplishment. I had unlocked no secrets of the ordered mysteries of the universe. I had drawn no closer to the mind of the God who had created them. Instead, I had memorized a gaggle of the man made constructs which had been devised to regulate the deviant aspects of human behavior.

It occurred to me that, in so many respects, an attorney is but a glamorized repairman. A well paid one, but a repairman nonetheless. I could not help but imagine myself, in a three piece suit, being utilized to repair someone's damaged promises. Is your business contract broken? Call a contract attorney. Is your marriage broken? Call a divorce attorney. Have you broken the law? Call a criminal attorney. Are you hoping to unlock the mysteries of the universe? Well, there is no attorney to call for that.

Still, I only needed to adjust my expectations from this practical, if not especially fulfilling, profession. An attorney is fulfilled by his compensation. There would be exotic automobiles, spacious homes, far flung vacations, and, as I still hoped, my Jenn. I would gladly make her the direct beneficiary of my success, her days being spent relaxed and carefree, reading by a sultry poolside, or galloping atop a loyal horse. Our evenings could be happily consumed with dining, socializing, and lovemaking. I would make her a perfect life, funded by a multitude of clients who insisted on living imperfectly.

I even amused myself thinking that I could still pursue an interest in physics. If the exams were any indication, I would be able to complete all of my future legal duties in only half of the allotted time. I could then use the remaining time to foray into the mysteries of the universe. Possibly I would attach a small observatory to my home, situated on a hill of course, perhaps even one that looked down on Dave Richard's pitifully smaller estate. I became intoxicated by thoughts of such a possible future, so much so that I called Jenn to tell her of my stellar performance in the final exams, and of the bright future which surely awaited me.

"If the exams are any indication," I told her, "working as an attorney will be trivial."

"Are you sure?" she asked. "That's not what I've heard."

I vowed that it would be. Jenn too had completed her own exams, and was preparing to return to the Eden Ranch. I dreaded the prospect of a summer without her. But I had not given up on winning her heart. So, putting down the phone, I consoled myself by thinking that these first few months with her had been only the opening act of our eventual life together.

****

During the few days before my summer internship began, I attended to some necessary chores. I cleaned my apartment for one thing, and I had the headlight of my car repaired. But mostly I anticipated my new foray into the confines of Ashton Tate. So much of my old life was quickly being mortared over by the happenings of my new one. Only my old outdated business suit remained as a last vestige of my former life, and, as I drove back in my recently repaired automobile, I resolved to put this too firmly behind me. Luckily, for this purpose Westwood village was littered with no shortage of clothing shops.

I needed at least two suits, stylish, modern, and befitting of my new role. Apparently not many people were clothes shopping on this particular day and I found most of the stores to be empty of customers. The attending salesman inside each one would shake off his boredom and approach me as I fumbled about. But in each shop I soon found myself confused, without the slightest notion regarding what to buy. I longed for the time when attorneys were expected to wear nothing more drastic than a dark woolen suit.

Having a female companion along might have helped to lessen my confusion. Jenn, Laura, or even Monica, with their feminine intuitions could have easily made the correct choices for me. But I was deprived of such a luxury, and, resolving to make a purchase before returning home, I decided to rely on advice from each shop's resident salespersons. With this new strategy, I entered another store, *The Eunique Male*, with a renewed hope. True to its name, the selection inside this particular store did indeed appear to be somewhat unique.

In typical pattern, I loitered for about ten minutes, before being offered assistance. The elderly salesman who approached me was dark, heavy set, and spoke with a pronounced accent. I described my dilemma to him. He listened, nodded, and, after giving the matter a further moment's thought, quickly sprang into action. Following his guidance, I soon stood before a rack of muted pastel suits, soft and lustrous, as he queried me about my particular size.

"Mate in *Eedalee*," pronounced the salesman.

I inspected the merchandise. The *Eedalian* suits were indeed beautiful and seemingly well made, proudly exuding the style and grace of their home country. I chose a lavender one and soon found myself draped in its soft silky shroud. Unlike my itchy wool suit, the wispy Eedalian material felt cool and smooth against my skin. It wrapped itself loosely about my body, quickly prompting the salesman to initiate some undue adjustments. He pinned the contours of the jacket and pants until the material fit snugly, perhaps overly so for my preference. I expressed a small note of concern regarding the snug fit, but in response he only clasped me, unexpectedly, on my buttocks.

"*Zee, nize and tide bag heah*," he assured me. "*Dhe vhimen, dhey lige dhad.*"

I inspected myself in the full length mirror. The suit did indeed seem to fit noticeably tighter. And although the fit was not as comfortable as it had once been, I consoled myself with the thought that *vhimen* would now find me considerably more appealing.

Of course one cannot buy such a suit without also buying the correct shirts, shoes, belts, neckties, and socks for it. Once the final amount for all of this was tallied I found that I'd spent most of my bank balance. It then only took the slightest bit of the salesman's further prodding to have me part with nearly the entire account. A second suit he suggested, perhaps in lilac and *haff-prized*, might also serve me well. As a result, I left the store overloaded with bags and boxes and the knowledge that in my bank account there were only enough funds for a week's worth of groceries. Both suits were to be altered, with the salesman assuring me that they would be ready first thing Sunday morning.

I retrieved the suits that Sunday, and, firmly ready for Ashton Tate, I found myself with no further obligations. But I was curious to know my exam grades, which by then were available. So I walked to the university campus and then to the law building. With the summer recess full underway, the campus grounds were depressingly desolate. Only the green lawns seemed cheered to enjoy a respite from the ceaseless waves of tramping feet.

I found a few other students mingling in the law school hallways. The grades were not publicly posted, but a teaching assistant, Judd Hansen, there for this exact purpose, could provide them. Hansen was a third year student and I recognized him from my mentorship group. He rummaged through cartons of graded exams until he found mine. With an undisguised smirk, he handed them to me. The grades were not good, with one, the contracts exam, being nearly disastrous.

"I can't believe that Ashton Tate made you an offer," Hansen added.

My spirits had sunk low enough on seeing the grades, but Hansen's comment dropped them even lower. However, the offer from Ashton Tate could not be revoked, and with any luck they would never learn of these grades. I skimmed through the exam books, and read the various annotations scribbled therein by the graders. It seemed that on the whole my answers had been indeed correct. But the annotations, in red ink, all consistently demanded a more detailed response.

"Please expound further!" chastened one annotation.

And, "*Brevity is not a virtue*!" suggested another.

Of the physics equations which I had included into the exam books, one comment simply read "*What is this nonsense?*" While another admonished that *"You are taking the wrong exam!!"*

I voiced a concern to Hansen that my exams had not been properly graded. As proof I handed him my contracts exam, and showed him that my responses were actually correct. He skimmed through the few pages quickly. An occasional facial gesture indicated that he was indeed contemplating the substance of what I had written. But at length he closed my exam book and handed it back.

"The grades stand," he said. "Too bad this wasn't a physics exam."

He explained that yes, my answers were correct, but that the successful practice of law extended beyond mere correctness. An attorney was required to demonstrate a necessary depth and breadth of understanding such that his opinion might then carry the undeniable weight of authority. A wise grandmother might also have provided the type of responses that I had. But a skilled professional attorney would have examined the cases from every conceivable perspective, and would have provided unrelenting citations to justify his chosen position. He suggested that I might have done better by even arguing an incorrect position, but with more substance.

"You'll never be successful your way," he advised. "For an attorney, both time and words are money."

But I could not accept the situation. It made no sense to me. My answers were correct, and I deserved a better grade. I argued my case to him, as a successful attorney might, for another half hour. But it was pointless to continue, as posting any change to the grades was well beyond his authority. I left the law building feeling cheated and abused, and, had this been a matter of any legal consequence, I might have contemplated retaining a proper attorney myself to seek justice.

****

I left the dark confines of the law building to find it a glorious day. But not even the cheering sunshine or the sweet scent of unfettered grass did much to lift my spirits. I wandered through the empty campus aimlessly, furious that such poor grades would now appear on my transcript. By lunchtime I had made my way to a small café on the north end, where I sat down, hoping to console myself with a lonely sandwich and a few cups of coffee.

The north end of the campus was home to the university's many science departments. As such it was still busy with graduate and postdoctoral students who, like Jonathan Schwarzchild, used the summer recesses to concentrate on their own research. The café was centrally located, within the proverbial stone's throw of buildings which housed the biology, chemistry, and physics departments. It was now past noon and I wedged myself amidst the small tables, so closely packed that I imposed onto graduate students and their heated discussions on all sides. To my right, in a quiet and deliberate manner, two students were arguing the topic that had intrigued me since my undergraduate days, the inherent expansion of the universe.

Edwin Hubble had first inferred this phenomenon from his observations. But after his initial, revolutionary discovery, as is typical in physics, more questions than answers began to emerge. Einstein too had been puzzled by this. So much so that he modified his fabled relativity equations, with a *'fudge'* factor, to account for the expansion. But the actual ingredients of Einstein's fudge had never been discovered. It was only postulated that a mysterious energy, a dark energy, was responsible for ever pushing the universe apart. This expansion was also inconveniently accelerating, with the universe condemned to unceasingly expand into the cold, lonely expanse of infinite, empty space until all of its stars had dimmed. Not a cheery thought really, and one that even cast doubts on the notion of a benevolent God.

I continued listening as the two students speculated that the mysterious dark energy was nonexistent, that instead the current theories of gravity themselves were flawed, and were in need of some unknown revision. Perhaps a new theory of gravity might be formulated to better agree with the observed cosmologic anomalies. But I shuddered at the thought of tampering with the sacred concept of gravity, which had ever dutifully maintained the planets in their proper orbits.

"Hubble was wrong," I blurted out to the two students.

I had questioned Hubble's original conclusions long ago. There, at that source, lay the corrupted concepts which had produced such a flawed view of the universe. One only needed to assume a different behavior for the properties of space itself, and, from this simple singular adjustment, all of the mysteries surrounding dark energy would then be resolved. I longed to convey this insight to the two physicists beside me. But the details which I might have provided them were merely my own stale speculations. To prove such ideas conclusively required climbing that daunting mountain of mathematics, the height of which had already proved insurmountable in my undergraduate days.

"What?" asked one of the students.

"Hubble was wrong," I affirmed. "The universe is not expanding."

I offered them a few details based on my thoughts from years ago. But they only stared back silently, in disbelief of such a sacrilegious notion.

"Are you a physicist?" one of them asked.

"No," I replied, "I'm a law student."

The students nodded politely.

"Well then," the other said at length, "maybe you can prove Hubble wrong in court."

They laughed, and it then was my turn to nod politely. I remained silent after that until the students had finished their lunch. Once they'd left I had nowhere else to go, and so I followed their trail into the physics building. I made my way to the library on the fourth floor, where the hardwood tables and the musty smell of old volumes had a familiar feel. Unlike the law library, this library was compact and intimate, like a cozy bookstore which catered only to a select clientele. Next to about half a dozen worn overstuffed chairs, I spied a collection of physics journals. I had not read a single journal since my undergraduate years, and I smiled as I again skimmed through the old familiar publications.

From stars to strings, heated debates still raged. I scanned through back issues for Jonathan's name, and found three of his papers from past years. Each one revealed a consistent progress along his line of research. But his name was noticeably absent among the recent publications. He had not been idle of course, and perhaps only Monica and I knew that his missing publications had been replaced by long lonely walks through late night hours. I felt a solace for him and for his struggles, which, like an unforgiving shipwreck, had left him alone and adrift in a tumultuous sea of uncertainty and doubt.

I immersed myself into the various journals, to the point of losing track of time. Scanning through articles in my own field of cosmology, I was infuriated that so little progress had been made during the last five years. The dark energy theory still persisted. I'd once hoped that my own speculations might have provided a breakthrough, even a minor one, for this problem. But scanning the various journals, apparently no one else had stumbled across a similar insight. With a fool's hope I located a pencil and some paper and began scribbling, into the night, the equations which had long ago been my adversaries. By the time that the library lights were flickered, the time was ten o'clock and I was the only soul remaining.

Walking back across the dark campus I felt emotionally drained, but strangely elated, my mind once again reveling in the same old mysteries which had fascinated me years before. When I arrived home I telephoned Jonathan with some questions. But instead it was Monica who answered. With a worried voice, she informed me that Jonathan had gone on one of his late evening walks. With my mind still swimming in physics, I needed to walk myself. But tomorrow would be my first day at Ashton Tate, and so, with equations still floating before my closed eyes, I begrudgingly forced myself to fall asleep.

11.

I had envisioned myself rising early for my first internship day. Then showering, shaving, dressing in my new lavender suit, and arriving at Ashton Tate with sufficient time for at least one leisurely cup of office coffee. Instead I awoke late, and found myself scrambling to arrive on time for the new employee orientation at nine. With my hair still wet I drove recklessly down Wilshire Boulevard to the first available parking spot more than two blocks from my employer's office. When at last I arrived in the Ashton Tate lobby, the fashion model receptionist, still all legs and stockings, directed me to a side room where the employee orientation had already begun. I sheepishly dissolved myself into the one remaining seat, and cast a bemused smile at the middle aged matron and her younger assistant standing at the front of the room.

"Ugh, so much traffic," I said, shaking my still damp head.

For added effect I also gestured a random hand flourish, the intent of which was to conjure visions of countless automobiles stacked atop each other all along Wilshire Boulevard. But the matron was not amused. In response to my smile she only returned a disapproving scowl. Her assistant, who seemed perfectly capable of a sympathetic smile, also followed her lead.

We were almost a dozen fresh interns seated about the conference table, each of us staring at the package of paperwork placed before us. Among the faces I recognized Bryce Davis, now dressed in full business attire and who, as our gazes met, only acknowledged my presence with raised eyebrows and pursed lips. I also recognized Miss Portfolio, from my interview day, now dressed in a different, but similarly snugly fitted outfit. She still carried her trademark leather portfolio, placed squarely before her.

As I skimmed through my paperwork, Ms. Nichols, that was our matron's name, announced that she would show a short video which recounted the illustrious history of the firm into which we had now become employed. I put aside my papers as the lights were dimmed, and, along with everyone else, turned my attention towards the front of the room.

"*The firm of Ashton and Tate has been a Hollywood institution since the nineteen fifties,*" the narrator informed us.

We learned that the firm of Ashton Tate had begun humbly enough as the two attorney practice of Robert J. Ashton and Laurence S. Tate. This practice had subsisted well enough for many years on the random scraps which fell from the legal tables of the large Hollywood movie studios, before the two attorneys then subsequently found themselves in an especially advantageous position. With the demise of the so called *studio system* major movie stars became suddenly free to negotiate their own contracts. As a result they suddenly needed their own legal counsel, and there was no firm better positioned to provide such counsel than my astute new employer. To reinforce this point, the video casually mentioned some of the many notable names which the firm had initially represented in those early years.

From these beginnings, the firm's reputation flourished. Driven by the ambitious talents of its founders, Ashton Tate grew, prospered, and grew even more. The stars it represented became wealthy. With each movie they starred in, Ashton Tate negotiated their film contract. When they bought and sold real estate, Ashton Tate negotiated their sales contracts. When they invested their wealth, Ashton Tate scrutinized the specific transaction details. When they owed exorbitant taxes, Ashton Tate found them convenient loopholes. When they married, Ashton Tate provided the prenuptials. And, when they subsequently divorced, Ashton Tate was there for them also.

The firm eventually established satellite offices worldwide. Ashton Tate became the first choice for celebrities in both film and music. More recent decades also saw the rise of the sports celebrity, that is, those photogenic athletes who eventually found their way onto Hollywood celluloid. Of the faces which now appeared in our video, I recognized that of a younger Bruce Robinson, flanked by a then middle aged Robert Ashton.

With a worldwide presence, the firm then exploited its commanding position in the arena of entertainment law by changing the long standing rules of the game. Ashton Tate championed the notion that all contributors to an entertainment product, including legal counsel of course, should share in the royalties from such a product. This allowed the firm to then profit handsomely as its clients' products generated not millions, but billions, in worldwide sales. And as for Ashton Tate's founders and partners, this new reordering of the industry's cash flows now assured them of becoming not merely wealthy, but fabulously wealthy.

The video eventually concluded by showing an early grayscale photo of the founders morphing into the thousands of other faces which the firm had become. The screen then faded to black while the narrator assured us that, whatever the possible future of entertainment law, Ashton Tate was certain to play a leading role. As we then sat briefly in darkness while Ms. Nichols' assistant struggled with the lights, I wondered how many of the squeaky fresh interns seated in the room had now firmly resolved themselves to becoming Ashton Tate partners, at whatever the cost.

"Are there any questions?" asked Ms. Nichols once the lights came on again.

Certainly the only question now worth asking might be "*So, how do I become a partner?*" But instead the room remained reticent, until only Miss Portfolio spoke up.

"Are the founders still active in the firm's affairs?" she asked.

No, Ms. Nichols informed us, they were not. Mr. Ashton had passed away several years ago, while Mr. Tate was officially retired, and dedicating his remaining energies to philanthropic pursuits. Ms. Nichols noted that other, younger family members were now active in the firm's affairs. But aside from this tempting bit of detail, she offered no further clues as to their identities.

We were prompted for other questions which, after a further silence, never materialized. Perhaps the video had now inspired everyone to immediately embark onto their partnership track, or perhaps everyone was merely tired of sitting. But as a result the orientation session quickly concluded, and we were subsequently led, carrying our packages of paperwork, through the lobby, and past the scrutinizing gaze of abstract

Lady Justice. We then entered into the heart of Ashton Tate, where I was overwhelmed by the sudden avalanche of frenetic activity.

As on my interview day, the firm's great atrium once again filled me with awe, now even more so as it buzzed with the furious energy of nearly four hundred employees. The vast open space teemed with lawyers, legal aids, secretaries, and assistants swarming about its main floor. People were talking and nodding, telephones were beeping and ringing, file drawers were opening and shutting, all of these sounds blending into one unrelenting drone of regimented purpose.

We were led to a corner area, where a grouping of cubicles had been arranged for us lowly interns. There Ms. Nichols gave us our first assignment - to complete our package of paperwork. A name tag on one of the cubicles already proclaimed me as its resident, and so I settled into it. I took inventory of the bare essentials provided me, a desk, a telephone, and a previously used computer. Armed with these, and with my well trained gray matter, I was now equipped to fight whichever legal battles the firm would dispatch me to.

The package of paperwork held many forms. There were forms inquiring as to my desired tax deductions, previous employment history, and marital status. Finally there were two substantial agreements which outlined the employee code of conduct, and the firm's confidential information policy. Like any good attorney, I thoroughly reviewed these documents, even though neither allowed for any renegotiation. Afterwards I returned the signed forms to Ms Nichols' assistant who, without having to answer to her supervisor, this time rewarded my efforts with a kind smile.

It was soon time for lunch, and I rummaged through our collection of cubicles looking in vain for one which might have contained Bryce Davis. But his name tag was nowhere apparent, and so I ventured alone to the outside streets searching for food. When I returned, the situation was no better. Bryce was still nowhere to be found. I seated myself back at my desk and then realized that, with my paperwork complete, I had not the slightest idea of what I should be working on next.

"You'll receive a daily schedule starting tomorrow," Ms. Nichols' assistant informed me.

But regarding what I might do until then, she offered no further clue. The salary being paid me was not so trivial that I should be kept idle, and it seemed that someone should have taken an interest in aligning me to some productive task. Some of the other interns had already been visited by a mentoring attorney, and had been given an initial assignment. But in my case no such visit, and no such assignment. I alerted Ms. Nichols about my idle situation and learned that my own mentor was none other than Andrew Jackson himself.

"He's very busy right now," she told me. "Just wait for *him* to contact *you*."

But I could not wait. It seemed harmless to pay my supervisor a brief impromptu visit, and, with that in mind, I soon found myself breathing the rarefied air of the atrium's upper tier, en route to Jackson's office. As on my interview day, the view from this height was thrilling, now even more as the frantic milling of a proper business day swirled below me. I imagined the sense of majesty which both Ashton and Tate must have once felt from this particular vantage point, as the creators of this small world, and as its veritable gods in their own right. They might have conversed on the very spot where I now stood.

"*Well done, Ashton*," Tate might have pronounced, with admiration.

"*Yes, very well done, Tate*," Ashton might have concurred, with sympathetic pride.

I daydreamed briefly in this manner, until I soon found myself standing before Jackson's office. His door was open, but Jackson himself was not there. Determined to wait for him, I loitered about, and explored the remainder of the upper tier. Here the offices were richly appointed. I glanced at attorneys and their clients as they filed past me, hoping to catch sight of some recognizable celebrity. But after ten minutes of loitering, it became painfully obvious, especially from the glances that I was receiving, that I should return to the lowly confines of my own cubicle. Jackson had never returned, but, arriving back at my desk, I found a handwritten note from Bryce Davis.

"*Looking for you. Where are you?*" asked the note.

I might have asked the same of Bryce, and, after enquiring about him, I learned from Ms. Nichols that he had been placed into a small office on the first tier. I made my way there, only to find him already gone for the day. I wondered why Bryce Davis, a summer intern like myself, had been assigned an office, albeit a small one, but a proper office nonetheless, while we other interns had not. I surmised that perhaps there hadn't been sufficient space in our cubicle community for him, and so he had been relegated to this tiny office instead.

So again I returned to my desk, still without a purpose. The day was not progressing as I had anticipated. But with still a few hours remaining, I was determined to somehow justify myself through some seemingly useful activity. I found a small reference library in a corner of the main level, and retreated there, out of desperation, to spend the rest of the working day skimming through law journals.

That evening I had not the heart to tell Jenn about my first day. For one thing, there was nothing to tell. Nothing interesting had happened, and, with such an inauspicious beginning, it would have been difficult for me to hide my disappointment. I could only look forward to the possibilities of my second day, and had resigned myself to an early bed, when the telephone's ring broke the silence of my two solitary rooms.

"Sorry to have missed you, but I was out last night," said Jonathan's voice.

He had gone on one of his long walks that night. But for this night Monica had persuaded him to remain at home. He had consented to do so for her sake, and for the sake of his own skin. With the summer there had come an increase in the local criminal activity. During his last walk Jonathan had even heard gunshots, seemingly too close and too disconcerting. So on this night he would instead pace back and forth in the confined safety of his small apartment.

Jonathan had more than enough to think about. He still lacked his breakthrough, and thoughts of Wilson's imminent publication provided no respite. I recalled my recent forage through the physics journals, and the absence of Jonathan's name on any of the current articles. But, until the remaining anomalies in his theory were resolved, he could not publish, and running now alongside Wilson, Jonathan was in the race of his life.

"I'm so close, damn it, so close," he veritably implored over the phone.

I felt desperately sorry for him. Given the scope of his problems, my first frustrating day at Ashton Tate was trivial in comparison. Even those problems which I might have encountered as an astrophysicist could never have been as severe. Whereas an astrophysicist could rely on an observable reality to guide his theories, in Jonathan's world there was no such crutch. Only through the correct formulation of excruciatingly complex equations might a string theorist even venture a glimpse into the behavior of entities which, for the present, existed fantastically beyond the reach of anyone's conceivable measurement.

"Why did you call last night?" he asked me at length.

"Oh, no reason," I lied. "Just wanted to see how you were doing."

I hadn't the heart to mention my own simple ideas, and so I only offered him my useless sympathy, and wished him a good night.

"And give yourself a break," I added, but knowing that this was impossible.

After the conversation, I could not sleep. Thoughts of physics again swirled inside me. I began jotting down the simple truths from my undergraduate days - the Planck-Einstein relation between energy and frequency, Hubble's equation for the observed cosmic red-shift, the speed of light as it relates frequency and wavelength. I folded these equations into each other, and finally tried to confront my long standing misgivings with Hubble's conclusion. What if Hubble had simply latched upon the most convenient explanation for the cosmic red shift? What if space where not expanding as Hubble had proposed, but rather space was simply a resistive medium instead? He would have observed the same red shift either way.

I followed this train of thought for several more hours until, at three in the morning, I had derived a set of rudimentary equations which described my ideas. The equations were simple, but elegant, and I could not help but wonder why, with such straightforward equations to deal with, this concept had not yet occurred to any other physicist. Most likely my thinking on this matter was flawed and needed reconsidering.

But with precious few hours remaining until my second day at Ashton Tate, I thought it best to trade my musings for a few hours of long overdue sleep.

12.

It seemed my life's fate to be perennially behind schedule. As such I arrived for my second day at Ashton Tate again late, and with little sleep. My watch showed almost ten o'clock by the time that I finally reached my desk, placed onto which that morning, just as Ms. Nichols' assistant had foretold, was my agenda for the day. I scanned the agenda to find myself scheduled for a meeting, called by Andrew Jackson himself, which had actually already started twenty minutes ago in an upper tier conference room. Driven by a sudden surge of adrenalin, I rushed to it. During the elevator ride up I pondered the meeting's possible purpose.

"Review Robinson Case," the meeting notice had read.

Here, at last, was confirmation that I was on board with the firm's most urgent case. I hadn't the slightest clue as to what duties I would be given, but this ambiguity did not seem to matter. All that mattered was that I was involved in a trial most likely destined to become the landmark trial of the year, if not the decade. I reached the conference room with my heart pounding. But before entering, I composed myself, adjusted my hair and jacket, and assumed a posture which belied not the slightest trace of tardiness.

I spied Andrew Jackson at the head of the conference table, and, surprisingly, also Bruce Robinson. Among the other dozen faces I also recognized, at the back end of the table, Bryce Davis and Miss Portfolio. There was an empty seat next to Bryce, which, I assumed, was intended for another insignificant attendee such as myself. This was only my second day at Ashton Tate but already I had come to understand the strict ordering of its legal universe, and in keeping with it I assumed my lowly place among the other interns. I received the usual raised eyebrows from Bryce as I sat down, but otherwise no one else took notice of my presence. Even Miss Portfolio, seated beside me, continued her diligent scribbling without the slightest interruption.

Eventually I came to surmise the identity of the other attendees. Next to Robinson was a young and dutiful assistant, provided for his benefit by the firm. Her responsibilities included attending to any of Robinson's particular needs, from managing his papers to fetching him a cup of coffee. Across from Robinson, and next to Jackson, sat another Ashton Tate partner, Elliot Reichert from the New York office. Reichert specialized in criminal litigation, and had been assigned exclusively to the Robinson case. Both Reichert and Jackson commanded a support staff of two associate attorneys and two paralegals. All together there were quite a few billable hours seated about the table, and with a quick calculation I estimated that Robinson's bill for this meeting alone would tally to what most anyone might consider a respectable monthly income.

"We are going to make their evidence seem ridiculous," asserted Reichert.

To win the case, Reichert was proposing a simple strategy based on a discrediting of the prosecuting evidence. An easy matter, he maintained, due to the ineptness of the government prosecutors, and their pressing need to settle the case.

For in a high profile case such as this one, there was usually tremendous pressure on the criminal justice system for a speedy resolution. The unwavering attention of the public, and a persistent scrutiny from the news media insured that such a case could not grow stale from insufficient evidence. As a result the District Attorney's office had pressed for a trial date, even though the police evidence was poor. But, in truth, from the District Attorney's perspective it did not matter whether Robinson was guilty or innocent, convicted or exonerated. All that truly mattered was for the case to be resolved, expediently, and with undue political repercussions.

"We'll cut them off at the knees," Jackson confirmed. "They've got nothing."

Reichert then presented an overview of the police evidence. The evidence was not necessarily weak, but it was not particularly strong. The police had found no murder weapon, nor had they found any accusing fingerprints. What they had found were footprints, or rather shoeprints to be more exact, in front of Nicole Robinson's door and in an adjacent flowerbed. The shoe was identified as an athletic shoe of Robinson's exact size, and of the type that Robinson was known to endorse. There was also another set of footprints, or rather boot prints, from a different pair of feet. The police also had a witness, someone who while walking his dog had seen a man of roughly Robinson's build in a jogging suit, but running, not jogging, through Nicole Robinson's neighborhood around the supposed time of the murder.

Based in this evidence, the police had formulated a theory for the events of that evening. It might have been the second man, they proposed, who had actually pulled the trigger, with Robinson's involvement only necessary for his estranged wife to unsuspectingly open her front door. Robinson's alibi was that he had spent the evening with a young actress friend of his, a certain Bambi Farinelli. But with her apartment a mere mile from the murder scene, the police maintained that this distance would have been a trivial jog, or run, for someone as athletic as Robinson. To further substantiate this theory, the police would rely on their dog walking witness.

There were gaping omissions in the murder scenario being conjured by the police, and it would be a textbook matter for Jackson and Reichert to expose these shortcomings to any jury. Reichert explained how this type of evidence, which was mostly circumstantial, could be easily discounted. The shoeprints could not be precisely linked to Robinson in a convincing manner, while the eyewitness sighting in those dark hours could be proved unreliable. And beyond this there was no further evidence of any merit. There were no fingerprints, there was no smoking gun. There was only a need by the authorities to remove this case from the public eye, regardless of its outcome.

But if the police were indeed correct, it seemed to me that the logistics of the murder had been brilliantly conceived, and flawlessly executed. Could Robinson have been capable of such a plan? As a football player he had been a running back, not a quarterback. As an actor he had read his lines well, but had never improvised. As a murderer, I myself could not imagine how he alone might have envisioned such malevolent details. The identity of this other possible master mind was a mystery, as was the identity of the supposed gunman.

Only Bambi Farinelli might provide exact insight into the details of that evening. But here Ashton Tate had acted quickly and decisively. The police's harsh interrogation tactics were well known by the city's legal establishment. So, to shield crucial individuals from any direct police questioning, Ashton Tate had successfully petitioned to have all pretrial interrogation conveyed exclusively through their office. The court had allowed this, but only for those individuals which were Ashton Tate clients. Immediately, Bambi Farinelli and other related parties were enrolled as clients, and with these key individuals sheltered under its legal umbrella, Ashton Tate had put the situation securely under its control.

"Thank you for protecting my friends," offered Robinson.

"Yes," said Jackson. "But of course, we're really trying to protect you."

Robinson sat back in his chair, apparently at ease. From the combined legal expertise of Jackson, Reichert, and their ample support staffs, to the unceasing attention of his nubile attendant, Robinson was being exceptionally well cared for. With confident smiles, both lead attorneys assured Robinson of their ability to conduct a winning trial. This confidence then proved infectious, and permeated itself through the entire room, until everyone was silently nodding, similarly assured that this case was already won. From one of the room's prominent portraits, the oil brushed visages of Robert Ashton and Laurence Tate had observed the proceedings approvingly, and they appeared satisfied that the precise workings of their firm were resolutely ticking as they would have intended.

****

Robinson and the senior attorneys departed for lunch once the meeting had concluded. We interns and paralegals, our fellow lower life forms in the Ashton Tate legal food chain, were left behind to fend for ourselves. Across the room, a carafe of lukewarm coffee and a collection of stale pastries offered some appeal. But I had been seated uncomfortably for nearly two and a half hours, and I desperately needed a change of air. Bryce Davis stretched and yawned. Only Miss Portfolio, even after so many hours of scribbling, still seemed capable of scribbling for many hours more.

Bryce, myself, and Miss Portfolio ventured outside, eventually finding ourselves at an outdoor table staring at overpriced sandwiches. There I learned that Agnes Cook, that was Miss Portfolio's real name, was studying law at the same university where Jonathan Schwarzchild studied physics. She had grown up in a neighborhood near that university, and her parents had always dreamed of her attending it. She had actually done so, and had then exceeded their expectations by progressing on to its law school. We both commiserated as to how dangerous that part of town had become. Like Monica fearing for Jonathan's safety, Agnes feared for that of her parents.

"When I'm an attorney, I'll help them get out of there," she told us resolutely.

Bryce Davis had remained silent during this conversation. His upbringing, filled with green lawns and tennis courts, had been insulated from any such inconveniences. Perhaps, through an eventual political career, he might begrudgingly acknowledge the existence of such concerns. But for now he showed no interest, and, as the conversation between Agnes and myself lulled, he redirected our thoughts onto the more immediate matter of the Robinson case.

"Jackson and Reichert aren't seeing the whole picture," he announced.

According to him, they were primarily focused on debunking the evidence, to the exclusion of so many other vital aspects of the case. For one thing, they were not actively promoting a positive image for Robinson in the media. They were not dissuading television networks from broadcasting his more violent films, at least in the markets from which the jury pool would be drawn. They had not arranged public appearances for Robinson in local charity events. They had not leaked information, or misinformation, about the city's police force, or about Nicole Robinson's personal life.

Bryce listed the many shortcomings of the defense team's strategy, speaking as though the he himself were a partner in the firm. Until now I had never seen him so animated, and so unlike his normally aloof self. For whatever reason, he seemed to have become personally engrossed into the affairs of the firm, such that all of the energies which he had held back through an entire indifferent year of law school were at long last being released. The force of his arguments seemed to defy containment, and I imagined him eventually confronting even Jackson with his particular list of grievances.

"And best of all," Bryce added, "all my suggestions will generate even more billable hours for the firm."

"The case is already going to cost Robinson millions," I noted.

"Yes, so what's another million more?" he asked.

But Bryce explained how Robinson's eventual legal bill was not as dire as it might appear. His wife's convenient death now spared him the financial damage of a costly divorce, and, once acquitted of murder, he could easily recover his legal expenses with a lucrative book or movie deal.

"He might actually end up making a profit from all of this," Bryce predicted.

I myself had never considered the Robinson case from such an alternate perspective, but there was something about Bryce Davis's upbringing, or perhaps his genetic makeup, which naturally inclined him to do so. There was more to Bryce's constitution than I had so far come to assume. He was indeed a spoiled rich kid, but one who still possessed his family's keen financial instincts. He had been nurtured in an environment of money, and probably instilled with a belief that everything could be measured and quantified into dollars and cents. I wondered what value he might place on our friendship, such as it was, or on Nicole Robinson's life, now that it was gone. I almost shuddered to think that, if he were actually asked to do so, Bryce probably could indeed produce an exact figure for these.

We rushed back to Ashton Tate after lunch. Agnes was eager to begin her assignment. She had been tasked with investigating past murder cases which had involved either circumstantial or insubstantial evidence. She was expected to present a preliminary summary of these findings in only a week. Myself, on the other hand, had been given no such duties, and the thought of spending a second listless afternoon browsing legal journals filled me with dread. I resolved to again seek out Andrew Jackson, perhaps to remind him of how much money was wasting by my sitting idle. Ms. Nichols hinted that Jackson might be available after a two o'clock meeting, and so I made it a point to unexpectedly find myself near his office at about three o'clock.

"Good, you're here," said Jackson, when I accidentally appeared at his door.

He invited me to sit down, apologizing for having neglected me so far. He had been indeed intending to meet with me, but the case was placing tremendous demands on his schedule.

"I'm ready to start," I offered.

"That's good," he said leaning forward, "because we're in desperate need of some declarations, fast."

From behind him, the photo of Jackson's dog, now resembling more Pit Bull than Labrador, seemed to reinforce his urgency.

"But declarations aren't legally binding," I said. "We really want depositions, right?"

"No, we don't," corrected Jackson. "We want declarations."

Declarations are the poor, non-legally binding cousins of depositions. But Jackson explained how they were going to be a crucial part of the defense strategy.

"We'll use declarations to send a clear message to the prosecutors," Jackson told me.

The testimonies of key individuals would be entered into the court records as declarations. These testimonies would clearly convey Robinson's innocence, and, in essence, would show the prosecuting team that their case was already lost. For this strategy then, declarations were the perfect legal vehicle - less formal than depositions, and with no liability to perjury, which, last I'd checked, was still considered a felony in the state of California.

Jackson suggested that I use the remainder of the week to acquaint myself with the proper techniques for obtaining a declaration. As a starting point, there were several trade articles which he referred me to. After absorbing those I might also solicit the advice of other attorneys in the firm. The declaration interviews were scheduled to begin next week, and he expected me to be fully ready by then.

"Bob Parker will be leading the interviews," Jackson informed me. "You'll work with him from now on."

After he'd delegated me into Parker's supervision, Jackson then nodded me away. Our meeting had lasted only thirty minutes, but I had benefited tremendously from it. Assured now that my time at Ashton Tate would not be wasted, I rushed to the law library and made copies of the articles which Jackson had recommended. Soon I not only found myself with over fifty pages of reading material for the next few days, but also with a clear sense of purpose for the weeks ahead. Later, with a bit of pride, I informed Agnes Cook of my new role.

"What a good assignment," she noted. "It will look great on your resume."

13.

I prepared for the upcoming declaration interviews with a newfound fervor, reviewing any related material I could find even into the late hours. By Wednesday evening however I was so bloated with reading about declarations and interview techniques that I put all thoughts of them aside. I was then detemined to embark onto a good night's sleep when the telephone's ring unexpectedly pulled me out of bed.

"I need your help," said a woman's voice at the other end of the line.

It was Monica, sounding worried and desperate.

"Jonathan's been gone for two days," she said. "Can you help me find him?"

She had not seen Jonathan since the night when he and I had last spoken. That night he had paced aimlessly at home, until the confines of their small apartment had almost suffocated him. He had then ventured out for a brief walk, and had not returned since. A call to the police had yielded nothing, and, with the university's physics department closed for the summer, Monica knew of no one else to reach out to. She had decided to search for him herself, and would I please be so kind as to accompany her?

"But it's past midnight," I pleaded, attempting a small protest.

"Yes, I'm well aware of that," she countered.

I needed rest for my next day at Ashton Tate, especially now that I had a definite assignment. But Monica insisted that she could not search for Jonathan alone, especially at such a late hour. And so, with my eyes half shut, I drove my groggy self to their apartment on the far side of town. The roads were nearly empty, but even so it was well past one o'clock when I finally arrived.

Monica greeted me with a gift cup of freshly brewed coffee already in hand. She was eager to set out. Her plan was that we should first scour their neighborhood, especially in directions leading to the university, for signs of Jonathan. I wasn't sure what signs we would be looking for, and in my sleepless state I began imagining gruesome visions of Jonathan's lifeless body crumpled into the dark corner of some remote alleyway.

The chilly air of the early summer night helped to revive my senses. But as Monica and I walked along, this particular night seemed unusually still. Even the neighborhood's many vigilant canines maintained a nervous silence, not caring if they were labeled failures as guard dogs, already knowing perhaps that their owners did not possess anything of value worth guarding. The rows of ancient bungalows too seemed to hover uneasily. Shrouded now in the menacing darkness, they seemed stripped of every vestigial charm from their former, kinder days.

I became increasingly worried as we walked, and fearful of what we might find. We soon reached a major intersection illuminated by streetlights, and populated on two corners by the young business men and women who engaged in the particular commerce of late night hours. A pack of youths, sporting jewelry and loosely fitting clothes, approached us. I shuddered at the sight of them. But they soon recognized Monica and greeted her. As the neighborhood's resident social worker, she was not a threat. She had helped many of these young men when they might have unexpectedly found themselves in jail, or when their girlfriends had suddenly become pregnant, or when their broken families might have been in need of critical financial support. In the framework of the local turf wars, Monica's rank was most likely that of a protected civilian, if not medic. I remained in her shadow, hoping that I too would be protected by it.

Monica asked about Jonathan. And yes they had seen him, two nights ago.

"He was walking to the college," said one of the youths.

This was not a significant piece of information. But, with only this one clue, we pushed on towards the campus. I myself was beginning to suspect that Jonathan was encamped somewhere in one of the university buildings, or buried deep in the shelves of one of its libraries.

As an undergraduate I had known him to do this when he had a particularly difficult problem to solve. He would quietly disappear, only to remerge several days later, grungy and in desperate need of a shower and shave, but with a solution cleanly in hand. I mentioned this particular habit of Jonathan's to Monica, but she had not known him to practice it during the three years they had been together. For her sake, he had always made it a priority to stay in touch, making this particular disappearance a certain cause for concern.

We walked four more blocks and arrived at another brightly lit intersection, similarly populated by young men and women conducting business. In this group however, only one youth greeted Monica. He had not seen Jonathan recently. Instead he recounted a recent incident in which a random pedestrian had been fatally shot. Lifting a ring adorned finger, he indicated the general direction of the shooting. I peered down the dark street, my mind filling again with morose images, this time envisioning Jonathan slumped over, a bullet hole in his chest oozing out the precious red essence of his life.

"No, that wasn't Jonathan," concluded Monica, "or the police would have called me by now."

But there were no further clues to be had from this crowd, and so we continued on towards the university. We reached the campus with me still thinking that Jonathan had returned to the habit which had served him so well in his undergraduate days. He would refer to this practice as going into a *dungeon* - a dungeon whose door could only be unlocked by a set of well bounded, convergent mathematical expressions. I was convinced that somewhere in the physics building, perhaps in the physics library, we would find Jonathan, in his self imposed dungeon.

I suggested that we thoroughly scour the physics building. We found the main door of that building to be unlocked. Inside, the hallways were minimally illuminated, and all of the lecture rooms locked, as was Jonathan's small cubby of an office. We proceeded to an upper floor, where the physics library resided. Here too we found the double glass doors locked. But a few lights flickered inside, and, as I peered past the glass, I spied a lone figure hovering in the distance. It was Jonathan, and, as I rattled the doors, Monica called out to him.

He approached us through the gloom, unkempt, unshaven, and unwashed. As the glass doors parted I found myself staring at the figure of someone whom I now hardly recognized. Jonathan's eyes were dull and distant, and completely devoid of any vitality. In his hand he carried a journal opened to a specific article. Silently, he handed it to me. It was the current issue of a theoretical physics journal, and the article in question was the long rumored theory from Wilson. I scanned through it, digesting what little I might in this late, now early, hour. With simple, pristine mathematics, Wilson's paper appeared to distill the myriad of discordant competing theories into one unified, all encompassing physical framework. His theory was precise, concise, and elegant.

I looked up at Jonathan and immediately understood his anguish. Monica was holding his hand and she stroked his arm gently. She understood that something was very wrong, but she said nothing. I searched for some way to console him. Perhaps his own theory could be formulated into a superset of the Wilson theory. Perhaps Wilson's theory would eventually be dismantled and ravaged, as so many new theories are, by the exacting glare of the physics community. Perhaps Jonathan just needed some rest for now, and, with a fresh start, the discontinuities inherent to his approach would soon become apparent.

"No," he said. "It's over."

I heard Jonathan's voice break as he said these few words, and, like a boxer whose legs finally buckle, he slumped down to the floor, hid his face in his hands, and began crying. Monica bent down to console him as I watched helplessly. The sound of Jonathan's tears cut into the surrounding stillness, engulfing us with his anguish. I was tired, but even so I felt an anger well up inside me, and, having no other recourse for it, I flung Wilson's article into the gloom.

Our walk back to their apartment was a slow and quiet one. Under the early morning sky we stumbled past the various street corners, all now deserted and closed for the night's business. We walked past the rows of old bungalows which, in the probing gray light of dawn, looked especially cheerless. Dogs now barked as we walked past, their silent vigil ended. There was no shred of conversation which seemed appropriate, not a word of encouragement which might be said. As the somber mood sunk deep even into me, I called on every force of my being to restrain the tears which wished to well in my own eyes. I looked at Jonathan, drained and stooped over, not in the least resembling the superhuman figure I had once known.

Monica and I put him to bed, seemingly already asleep. I learned later from Monica that Jonathan would continue sleeping for a full twenty eight hours, and that when he at last awoke he no longer knew what day it was. I too was exhausted, but unlike Jonathan, I could not afford the luxury of an entire day's sleep. Before leaving, I shared some lukewarm coffee with Monica, and attempted to explain Jonathan's dilemma to her. But she had seen it many times before over the years, where Jonathan had found himself at an impasse, only to eventually surmount it. She confidently predicted that, after some rest, Jonathan would indeed find a way to salvage his broken theory.

"Don't worry," she said. "I know him. He won't give up."

I left her in optimistic spirits, and returned to my car, finding it, surprisingly, still where I had parked it, and still fully intact. But the morning traffic was not as forgiving as it had been a few hours before, and I soon found myself crawling on the westbound highway amidst a sea of similarly floundering vehicles. Back home I treated myself to a quick shower and shave before going to work. When at last I arrived at Ashton Tate, it was well past ten thirty. Luckily I had no morning meetings scheduled, nor any afternoon meetings for that matter, so no harm done. But still, my late arrivals were not going unnoticed.

"They're starting to call you *Mr. Tardy*," Agnes noted, when she saw me that morning.

Later over lunch she explained how Ms. Nichols and her staff were always monitoring the summer interns. It was no coincidence that we had been seated in such close proximity to her people, for now they could easily observe anyone's poor work habits. Another intern had already been reprimanded for distracting other interns by being too *'chatty'*. Agnes was certain that I, as *Mr. Tardy*, would soon be next. I was about to explain the various reasons for my tardiness, but my mind was so dulled by lack of sleep that I didn't bother. At this point I merely wished to return to my desk for a nap, not caring if I were then possibly re-branded as *Senor Sleepy*.

"By the way, have you noticed that Bryce Davis doesn't sit with us?" asked Agnes.

"I have," I said. "Probably there weren't enough cubicles for all the interns."

"No, the cubicle next to mine is still empty," she countered.

This strange anomaly had caused her to initiate some investigative work. And it was Ms. Nichols' assistant, who made a study of the firm's eligible bachelors, who had finally shed light on this particular mystery.

"He's a *Tate*!" Agnes whispered. "On his mother's side. That's why he has an office!"

So Bryce Davis was a Tate, or at least half a Tate. This explained so many things. His having an office, his not interviewing for a summer position, his relaxed demeanor at the firm, his apparent ease around even the most senior of partners, all now made perfect sense. It occurred to me that Bryce's situation was a clear example of Einstein's theory of relativity, as applied to human beings. That is, one's position in time and space is strongly determined by one's relatives.

Back at my desk after lunch, only willpower and three cups of strong coffee kept me from an afternoon nap. I forced myself to review the last of the articles which Andrew Jackson had referred me to. I muddled through it. But by five o'clock the printed lines had turned themselves into a jumbled blur of words that I could no longer decipher. I went home exhausted, and, determined to finally have a good night's sleep, I disconnected my phone and dropped myself into bed.

14.

I arrived the next day well rested, and early, to work. I walked by Ms. Nichols' desk, intentionally, several times, hoping that she might see that *Mister Tardy* had now suddenly transformed himself into *Mister Early*. I then plunged myself into my assignment. This time, with a clear mind, I summarized the salient tactics that were necessary for obtaining an accurate declaration. At the end of the day I reviewed the neat and tidy list that I'd compiled: *visually engage the witness, observe body language, speak in a clear and concise manner, do not lead the witness to a predetermined answer, interrogate further to clarify ambiguous responses, record responses accurately.*

I even reexamined my list to see if it revealed any great mystery beyond the simple guidelines which I had written. But it did not, and, given these guidelines, the interrogating procedure seemed to be a glaringly straightforward process. I worried that I had overlooked a critical element, and so I tracked down Bob Parker and asked for his advice. Unfortunately he only reaffirmed that my simple list was indeed complete.

"But beyond the procedure, it's also the questions themselves that are crucial," he informed me.

Parker noted that he would be the one devising these crucial questions, and, for my part, I was to assist him by taking notes, and then formatting them into the required declaration documents. Considering my inexperience, this seemed like a proper arrangement, and I looked forward to being mentored by such a seasoned attorney as Bob Parker.

I had planned to solicit further advice from a few other attorneys. But that day after lunch I suddenly felt especially fatigued. The strains of the past few days had finally caught up with me, and I decided that perhaps it was time to declare victory for my first week of struggling in the legal world. I had enough to be proud of. I had perched onto the lowest rung of the Ashton Tate ladder for an entire week, and had not fallen off, and for accomplishments I had my list of interrogation techniques. And so, with a well deserved flourish, I filed the list away, neatly and securely, into its own little folder. I dared a silent congratulation to myself for this small achievement, and, as celebration, I rewarded myself with a final cup of stale office coffee before going home.

I walked to the atrium's western wall and stared through it, wistfully sipping my coffee and taking inventory of my situation. I had come so far over the last year that I found the course of it overwhelming. I had never planned to intern in a such renowned firm as Ashton Tate, but somehow it had happened. I had never planned on being involved in a preeminent case such as Robinson's, but somehow I was. I had never planned on driving about in a classic convertible, but somehow I did. I had never planned to meet someone like Jenn, but somehow I had. I considered the thread of these events, and, searching for a possible explanation, concluded that the universe itself must have long held a plan for me which was at long last being revealed - a comforting thought if one believed in such things.

I continued gazing through Ashton Tate's western wall. From such a vantage point I could spy over all the rooftops of the western side of the City of Angels, clear to the shimmering waters of the Pacific. I made a note of the places that I was familiar with. I sought to locate the neighborhood, somewhere near the confines of Santa Monica, which nested my small apartment. I traced out the route that I had once used to bicycle to the beach. I located the university campus, and made a visual inspection of it. Looking closer in, I also spied the Page Museum, and next to it the LaBrea tar pits, still bubbling, still holding its forlorn mastodon captive.

****

That weekend I sought to completely clear my mind of anything related to Ashton Tate. I desperately longed to be with Jenn of course. But after the star party disaster I dreaded speaking with her. I thought to reach out to whatever other friends I possibly had. But loyal Laura was still in Russia, and, aside from a postcard stating that all was well, I'd heard nothing else from her. I thought of Dave Richards. But after my drubbing on his squash court, it felt uncomfortable to call him. So, and prompted also by concern, I reached out again to Jonathan.

"We're leaving for New York next week," Monica informed me over the phone.

Apparently Jonathan had decided that he needed a change of air, even if that air was to be found three thousand miles away. He had physically recovered from his dungeon ordeal and now wanted only to clear his mind, with a change of scenery and the help of some home cooking. Over the phone I wished him a good and restful trip.

"We can talk physics again when you get back," I said.

For I had so many new ideas that I wanted to tell him. In fact I spent the remainder of that weekend pulling them together into the germinal form of a publishable paper. I relished the mental change from legal matters, and, without Jenn, what else had I to do with my spare time? I missed her, desperately even, to the point that I found myself almost wishing that her father might pass away so that we could be together. I quickly banished such an unanticipated and shockingly horrific thought, but it only underscored how much I sorely missed her.

I thought of Jenn that entire weekend until, that Sunday evening, she unexpectedly called me. Apparently her father had recovered enough to care for himself, and she suggested that we might now plan an outing together. My heart leapt at the thought, even as my mind stumbled for good ideas.

"What about your friend Dave?" Jenn asked. "Remember that he invited us to go sailing?"

Yes, Dave had indeed expressed this possibility. And I myself longed to sail again. Perhaps I could also impress Jenn with my latent, although somewhat rusty, nautical skills. So this possibility became more appealing as I thought of it, not to mention that it seemed a sound strategy for pleasing a girl friend - that is, simply follow her wishes and not your own.

"Yes," I said, "that's a great idea. I'll call Dave and make all the arrangements."

I now hoped that a beautiful day spent on the open water might restore Jenn's spirits. I had always been a natural problem solver, but, for those problems rooted in the human heart, I hadn't a clue. There were no equations there from which I could derive an answer. I wanted desperately for Jenn to be happy, and, had I some magic wand of happiness which I might wave over her, I certainly would have. But short of possessing this particular power, all that I could conjure for her was a weekend diversion and the promise of a better life in the unspecified future.

****

The next Monday found me again early to work as I sought to erase my Mr. Tardy moniker. Given the early hour it was easy to find a good parking spot, and I proceeded unobstructed from my car, through the cavernous lobby, and up an empty elevator. Upon reaching my desk, it was either my demeanor or my early arrival time that elicited a note of surprise from Ms. Nichols' assistant.

"Well, look at you!" she chimed while dropping off my day's schedule. "Aren't you the early one?"

"Yes," I said, "and please make a note of that if you will."

"Oh, no need for that," she reassured me. "We don't take attendance here."

My agenda for that day had me in an afternoon meeting with Bob Parker, and a certain Ms. Gomez. I now had the first of the declaration interviews to look forward to, although I hadn't a clue about Ms. Gomez's identity.

Eventually more employees filed in, such that in short order the Ashton Tate legal beehive was again buzzing. From over the walls of my cubicle there spilled the usual assemblage of morning banter, until everyone had finally settled into their day's agenda. I went to see Bob Parker, and asked him about the afternoon's meeting. He mentioned that Ms. Gomez was Bruce Robinson's housekeeper and that we would be questioning her about the events relevant to the night of the murder. Parker of course would be in charge of the actual questioning.

"But you be prepared to take notes," he advised me.

So with little else to do I spent the rest of that morning becoming prepared. Over lunch with Agnes I expressed my satisfaction with my current assignment. Regarding her own however, she voiced the exact opposite tone. She had been tasked with researching and summarizing the case histories of murder trials which had involved circumstantial evidence. But there had been thousands such trials over the past decade alone - an overwhelmingly impossible assignment. Another intern had been tasked with researching those cases which involved a husband accused of murdering his spouse.

"So, why not combine the two?" I suggested.

I proposed that it would significantly simplify the research if only those cases involving *both* a murdering husband *and* circumstantial evidence were considered. I argued that this subset would also have greater relevance to Robinson's particular case. Agnes gave my suggestion some thought, and, by the time that we had returned from lunch, she had agreed to it.

"That's a good idea," she told me. "I think I'll follow your advice."

That afternoon Parker and I met with Ms. Gomez. At the appointed time I found myself seated alone in the empty stillness of a conference room, holding my notepad, and waiting for Bob Parker to arrive. It was nearly a quarter past when he finally appeared, escorting the long awaited Ms. Gomez who, upon finally materializing, was not at all what I'd imagined. For whatever reason, I had expected her, given her duties as maid and cook, to be matronly and portly. But the actual Ms. Gomez was hardly that. Still in her twenties, she lacked any matronly qualities whatsoever. She was slim and pretty, and had worn today what was most likely her best dress. As she seated herself, alertly and upright, she seemed eager to be questioned. Parker introduced her. Her name was Inez, Inez Gomez.

Parker initiated some informal chatter to put Inez at ease before questioning her. He then followed the standard procedure, and began reading from his list of prepared questions. Since we were only capturing a declaration, there was no need for Inez to swear an oath. But her answers would be captured in writing, by me in this case, before being later formatted into the final document which would then be signed and witnessed. For completeness, she would also sign the meeting notes that I was transcribing.

Ms. Gomez's declaration would serve as a reference point for her eventual testimony. In essence, this was the script which she would follow, and woe to any prosecuting attorney who might seek to rewrite it. Another benefit of the declaration, I soon realized, was that it allowed the subject's responses to be made grammatically correct. And for Ms. Gomez, this seemed especially necessary.

"*Oh jes*" she replied to one of Parker's questions, "*Meeztor Roebeenzon, he berry nize to me. Bud Meez Roebeenzon, she berry crasee. She dreeng too mudge. And otter teengs too!*"

I struggled to capture such a response, and motioned to Parker for more time. Luckily Parker seemed in no rush with his questions. He became intrigued by this mention of "*otter teengs*", and decided to pursue the matter further.

"What *other things* do you mean?" he asked.

Here Ms. Gomez hesitated slightly as she leaned closer towards Parker and me.

"*Well, jou know,*" she said, "*Mees Roebeenzon, she tage drukks sometimez.*"

Ms. Gomez seemed greatly relieved to have finally gone public with this great secret. Having now let it out, she once again sat back in her chair. This was crucial testimony, from a firsthand source, which could be exploited. Bruce Robinson was no angel himself of course. But for his defense it would be necessary to tarnish his wife's image, in every possible way.

"Did the Robinsons appear to have a happy marriage?" Parker asked her.

Inez recounted how the Robinson marriage did not appear to be a happy one. She recalled how the Robinsons were constantly fighting. Only after the couple had separated did peace return to the Robinson household. Afterwards, *Meeztor Roebeenzon* was no longer discreet about his many mistresses, often bringing them to his empty, but more peaceful, home. Inez offered to provide further details on this particular topic, but Parker indicated that this would not be necessary.

"Mr. Robinson's love interests are not relevant to his defense," he assured her.

Relevant for Robinson's defense, however, were details surrounding the night of the murder. But here Inez had no shocking new information to convey. Her recounting of that evening matched Robinson's story perfectly. He had eaten the dinner prepared for him - lamb shanks, potatoes, and asparagus - between five and six, and had left the estate at about seven. Inez did not know where Robinson might have gone that evening, but he had returned the next day, driven by his chauffer.

"*Jou teenk Meestor Roebeenzon OK? No murder, no*?" she asked with genuine concern.

Parker assured her that her employer would eventually be acquitted of all charges - no murder. Upon hearing this Inez beamed a relieved smile, seemingly confident that the two well dressed men before her were infallible in this particular matter. The interview then concluded, and I motioned Ms. Gomez to witness my interview notes with her signature. Parker then escorted Ms. Gomez out of the conference room, and instructed me to compile the notes into a formal declaration for his review.

"We'll be doing another interview tomorrow afternoon," he alerted me on the way out.

I told Parker that I would be ready for it, no problem. I also thanked Ms. Gomez for her time, collected my notes, and then spent the remainder of the day, and most of that evening, translating Ms. Gomez's version of *Eengleez* into its standard form.

****

The next morning, after I'd submitted my annotated transcript into the secretarial pool for typing, I reviewed my agenda for the day. Just as Parker had forewarned, I was scheduled for another interview, this time with a certain Ed Willis. I beamed to think that I was at last tightly entwined into the inner workings of the Robinson case. Over lunch I told Agnes of my recent doings, and that, with more declarations coming, I was soon bound to be as harried as she was. In fact everyone involved with the case was now frenziedly busy, as the Ashton Tate army mobilized itself to Robinson's defense.

But reports of the Robinson case had diminished to a trickle in the news media, and the outside world seemed to have lost track of the case completely. Agnes however hinted that this would soon change.

"Jackson is initiating a media campaign next week," she informed me.

"That should be interesting to watch," I said. "How did you find out?"

"From Bryce," she said. "He's helping Jackson with it."

I should have gotten this information first hand from Bryce himself, could I ever find him. The case was now at a crucial juncture. The trial was scheduled to begin in three months, and the jury selection process would soon commence. This was the point where public opinion was to be strongly bent in Robinson's favor. A positive image of Robinson had to be impressed onto the public's mind, and onto the minds of any potential jurors. Jackson's media campaign would enable this. In contrast, the District Attorney's office did not conduct, and was not allowed to conduct, any such campaign, a deficiency which Andrew Jackson, and Bryce Davis I assumed, eagerly sought to exploit.

That afternoon I found myself in the same conference room as the day before. Almost reenacting the prior day's routine, I again awaited Bob Parker and that day's interviewee, Ed Willis. Unlike Ms. Gomez, I had no preconceived notion of Mr. Willis, which, as it turned out, would have been a waste of my time. Mr. Willis, once he'd arrived, defied any notion that I might have had of him. He was a tall man, lanky and turned turtle brown by many hours spent in the sun. Unlike Ms. Gomez, Mr. Willis had not taken the trouble to dress in his best attire. He was employed as the groundskeeper for Robinson's estate, an activity which, by his appearance, he had been seemingly pursuing only minutes before the interview.

Willis immediately impressed me as a man of few words. It was unclear as to his exact background, but most likely it had contained little formal education. I did eventually learn that he had been groundskeeper of the Robinson estate long before it had become the Robinson estate. He resided in the estate's guest bungalow, and, like it, had simply come with the property. Willis took a seat at the head of the conference table, eyeing both Parker and myself suspiciously, as though we had some cruel trick planned for him.

"Please feel at ease," Parker suggested. "I just have a few questions for you."

But Willis's demeanor never grew any easier, even as Parker ran through his list of questions and it became obviously clear that no cruel trick had been planned. Parker's questions however revealed that Ed Willis had ever only marginally interacted with either Mr. or Mrs. Robinson. At one time, Nicole Robinson had asked him to install a row of rose bushes along the southeast line of the property. And later, Mr. Robinson had asked him to gather an assortment of these roses after Mrs. Robinson had moved out. But aside from that, his life on the property was a monotonous routine which apparently suited him just fine.

Regarding the events surrounding the time of the murder, Mr. Willis had nothing to contribute. He had seen nothing abnormal, had heard nothing abnormal, and he remembered nothing abnormal. Parker nodded approvingly to hear this. In a way, this absence of anything abnormal would make for good testimony.

Ed Willis seemed to favor monosyllabic responses when queried, mostly *Yep* or *Nope.* As a result the interview proceeded at a rapid pace, and Parker quickly exhausted his queries. With ample time remaining in our session, he then unexpectedly turned towards me and asked if I myself had any questions. No, I really had nothing to ask Ed Willis. But, given this opportunity, I felt pressured to conjure some sort of insightful question.

"Well, do *you* think that Bruce Robinson is guilty?" I asked Ed Willis.

In the ensuing silence I quickly realized that this had not been an appropriate question to ask. As confirmation, Bob Parker cast a quizzed look in my direction. But I was curious to see if Ed Willis, like Jenn's father, was a man of few words but of perhaps many thoughts. I had asked this question in the hopes of possibly scratching below his sun hardened surface. As Willis then thought for a few moments, I wondered if he would possibly reveal anything that might prove disturbing to his undisturbed lifestyle.

"What I think about all this is not important," he pronounced at last.

"Yes, absolutely right Mr. Willis," confirmed Parker. "Bruce Robinson's innocence will be for a jury to decide."

And without offering me a chance for a follow up question, Parker quickly concluded the interview. Ed Willis then witnessed my notes with his signature and extracted himself from his seat, seemingly relieved that this intrusive ordeal had finally ended. He moved towards the door with the same expressionless face that he'd maintained through the entire meeting, and I bid him goodbye. Willis said nothing in response, but Parker glared at me with a concerned look.

"I'll have the transcripts to you by tomorrow," I said to him as he left.

Formatting the meeting notes took little time, as Willis's monosyllabic responses, already in English, were trivial to transpose into a final form. And so, without rush, I submitted my draft for typing before going home. The next day I received typed versions of both the Gomez and the Willis declarations. I inspected the documents, found them to be correct, and personally delivered them to Parker's office.

"Is there anything else that you need from me," I asked him.

"Nothing for now," he told me. "But we have two more interviews scheduled for next week."

Next week we were scheduled to interview Robinson's chauffer, and his supposed mistress - the now infamous Bambi Farinelli. Both were crucial witnesses. But until then I had no duties for the remainder of the week, and it was only Wednesday. There were other interns, such as Agnes Cook, who were greatly overloaded and who could possibly benefit from my help.

"Do you want me to help Agnes Cook in the meantime?" I asked.

"No, don't bother," Parker suggested. "Just remain prepared for next week."

Back at my desk I braced myself for eventually interviewing the individuals who had been closest to Robinson on the night of the murder. Robinson's would fate hinge on their testimony. But I suspected that, with their interests so closely aligned with Robinson himself, these two would offer no incriminating evidence. Rather, their testimonies would most likely guarantee Robinson's acquittal. And to counter them the District Attorney's office had only some unidentifiable shoe prints, and the dubious testimony of a man walking his dog along the dark streets of Nicole Robinson's neighborhood.

15.

For the remainder of that week I did my best to remain prepared. I tried to think of questions that I might ask, if again prompted. But remaining prepared eventually became essentially an exercise in drinking coffee and appearing busy. And when I was not busy appearing busy, I spoke with anyone else who seemed to have some spare time. This mostly consisted of speaking with the paralegals who, unlike the attorneys, were more inclined to have a free moment, and were more inclined to speak about whatsoever matter in particular.

Invariably however I found that the topics which fascinated paralegals most were those related to the monetary aspects of the legal profession. Few paralegals desired to be attorneys themselves. But most, of course, would not mind being compensated like one. They seemed to be familiar with every nuance of the firm's finances, and from them I gleaned the many details of the firm's billing structure. For example I learned that an hour of Jackson's time, as partner, would cost at least eight hundred dollars. In comparison, an hour for a staff attorney, such as Bob Parker, was a relative bargain, at only half that rate. My own time as an intern was not even billed, but once Parker had reviewed and approved of my work, my collateral could then be billed as though Parker himself had produced it. Through some quick mathematics I quickly concluded that, even if I only worked but one day in a week, I still produced a profit. I thought of Agnes Cook, and of the many hours being billed from her activities. She herself was bringing in her own weight in gold.

But the firm's exorbitant billing structure was just the tip of the iceberg. Attorneys could also bill the time they spent while traveling for a client. The cost of an attorney's hotel room could also be billed, as could the cost of meals. The fact that attorneys needed to eat regardless of their clients was not ever taken into consideration. Often clients were not even billed for an attorney's actual time, but for his *equivalent* time. This was especially true of the firm's contractual work when one of the firm's standardized contracts was easily customized in a just few hours' time. But the client was then billed for many more *equivalent* hours, as though the contract had been written from scratch, a perfectly acceptable practice apparently. Clients were also billed for a myriad of other services, ranging from the use of conference rooms to the production of sometimes unnecessary paperwork. The charges for paper documents alone allowed the firm's many copying machines to print money as easily as a government mint.

With this new information gleaned from the paralegals, I began to consider the workings of the firm from an entirely different perspective, and it was with this perspective in mind that I entered Parker's office Friday afternoon. He had requested that we meet for about two hundred dollars worth of his time. He had reviewed the two typed declarations and had found them for the most part acceptable, short of a few minor corrections. For the Gomez declaration he simply suggested that her final inquiry regarding Robinson's supposed guilt or innocence be struck from the transcript.

"The matter of her personal curiosity is of no consequence here," observed Parker. "Don't you agree?"

I did agree with him. He also suggested the same fate for the question which I had asked of Ed Willis. Willis's answer to that question appeared to be more a matter of personal opinion than of actual fact, and so it would be proper to strike it from the declaration. Again I agreed, as even with my limited, if nonexistent, experience in these matters, I easily grasped the validity of Parker's adjustments.

"And I'm going to suggest one final, slightly editorial type of correction," said Parker leaning back in his chair.

Parker smiled at me with an air of relaxed confidence. He cautioned me that this final correction was based on his own professional discretion, but that the firm normally considered this an acceptable practice. He leaned back further, as far back as his chair would allow, and exposed a photo of his wife and young daughter on the credenza behind him. They also smiled at me, and, could they speak, they might probably express their desire that Bob Parker, loving husband and father, should someday become a partner in the firm.

"I'm proposing that we modify only one word in the Gomez testimony," he said. "I've already marked it in the declaration. Take a look."

I looked through the document and found the proposed modification. Parker had changed Inez's statement that the Robinsons were *constantly* fighting, to one in which they were *occasionally* fighting.

"It's hard to imagine that two people would be *constantly* fighting, now isn't it?" he conjectured.

True, perhaps the phrase "*constantly fighting*" did conjure an image more akin to a boxing match than to a domestic relationship. Perhaps this statement might have indeed been a bit of an exaggeration by Ms. Gomez. I gave Parker's proposal a bit of thought and concluded that I actually had no bias in this matter. I would be perfectly fine with his suggested correction. He did after all have more experience then I had, and, when it came time for Ms. Gomez to add her formal signature, she too would have the opportunity to approve or reject the corrected declaration before signing it.

With this bit of business now concluded, I went to submit the modified declarations into the secretarial pool for about eighty dollars worth of retyping. On the way down, I stopped by to chat with Bryce Davis. But again he was nowhere to be found. I had not seen him at all that week, and perhaps, like Agnes, he too was overloaded with various assignments. I became saddened to think that his duties had left him no time to spend with me, his recent old friend from law school. I went to ask the ever prescient Ms. Nichols if she knew of Bryce's whereabouts.

"He's gone for the day," she said, "to play golf with Mr. Jackson."

The thought of Bryce now playing golf, rather than slaving away like the rest of us interns, left me dejected. But it inspired me to also leave for an early weekend. And so, just as Bryce Davis had left to improve his golf game, I left to improve my physics paper. That weekend I heard nothing from Jenn, or anyone else for that matter, and fell back again into my student routine. I biked to the beach and spent the days reading on the sand, this time studying not the laws of men, but rather, the laws of the universe.

I also made good on my promise to Jenn about contacting Dave Richards for a possible sailing outing. I was unsure of how much to impose on him with this request. So for starters I offered the looming long Independence Day weekend as a possible date. Dave was agreeable to this suggestion, even recommending that we do a proper sail, an overnight one, all the way to Catalina Island.

"And would your friend Jenn also care to come along?" he asked.

"I'm sure she would," I said.

"It's a date then," said Dave, "and actually, you'll be doing me a favor."

"I will?" I asked. "How's that?"

Apparently it was fortuitous that I had called, as Dave had originally planned to sail with Bruce Robinson that weekend, but Robinson had unexpectedly pulled out. All of the arrangements for this cruise were already in place, and Dave had not wished to cancel them.

"Robinson's been roped into doing some useless charity event instead," said Dave.

"Probably not so useless," I suggested. "He needs to work on his public image for now, or at least until his trial. Is he going to do your exercise video? "

"No, he declined it," mentioned Dave. "Crystal's been heartbroken. But we'll go ahead with someone else, a fresh face."

Most likely Ashton Tate had expressly forbidden Robinson any damaging nonsense like appearing in an exercise video. Such a thing would have certainly cast a remorseless shadow onto his image. But Dave did not sound defeated. Already he and Robinson were formulating a new project.

"After the trial we'll dramatize his entire ordeal into a movie," Dave told me.

And the funding for this film was already in place. All that was now needed were a few more fresh faces to appear in it, and, of course, Robinson's eventual exoneration.

16.

The next Monday found me rising late, with my mind muddled. The night before, as all that weekend, I had worked into the late hours on my physics paper, trying to complete it before Jonathan's eventual return from New York. I arose out of bed, already resigned to arriving late to work. So, like a self fulfilling prophecy, it was almost noon before I finally reached my desk. Ms. Nichols was quick to note that my absence had not gone unnoticed.

"Bob Parker has been looking for you," she informed me.

I examined my daily agenda. There was the usual weekly status meeting scheduled for the afternoon. But aside from that, my schedule was empty. I went looking for Parker, without finding him anywhere. In fact, it seemed that the entre Robinson defense team had gone suddenly absent. Only after I'd returned from lunch did I learn that everyone had been called to a spontaneous lunch outing.

"You missed a good time," whispered Agnes during the afternoon meeting.

They had dined in a fairly pricey restaurant. I suspected that the tab for this impromptu affair would eventually find its way onto Robinson's slate, classified as a strategy meeting. But in the large scheme of things, this bill would be a trifling sum, and would pale in comparison to Robinson's charges for the next three hours. The entire defense team, nearly four thousand dollars per hour strong, had been assembled into one conference room for the sole purpose of reviewing everyone's current status.

Jackson usually managed this meeting in a straightforward manner - he simply solicited the status of everyone in the room. Jackson solicited himself to start with, and he gave an update on the media campaign which was soon set to begin. Robinson himself would be the star of this campaign. In his first appearance he would host a sports camp for underprivileged youths during the upcoming Independence Day weekend. Also in the works were events which featured Robinson feeding the homeless, helping unwed mothers, and raising money for the beautification of those especially rundown sections of the inner city. Jackson noted that many of these events had been conceived by Bryce Davis.

"We'll have Robinson looking like Mother Teresa by the end of all this," Bryce added.

Jackson smiled confidently on hearing Bryce's remark. His golf partner was doing well, as one would expect from an actual Tate. Jackson then turned his attention to Bob Parker who reported that the declaration activities were also proceeding well. Declarations had been successfully obtained from Robinson's maid and groundskeeper. Still pending were the interviews with Jack Engels, his chauffer, and with Ms. Bambi Farinelli.

"We'll do Engels and Farinelli this week," said Parker, casting an inclusive glance towards me.

"Good," noted Jackson, "those declarations will be especially crucial for Robinson's alibi."

"I agree," said Parker, "especially the one from his mistress."

But on hearing this, Jackson grimaced.

"You know what?" he asked. "Let's not use the word *mistress* anymore. How about we refer to Ms. Farinelli as a *protégé* from now on?"

Everyone, especially Parker, nodded their concurrence to this suggestion. Jackson then solicited Reichert for the status of the pretrial team. Reichert reported that there had been tremendous activity in this area. To discredit the police evidence they were investigating the prevalence of the particular shoe types, from the incriminating shoeprints, among both the local and the national population. The popularity of the athletic shoe, the type endorsed by Robinson, was, as expected, found to be relatively high. If a pool of suspects were to be selected based on that sized shoe alone, then the number of possible murderers would range into the tens of thousands. Even worse for the other shoeprints, the combat boots, a generic type, of which hundreds of thousands had been sold. Possibly the police might attempt to link the boot prints with Robinson's chauffer, Engels, as he himself was an ex-Marine. But here the boot size did not match – Engels' foot was far too big.

"So, if the boot does not fit, then they must acquit!" quipped Reichert.

Reichert's remark elicited a round of chuckles. But once these had subsided, he then addressed the matter of the dog walking eyewitness. He maintained that this sighting, at twenty yards' distance, of a man having roughly Robinson's build running through the neighborhood could be easily discredited. Already Reichert's team was arranging testimony from a night vision expert who would assert that, in the dim light of a dark suburban street, any sighting beyond a distance of five yards could be considered unreliable.

"It's still looking like circumstantial evidence," concluded Reichert, "easily contested and disproved."

Reichert maintained that, barring the sudden appearance of new evidence, there was nothing to fear. To reinforce this point he referred to the data recently collected by Agnes Cook. The preliminary results of Agnes' work implied that, in previous spousal homicide cases involving circumstantial evidence, there had been a conviction only in those cases where the spouse had a flawed alibi. Based on these findings, Reichert concluded that maintaining Robinson's rock solid alibi was now the key to the entire case.

"And I want to thank Agnes Cook personally for greatly simplifying the research problem," added Reichert.

Apparently Agnes had greatly simplified this problem by suggesting that only those spousal homicide cases which had also involved circumstantial evidence need be investigated, thus saving tremendous time and effort. Everyone in the room acknowledged her contribution with brief applause, as did I, although I could not keep from wondering where her next great idea would be coming from. After the meeting I offered her further congratulations.

"That really was a great idea that *we* had," I pointed out.

But to this particular remark Agnes Cook made no response, and after I'd returned to my desk I only wanted to close out for the day. My meeting with Engels was scheduled for the next morning, and I already felt sufficiently well prepared for it.

****

The next morning found me only slightly late to work. I was failing miserably in my bid to become *Mister Early*. The night before, I had again returned to contemplating physics, this time until near midnight. I was feeling compelled to complete my paper, publish it, and relieve myself of the ideas within it, gladly passing my thoughts on to the general physics community in the hopes that, like a relay race, another more capable hand would pick up the baton and run with it. I could then fully focus my life solely onto practicing law, spending time with Jenn, and, when the urge came over me, peering at the mysteries of the universe through an available telescope.

Both Parker and Engels were already seated when I arrived in the scheduled conference room. I was immediately struck by the physical enormity of Jack Engels. He was of nearly the same proportions as Bruce Robinson, but larger, as though someone had inflated Robinson's body like a balloon into a new and significantly bigger size. He wore tan slacks and a white short sleeved polo shirt, both of which strained over the contours of many oversized muscles. His forearms sported various tattoos, prominently displayed like medals of valor. "*Semper Fi*," one of them declared.

"You were a Marine?" I asked while shaking his hand.

"Yes, Special Ops," he said blankly, as though but mentioning his cuff length.

I wondered if Engels might have actually ever killed anyone, but this notion would remain unanswered. However, throughout the course of Parker's questions I instead learned that, before enlisting as Robinson's chauffer, Engels had spent nearly a decade in the United States Marine Corp. He had come to the City of Angels afterwards to become a celebrity fitness trainer, only to find several thousand other aspiring celebrity trainers already ahead of him.

But Engels did eventually land a celebrity client, Bruce Robinson, and, as the two men became better acquainted, Engels also became his chauffer and, as the occasion might require, his personal bodyguard. I also learned that through Robinson's connections Engels had now also initiated a possible new career in exercise videos. The first such video was scheduled for release next month.

"It's called *Jumping to the Classics*," Engels volunteered, "and it's going to sell millions."

The title sounded familiar, and I suddenly realized the identity of Dave Richard's *fresh face.* I examined Engels' face a bit further. It sported a pair of steel blue eyes set confidently beneath a spiked jarhead haircut. He sat unmoved and unnerved, easily answering whatever question Parker asked of him. I could only imagine the harrowing situations that his military years might have exposed him to, so that sitting here now, answering these trivial questions, was no more strenuous for him than taking a nap.

For the night of the murder, Engels had a simple story to tell. He had driven Robinson to Bambi Farinelli's apartment, arriving there at about eight o'clock. Afterwards Engels had simply gone home. The next morning he retrieved Robinson at nine o'clock and drove him to a favorite gym for their morning training routine. Engels could not corroborate Robinson's alibi for the night of the murder. But no matter - it was the police's burden to disprove that story.

I imagined that Engels would simply recount this same testimony when called to the witness stand. I doubted that any cross examining attorney could sway him from telling otherwise. Even from my inexperienced perspective I sensed that Parker had asked questions which were very simple and direct. When matched with Engels' confident and uncomplicated persona, this testimony would then become one of undeniable dogma, sure to be accepted by even the most skeptical jury.

Thus, in little time, Parker had obtained a distilled essence of the indisputable events which would be crucial for enabling Robinson's acquittal. Parker's questioning had been efficient, and again plenty of time still remained in the scheduled interview session. But my initial musing regarding Engels' background still haunted me. So much so, that in the ensuing lull my curiosity overflowed.

"Have you ever killed anyone?" I blurted out. "I mean in the military, that is."

I fixed my sight onto Engels, waiting for his response. But Engels remained unmoved, his steel eyes calmly returning my gaze without a waiver. Off to the side I caught a glimpse of the grimace which had settled onto Parker's face.

"Of course I have," Engels replied casually. "But I was simply following orders."

I did not press him for any more details. I simply nodded to indicate that his actions must have been perfectly justified at the time, and that he had acted as any good military man would have. I was curious to also ask exactly how many people he might have killed, but Parker quickly interrupted me.

"You'll have to excuse that last question," he interjected. "He's one of our interns."

But Engels merely shrugged. I imagined how the business of killing had simply been his livelihood through all those secretive military years, and that he had become accustomed to it, as a taxi driver might become accustomed to driving a cab. His matter of fact demeanor even imparted a gentle legitimacy onto his past actions. But still, I could not banish the unnerving image of this past Engels that had suddenly come into my mind - shadowy, hulking, and fully arrayed with the menacing tools of death.

"No problem," he said, "lots of people ask me that."

****

Parker called me to his office after the meeting. The interview with Bambi Farinelli was scheduled for tomorrow morning, but he mentioned that a conflict had unexpectedly arisen with his own schedule. As a result I would have to carry out the interview myself, serving as both interrogator and scribe. I was delighted to hear of my new responsibilities, but Parker quickly capped my enthusiasm. He would be providing me the list of questions to ask.

"Ask those questions, and *only* those questions," he advised. "Do you understand?"

I nodded that yes, I understood.

"And also, there's a degree of professional restraint that you need to cultivate," he suggested.

"What do you mean by that?" I asked.

"I mean, don't ask any other questions!" he emphasized. "Just stick with the script, OK?"

He suggested that I again review the Ashton Tate interview protocols, and prepare myself to conduct myself professionally. I did not know what to think. In so many ways I now felt like Parker's legal automaton, executing his preprogrammed routine. Perhaps this was the designated lot of a legal intern, with little recourse otherwise. So I resigned myself to my rote assignment. But even then, after I'd submitted the Engels' transcript into typing, I was quick to tell the other interns of my significantly increased responsibilities.

17.

The next morning, just as Parker had foretold, I found the list of questions to be asked of Ms. Farinelli, typed and almost two dozen in all, placed onto my desk. Following Parker's typical pattern, the queries began by soliciting information about the subject's background, before proceeding onto their personal involvement with Bruce Robinson during the night of the murder. The interview was scheduled to begin at ten o'clock, and until then I sat at my desk rehearsing the questions in the straightforward, detached demeanor that Ashton Tate protocols required.

The receptionist was instructed to phone me once Ms. Farinelli had arrived. I would then escort her from the lobby, and to our appointed conference room. But by half past ten I had not yet received any call. Dreading a mix up, I nervously made my way to the reception area, only to find that, no, Ms. Farinelli had indeed not yet arrived. I returned to my desk. When my phone finally rang, it was just past eleven o'clock.

"Ms. Farinelli is here," the receptionist informed me.

I rushed to the reception area, disturbed by her tardiness. I imagined how uncomfortable the situation might have been if Parker and I had been waiting for her, both of us sitting anxiously in a silent conference room. But luckily it was just me that day, and I had no other pressing duties to attend to.

I had eagerly anticipated my meeting her. As Bruce Robinson's fateful companion she had become somewhat of a celebrity. Through magazine photos I knew her to be the same stunning fertility goddess that had clung onto Robinson's arm during the university's homecoming parade, the same one who had instilled me with an urge to start a large family. Now I would be spending an entire hour with her.

I recognized Ms. Farinelli immediately on entering the lobby. She arose as I approached her, almost jumping up to greet me. She seemed imbued with more than a normal allotment of exuberant energy. She wore a pale pink exercise suit, loosely fitted, but still hinting at the enticing contours beneath it. Her hair, sun bleached and curly, was drawn back into a loose bun, and, except for two studded earrings and two strokes of glossy pink lipstick, she had not bothered with any other jewelry or cosmetics.

"I'm off to the gym right after this," she said, trying to explain her attire.

"Yes, no worries then," I said. "This won't take long."

I motioned that we should proceed, and she lifted a cloth bag beside her chair, also pink, up from the floor. In mid flight the bag let out a tentative whelp, and from inside it a small mound of pink fluff sporting two darting dark eyes suddenly appeared. The pink fluff peered about examining its new surroundings, before finally announcing itself to the entire room with a loud emphatic bark.

"Do you mind if I bring my dog?" inquired Ms. Farinelli.

She stared at me intently, her two moon eyes wide open, pleading an affirmative. So did the receptionist, who seemed to be dreading the prospect of a noisy dog suddenly relegated into her care. In their matching shades of pink, Ms. Farinelli and her dog seemed inseparable. Our intended conference room would certainly be spacious enough to also accommodate a small pink poodle, and so I obliged her.

"Bringing your dog shouldn't be a problem," I said to the receptionist's relief.

As we made our way to the conference room, Sparky, that was the dog's name, suddenly became enamored with the sound of his own barking, and it echoed through the entire inner enclave of Aston Tate. Needless to say, his outbursts drew a fair share of curiosity towards our direction. But to all inquiring eyes I merely smiled in return, showing them that there was nothing here of any concern.

While escorting Ms. Farinelli, I took notice of her pink attire, her pink lip gloss, her pink tote bag, and her pink dog. Possibly she was partial to the color pink. By an odd coincidence I had worn my lilac silk suit, a cousin shade of pink, so that we now comprised a fully coordinated pink entourage. She was kind enough to take notice of my suit, the first to ever do so.

"I see that you like pink too," she said.

"Not so much pink," I countered. "Technically, this suit is considered lilac."

"Well, it's almost pink," she said. "And I like it."

She had a lighthearted voice, and I wanted to hear more of it. So, to keep the conversation going, I took notice of Sparky.

"I didn't know that poodles were pink," I remarked casually.

"No, they're not naturally pink," she said. "But I had Sparky dyed."

Ms. Farinelli informed me of a grooming shop in town which specialized in this type of service. Upon first hearing about it she had rushed Sparky to it. I heard the tale of how, as a small girl, she had always wanted a pink poodle, only to be disappointed when her mother insisted that there was no such thing. But now poodles could be had in any color one desired, as could most any other dog. In fact, Bambi knew of one couple who had dyed their sheep dog blue so as to better match the interior décor of their home.

"They had spent a fortune decorating," she told me, "and it was a shame that their dog clashed with it."

When we arrived in our conference room, I wondered what shade of dog would have matched well with its décor. Possibly a muted burgundy dog in this case, as Sparky, in his bright pink, clearly clashed with the leather and walnut trimming which surrounded us, as did his unmuted barking, which by then had evolved into more of a high pitched yelp. I closed the conference room door firmly behind us to contain it.

Luckily, our particular room was adorned with a prominent bust of Laurence Tate, and upon spotting it, Sparky leapt from the folds of his pink tote bag to bark at it exclusively. But the bust remained stoically unmoved, and so Sparky stationed himself before it to maintain a close, and thankfully silent, vigil. I then moved to offer Ms. Farinelli some water or coffee, but she instead reached into her bag and produced a drink of her own.

"It's my pre-workout energy drink," she told me. "And please, feel free to call me Bambi."

I greatly doubted that Ms. Farinelli - that is, Bambi - needed any more energy. Regardless, she raised the concoction to her pink lips and took a determined gulp of it. But in seeing her close, she impressed me as the type of woman who needed to exercise, possibly daily, as the means for keeping the curves of her fertility goddess figure firmly in check. It was an enticing figure, and I again began pondering the possibility of siring a large family.

But beyond her intoxicating form, Bambi exuded a vivacious spirit which left me feeling, like a good brandy, excited and light headed. She was friendly and unpretentious, and I started liking her. There was also something uncharacteristically familiar about her demeanor, unidentified, until it eventually came to light that she originated from the same Long Island north shore, one county over, from where I had been raised. Like me, she had lost all trace of that accent, mine having disappeared during my university days as a means of fitting in, hers through more formal means.

"*Brucee* had me take elocution lessons," she informed me.

She savored the four syllables of the word *elocution*, making sure that she had indeed correctly elocuted each one. I gathered that *Brucee* was a reference to Bruce Robinson, and, that, in addition to elocution lessons, Brucee had also arranged for poise and acting lessons in order to develop his protégé. Brucee was grooming her for fame, and had assured her that it was but a matter of time, and the right film project, before her star would eventually shine. Bambi spoke of this inevitability with such an infectious confidence that I too imagined tabloid covers adorned with her smiling image as she rushed energetically to various gala events, with Sparky the pink poodle firmly in tow.

"What is your full legal name?" I asked, as the first of Parker's questions.

"Angela Irene Farinelli," she said. "But everyone calls me Bambi."

"And how did you meet Bruce Robinson?" I inquired, as the next question on Parker's list.

"Oh, I met him back in New York," she said, "when I was a model."

Bambi then recounted that, before becoming a protégé, she had worked in New York City as a model, of sorts. Bruce Robinson had discovered her there in a night club, where, to earn extra money, she sometimes moonlighted as a dancer. But Robinson had quickly recognized her other talents, and he suggested that she might try for an acting career out west in the City of Angels. He would help her with this endeavor, with both financial support and with his film industry connections. For Ms. Farinelli this sudden proposal had seemed as an unexpected gift from heaven.

"Brucee was still married then," Bambi said. "But he told be that things weren't going well."

In fact, Robinson had assured her that a divorce was inevitable.

"She wasn't a kind woman," Bambi said in reference to the former Mrs. Robinson. "And Brucee needed to get away from her."

"How do you know that?" I asked, mostly from personal curiosity. "Did you ever meet her?"

"No, but Bruce told me all about her."

Hence, in the months before the separation, Robinson had dedicated much of his time to his newfound protégé, rather than to his unkind wife. He had fallen into a routine, similar to the night of the murder, where he would spend his evenings with Ms. Farinelli rather than in his own home. Even after Nicole Robinson had filed for divorce, Brucee had continued to do so, in spite of the state's unforgiving divorce laws. But, with Ms. Farinelli seated so radiantly before me, I understood how such dangerous hubris could have been so easily justified.

For the night of the murder Bambi recalled nothing out of the ordinary. Brucee had arrived at her apartment around eight o'clock, corroborating Engels' account. They had chatted for a bit, and at nine he had stepped out for his evening jog. This was a typical routine for him, as he usually brought along an overnight bag with his jogging suit. Robinson had returned from his jog by ten, and, following a quick shower and a few drinks, he and Bambi had simply retired for the remainder of the evening. The next morning Robinson's chauffer had arrived after nine to shuttle him away.

"So you see," Bambi summarized, "Brucee spent that entire night with me, just like he said he did."

"Yes, I see," I said.

"Oh, but there was one other thing," Bambi then suddenly recalled. "I was a little angry at Brucee that night, for tracking dirt on my carpet, my pretty pink carpet!"

I made an accurate note of her final statement, even including that her carpet was of a pretty pink color. I had now diligently marched Bambi through Parker's full list of questions, and I had dutifully captured her responses, all in proper accordance with Ashton Tate's recommended procedure. Bambi's testimony had corroborated Robinson's own alibi for the night of the murder, that he had spent the evening with Ms. Farinelli, leaving only the one hour's time between nine and ten unaccounted for. But there Ashton Tate could easily argue that there was nothing out of the ordinary. It was Robinson's usual habit to go for an evening jog, and he had again done so that particular evening.

"Are there any other questions that you need to ask me?" inquired Ms. Farinelli.

At that point there weren't. But I was still intrigued by the vague familiarity which I felt for Ms. Farinelli, and wanted to probe further. Parker's admonishments however had strictly forbidden me from deviating from his list, and so I put my curiosity aside. Bambi had finished her energy drink, and I had promised her a speedy interview. Sparky too appeared disenchanted with Laurence Tate's unwavering visage, and he too seemed eager to leave.

So, according to protocol, I captured Bambi's signature onto my notes and concluded the interview. After I'd escorted her to the elevator, our party of pink disbanding, I suddenly already missed her company. From the confines of her pink tote bag Sparky let out a farewell whimper, and, as the elevator door closed between us, I too felt like responding with a sympathetic whimper of my own. I would see Bambi Farinelli again next week when her signature for the final typed declaration would be required. But until then I would endeavor to recover from the intoxicating effects of her alluring form. I mentally contrasted her to Jenn, and whereas Jenn's presence might have typically left me, like a Mozart symphony, feeling calmed and refreshed, Ms. Farinelli's presence had affected me more like the fervent beatings of hot jungle drums.

****

Before submitting Bambi Farinelli's transcript into the typing pool, I corrected a few illegible portions. I also made a copy for myself, and filed it as credible proof of a job well done. For all practical purposes my work week at Ashton Tate was now complete. It was only midweek, but again I had no further duties. The long holiday weekend loomed ahead, and already it had noticeably reduced the number of worker bees swarming about the Ashton Tate hive. I too began to feel the alluring pull of the long weekend, when Jenn and I were to be together again, cruising on Dave Richard's yacht.

During the rest of that week I did manage to finally locate Bryce Davis. He and Jackson had been busy finalizing the first phase of their media campaign. It would be launched over the course of the upcoming holiday weekend, when a vacationing, news hungry populace was bound to be receptive to it. As anticipated, the campaign had been structured to not only bolster Robinson's public image, but to also disparage that of his deceased wife. This left me wondering what nefarious activities Nicole Robinson might possibly have been involved with. I had access to Ashton Tate's files, and so, out of morbid curiosity, and lacking a better purpose for my time, I delved into all of the documents which remained from Robinson's mooted divorce case.

The state's no fault divorce laws allowed any grounds for divorce, even something as trivial as dissatisfaction. Hence Robinson's penchant for infidelity was immaterial. The Robinson marriage had produced no children over its many years, so the case files dealt mostly with the financial aspects of the divorce. The exact value of Robinson's estate, and the amount due his wife, had become the primary issue in the case. For whatever reason, the Robinsons had devised no formal prenuptial agreement, and so the division of their community property would have been decided by the malleable whims of a divorce court jury. Given this eventually, Robinson's penchant for infidelity would then definitely have not been immaterial.

In going through the files I was astonished by the extent of Robinson's wealth. His yearly income alone from endorsements, royalties, and public appearances significantly dwarfed any sum that an Ashton Tate partner might ever hope to earn. There were also investments in stocks, bonds, oil trusts, and real estate, from which the residual income alone could have easily provided for an entire village of Bambi Farinelli protégés.

However there were also expenses. The Robinson's primary home, their two vacation homes, and the staff required to maintain them, were a large drain. Each home had a maid and a groundskeeper assigned to it, duplicates of Inez Gomez and Ed Willis. But as for personal trainers, chauffeurs, and bodyguards, Robinson employed only one – Jack Engels. And for serving in that capacity, I was startled to see the actual amount of Engels' salary.

But after I'd reviewed the case files I still had no idea who Nicole Robinson was, exactly. The docket had provided only a few details – she had been Bruce Robinson's wife for almost fifteen years, having landed him early in his sports career. Since then it seemed that she had dutifully persisted in being his wife, nothing more, nothing less. From Robinson's finances I did get the impression that Nicole Robinson had been well taken care of, in spite of her husband's apparent transgressions. It would have been conveniently practical for her if she could have just turned a blind eye and carried on. But she hadn't.

I wanted more of her story, and with time to spare I went looking for John Corsini, the attorney who'd been Robinson's divorce counsel. I found him in his office, and he beckoned me in. Of the various Ashton Tate attorneys, Corsini had always impressed me as the most personable, perhaps out of necessity from the nature of his practice. His office was adorned with photos of a young girl, his daughter I presumed. But there were no photos of a Mrs. Corsini, and I would later learn that, appropriately enough, Corsini himself was divorced.

"So what brings you here?" he asked, after we'd chatted for a bit.

"I'm just a little curious," I said, casually, "about Nicole Robinson. That's all."

"Yeah, shame what happened to her," he said, sounding almost relieved.

And in many ways Corsini seemed thankfully relieved to be relieved of Robinson's divorce case. He confided that resolving that case in Robinson's favor would have been nearly impossible. To emphasize this he went to a locked cabinet, and extracted a collection of photographs.

"Here," he said handing them to me, "not clean enough for our regular files."

They were copies of police photos of Nicole Robinson, and, as he'd warned, there was absolutely nothing '*clean*' about them. The photos showed Nicole Robinson in a disfigured state, and horrendously so. Corsini informed me that during her marriage she had been repeatedly abused, although *abused* was hardly the word. *Assaulted* would have been the more appropriate term. In one photo the entire left side of her face was bruised and swollen, with both her nose and jaw seemingly offset from their natural positions.

"Honestly kid, she was a saint to put up with that bastard," Corsini volunteered. "But that's off the record, of course."

These self same photos would probably appear again during Robinson's murder trial. The prosecutors would roll them out in an attempt to bias the jury. But it would serve them no purpose. As evidence for murder, the photos were irrelevant. Plus, Andrew Jackson had already devised a counter.

"He'll say that Robinson lost his temper because of Nicole's drug habit," Corsini predicted.

Apparently Bruce Robinson had a poor memory about this drug habit, because Nicole had been repeatedly assaulted on several more occasions. But this too would be favorably spun as indicative of Robinson's ongoing concern for his wife's well being.

"But she did have a drug habit, right?" I asked, handing back the photos.

"Sure, but you would too under those circumstances," Corsini proposed.

I departed Corsini's office with even more questions about Nicole Robinson swirling through my mind. Now I wondered what transgression on her part had led to her murder. Perhaps it had indeed been a random crime. Or perhaps a crime related to her drug habit. But if so, then how had she brought it upon herself? Here I had no obvious answer. No one had. For the longest time I sat at my desk imagining her, until she almost appeared standing beside me. But she too offered me no clue. In the end, all that I surmised was that she had simply longed to be free of Bruce Robinson, and that the universe had granted her that wish, except not in a way she would have intended.

Eventually I came to feel sorry for Nicole Robinson. I came to regard her as being so desperate and so alone, with no one concerned about her dignity. Even the District Attorney's office, supposedly her protector, had seemingly adopted her cause only as a political tool. Nicole Robinson as a person no longer mattered really. She had entrusted the memory of herself to those still living, who, in the final analysis, were only concerned about themselves.

18.

By that Friday, the halls of Ashton Tate had become desolate, and I wanted no more thoughts about the Robinson case. So after lunch that day I simply went home, contenting myself with dreams of sailing in the weekend ahead. Everything was now nicely planned for it, with all of us scheduled to rendezvous at Dave's marina early next morning.

That Saturday morning dawned uncharacteristically hot and dry. The Santa Anna winds were blowing from the eastern inlands, bringing the hot sirocco climate which the locals hated, but which the tourists all seemed to love. It was typically a shock for most novice visitors to the City of Angels to find themselves both hot and cold in the same day. But the Santa Anna winds relieved them of this inconvenience. The winds guaranteed that the entire day would be hot, consistently and predictably hot. Record temperatures were forecast for the inner city and for most of the interior valleys, making me glad that I would soon find myself engulfed in cool breezes offshore.

"Do you know how to sail?" Jenn asked me as we waited for Dave and Crystal at the marina.

I did indeed know how to sail, or at least I had known, years ago on my father's boat. He sailed the waters off Long Island. But neither of my older siblings had cared much for this activity, so it fell on me to keep the old man company, and out of trouble, during his haphazard weekend excursions. He sailed an old, rickety wooden sloop which was constantly in need of repairs. In our final outing together we risked a trip across Long Island Sound clear to Connecticut. On the return leg, the sloop's bilge failed and we suddenly found ourselves taking on water. When we finally, and miraculously, reached home dock the gunwales were sunk almost halfway to waterline. My father's spirits were sunk even lower. He let the boat flounder in its slip after that, until an early winter storm mercifully sent it down for good.

"Yes, I know how to sail," I told Jenn as Dave's red convertible came into view.

I watched as Crystal strove to readjust her disheveled shock of red hair, again wind tossed by the open air drive. She waited while Dave secured the car, and then together they came down to join us. Crystal seemed to have added a few pounds since I'd last seen her. To my eyes this extra weight agreed well with her naturally sturdy frame, but in a town where superfluous ounces were akin to unrepented sins, she had conspicuously placed her soul in dire jeopardy. She coolly greeted us, with hardly an acknowledgement towards Jenn. Dave was a bit more enthusiastic.

"Glad that you could make it," he said, reaching for Jenn's hand.

"My pleasure," said Jenn. "Which is your boat, by the way?"

"It's that one," said Dave, pointing, "the *Pacific Pirate*."

"But there were no pirates in the Pacific," I observed.

"Why of course there were," Dave affirmed. "Pirates are everywhere."

We made our way to the docks, where the *Pacific Pirate* had been prepared in advance by the marina's staff. Like two floating hotel suites, Dave's catamaran had been thoroughly cleaned and fully provisioned with food, fuel, and fresh towels. We followed Dave below deck, where he pointed Jenn and me to the starboard stateroom. He and Crystal would inhabit the port side. Both cabins were conspicuously appointed in supple leather, lustrous mahogany, and brushed nickel. I tossed my overnight bag onto the awaiting bed and watched as it landed there without a sound, cushioned by a heaped mass of quilted down.

"It's going to be a great sail," Dave augured as we emerged again topside.

"Yes, it's going to be *delightful*," Jenn replied with a radiant smile.

I nodded in agreement, although, by my judgment, the hot dry inland winds were blowing exactly opposite of what was required. The Channel Islands lay to the west, and, due to the convoluted mechanics of sailboat propulsion, we needed winds originating from there. But I refrained from voicing any discord, and relinquished the matter into

Dave's capable hands. My chosen strategy for this trip was to simply relax and enjoy it.

I offered Dave some assistance to get us underway, but apparently none was needed. Unlike my father's sloop, Dave's floating hotel was fully motorized. After pressing a red button, the inboard engine gurgled to life, and whisked us out of the marina and into the open water. At the press of another button, whirring, hidden, motors unfurled the mainsail, which ruffled loudly in the wind until the whirrings of other hidden motors trimmed it to perfection. A second set of buttons and motors then did the same for the jib. This motorized crew could even tack and jibe automatically, so that no sail sheets need ever rip through a human hand, nor any stubborn winch ever strain a human shoulder. Hence, the human crew's main duty was relegated solely to preparing a pitcher of martinis, and remaining watchful that it did not spill.

We were soon under full sail, being pushed, somewhat slowly, by the hot inland breezes. My premonitions about having inappropriate winds were apparently correct until, about two miles offshore, an abrupt swirl zone suddenly shook all of the riggings. After this violent shudder the hot sirocco winds immediately vanished, and were replaced by a fresh, almost frigid, westerly breeze blowing strong and steady. Dave made the necessary adjustments to the sails and, like a race horse under the whip, the boat responded with graceful speed. Dave ran another half mile past the swirl zone before pointing the boat onto its final line. He then re-trimmed the sails, and the *Pirate* settled into a comfortable glide over the slight chop, its speedometer showing twenty five knots, and begging for more wind.

"I had custom keels installed last year," Dave told us. "The boat will do forty knots, no problem."

We now moved effortlessly atop the water, and, with our course comfortably set, there was nothing left to do but relax. We lunched on deck over martinis and small sandwiches which had been raised to a delicate art form. I breathed a sigh of relief to see no aloe juice anywhere in sight. Jenn too seemed to be at ease and enjoying herself. I crossed my fingers, hoping that this sail would finally absolve my sins from the disastrous night of the star party.

The cool Pacific wind blew into us as we sailed, but the golden rays of the afternoon sun kept us warm. Jenn let her hair blow free, and I watched it undulate behind her in silky, weightless waves. Crystal on the other hand had no such luck. The wind only distressed her hair, tangling it further into her bushy red mess of a bird's nest. Eventually the bare sun also annoyed her, and her anemically pale skin hinted that it might soon be scorched into a painful red. Jenn however seemed naturally adept to life on deck.

"Look at you," Dave said to her. "The sun doesn't bother you at all, does it?"

Jenn's ranch tanned skin appeared untroubled by the rays of any sun. As when I'd first met her, she basked in these rays, absorbed then, and then seemingly sent them back out redoubled. After lunch the girls had dressed down to their swimsuits, and Jenn proceeded to augment her tan even further by splaying herself out on the bow trampoline. Crystal had almost followed her there, but had then thought better of it. Instead, she stood up abruptly and informed us that she'd completely exceeded her tolerance for the natural elements.

"I think I've had quite enough sun," she announced.

She then lifted the half full pitcher of martinis with an annoyed huff, and disappeared below deck. We men were then left to ourselves, and Dave deemed it appropriate to instruct me in the masculine duty of piloting of his boat. But I soon found this to be a trivial matter. The pilot's console was fully equipped with every electronic aid. Oversized gauges prominently displayed wind and nautical speed, water depth, and direction. The sails of course were easily trimmed by the flip of a switch.

"Here, take control," Dave suggested as he handed over the wheel.

He stepped aside and let me settle in as first mate. I turned the wheel slightly port and then starboard, noticing how the boat effortlessly responded. With the steady wind it was a trivial matter to maintain our course, and Dave nodded approvingly, confident that the boat was now in adept hands. He then removed his shirt, and went forward to also absorb some sun on the trampoline.

"Any problems, just shout," he called out.

"Don't worry," I responded, with a thumb's up. "This isn't sailing, it's driving!"

And indeed, the boat almost sailed, or drove, itself, taking we passengers along merely as an afterthought. The hours spent aboard my father's deathtrap of a tub now seemed but painful drudgery in comparison. I gazed upward to the heavens in acknowledgement of this particular moment. I stood happily at the helm, with Dave and Jenn chatting lazily in the sun. Crystal was still below deck and, I assumed, contentedly sheltered from the elements. I let out a relaxed sigh, as all things known to me were seemingly settled into their proper orbit.

I scanned the vast expanse of the Pacific as it stretched out before me. Standing at the westward edge of the continent I had felt as though I could go no further. But with help from Dave's yacht it was now possible to go a bit more. Our final destination was less than a three hours sail away - Avalon, an old resort town nestled into the main harbor of Catalina Island.

I held the helm for the entire stretch, maintaining the course under a boringly steady wind. Dave and Jenn lounged on the trampoline the entire way, and when Catalina at last came into view I called to Dave for relief. It was one thing to pilot the boat through easy open water, but quite another, and more difficult thing, to bring it into harbor. But Dave only waved me off, and indicated that I should continue sailing for a just bit longer. Not until Avalon loomed but a scant quarter mile away did he finally return to the helm. With the casual flick of a switch, he rolled the sails back into their shrouds. He then brought the engine to life, and routinely piloted the boat into the awaiting harbor.

At least two hundred other yachts were crowded into the Avalon marina, and Dave's big catamaran found good company there. None had a span of less than fifty feet, with one notable standout, a monstrous three-masted schooner which must have spanned at least a hundred and twenty. This was the type of boat which in former centuries had discovered new worlds. As proof of its prowess, this particular schooner proudly flew the Aussie Jack, veritably daring any of the other boats to attempt such a crossing.

"That's at least forty million dollars floating there," Dave remarked in reference to it.

I stared at the schooner, admiring everything that the forty million dollars had purchased - its sleek black hull, its towering masts, the expanse of its rigging, its many decks. On the main deck I spied an especially dignified looking older gentleman who, I surmised, had been the source of the forty million. He sported a thick mustache and a full head of silver hair, staunchly combed back. Seated in a deck chair, he shared drinks with two other gentlemen, and several bikini clad deck hands, none of whom appeared older than twenty five.

I thought of my father's old boat, and how there had been no similar crew, not that my mother would have ever allowed any such thing. But with boats of a certain caliber, such as the Aussie boat, an appropriate amount of feminine rigging is an absolute requirement. Crystal normally performed this duty on Dave's boat, but now, in the heart of the marina, she was nowhere to be found. So, as Dave maneuvered towards our dock, Jenn stood up, as though on cue, and assumed a position at the front of the boat. Grasping some rigging for balance, she tilted her frame back and assumed the demeanor of a sculpted automobile hood ornament. Gracefully, Dave slid the boat into an awaiting slip, as I jumped off to secure the dock lines.

"Can you go see what Crystal is up to?" Dave asked me once we were tied in.

I could not imagine what, if anything, she might possibly have been *up to* below deck. But it did seem strange that Crystal had spent the entire sail down there. I went below to find her. The main cabin was empty but I found her in her stateroom sprawled across the bed, asleep but still clutching an empty martini glass. On the nightstand the martini pitcher, it too empty, was also resting comfortably. Crystal would have most likely remained blissfully asleep had I not first nudged and then shaken her back to life.

"Are we there?" she asked with eyes half open.

I assured her that we were indeed actually there, and that she should come join us. But in response Crystal only closed her eyes, rolled onto her side, and waved me away.

"Tha's great," she mumbled. "I'll be up soon."

By the time that I'd reappeared topside, Dave and Jenn had jumped into the water and were frolicking like young seals. In the late afternoon hours the harbor traffic was starting to subside. All along the beach large overheated umbrellas were being closed, and sand soaked beach towels were being shaken clean and packed away. In deference to the upcoming evening, the beach crowd was dispersing back into town, or back towards the docks and onto waiting boats. A temporary peace descended onto the harbor as the frantic sounds of the day gave way to rippling splashes of soft summer music, or to the random giggles of the afternoon's last swimmers. The shifting harbor wind now carried with it the savory scents of dinners being prepared below deck in busy hidden galleys.

"Break out the mess, mate!" Dave shouted from a nearby patch of water.

It seemed that sometime during the past hour I had been summarily demoted from guest to deck hand. I did not mind being useful, but suddenly I was starting to feel like a designated servant. Would Dave have ordered Bruce Robinson about like this had he come on this trip as planned? It was only the sight of Jenn, so apparently enjoying herself, that kept me from voicing my complete disdain. But still, it was with pursed lips and raised eyebrows that I begrudgingly went below deck to do the captain's bidding.

Luckily, our meals had been prepared in advance by the catering staff in Dave's marina. So it was a trivial matter for me to simply unwrap them, and place them onto the galley table. I called out to Crystal to join us, but she gave back no response. Only the sound of water running in the port washroom announced that she had at least gotten off the bed. With dinner laid out, I finally attended to my own needs. I took up one of the meals and carried it with me to the main deck. By the time that Jenn had eventually climbed out of the water and onto the rear transom, she found me contentedly chewing.

"Well, you could have at least waited for us," she complained.

Only a mouthful of fried chicken prevented me from responding, and I merely shrugged my shoulders with feigned innocence. With a flourish of half eaten drumstick I indicated that there was more food waiting below deck, and that she should simply help herself to it.

19.

Since its founding at the turn of the century by the chewing gum magnate, William Wrigley, Avalon was jokingly referred to as a town built on chewing gum. As the many streets, roads, terraces, coves, and lanes bearing his name indicated, Wrigley had originally owned the complete extent of Santa Catalina Island. I marveled briefly at the thought of this, that any man might have sufficient wealth to purchase an entire island, and also that any man could sell enough chewing gum to accumulate that much wealth in the first place.

Probably even Edwin Hubble might have purchased some of Mr. Wrigley's gum, and had chewed it while scouring the heavens for remote stars, which, as the sun set behind Avalon's brown hills, started to glimmer in the early evening sky. Catalina's air hung brisk and clean, and, unlike the hot dusty day on the mainland, the chill Pacific waters had maintained our island's climate at comfortable air conditioned temperatures. The harbor traffic had now almost completely subsided. Only the odd, daring craft was still out bobbing in the open water. I had finished with dinner, and was enjoying the sounds of the many halyards chiming against their masts when Crystal finally appeared, awake and showered, and carrying a fresh pitcher of martinis.

"More drinks?" remarked Dave, apparently annoyed.

The three of us topsiders had already shared some wine with dinner, and so it fell upon Crystal to dispense of her martinis. She did not care for food, announcing the beginning of a strict eating, or rather non-eating, regimen. But drinking, apparently, was still allowed. Since completing her exercise video Crystal admitted to having become too casual about her diet. And ten pounds later, it was now time to undo this unfortunate lapse.

"You know, last week she downed an entire chocolate cake," remarked Dave.

"Yes, but not all at once," added Crystal. "You make it sound like it was all at once."

I scanned the white linen slacks which Crystal wore, and noticed several obvious pinch points in the vicinity of her thighs and buttocks. I surmised that these had become the final resting places of that particular chocolate cake. This was indeed the devil's food, ever to be wary of.

Dave recounted Crystal's other food related lapses of the last few weeks. In addition to the devil cake, there had also been various weaknesses involving cookies, cupcakes, pastries, and, in general, baked goods of all kinds. Ice cream too was a particular temptation which she had many times failed to resist.

But seemingly distrusting all food, Jenn had only pecked at her own dinner. She had placed a few nibbles onto her fried chicken, consumed only a few stalks of her asparagus, and had completely avoided any of the evil, butter drenched, mashed potatoes.

"I don't even think to diet anymore," said Jenn. "*Not* eating is now just a habit with me."

This was a habit which Crystal again had to practice. The release party for her exercise video would be in two weeks, and she desperately needed her best figure by then. The party would expose her to the scrutinizing mechanisms of the health related media, and the Crystal which attended this party needed to be the same slim Crystal which had appeared in her video.

"Why don't you two also come to the release party?" suggested Dave. "Bring some friends if you'd like."

The invitation seemed to be in keeping with Dave's *more is merrier* philosophy. Jenn was quick to nod an acceptance to it, and so I too followed along. I was becoming encouraged that we had engaged into a social network more to Jenn's liking, and that she had forgotten, and forgiven me for, the disastrous night of the star party. But I could hardly blame her for preferring the touchable wonders of this world over those of remote unreachable galaxies. While gazing at the boats bobbing in their slips, the gentle lights of town emerging through the dusk, and the soft golden hills of Santa Catalina rising up out of the Pacific, I almost agreed with her.

Crystal had downed the entire pitcher of martinis by the time that evening had fallen full upon us. And after the last rays of setting sun had disappeared from the evening sky there then arose a scattering of music, as though on cue, from the heart of the town. The wind now carried the strains of jazz from a lost age, perhaps the same melodies once favored by William Wrigley himself, long ago. We had by then changed out of our swimsuits, and so the suggestion was made to walk into town towards the source of this music.

"They've held summer concerts here since forever," said Dave.

The evening hours were just getting underway, and, as we stepped onto the narrow streets, I felt as though we were stepping back in time. Avalon seemed to have remained little changed since Wrigley had walked its selfsame byways. Even now, no automobiles were permitted on these streets. Everyone got about on bicycles or scooters or through the forgotten use of their own two feet. For those incurably addicted to four wheels, it was possible to obtain a license, strictly controlled by the town council, for a tiny two seat contraption, an embellished golf cart really, that one might use for jaunts around the island. As a result, the town nurtured an eerie ambience, wherein the sounds of waves and wind and music reigned supreme.

We traced the source of the music for a few blocks to an open park, illuminated and buzzing with the excitement of the evening's concert. A substantial crowd had already gathered, tourists, like us, who had naturally gravitated there. In the grassy areas, children, oblivious to the event, played their chase games through the evening shadows.

Beyond the throng of heads I spied the jazz ensemble, formally dressed and at least a dozen strong, hovering on a raised platform. A makeshift dance floor before them awaited anyone with sufficient courage to venture onto it. Two older couples had been so brave, but their listless fox trotting failed to convey the magic of years gone by. So, in an attempt to incite the crowd, the band raised its tempo, and with horns charging embarked onto a medley of old swing tunes.

"Swing music! I love swing music!" announced Jenn. "Who wants to dance?"

Clearly this question was aimed at the two men in our group, and, although I wanted to dance, had always longed to dance, whether I actually could dance, without inciting laughter, was an altogether different matter. My own upbringing had not favored the cultivation of such seemingly trivial pursuits, and so, in response to Jenn's request, I could only offer her a bemused shrug of my shoulders. This left Dave to oblige her.

"I love swing dancing too," he said, offering his hand.

Dave and Jenn made their way through the crowd. Crystal and I followed a few paces behind until we found ourselves standing by the dance floor rail. The up tempo music had by then motivated other couples to try their luck, and Dave and Jenn rushed to an empty spot among them. As they aligned themselves to the downbeat, I could only watch and marvel at something that I had long wanted to do myself. Honestly though, in the culture of my upbringing the mere effeminate hint of such a thing as ballroom dancing would have produced instant derision from my peers. Such things were simply not done on Long Island, and so I did not. As a result, I now found myself standing awkwardly by the dance floor's edge, wishing that I were Dave.

Dave was not an especially proficient dancer, but he was adept enough to guide Jenn through a moderate routine. She easily followed his lead, taking every opportunity to add her own embellishments, most likely culled from her former trophy winning days. In response, Dave found encouragement to push the limits of his own abilities. He attempted a type of rollover step but failed miserably, which only caused Jenn to laugh. Undaunted however, he persevered, perfectly content to let Jenn showcase her own obvious talents. Even more dancers then joined the throng, and, enthused by the rave response, the band kept playing one swing tune after another. I glanced at Crystal, and noticed how glum she looked.

"Would you like to dance?" I asked her. "I'll give it a try if you do."

"No thanks," she said dryly. "I don't care for this type of music."

And so we both continued standing on the dance floor sidelines, dutifully playing our roles as overlooked onlookers. Jenn and Dave showed no inclination that they might ever again rejoin us, and eventually I became bored with just loitering about. I felt compelled to find some sort of distraction.

"Care to go find a drink?" I suggested to Crystal.

She nodded a yes, and together we made our way to one of the cafés at the edge of the park. We jammed ourselves into two lonely seats in a dark corner, as an attentive waiter made sure that Crystal and I, in our corner, were not ignored. Crystal ordered a martini, with me desperately hoping that it would lift her spirits. Trying for some conversation, I asked her about her new exercise video.

"It's going to be a disaster," she declared flatly.

She was holding out little hope for its success. Bruce Robinson had declined to do the project, and, as a last minute substitute, Dave had recruited, of all people, Robinson's chauffer.

"Jack Engels," I affirmed, nodding.

Crystal flinched at the sound of the name. She told me that she and Engels had not gotten along well, and, according to her, he had been completely unsuited for the part. He had no star appeal. He could not act. He had not learned the exercise steps correctly. He and she had generated no natural chemistry. On and on Crystal fatalistically recounted how *Jumping to the Classics* was destined to fail. I had difficulty imagining how any of Dave's ventures could possibly turn bad, but in this case Crystal seemed convinced of it. The exercise video would be a money-losing flop, and Crystal was certain that she would be inevitably blamed for it.

"But it's all *your* fault really!" she suddenly exclaimed. "All of my problems started because of *you*!"

I looked about to see who Crystal was possibly accusing. But, with no one else in the vicinity, this remark was aimed right at me. I had been involved not in the least with the making of her damned video. But, at this late hour, I hadn't the inclination or the energy to confront her about such an unexpected remark. Whatever goodwill had motivated me to reach out to her was now summarily dissipated. She had been drinking too much, and it was probably best that I should return her to standing quietly by the dance floor.

****

Crystal and I pushed our way through the crowd back to the pavilion. I scanned the dance floor, but Dave and Jenn were nowhere to be seen. The band had stopped playing and the floor was desolate. We stood about like lost puppies until an announcement informed everyone that the fireworks would soon commence, and I suddenly remembered that it was Independence Day.

Jenn and Dave had seemingly vanished, and I couldn't imagine where to next look for them. The most obvious strategy suggested that Crystal and I should remain in place, and wait to be found ourselves. People were sitting themselves onto the grass to view the upcoming fireworks, and without exchanging a word Crystal and I did the same. I continued scanning the crowd for signs of our lost comrades.

For me Fourth of July fireworks had, like a birthday, always seemed a good time for reflection. Each year, as the observance of this ritual was dutifully accommodated, all activity ceased for the one hour that the fireworks required. During that hour I would try to recall the fireworks of past years. But after twenty seven years, all of my prior Fourth of Julys had become merged into one identical image of me sitting in a grassy patch amongst family or friends as fireworks exploded violently overhead - unlike this year, which found me watching them virtually alone.

Beside me, Crystal had become completely silent, seemingly lost in far away thoughts. The missiles burst overhead, their light illuminating the pale palate of her face. At some point during the barrage I noticed that she had started crying, silently and unmoving. I pretended not to notice, and eventually, while the show still continued, she simply rose up and walked away. I was now officially alone, and left to ponder this mysterious tendency of mine that seemed to so often put me into the company of weeping women.

I made my way back after the show, moving with the crowd, and in no particular hurry. Arriving at the boat I discerned the faint sounds of Crystal sobbing from her stateroom. But I dared not disturb her for fear of suffering yet another irrational accusation. Instead I remained topside and maintained a lonely vigil for Jenn and Dave. They eventually appeared, both humming an old swing tune. With a casual flourish, Dave spun Jenn off of the dock, and onto his boat.

"Where were you two?" I asked. "I looked everywhere for you."

"Well, we *were* everywhere," said Jenn. "You should have found us."

She brushed by me, and, throwing an obvious yawn, made her way below deck.

"Well it's been quite a day hasn't it?" announced Dave. "I'm going to turn in. Happy Independence Day!"

I nodded a happy one to him also as he too disappeared below deck. An exhausted stillness had now descended onto the harbor. I too felt exhausted, and so I dragged myself to my cabin. But I was not yet ready to sleep. In our stateroom, Jenn was already tucked into bed. She had rolled onto her side, curled herself into a tight little shape, and was seemingly in the process of falling asleep. By the time that I too laid down, her breathing had assumed a deep, slow rhythm. From the other cabin I heard sporadic bickering, faint but still somewhat annoying. The sound of it rose and fell, and rose and fell again, until it abruptly ceased, leaving the boat completely silent.

But a lingering tenseness had settled into me, and I could not sleep. Of course, trying to force oneself to sleep is the easiest way to remain awake. So, resigned to my fate, I donned a robe and went again topside. Along the way I spied Crystal's empty pitcher of martinis sitting neglected. I filled it again, mostly with gin, and took it with me above deck for company.

I do not know why I decided to drink the entire contents of that pitcher. It began innocently enough with a few drinks and the hope that they would help me fall asleep. But before long the spirits had imparted their usual spell, and I was soon lost in that state of mind where nothing, and yet everything, made sense. The stars hovered brightly overheard as I drank, while all around me noisy halyards drenched the harbor with their soothing chimes. The cool night air soon bit into me, but I didn't mind.

The Aussie yacht floated only a few docks over, and I had a perfect view of it. One by one, the lights of its many staterooms went out, until only one remained undimmed. On its deck I discerned a solitary figure, seated and possibly contemplating like myself nothing in particular and yet everything imaginable. We were both ingredients in the same cosmic soup, as were Jenn, and Dave, and Crystal, and Bruce Robinson, and Jonathan Schwarzchild. All of us were just a part of the whole, the vast uncaring whole into which our random little lives had fallen.

If there was any sense to be made of our existence I did not know, and in my drunken state I could not fathom. Perhaps my Aussie companion, with his wealth and age, had garnered a better insight than me. But he remained silent, and eventually he too made his way below deck, and I was left alone with my empty pitcher and my unsettled thoughts.

Looking at the heavens above, I felt the stars literally swirling about me, and only adding to my confusion. By then both the drinks and the cold had turned my body numb and rigid, and it was only with strained effort that I finally stood up and stumbled my way down to bed. Like the stars, the stateroom ceiling also swirled, and this was my last conscious memory of it as I shivered myself into a deep and uncaring sleep.

20.

I awoke the next morning with the sounds of a freight train roaring through my ears. As I gradually regained consciousness, I wondered where that pleasant numb feeling of the night before might have possibly gone to. Everything above my neck was drenched in excruciating pain. It hurt to hear, it hurt to swallow, it hurt to open my eyes. My pounding brain felt as though it were four sizes too big for my skull. The light outside showed that it was already well into the morning and time to be about. But I remained in bed unmoving until Jenn came into the stateroom, her swimsuit still dripping water from a morning swim.

"We're going to the harbor café for brunch," she murmured. "Care to join us?"

I motioned that everyone should go on ahead without me. I would join them just as soon as that annoying freight train had pulled out of the stateroom. It eventually did, taking with it my dry mouth and unsteady hands. Unfortunately there was no room on this train for a throbbing headache, which stayed behind, having seated itself comfortably into a berth just between my eyes.

My holistic wonderment from the night before had dissipated, and was now replaced by a dire need for unlimited cups of strong black coffee. I reached the café just as a smiling waitress had appeared with three full brunch plates. Just the sight of this food disagreed with me, as did our waitress's bright and cheerful demeanor. I would have rather preferred that everyone could have also felt as miserable as I did. But on this cool, sunny morning, even Crystal seemed to be wearing a positive disposition. The waitress chirped at me for my breakfast order.

"Just black coffee," I grumbled. "Lots of it."

I slumped into my chair and tried to feign an interest in Dave's current ramblings. He seemed to be complaining about the service at his own marina, and how, due to their unrelenting cost cutting, it was impossible to have them stock his boat's bar with any decent liquor.

With my head throbbing from last night's gin, I sorely wished that they would have listened to him.

"I've asked them many times to give me the good stuff," he whined.

"So what do they give you instead?" asked Jenn.

"Oh it varies," said Dave. "But sometimes they give me the vilest bottom shelf stuff you can imagine."

"Oh, I can imagine," I added.

By the time that my lifesaving coffee arrived, everyone was well into their own fully heaped plates of eggs and potatoes and breakfast pastries. As usual Jenn hardly touched her food, unlike Crystal, who, despite her solemn proclamations of the previous day, seemed to be actively indulging a healthy appetite. Before long, every calorie on her plate had vanished, and she began eyeing those that still remained on.

"Care for one of mine?" asked Jenn, offering Crystal an untouched pastry.

Crystal briefly hesitated, but the allure of raspberry and cream cheese soon won out.

"Well, maybe just one more," she said.

Crystal's mood appeared noticeably improved from the night before, and she seemed to have forgiven herself for her few extra pounds. But I still eyed her suspiciously, wondering if I might be eventually blamed for those also.

I began to feel a bit hungry myself, and, with no food of my own, I made a bid for Jenn's remaining pastry. But the few bites of it did nothing to alleviate my headache. Even the strong black coffee, delivered steaming hot, did little good. Rather, it had the opposite effect of heightening my senses, so that I was even more acutely aware of my painful condition. So, with little hope of feeling better anytime soon, I buried my face into my hands and simply prayed for the world to end.

"Look, there's Bruce Robinson," Dave announced suddenly.

I looked up, as we all did. In the general direction which Dave had indicated, towards the rear of the café, a television screen displayed Robinson's image. The morning news broadcast was running a human interest piece showing Robinson with a throng of inner city youths. He was teaching them the nuances of how to correctly handle a football, the proper mastery of which would undoubtedly provide them with an escape from their underprivileged condition. He showed them how to grasp the ball, how to throw it, and how to run with it. The piece closed with a touching final scene wherein Robinson was tackled by a clinging mass of nearly two dozen underprivileged bodies.

Here was the invisible hand of Ashton Tate busily working. It was impossible to associate that final image of Robinson, smothered by a swarm of laughing children, with that of any killer. He had devoted his entire holiday weekend to raising badly needed funds for these poor children, an act of kindness which no genuine criminal could be even remotely capable of. No, some other unknown evil, far removed from Bruce Robinson, was culpable for the regrettable murder of his poor wife.

A follow up story quickly underscored this point. With professional alacrity, the news broadcasters quickly shifted their mood from playful to pious as they reported on recent police suspicions that Nicole Robinson had been nurturing an illegal drug habit before her death. No concrete facts were actually presented, but the story did leave one with an impression that she must certainly have been involved with a cast of unsavory characters as a result.

"She probably got what she deserved," observed Crystal.

Indeed, from the second report it was difficult for anyone to conclude otherwise. One was only left to imagine Bruce Robinson out and about doing good deeds, while his wife, when still living, had lingered behind in dark shadows coddling her nefarious drug addiction.

"Paul has the inside scoop on all this, I'll bet," Dave surmised enticingly.

Yes, I was privy to information far beyond that presented by the television news, and the air hung thick with an anticipation of what hidden details I might possibly reveal.

"Sure," I offered, "but what I know, I can't tell."

Still, so as to not disappoint my audience, and between ongoing spasms of pain, I let on that Robinson's fate would probably rest on the testimony given by his protégé, Bambi Farinelli. She had become the key witness in the case, and Robinson's only true alibi.

"Well, Robinson is as good as acquitted then," Dave speculated. "She'll say anything they tell her to."

I nodded in painful agreement, with a tacit indication that I had perhaps revealed far too much already. I declined to say anything more, and, with brunch behind us, Dave proposed a brief stroll through the Avalon streets. But as we made to go, the television screen began showing footage of the wildfires which were then raging, uncontrolled, through the southern California inlands.

Far removed on our temperature controlled island, we had remained blissfully unaware that, back on the mainland, the Santa Anna winds had been fanning flames all the way from San Diego to Malibu. The television showed one particularly bad fire which had completely engulfed a large portion of the Cleveland National Forest. Nearly a dozen planes, each dutifully dropping smothering clouds of red fire retardant, were relentlessly trying to contain the blaze.

"My God," exclaimed Jenn, "that's near the Eden Ranch. My father's there!"

She seemed noticeably concerned, if not outright distraught. The thought of a leisurely stroll through town was quickly abandoned as Jenn rushed to a phone at the back of the cafe. With trembling fingers, she punched her father's number and waited for seemingly countless rings. But there was no response, and when Jenn returned to us she was almost ashen, and trembling.

"I'm sorry," she announced, "but we have to go back."

And with that, we made quick preparations for the return sail. Dave rousted the boat's mechanized crew and they whirred themselves to life. We rushed to the open water, and sought to make a fast line over the ocean chop. We found good wind, and so the bobbing masts of Avalon harbor quickly receded into the distance, as did the contours of Wrigley's island, which soon enough resembled nothing more than a discarded mass of golden chewing gum floating atop the blue waters of the Pacific.

For most of the return journey I slept below deck, not very well, and troubled by the strange, chaotic dreams of an uncomfortable midday nap. I awoke feeling somewhat better, but still not completely recovered from my bout with a pitcher full of bottom shelf gin. When I'd finally dragged myself above deck, I found the mainland coastline looming before us, with Jenn piloting the boat towards it. Dave stood behind her at the helm, reaching around so that his hands were also on the wheel.

"She's a natural sailor, this one," he said as I appeared back on deck.

Apparently Jenn had piloted the boat for most of the return stretch. After I had gone below, so had Crystal, leaving Dave to entertain Jenn with some impromptu sailing lessons. She had proved a capable learner, and so Dave had entrusted her with the helm over most of the open water.

Jenn's anxiety had seemed to lessen at the helm. But as the coastline drew near, a look of concern again returned to her face. Past the blur of the shoreline, to the north and south, but especially to the south, a menacing brown haze could be seen hovering over the horizon.

"I hope he's alright," Jenn offered to no one in particular.

We made for Dave's marina as quickly as possible, docking the boat so haphazardly in its slip that it crashed to a stop with a resounding shudder. Crystal had slept during the entire return trip, but this final jolt must have certainly awoken her. Dave went below to fetch her, while I hastily secured the dock lines. When Dave and Crystal reemerged, Jenn signaled them a rushed goodbye, before racing off to the parking lot.

"See you at the video party!" Dave shouted as she ran out of sight.

The rest of us finished tending to the boat. Eventually, with Crystal still somewhat groggy, we made our way to the cars and said our own goodbyes. During the return drive, I reflected on how the weekend had not truly developed into what I had originally anticipated. It had not been a disaster similar to the ill fated star party. Jenn had clearly enjoyed herself. But we had spent far too little time together, and, as on the night of the star party, events beyond my control had again seemingly conspired to keep us apart.

21.

The wildfires threatening the Eden Ranch were the next happenstance to come between Jenn and myself. I had hoped to spend the third day of the holiday weekend with her, but even Nature was seemingly set against me. My calls to the ranch went unanswered, and I could only retreat to an optimistic hope that nothing disastrous had occurred. So with no other plans for that day, I filled a backpack with food and my unfinished physics paper, and bicycled to a secluded green space. There, under the sheltering shade of a friendly Spanish oak, I nudged my physics paper into what appeared to be a publishable form.

But at this point I could no longer work in a vacuum. I needed to have the paper reviewed for whatever errors might be lurking inside it. Jonathan was scheduled to have returned from New York. So that evening I called him, hoping to enlist his aid. But it was Monica who answered the phone.

"Jonathan is still in New York," she informed me.

Apparently he had decided to remain longer than originally planned. His fallen spirits had not yet recovered, nor had he received any further inspiration. So he had remained with his parents, lounging about their house, making no particular plans for any given day. He was planning to return next week, to prepare for the fall semester. Monica suggested that I might wait until then, or I might call him directly if the matter were pressing.

"No, it can wait," I said. "It's hard to review a physics paper over the phone."

But in truth, the matter could not wait. I desperately longed to submit this paper for publication, have it accepted or rejected, and, in either case, bring a sense of closure to my foray into the world of physics. I wanted so desperately to achieve this one thing, however feeble it might be, as a tangible proof that my undergraduate years had not been wasted. Frustrated now by Jonathan's unavailability, I spent a few more hours, well until midnight, scouring my pages one last time for possible errors. As a result I arrived late the next morning, past ten, to my desk at Ashton Tate. This transgression did not go unnoticed by Ms. Nichols, as most likely I was back to being *Mister Tardy* in her eyes.

"The work day here starts at nine," she mentioned as I walked by her desk.

That morning I found the typed declarations for Jack Engels and Bambi Farinelli already waiting for me on my desk. Attached to them was a handwritten note from Bob Parker.

"*Come see me*," the note instructed.

Up in Parker's office I also found Bryce Davis. Parker was congratulating him for the success of the recent media campaign.

"Did you watch the news at all this weekend?" Bryce asked me with obvious satisfaction.

I refrained from providing any details of my physical state at that time, but, yes, I had, through bloodshot eyes, seen the news this past weekend. Bruce Robinson had played his saintly role perfectly, such that no one would ever imagine him pulling the trigger of even a garden hose, let alone a loaded gun. However I had found the story about his former wife less than credible.

"It's never been proved that Nicole Robinson had a drug habit," I remarked.

"Well, the story speculated that she *might* have had one," Bryce corrected. "That's different. And it's certainly possible she did have one, isn't it?"

The substantial sway which Ashton Tate imposed onto the news media was indeed remarkable. Through their influence, chance speculation had been so easily elevated to the status of creditable fact. Bryce veritably beamed from his newly acquired ability to create whatsoever plausible reality he wished. I suspected that Jackson, of course, had also been involved, perhaps on a putting green, or in the dim corner of a secluded restaurant, where, with a few persuasive words, he would have facilitated a favored proposition. I was curious to hear more about all of this, if I could.

"Do you want to meet for lunch today?" I asked Bryce.

"Not today," he said. "Jackson and I are working on something else. Can't tell you what it is though."

So while the typical summer intern was rummaging through stale case histories gathering data, Bryce Davis, in his privileged circle, was being exposed to altogether different aspects of the legal profession. But I too almost felt a part of that select circle. There had been no tedious research that I had been asked to compile, no eleventh hour reports that I had been summoned to deliver. Like Bryce Davis, my assigned duties had been relatively light, and devoid of drudgery.

"All done with your declarations?" inquired Bryce as he left.

"Almost done," I said. "Only the formal signatures are needed."

These I would obtain over the next few days. Parker had scheduled me to visit the Robinson estate that very afternoon, where, in one swoop, I would obtain signatures from Inez Gomez, Ed Willis, and Jack Engels. The next day I would visit Bambi Farinelli. I had previously assumed that these witnesses would again bring themselves, and their signatures, back into our offices. But, as the use of my own time was effectively expendable, Parker's suggestion that I instead visit them had seemed perfectly practical. My own time, of course, would still be billed at his rate.

Hence, that afternoon found me breathing the expensive air of Beverly Hills. From Ashton Tate I had driven westwards along Wilshire Boulevard, through Westwood Village, over Sunset Boulevard and eventually into the privileged hills which nurtured the obscured enclaves of the well known. I followed a sinewy road upward to the crest of a prominent hill, to Robinson's four acre estate.

I announced myself at the gate, an imposing wrought iron affair, which then automatically swung open with hardly a sound. I proceeded along a white gravel drive, through a sparkling green lawn, and up to a miniature version of Louis the Fifteenth's home. Like Versailles,

Robinson's own palace was framed by imposing lines of tall cypresses, and surrounded by expanses of meticulously pruned topiaries. The home itself seemed perfectly planted into the surrounding gardens, so that it too appeared to have naturally sprung up from the fertile soil of the underlying hill. I drove my car up to the front entrance, where Jack Engels already stood waiting for me.

"You can't leave that here," he said with reference to my car. "Pull around to the side."

At the side entrance, I again found Engels standing on duty. Now he let me in, and escorted me towards a far wing of the house, and into a darkly paneled room filled with books and overstuffed chairs. After he'd left to fetch Ms. Gomez, I sunk into one of the chairs and looked about. The room was quiet and peaceful, and I began imagining a serene afternoon scene whereby, with tea and sandwiches, the Robinsons might have spent some leisurely time together reading their favorite books. He reads the biography of some memorable sports figure, while she reads a book on gardening. I imagined how Robinson might have then suddenly risen up, his eyes filled with an overdue revelation.

"You know, it's time that I wrote my own memoir," he muses.

"Why yes dear, you should. It would be a wonderful book!" his loving wife assures him.

She smiles, a fond glimmer in her eyes, knowing that the book will certainly contain, as its opening dedication, an expression of her husband's undying love and gratitude for his devoted wife. They then arise, leave their books behind, and, leaning close against each other, exit the room through its large paneled doors. I daydreamed in this manner until those selfsame doors again swung open, and Ms. Gomez appeared.

"*Hello, I am reddy for dee seegnatoor,*" she chimed.

"Yes, so you are," I said, coming back to the moment.

But my thoughts were still with the Robinsons as I prepared the paperwork. I wondered if they had indeed ever spent the happy moments that I'd just imagined.

"Did the Robinson's spend much time in this room?" I asked Inez, curious.

"*No,*" she replied, "*Meez Roebeenzon, she haded dees room*!"

Inez then glanced about the room, possibly assuring herself that it was indeed still the same room that *Meez Roebeenzon* had once *haded*. I also glanced about, wondering what exactly there was to hate about it.

"Why?" I asked. "The room seems perfectly fine."

"*I don' no,*" she said. "*Dees ees Meestor Roebeenzon's rume.*"

I wanted to probe a bit further, but Inez's declaration called out for a signature. So I nodded a feigned understanding of the matter, and motioned Inez to sit at a table that was once perhaps particularly despised. I then handed her the document, and, as she flipped through its four pages, it occurred to me that she probably could not read even a single word of it.

"I can read that for you if you'd like," I offered.

"*No, ees fine,*" she said. "*I sine.*"

I watched as Inez carefully traced her name onto the document. I then added my own signature as the witness of record, and the declaration was complete.

"*Dees weel help Meestor Roebeenzon, jes*?" she asked.

I told her that, *jes*, this declaration was invaluable to Mr. Robinson's case. Her statements agreed well with his own recounting of the night of the murder, and so any corroborating testimony would greatly aid his defense. She smiled to hear this, and I smiled back to reassure her. Before she left I asked her if Ed Willis and Jack Engels might also come to sign.

"*Jes,*" she said, "*I ged dem!*"

I placed myself back into the overstuffed chair and waited for Ed Willis. But it was nearly a half hour before he eventually materialized. In that interval Inez had been considerate enough to have brought me some coffee, and I occupied the time by inspecting the contents of Robinson's bookshelves. Unlike Dave Richard's collection however, Robinson's many books, seemingly well bound and perfectly organized, turned out to be nothing more than a well fabricated façade.

I tapped across the span of the wall, knocking from Plato to Poe, hoping to find an actual book. But each time my tapping produced only a hollow thud. Out of boredom I contemplated that a secret chamber lay concealed behind the shelves. I began searching for whatever hidden button might perhaps retract this façade of books like a pocket door, when Ed Willis suddenly appeared beside me. I jumped back startled, while he remained standing and completely unmoved.

He seemed annoyed. Wearing a soiled uniform and hair still damp with sweat, he had been obviously interrupted to have come here. As the sole groundskeeper, I imagined that maintaining all of Robinson's acreage was not a benign responsibility. But still, sparing a few moments to keep his employer from a long prison stay should have been no hardship.

"Is this exactly what I said?" he asked as I handed him the thin declaration.

I assured him that indeed it was, and that, in the entire two pages of it, I had accurately captured every *Yep* and *Nope* that he had uttered. I had brought along my handwritten transcript of his interview, and so I also handed him those pages to scan through. For a man with so little apparent involvement with Robinson's affairs he seemed overwhelmingly cautious. He scrutinized the two pages of the formal declaration and of my original transcript, not once but twice, before finally offering to sign.

"Give me that pen," he said at length.

He scrawled a mark onto the declaration, and, with a conviction that this inconvenient ordeal was now firmly behind him, he turned and left the room. I witnessed the document, and then waited for Engels, assuming that he would be next to come see me. But after ten minutes of waiting no one had arrived, and I returned to amusing myself by hunting for the library's imagined secret passageway.

Were the books to have been genuine, Robinson would have had a wonderful collection. Mostly it would have been an assortment of fiction, with a smattering of classic philosophy. I scanned across the many volumes, speculating as to which one, when correctly actuated, might possibly set the wall in motion. I was about to toggle *Through the Looking Glass* when a stern voice suddenly resounded behind me.

"There's nothing there for you," the voice suggested.

Startled, I turned to unexpectedly find Bruce Robinson standing in the doorway. I suddenly felt like a movie villain, caught red handed. If this had been one of Robinson's films, he would have most likely shot me by now. I tried excusing myself with an appropriate apology, but all I could muster was a bemused, wordless expression. With effort I reclaimed my composure, and, as I backed away from the bookshelves, Robinson's demeanor seemed to soften.

"I just wanted to thank you for what you're doing," he said. "These declarations will be crucial to the case."

"No problem," I blurted out, still half tongue tied. "I'm just doing my job."

The ability to speak had fortunately returned to me, and we began chatting. I found Robinson to be casually charming, although noticeably distant. In speaking with him there was always the sense that, in keeping with the natural order of the universe, he was Bruce Robinson and everyone else was not. I expressed an admiration for his property, and we spoke a bit about it. It was clear that he was very proud of it. The grounds had originally belonged to Janns, the orchard king, in the time when this particular part of California had produced figs and not film.

"I had the original home torn down to put up this one," Robinson informed me.

There was an insinuation that the original *home* must have appeared as a mere shack to his eyes, and worthy of demolition. In its place was now a residence more befitting the stature of Bruce Robinson, who had countless times rescued the entire planet from every sort of menace imaginable by Hollywood screenwriters. From my study of his divorce docket I recalled that Robinson had been lobbying fiercely for ownership of his estate. He had attained his rightful place at the top of this hill and, like one of his film characters, he would seemingly fight to the death to defend it.

"We have a common acquaintance," I said at length, "Dave Richards."

"Ah yes," Robinson recalled after a moment, "the aspiring film producer."

"No," I said. "He already produces films, lifestyle films."

"Ah yes, he does," affirmed Robinson.

Perhaps Robinson had seen so many such aspiring producers over the years, gamblers really, who were willing to bet on a dubious future in such an unpredictable business. Dave was just the latest to have come along to try his luck. But Robinson did not seem inclined to discuss the subject of Dave Richards much further, and so I let the matter drop. I merely added that Dave and I had attended the same college together, and that by chance we had found ourselves here in the same city. Our conversation then lapsed into silence and I was about to enquire about the façade of books, when Jack Engels' piercing blue eyes appeared at the door.

"Well anyway, I just wanted to express my thanks," Robinson said before leaving. "If there's anything that I can ever do for you, just let me know."

I nodded and smiled in response as he departed. I was then left alone in the strict confines of Engels' steely blue gaze. From the former Marine's rigid stance I surmised that the time for pleasantries had ended. I almost expected him to bark out an order that I should proceed in double time to conclude my visit. So I quickly produced his declaration, and watched as he scanned through it. I pointed out that we had struck the record of my last question to him.

"Good," he said as he signed the document. "That's not important here, right?"

"No, no it's not," I said.

He signed, and afterwards I witnessed the signature. Engels then escorted me, like any other household servant, back to the side entrance. Along the way we walked through the kitchen, and past Ms. Gomez. She was busily wrapping a small package in pink chiffon paper, while beside her lay a loose bundle of seemingly freshly cut roses. She was engrossed by the intricacies of impressing a perfect fold onto the pink wrapping paper. But as I walked by, she looked up and acknowledged my departure with a bright smile.

"*Vaia con Dio!*" she chirped out to me.

"*Si*," I said. "I will."

****

That evening I allowed myself a fleeting moment to savor the satisfaction of my day's accomplishments. With the three signed declarations I had produced my first credible contributions as an intern. Were I not alone this might have been cause for a minor celebration. But I was alone, alone and with little prospects that any friendly face might suddenly materialize on short notice. I had once planned that Jenn and I were to have grown closer over the course of the summer. Except that this plan had never congealed, and I now pitifully longed for her even more. I attempted a call to the Eden Ranch, and my heart leapt as the receiver was lifted. But hope quickly turned to confusion, as an unexpected voice came over the line.

"Who am I speaking with?" I asked.

"This is Dave," said the voice, "Dave Richards. Paul, is that you?"

For a moment I almost believed that I had dialed Dave's number by mistake. But I had not. Dave was indeed at the Eden Ranch, along with his maid and his groundskeeper, helping to clean things up.

"You should see this place," Dave said. "It's a disaster!"

Just as Jenn had suspected, the wildfires had posed a real threat. They had continued advancing towards the Eden Ranch, eventually blowing over the north ridge break line and spreading onto the ranch property. When the rescue crews had at last arrived, they had found Mr. Devaine, garden house in hand, standing ready to defend his home. Only through concerted persuasion did they finally convince him to evacuate before the fire planes began drenching his property with fire retardant. Most of the ranch was now splotched with bright red dust, and enough of it had drifted into the house to coat a fine red patina onto most everything inside. Dave's maid had busy been at work here, while his gardener had attended to the outside.

"Is Jenn there?" I asked. "I'd like to speak with her."

"No, she's at the hospital," Dave said.

"She's in the hospital?" I remarked

"Yeah, her father's there," Dave told me.

The fires had taken their toll on the old man, and he was recovering from exhaustion. After being evacuated to a nearby shelter, the day's exertion, combined with his already fragile condition, had suddenly overwhelmed him, and he had collapsed.

I got the entire story from Dave. After our sailing excursion, Jenn had returned to the ranch to find it a scorched shambles, devoid of humans and of horses. Everything, save the house, had been touched by fire. The stable was gone, and so were the horses. She eventually found Ariel on a local road. But Duke was not so lucky. He, or his remains rather, were found beneath the stable's charred timbers.

This was the first that I'd heard of all this. Jenn had not bothered to call me with the news, and, unbeknownst to me, she had apparently sought help from Dave Richards instead. But this almost made perfect sense in a way - I had no maid, no groundskeeper, at my disposal that I might dispatch to help her. All that I had consisted solely of my old red convertible, and a desire to be with her.

I fell asleep that evening with many unsettled thoughts, and even asleep my dreams were not very pleasant. In one of them I found myself back in the Mount Wilson observatory. Edwin Hubble was there, as was Albert Einstein. The observation chamber was ablaze with the crimson hues of the viewing lights, and after the two physicists had finalized their adjustments to the telescope, they beckoned me to the eyepiece. I peered through it hoping to view a remote star. But instead I discerned an image of Jenn, my Jenn, as beautiful as any star, staring back at me from the recesses of deepest space. She smiled at me briefly, and, as I sought to return her smile, a whirlpool galaxy suddenly appeared and swallowed her, like a wisp of cosmic fluff, into its swirling mass. And with that, she was gone.

22.

I awoke the next morning feeling not particularly well rested. I shook the stupor out my head and tried to embark on my day. Later that morning I was scheduled to visit Bambi Farinelli for her signature. There was no point in my having gone to the office beforehand, and so I had taken her unsigned declaration and my copy of the original transcript home with me the day before. We were scheduled to meet at ten, and so until then I treated myself to an extra unhurried cup coffee, and sought to recover from the lingering memories of my troubled dreams.

As a distraction I reviewed the typed declaration for any last minute errors. The document appeared to be in good order, but it somehow struck me as being strangely incomplete. I compared it to the original transcript, and indeed, scanning through the two documents line by line, some discrepancies did stand out.

For example, all references to Robinson's evening jog had been summarily removed. There was no mention of the hour that he had spent away from his protégé, or of the soil that he had tracked onto her pretty pink carpet. Instead, the declaration painted a picture of the two of them, cozily cocooned inside the apartment from dusk until dawn. But with so little time remaining before my visit, I didn't know how to react to these unnerving omissions. Out of desperation I called Bob Parker. I explained how certain sections of the testimony, and which ones, had not made their way into the final document.

"Those parts are irrelevant," he suggested over the phone. "Just get her to sign it."

"Irrelevant?" I asked. "But that was her testimony!"

"I don't have time to explain, but they're irrelevant," he affirmed. "Do you understand?"

The tone of his voice left little leeway for any further discussion, and so, with my marching orders made so apparent, I rushed out the door.

But on the drive to Ms. Farinelli's address, an uneasy feeling still lingered. The deleted sections might have been irrelevant, but they were also not at all incriminating. They were merely circumstantial. Perhaps it had been no sin to delete them. But to my rigidly scientific mind, it seemed disdainful that the truth in Ms. Farinelli's declaration had been so easily disregarded. I was also angered to think that someone had so casually modified the transcript, my transcript, without even bothering to consult me beforehand.

"But no matter," I thought as I parked my car. "With these omissions, she won't sign."

Bambi's apartment was located in one of the few remaining traditional sections of the Hollywood hills. Here the streets were still tree lined, and banked by blocks of older well maintained buildings, all probably inhabited by many more protégés just like Ms. Farinelli. As I made my way up the steps to her building, I imagined arriving at a door that would be painted a bright cheeky pink. But it was not. Instead I rummaged past various doors, all painted the same muddy brown, until I at last knocked, only ten minutes late, on the one that was Ms. Farinelli's.

"Oh, and you wore your pretty pink suit again!" she observed upon letting me in.

I hadn't planned this, but by chance I had again worn my lilac suit. I then blended perfectly into the décor of her home, which, from drapes to divan, was strongly biased towards her favorite color. The coup de grace came in the form of an indoor tranquility fountain, fashioned of white glass but spouting an iridescent pink fluid. We made our way past it to a living area, which I unexpectedly found to be in complete disarray.

"Careful where you step," Bambi advised. "The carpets were just replaced yesterday, and the rooms are still a mess."

She guided me around the haphazard furniture to a pink couch in the middle of her living room. As I sat onto it, one of its pink cushions suddenly rustled and began to sniff at my sleeve. Apparently, Sparky had been resting there, his color blending almost perfectly into that of the underlying fabric. He seemed to remember me, and, after determining that I was neither treat nor threat, he snuggled himself back into the shape of a sleeping pink pillow.

"Will this take long?" asked Ms. Farinelli. "I have my morning workout you know."

"Not long," I said. "Just review the declaration and, if everything looks correct, sign it."

She placed the document onto her lap and, assuming an erect posture, lifted the sheets to read them. In such a pose, the obvious fertile qualities of her frame were not again lost to me. I sought some distraction from it, and I so glanced about the room. All around me, there was no relief from the pink onslaught of the apartment's décor. Only one area, an oasis of framed photographs beside the tranquility fountain, offered some respite.

Inside the frames were the usual photos of family members and friends, except nowhere was there any image of Bruce Robinson. Instead there were many photos of Ms. Farinelli as she had progressed along life's path. One photo in particular however, of her as a former cheerleader, struck me as having a familiar tinge.

"I know that uniform," I mused, loudly enough to catch Bambi's attention.

"What?" she asked. "Which uniform?"

"That one," I said, "that cheerleader uniform."

We got to talking about it, and she mentioned the Long Island high school which she had attended, a rival school to my own. Bambi also mentioned the year that the photograph had been taken, and it was a year that I still remembered.

"Your school beat us in the region finals that year," I recalled.

"We did," she confirmed. "Were you there?"

Yes, I had been there. I could almost replay the entire day of that game, a dreary, windswept day typical of late northeastern autumns. We had all huddled together in the stands for warmth, especially into the last minutes as it became apparent that our team would be eliminated. As a lonely teenager I had probably cast longing glances towards the cheerleaders then prancing along the sidelines, lacking the courage to actually speak with one, let alone have one as a friend. But now, with only a pink poodle's separation between us, I found myself close enough to touch one of those very creatures whom I had so admired, if not desired, so long ago.

"You know, that uniform still fits me," Bambi mentioned casually.

"It does?" I asked.

"Still does," she affirmed. "But now I only wear it for my Brucee."

"Uh-huh, and does he also wear *his* old uniform?" I added smiling.

Bambi and I chatted a bit more as costumed visions of the two of them flashed through my mind. We marveled at how the world was indeed a small place after all. But this was untrue of course. In truth the world is an immense place, easy to hide in, and disappear into. But we were apparently both children of the same storm, and that we now found ourselves seated onto the same pink divan so far from our childhood homes marked us as victims of those selfsame indifferent storm currents.

We eventually concluded our reminiscing, and Bambi returned to examining her declaration. I watched as she glossed over the sections where some of her testimony had been deleted, and I waited for her to voice an objection.

"Well, I'm ready to sign," she announced after scanning the last page.

She was already dressed in exercise clothes, and seemed eager to be going. I produced a pen from inside my briefcase, but before handing it to her I felt obliged to point out the many deletions from her original testimony. I dutifully informed her that if the declaration did not seem correct, she was not required to sign it. She nodded intently while I spoke, even as her eyes searched for a glimpse of her wristwatch.

"No, everything looks fine," she pronounced. "Just let me sign it."

But I couldn't just let her sign it. I wanted to rally her to the side of correctness. It was as though I suddenly wanted her to don her cheerleader's uniform again and cheer enthusiastically for the cause of truth.

"Yay truth! Go truth!" I wanted her to shout.

"*One, two, three, four, Brucee tracked dirt onto my floor*!" I wanted her to cheer.

But she did not. Nor did she show any inclination to do so. I pushed the matter a bit further, until it was clear that Ms. Farinelli was becoming uncomfortable, and I had no choice but to then place the pen into her hand.

"Whose side are you on, anyway?" she asked while signing the document.

I should have been on the side of justice. But justice was not the source of my weekly pay. Nor was justice paying the other salaries at Ashton Tate, or its lighting, stationary, and travel expenses. Until Ashton Tate could pay these expenses by billing Justice directly, these would be paid in the interim by its clients instead. Any appeal to Justice could only be made by the offended party, who in this case was unfortunately deceased, and unable to speak for herself.

****

The document which I took away from Bambi Farinelli's apartment was affixed with only her signature. After she had returned my pen, I found myself tucking it, along with the half signed declaration, back into my briefcase. As I then arose from the couch with a forced smile, Sparky had lifted his head slightly in an unceremonious gesture of farewell. And as we made to say our goodbyes at the door, I struggled, and failed, to produce a lighthearted remark.

"Well, have a good workout," was all that I could conjure as we parted company.

During the drive back to Ashton Tate I stopped into Westwood Village for a brief lunch. While sitting in one of its obscure little restaurants, the matter of my half signed declaration still so clouded my mind that I hardly noticed the waiter asking for my order. Outside, seemingly pampered and well kept middle aged women shuffled past, determined to complete their day's nonessential shopping. I wondered how many times Nicole Robinson, in a silk sundress, might have continued to walk these self same streets, focused on these self same errands, had she lived. As I stared into the street, my confused mind almost imagined her passing by, not once but several times.

"Your lunch sir," the waiter said as he set a plate down.

While I listlessly consumed my food, I envisioned myself standing before Bob Parker, holding Bambi Farinelli's fully signed declaration in hand, and eagerly anticipating my next assignment. But as the details of this scene coalesced in my mind, it became clear that the hand which held the declaration was not my hand, and the face which was staring at Parker was not my face. For that face to become my own, the declaration would have to be changed. I thought back to one of my law school lectures on procedures, for the legal term which described the current situation.

"Ah yes," I finally recalled. "There's been a *breach*, a breach of procedure."

Later that day Parker accommodated my request for a brief meeting. As I made my way to his office, I struggled with how to best initiate a discussion about the disconcerting *breach*. I had successfully obtained Bambi Farinelli's signature, but now it was my own signature which posed a problem. Certainly he would sympathize with my concerns, and help me remedy the matter.

But as I stepped into Parker's office, my previous image of Nicole Robinson, prowling through the Westwood streets, returned to my mind. After nearly a full day's shopping, two brimming bags now swung by her side as she walked. I sat down in front of Parker's desk, and as I did so, it seemed that Nicole Robinson had suddenly sensed that Parker and I were about to meet. She turned abruptly, and began walking briskly towards the offices of Ashton Tate. I began dreading that she would actually arrive.

"I assume that all the declarations are now in order?" Parker asked as his gaze lifted to meet me.

"Well, almost in order," I started.

And with that, and probably sounding like one of my law school textbooks, I proceeded to describe the apparent breach of procedure in the Farinelli document. Parker leaned back in his chair and offered the courtesy of listening intently. Behind him the smiling images of his wife and daughter also gave me their undivided attention. Parker nodded understandingly as I described the two omissions in detail. By now, Nicole Robinson had made her way onto Wilshire Boulevard, and was rapidly advancing towards Ashton Tate.

"So the correct thing to do is to restore the original testimony," I concluded. "It still won't incriminate Robinson in any way, and the declaration will be accurate."

Parker had listened to my argument like a trial judge. He then leaned back in his chair even further and, biting his lip, contemplated the case that had been set before him. Behind him, his wife and daughter seemed to be holding their breath, eagerly anticipating his verdict. Outside, the California sun, oblivious to the tension I had created, was starting to wane, its daily duty once again nearly fulfilled. By then Nicole Robinson had made her way into the atrium of our building, had pushed aside the security guards, and was summoning an elevator for her ride to the fortieth floor.

"Let's not focus so much on the transcript," suggested Parker, leaning towards me.

"What matters most here," he began to explain, "is not so much the declaration, but the reputation of our client, Bruce Robinson."

He agreed that there was indeed the matter of correct procedure. But that was not the complete picture. In any given case, the greater responsibility of the attorneys was to weigh the interests of all of the affected parties, and then act accordingly. For this case, there was the matter of Bruce Robinson, a respected member of the local, if not the global, community, and of his reputation in that community. Part of

Ashton Tate's mission, Parker continued, was to serve as a healing force for this reputation. I listened intently as Parker argued his point calmly and convincingly. Behind him, I could sense his wife and daughter almost nodding in agreement.

"So do you understand what I am saying?" he asked.

"Yes, I understand," I replied, also nodding.

"And so you'll witness the declaration, right?" Parker asked.

On the fortieth floor, the elevator door opened and Nicole Robinson stepped out. She was no longer carrying her shopping bags, but instead she had transformed into herself as on the night of her murder. Gone was her spotless silk sundress, replaced instead by a splotched lavender pants suit. Of the bullet wounds which she had received, three in her torso, and one through her neck, each still oozed blood. She made her way through the Aston Tate lobby, pushed aside the receptionist, and entered into the hallowed confines of the inner sanctum. A clear trail of blood now marked her way, a trail which, I suspected, would soon lead directly to Parker's office on the second tier.

"Think also of your own reputation, and of your career," continued Parker.

There was much more to the practice of law than what was taught in law schools, he suggested. The law schools provided an initial foundation no doubt, but one which real world experience was meant to build on. Ashton Tate was providing me that experience, and I should not dismiss such valuable training so lightly. With this advice Parker's discourse had seemingly evolved into more of a sermon expounding the rightful path that an aspiring legal intern should adhere to.

"I just think that it would be a simple matter for Bambi Farinelli to sign a corrected declaration," I countered. "And that's the document that I'll witness."

"Listen," Parker offered, "that bimbo will sign whatever document we decide to give her, and it happens to be this one."

Parker now glared at me. His wife and daughter glared at me. With the correct choice laid out so clearly, and obviously, before me, why was I being such a fool? Didn't I know that they had already made plans to celebrate Parker's eventual promotion into partnership?

"Again, you'll sign *this* declaration, right?" insisted Parker.

His remark felt like more of an order than a question. I drew a deep breath and leaned back in my chair. I felt like a fish on a line, the hook sunk deeply into me. I searched for a way to spit it out. But it was becoming clear that I could not, that I was required to sign the declaration, that I had been hired to sign the declaration.

It was at about this time that Nicole Robinson finally appeared in Parker's office. She came in silently, and assumed a place beside me. I did not have to turn to see that she was there. The image of her in my mind was not horrifying, but pitiful. She was tired from her march across town, and sad that, in this entire world, there was no one thinking of her. But I was thinking of her. As I imagined her standing beside me, sad, pitiful, friendless, and not to mention dead, I not only felt her sorrow and helplessness, but also the kinship and compassion that one fellow victim might feel for another.

Parker's question hung in the air between us. Parker, and his wife and daughter, all stared at me, awaiting my response. I knew that there could only be the one acceptable response. Parker's wife was already dreaming of the larger home they would purchase once her husband had made partner, and how could I be such a monster as to interfere with that?

"Let me think about it," I said at length. "Let me get back to you on this."

"Sure, sure, sleep on it if you wish," said Parker with hesitant consolation. "But I need your answer by tomorrow morning. No later. Got that?"

I nodded a silent acknowledgement, and got up from my chair, with Parker's wife and daughter still glaring at me. I looked about for Nicole Robinson before making my way towards the door. But luckily she had already left, and had taken her blood stains with her.

23.

That night I did indeed sleep on my decision, but I did not lose any sleep. In fact I slept soundly and peacefully, and awoke feeling strong and well rested. I already knew what my decision would be, and as such I did not rush myself into the office. I savored an extra cup of coffee, shaved a bit closer, and fussed with my necktie until it was just right. The commuting traffic had already eased by the time that I set off to work, and when I arrived I made the way to my desk with no particular hurry. I was not worried about being tagged late by Ms. Nichols. My real dilemma that morning was how to approach Parker with the news of my decision.

"*After deliberating, the jury has decided….*" might have been a lighthearted way to have communicated the news.

But this approach seemed inappropriately flippant. I suspected that any pronouncement on my part would have to contain the word *sorry*, and that I should intone it so as not to also disappoint Parker's wife and daughter. But still, there was no easy way to convey the news, and after an hour's struggling with the matter, I decided to approach Bryce Davis for his advice.

"Sign the document," he advised after I'd sought him out. "That's your job."

"I can't," I said. "The declaration's not accurate."

"Don't be a fool," he said. "Just sign it."

Yes it would have been an easy matter to just sign it. But which choice represented the path of the true fool I wondered? I suspected that Bryce Davis was not naturally inclined to engage in philosophical debates, so I did not pose that question to him. But on returning to my desk I seriously considered his advice. I even took up a pen and placed it onto the line that I was required to sign. I braced myself and closed my eyes, as though I was about to ingest some bitter medicine. But eventually, I retreated. For me this medicine would have not been beneficial, not, at least, for the health of my soul.

Eventually I went to lunch, still without signing. When I returned, I was again calm and resolute. The anxious feeling that had overwhelmed me earlier was gone. I was no longer agonizing over the matter, and I said a quick, heartfelt prayer that some higher entity would now resolve it for me. I then passed the remainder of the day in the law library, where no one came looking for me. I did not hear from Parker, nor did I attempt to contact him.

By the end of that day I assumed that the matter was in the process of blowing over, of healing itself by simply being left undisturbed. Perhaps Parker had even reconsidered his own position so that it might coincide with my own. In any event, I found the continuing truce reassuring, a positive sign that my concerns were being appreciated. By all indications my employment with Ashton Tate was still intact, and if not, I most certainly would have heard about it by then.

The next day, a Friday, I debated whether I should go to the office at all. I had no new assignment to apply myself to, and it would have been pointless for me to sit there listlessly. That morning, still lounging at home with a third cup of coffee, I made a mental list of my accomplishments during these summer months, now more than half consumed. My internship at Ashton Tate had progressed to its current point, and had provided me invaluable experience. I had, unexpectedly, also developed my tentative physics theory, with a publishable paper to show for it. Only my relationship with Jenn, which I had hoped to nurture through the summer months, stood out as having withered from neglect. So I decided to call her.

"I'm coming to see you today," I said over the phone. "You know, to help out around the ranch."

Dave Richards and his entourage had left days ago. But certainly, I suggested, there still remained many more chores which needed doing. In truth of course I merely wanted to see Jenn again, regardless of how much manual labor I would have to endure. She mentioned that the situation at the Eden Ranch was now mostly under control. But I pressed my case, as any good attorney might, until she finally relented.

"But don't you have work today?" she asked.

"No, not today," I said. "I'd rather be helping you if I can."

I assured her that things were going well at Ashton Tate, and that, after so many weeks of diligent work, I had decided to reward myself with a spontaneous Friday holiday. This line of reasoning immediately struck my own sensibilities as sounding somewhat artificial, and I struggled to recover by adding, truthfully, that I also longed to speak with her about a few things.

"Yes," she concurred, "there are definitely things that we need to talk about."

And so that morning I found myself driving, not to Ashton Tate, but south along the Pacific Coast Highway, my heart lifted by thoughts of seeing Jenn once again. By the time that my car was pointed eastward and inland, all thoughts of Ashton Tate had vanished from my mind. There was too much to look forward to, not just this few days' visit with Jenn, but also the future that I still hoped we would spend together.

The ravages from the recent fires became more apparent as I drove further inland. Vast swathes of hillside, normally turned gold by the dry summer sun, were now a charred black. On the barren slopes, any of the lone dotting oak trees had been summarily consumed, their remains visible only as heaped mounds of broken charcoal. Occasionally, fervent red splotches of dropped fire retardant would appear like open sores on a body that had been irreparably burned. The Cleveland Forest especially, which had suffered the worst of the fires, had been transformed into a hellish and unworldly landscape. Nothing had been spared. Even the ranger's station, and its lone stand of pines, was gone, having been engulfed by the unstoppable flames of the ever advancing desert.

I began dreading the ravages that I might find at the Eden Ranch. As I approached from the ridge road, the landscape left little impression that anything had been spared. Gone were the sultry scents of eucalyptus trees. Instead, the acrid odors of scorched vegetation filled the air, and, as I turned onto the Devaine property, the damage that came into view was overwhelming.

"My God," I shuddered, as the full impact of the scene fell upon me.

Almost nothing had been spared. The fury of the fire, as it had swept over the north ridge, had been unrelenting. I envisioned the flames feasting on the lush silvery grass, and the terror of the horses as their safety became ever more threatened. Blackened earth surrounded their former stable which, like the many burnt oaks, was now only a charred disheveled heap. Beneath that heap was Duke, the horse I had once ridden, so joyfully, through the cool breezes atop the ridge.

Mr. Devaine's house had been spared the flames, but only by a saving rain of fire retardant. The home stood forlornly, like a wounded survivor amidst a bloodied battlefield. The grounds around the house were covered by a bright red carpet of lingering chemical, which gave no indication of wishing to dissipate. An attempt had been made, I suspected by Dave's man, to wash the roof clean of this chemical. But, as the red compound had drained downwards, it had merely dripped into obvious red streaks running down the sides of the house.

At first there were no signs of life. But, as I approached the house, a loud snort from behind it alerted me that something was there. Tied to a post in the rear yard, Ariel lifted her eyes towards me. She pranced slightly as I drew closer, recalling perhaps, in her equine mind, the happier time when I had ridden alongside her. Like the house, she too floundered amidst a red sea, atop a small raft of compacted straw.

"You'll be fine," I told her while rubbing her snout. "You're a survivor."

I approached the house, hoping to find Jenn. I then noticed that my breathing was becoming somewhat labored, my eyes somewhat itchy, and my nostrils slightly tender. When a sudden gust of wind stirred a random plume of red dust into the air, my breathing became nearly impossible. I bent over, choking for air amidst surges of involuntary coughing.

"Quick, come inside!" I heard Jenn shout.

She hurried me into the house where the air inside, slightly cleaner, but not by much, helped to alleviate my coughing.

"It's this red dust," I gasped. "I must be sensitive to it."

"You shouldn't have come," said Jenn. "Look how terrible everything is. Really, you shouldn't have come."

But, regaining my breath, I insisted that I had wanted to come, that I wanted to help. This sensitivity to the red dust would soon pass, I assured her, just as soon as I became used to it. But Jenn only shook her head skeptically.

"Come," she said, "have some lunch."

We shared a quiet meal. Our conversation did not seem to flow as easily as it once had. There was much that we needed to talk about. But, without an easy mood between us, nothing could be said. I sought to remind her of the few good moments that we'd had together.

"Yes, those were fun," she agreed with a passing smile. "It seems like forever now."

I wanted to convince her that our future together could be as much fun, if only she would let it. Soon the fall semester would begin, and we would be together again like before. We could share an apartment, and all the trivial little details of living - morning coffee, evening walks, books, conversation, warm smiles. To me, this sounded like a heaven on earth.

"Except that I'm not going back to school this year," she informed me.

"But, you have to," I replied. "You have to."

No, she didn't have to. Nor could she really. The state of her father's health, until it resolved itself, prevented her from pursuing any further studies. Beyond this, there was also the matter of her dissertation. Not only had she made no significant progress with it, but she had also lost all interest in it. Her little girl's fascination with the Russian language was gone. And, like a toy outgrown, Pushkin too was to be pushed aside, and forgotten.

"But what will you do?" I asked.

"I don't know," she said. "Probably I'll just take care of my father for now."

My spirits sank. As much as I cared for Mr. Devaine's welfare, I cared for being with Jenn even more. After lunch, with my mind still confused, I sought to make good on my promise to help. With my breathing recovered, I convinced Jenn, and myself, that I was ready to perform some useful task. But what was there to be done?

"Why don't you clear all of the red dust that's around the house?" Jenn suggested.

"All of it?" I asked.

"Well, you said you wanted to help," she reminded me.

The thought of possibly shoveling so much toxic chemical suddenly overwhelmed me. But Jenn's gauntlet of a suggestion had been thrown down before me. Certainly she couldn't be serious about the request, could she?

"No, I'm perfectly serious about it," she assured me.

Jenn's redoubled challenge left me little choice. There was nothing that I wouldn't do for her, and surely she must have understood that. So I located an old shovel in the back shed and set to work. It was unclear how to collect all of the fire retardant, nearly a half acre's worth, into one single pile. Instead I envisioned collecting it into a number of smaller piles to be removed by some unspecified person, hopefully not me, at some future date. So, with this plan, I began gathering the first pile, carefully staging my breathing so as to avoid the red plumes being launched airborne by my digging.

But only half a dozen piles later, I was already spent. In spite of my measured breathing, I had ingested enough dust to turn my eyes and throat unbearably sore. The hot afternoon sun had started to bake, and my forearms had turned bright red, not from the sun, but from the dust which had clung to me. I retreated to the porch in need of a break, and sat down, shaking my head in despair. Only my desire to please Jenn made me want to continue.

"Quitting already?" asked Jenn, peering out from the house.

"No, just resting, not quitting," I grumbled, choking back a cough.

I was thirsty, and Jenn obliged me with a desperately needed drink. But as I drank, the traces of fire retardant in my mouth suddenly came to life. This was nasty stuff, and it eagerly burned itself into any unguarded tissue of my being. After the pain had subsided, I took inventory of the six pathetic piles of red dust that I had gathered. To clear the entire property would have required more than six hundred such piles, a superhuman effort.

Still, I was determined to persist in fulfilling my futile promise. Driven by stubborn, senseless pride, I returned to my digging. My already sore limbs let out a painful complaint as I again took up my shovel. But the next two hours were a pointless exercise. When is it that a man is defeated? Probably not when he ceases a chosen endeavor, but rather when he ceases to believe in it. In that field, under the hot sun, with my eyes burning, my back aching, and each breath a labored affair, I ceased believing.

"I need a shower," I told Jenn after going inside.

"By all means," she said, and then adding after a pause, "because you look awful."

She was right. In the bathroom mirror there was indeed a frightful image staring back at me. I was immediately struck by the macabre hue of my skin, not a sun painted red, but an intense chemically tinged red, stained onto my arms and face. Even after furious scrubbing under a hot shower, the color had stubbornly remained, except with a heightened sheen. Rejoining Jenn, I wondered if my newfound color, in a dim light, might possibly have had any romantic appeal.

"Now you look like a rhubarb!" she exclaimed on seeing me again.

She had been setting the table for dinner, but the sight of me caused her to almost double over with laughter. From her reaction I realized that there wasn't a light dim enough to make me appear, in the slightest way, romantic.

"Are you alright?" she asked once she'd recovered.

"I'm fine," I said. "Maybe just a little embarrassed."

Probably I was indeed blushing, although now impossible to tell. Jenn had set three places at the table, so I surmised that Mr. Devaine would be joining us for dinner. He had remained in bed all day, and I had yet to see him. But I almost dreaded seeing again, and what he might look like.

"He still insists on eating dinner at the table," Jenn told me.

In a way I understood this. Perhaps dinner with Jenn constituted a last remaining vestige of his former life, and he was tenaciously clinging to it. His ill health had changed his life considerably, and I grieved for the enthusiastic, active life force which had become so diminished.

"Does he still drink scotch?" I asked.

"Still does. Every night on the porch," Jenn assured me, "in spite of his doctor."

My heart lifted as I heard this. *"That's the spirit!"* I thought. There was still plenty of fight left in the old fellow. I did not dread seeing him now. I even began looking forward to the day when he would be fully recovered. This was only a temporary setback to his health, which, with a proper amount of rest, care, and scotch, was certain to be restored.

Jenn went upstairs to assist her father. But almost half an hour passed until they both appeared, moving like careful inchworms, through the kitchen doorway. At first Mr. Devaine seemed like his old self, only more stooped. Except as he drew closer, further into the light, I was shocked to see how little of him remained. He appeared gaunt and distant, a faint shadow of his former self. I struggled to offer him some encouragement.

"It's good to see you," I remarked. "You look fine!"

"And you look…..sunburned," he replied after some scrutiny, "very sunburned."

Over dinner I explained the cause of my apparently sunburned skin. He seemed to listen intently, but, behind his hollow eyes, I wondered if he truly heard. After dinner we moved on to dessert, which, I discovered, was usually served in the form of scotch whiskey. I poured out two glasses and brought them out to the porch, where Mr. Devaine was already seated in his usual chair. I sat beside him and, with whiskey in hand, we both stared out towards the expanse of his property.

But the view from the porch, once of lush grass under a sultry moon, now showed only desolation. The abundant moonlight on this clear night was completely absorbed by the charred landscape. The former sweet scent of eucalyptus was but a distant memory, now replaced by the acrid smell of fire retardant.

"Don't worry," I told Mr. Devaine. "It will all grow back, you'll see."

"No. I won't see," he said. "By then I'm sure to be gone."

I nodded silently, took a quick sip of scotch, and swallowed it hard. Any words that I might have uttered seemed to get stuck in my throat, going no further. Mr. Devaine and I went on to pass the time in silence. We each had our own particular concerns to ponder. Most likely Mr. Devaine could now only stare at the barren remains of his property with a hard acceptance. Perhaps he had found shelter in the deep confines of the distant place that he had retreated into. But as for myself, I had no such place, and could only stare out, with pained and labored breath, at the futile, lonely piles of dirt that I had heaped together that afternoon.

"It's time for bed now Daddy," announced Jenn, as she reappeared on the porch.

Jenn then brought her father upstairs, and I got myself another drink. From her makeshift paddock, Ariel sent a lone snort into a night which was devoid of all sounds save that of the wind. Eventually Jenn joined me out on the porch.

"Red is really not your color," she observed smiling.

I smiled back, glad to see a small trace of the loving Jenn that I had once known. Back here she was different, so much so that I wished we could spend the rest of our lives on the ranch, nestled in a small cabin, living on love. Here was the Jenn that I had fallen in love with, that I wanted to be in love with. Gazing into her eyes it occurred to me that we still needed to *talk*, to talk about things that actually should have required no talking about to begin with.

"I really want to be in love with you, you know," I said softly.

"I know," she replied. "I know."

She smiled at me again, a half smile this time. But as I moved to draw her closer, she looked away. And with that I knew that there was really nothing for us to say. So quickly and easily, we had done our talking, and had come to an understanding. Jenn was a jewel, a golden prize, and it would be her decision as to who possessed her.

The next morning after breakfast I told Jenn that I would be leaving. She had been right - there really was nothing for me to do on the ranch.

"But you're still going to Dave's party, right?" I asked her.

"I am," she nodded. "Count on it."

"Want to go together?" I asked.

"Sure," she said, obligingly. "Let's do that."

She offered me a parting kiss, and I drove away from the Eden Ranch with mixed emotions. My future with Jenn seemed to be slipping away from me. But I could not let it go so easily. She was a prize worth fighting for. Over the course of the summer I had become aware that so much of life, especially my own it seemed, lay beyond my control. But I still wanted a chance to win her, and, as I drove again through the charred ravages of the Cleveland Forest, I recommitted myself to the dream of spending the rest of my life with her.

24.

Except for the red tinge to my complexion, the following week at Ashton Tate began normally enough. I arrived promptly on Monday morning to find that, in spite of my last Friday's absence, there were no inquiring messages left on my phone, no urgent notes placed onto my desk, and no notice of dismissal. I took this as a sign that Parker and I had come to an unspoken agreement regarding the Farinelli declaration, and that nothing was amiss. However, while sitting in my usual place at the back of our regular Monday afternoon status meeting, I was met with more than a few inquiring stares. Eventually it occurred to me that my newfound complexion was attracting all of this attention.

"Fell asleep in the sun this weekend," I explained tragically. "Don't ask…." And luckily no one did.

We were treated to a surprise in that particular meeting, or at least I was, as Bruce Robinson was also in attendance. He had come to receive a full report regarding the current status of his case. His interest in every slight detail soon became apparent. He listened, approved, disapproved, and even offered his own advice to his highly paid team of advisors. Like a paranoid gambler fixing a game, he sought to insure that nothing was being left to the unpredictable whims of mere uncontrollable chance.

Robinson came to learn that the progress in his defense case had been stellar. The publicity campaign was proceeding especially well. In addition to the Independence Day events, subsequent ones had been planned. In one particular event, scheduled to coincide with the jury selection phase of the trial, Robinson would be giving out countless autographed footballs to the city's homeless. I imagined the television news reports as these unfortunate people, equipped now with prized footballs, would be shown organizing themselves into teams and playing an impromptu game.

Regarding the expert witnesses, a full cadre of them had been assembled. Their expertise ranged from athletic footwear, to the capabilities of human night vision. There was even an odd expert, I thought, an astrologer who would testify that, on the night of the murder, Robinson's stars were aligned such that he would have naturally remained indoors after sunset. But Jackson and Reichert quickly noted that they planned to hold such an esoteric expert in reserve, to be used only if absolutely needed.

"Be sure to select jurors who also believe in astronomy," advised Robinson, "just in case."

The lead attorneys nodded in agreement, and duly noted this crucial request. As a former astronomer, not astrologer, I knew exactly which stars would have shone on the night in question. Most prominent would have been my old friend, Orion, hunting for Drago, the dragon constellation which skulked about on the opposite edge of the night sky. But in all my studies of cosmology nothing about Orion and Drago had ever indicated that one should have remained indoors on such a night. If anything, I thought, one might have ventured outside, especially if they had wished to hunt.

"What else?" demanded Robinson.

There were still a few more items remaining. For example, Agnes Cook had finally concluded her exhaustive research, and she presented a summary of it. Her data, gleaned from many precedent cases, indicated that the odds for an acquittal were excellent, at least ninety two percent, in the event that the incriminating evidence was shown to be circumstantial.

"Ninety two is not one hundred," observed Robinson. "What about the other eight percent?"

"In the remaining percentage, the defendants had weak alibis," Agnes informed him. "So the jury was moved to convict. Having a strong alibi is the key."

Agnes had done her homework well, and her cache of research clearly indicated how to proceed with Robinson's defense. Just as the lead attorneys had suspected, the police's evidence could be easily discredited by the hired experts, and made to appear circumstantial. What was also needed was a strong alibi, and luckily Robinson had one, in the form of Bambi Farinelli's supposed testimony.

"What about the declarations?" asked Robinson. "The filing deadline is this week."

An immediate silence now filled in the room. Robinson's eyes, which had been focused on Jackson, turned squarely towards me. I was then unexpectedly scrutinized by the same condescending gaze that had threatened me just a few days prior.

"What about that red fellow over there?" Robinson demanded. "Wasn't he supposed to have done this by now?"

This was clearly my moment. Like Agnes, I now had an opportunity to drop my own comments into the meeting, to impress everyone, to make myself known. I could explain to Robinson the cause of the delay, the current shortcomings with the Farinelli declaration, and how the declaration might be easily corrected and brought into accordance with proper legal protocol. I had raised my posture slightly to begin this discourse, when Jackson, rushing in as though to catch a falling vase, suddenly spoke up.

"The declarations will be filed this week," Jackson assured him. "There isn't any problem here."

Robinson then withdrew his attention from me and looked at Jackson. Jackson nodded, as though acknowledging some unspoken contract. The tension in the room lingered briefly, but then dissipated as I slumped back into my seat and remained silent, deprived of my chance to speak. After the meeting, Jackson asked me to stay behind, and, once the room had emptied, he took a seat beside me.

"Parker's given up on you," announced Jackson. "But I believe in giving second chances. And, really, we all want you to succeed."

"What do you mean?" I asked.

"What I mean is that I'm giving you one more chance to sign the declaration. You have until the end of today," he informed me. "Is that fair?"

With this statement, he looked at me intently, reassuringly. But I looked past him. Behind Jackson was not the photograph of his loyal Labrabull, but, rather, of a very patrician Robert Ashton, whose stern visage also advised me to not disturb the well ordered workings that he and his partner had put together. But still, I felt compelled to offer a remaining bit of resistance.

"The original declaration doesn't incriminate Robinson," I protested. "Why not just let the jury decide?"

"But the jury doesn't decide," intoned Jackson, as though sharing a great secret. "We decide for them. Don't you understand?"

Like Parker, Jackson too had asked me if I understood. Ashton's portrait continued admonishing me, probably also curious as to whether or not I understood. Yes, I understood. I understood it now all too well. I searched about the conference room to see if Nicole Robinson had perhaps also made an appearance. But this time she had not, and she did not have to since, if anything, I had come to understand her and all of these people she had known, who so casually took what they wanted, regardless of the casualties.

"Yes, I'll let you know by the end of today," I said, again not knowing what I would tell him.

"Good," he said. "I know you'll do the right thing."

Jackson stood up to go. But before leaving he offered one last bit of advice.

"By the way," he added, "I've faced many similar choices myself. But this is how careers are made."

I returned to my desk, frustrated that this matter refused to settle itself. I wondered if a trusted opinion might provide some help, and so I asked Agnes Cook to meet with me. In a closed conference room, I described the situation to her. I explained how in comparison to her own assignment, mine posed more of a personal dilemma. She listened intently, all the while nodding sympathetically.

"You should do the right thing," she counseled. "Myself, I wouldn't sign it."

I felt overwhelming relief to hear this. It was an honest opinion, plainly spoken, and I thanked her for it. Finally, in the entire universe of Ashton Tate, here at last was someone I could rely on for reassuring advice, a trusted friend who also valued that ephemeral concept known as integrity.

"Just tell Jackson that you can't bring yourself to sign it. He'll understand," she advised, then adding with levity. "Tell him that for now you have to attend to your sunburn."

I appreciated her sense of humor, or at least her attempt at humor, and I returned to my desk feeling more at ease to have the support of at least one other fellow human being. I already knew of Bryce Davis' opinion on this matter, but wondered if perhaps he'd had a change of heart. With the publicity campaign winding down, he was more available lately, so I found him this time in his small cubby of an office.

"If you do the right thing now," he advised, "you'll be hired again next year. That's just how it works."

I could always rely on Bryce for his practical assessment of any situation. From his mindset, signing the document was the only acceptable, if not the natural, course of action. At least this time he hadn't called me a fool.

"Listen, don't be a fool," he added. "Do you think you'll be rehired based on your grades? Yes, they know all about those, you know."

Bryce had offered me no support, and my spirits again sank. Jackson's end of day deadline was rapidly approaching. I was still so confused, but mostly I was confused as to why this decision was causing me so much confusion. It was simply a bit of bitter medicine, to be quickly swallowed with eyes closed, and forgotten. Outside, the fresh air and bright sun beckoned, urging me to join them, offering the promise that a brief walk through them might clear my troubled mind.

"*It's just a damned signature....*" I reminded myself in the elevator down.

I made my way out of the building, with my mind swimming, floundering actually, to arrive at the heart of the matter. I was not so high minded as to believe that the problem was rooted completely in my own code of ethics. I'd usually found those types of decisions to be simple and straightforward, much easier than this one. There was something else at work here, and in the glaring light of late afternoon I needed to find it.

Instinctively, and without thinking, I found that I had walked the customary route to my parked convertible. Perhaps I wanted no more than to simply jump into it and drive away. But I did not. I might have driven to the beach, but then, at the edge of the continent, there would be no further place for me to drive on to. Turning away from the car, I let out a desperate sigh, and walked another block to stare at the eternally bubbling pool of the LaBrea tar pits.

The one poor mastodon was still firmly ensnared by the unforgiving asphalt. Over the past few months, as I'd driven my car past, I had felt forever sorry for the unfortunate creature. But now my gaze chanced unexpectedly onto its mate, who called from the edge of the pool. I realized that this other creature was also as much deserving of my sympathy. Its expression was also one of grief and confusion. It too was trapped in a way, trapped between a longing for its mate, and by its own desire to survive.

Gazing at this other creature, I realized that here was the key to my dilemma, the reason why I had been torn by the Farinelli declaration. The matter was not solely about ethics, or about myself, or even about Nicole Robinson, but it was about Jenn and myself, and about the future that I had hoped for us. What was the price that I would be willing to pay for that future? Or even for the slim chance of that future?

I stared at the two hapless creatures, until their lengthening shadows had become noticeably apparent. All around me the increasing din of furtive traffic signaled the end of another business day. Finally, I drew a deep breath and walked back to Ashton Tate. It was only Jenn and myself, and our future together, that I was then thinking about.

The cavernous lobby of the Ashton Tate building teemed with bodies rushing toward the exits. The elevators were painfully slow to come down as they made stops on almost every floor. But the one which carried me up was completely empty, except for me. I stepped out onto the fortieth floor intent on going directly to Jackson's office, and knowing exactly what I would tell him.

The receptionist was closing out for the day as I rushed past her, hoping to catch Jackson, un-lured by any after hours' golf game. Alighting onto the third tier, I saw the door to his office still open, and my heart leapt when I found him at his desk. His gaze was fixed onto a document, and, as I cleared my throat softly, he looked up and smiled at the sight of me. I knew what to tell him. I knew what to say to save both Jenn and myself.

"About the Farinelli document," I said standing at the door, "I'm sorry, but I just can't sign it."

"I see," Jackson acknowledged, seemingly unsurprised. "We'll have to find some other assignment for you then."

And with that Jackson's smile faded, and he dropped his gaze again onto his document, apparently having nothing further to say to me. Back on the main floor, as I made my way to my desk, I ran into Agnes Cook and told her of my decision.

"Good," she said with a satisfied tone, "you did the right thing."

At least I still had Agnes's support, and as I left for the day I felt both relieved and excited. I longed to tell Jenn about all of this, to make her understand that I had done this for the two of us, and for our future together. Were we to ever have a future together, I would have preferred it to be one in which I had Jenn's respect. But how could this have been possible without my first having any trace of respect for myself?

That evening I telephoned Jenn. I told her all of the day's happenings, my voice still tinged with a lingering excitement. I made no mention of the plastic mastodons struggling in the tar, thinking to defer this particular sidebar for a future, more introspective, circumstance. But I did tell her all else. She listened intently, not saying much, and I imagined her absorbing all of my details with a newfound regard for me.

"But isn't this bad for your career?" she eventually asked.

"No, it shouldn't be," I said. "I'll have other assignments. It's more important that I did the right thing, don't you think?"

This question might have easily launched a rudimentary discussion on the philosophy of ethics. But in this case it did not. Jenn, like her father, was mostly inclined to approach the business of living from a practical standpoint.

"Well, I hope that you won't be fired," was all that she could conjure.

This was not the reassuring sentiment of support from a kindred soul that I had been hoping for. Still, simple spirits such as my own stubbornly cling to dogged optimism. So, deep inside I deluded myself into believing that Jenn would eventually come to understand the wisdom of my actions.

"Are we still going to Dave's party this Saturday?" I asked.

"Yes we are," she affirmed. "Expect me by seven."

The following day at Ashton Tate I did not know what to find. But it proved uneventful. I spent it noticeably unoccupied, in an uncomfortably solitary state. There were none of the Robinson team members to be found. Agnes especially seemed to have suddenly evaporated from her desk. With the Farinelli matter now officially settled, I had little choice but to wait for my next assignment. Meanwhile, to occupy my time, I fell back on my usual habit of bantering with the paralegal staff, hoping to catch up on the latest office gossip. I found, to my surprise, that most of it was now about me.

"What you did was suicide," one of the paralegals informed me.

"We'll see," I said. "Jackson has promised me another assignment."

I sensed that I had become somewhat of an impromptu celebrity among this lower caste, and my loyal fans hounded me for more notorious details. I explained the matter of the breached declaration to them, and how I had been troubled by the thought of signing it, and how I had arrived at my conclusion to not do so. But again I made no mention of Nicole Robinson's apparition or of the plastic mastodons in the tar pits, such effusive details being better suited for literature, than for office conversation. I did however present a strong case for my actions, and I described, perhaps with some deluded vanity, that I had prevailed in doing the *right* thing.

"The *right* thing here is to just do what you're told," one of the paralegals advised.

The practical wisdom of this last remark stayed with me for the rest of the day, which I again spent secluded in the firm's reference library indifferently skimming through various legal journals. The paralegal was right of course. Inside the rigid confines of Ashton Tate, the concept of ethics was indisputably redefined for the benefit of its clients. There had been a breach with the Farinelli declaration, true. But I had breached the trust that Bruce Robinson had indirectly paid me for. I had accepted his money as my salary, only to refuse performing the services which he'd required of me.

But my own mind has always been most comfortable when dealing with absolutes. The existence of an absolute truth is a notion which has always appealed to me, not only from an intellectual perspective, but also from an emotional one. There is some comfort to be gained from the acceptance of an absolute truth, and the belief that such a thing has been preordained by a benevolent God. Unfortunately, I suspected that were I to persist with this mindset it would be impossible to perform so many of the duties which a firm such as Ashton Tate would be forever requiring of me.

****

That evening I inspected the two folders which I had filed away at home - my physics paper in one, and my transcripts of the declaration interviews in the other. One contained an absolute truth spelled out in unassailable mathematics, the other contained a very malleable truth. One attempted to draw closer to the lofty mind of God, the other left one stranded in the mire.

I put the declaration notes aside, and reviewed my physics paper again, realizing how I had become very proud of it. I longed to have Jonathan examine it, so that I could then submit it for publication. I decided to phone him, expecting that he had now returned from New York.

"Jonathan's decided to stay in New York," Monica informed me. "And I'm moving there to join him."

"What?" I asked. "What are you saying?"

I did not want to hear what Monica was telling me, that Jonathan, in essence, was abandoning his physics research. There was a chance that he might someday return to it she said. But until then he had taken a position with his father's brokerage firm. All that remained was for Monica to join him. She had already packed their few things, and would be leaving for New York next week.

Monica's news left me devastated. The Wilson paper had indeed been a setback to Jonathan's research. But apparently he had concluded that it was one from which he could never recover. He had dedicated more than seven years to his theory. Seven years seemingly wasted, and, like an investor holding a losing position, he was simply cutting his losses.

"I'll need a ride to the airport," Monica said. "Can you take me?"

"Yes, of course," I said, recovering myself.

But after the phone call, I almost fell into grieving. Jonathan's departure from the realm of physics was a great loss, and in the ensuing days it saddened me each time I thought of it. For I now had much time to think. My duties at Ashton Tate had been reduced to waiting for my next assignment, and over that week I found the aimless days of waiting unbearable. I felt no incentive to appear at my desk early, or to remain at it late. Finally, by Friday, I strolled in to work no earlier than just before lunchtime.

"You definitely need something to do," observed Agnes on seeing me.

But in response I could only shrug my shoulders helplessly. Surprised to see her back in the office, I was curious as to where she had recently disappeared. Over lunch she explained how, in a last minute scramble, she had helped Parker with the all of the declarations. They were now complete, and Parker himself was currently en route to file them into the court records before the day's deadline.

"So, what finally happened with the Farinelli declaration?" I ventured to ask her.

Agnes only offered a nod and an unexpected smile. I did not press her for any more details, and I suspected that the relentless mechanisms of Ashton Tate had probably obscured my small, feeble homage to the gods of absolute truth. All was again working as the founders had intended. The small wrinkle that I had impressed onto Ashton Tate's fabric was now firmly ironed away. I sent a small mental note to Nicole Robinson, apologizing to her, not so much for having failed her in my small way, but for the fact that, among those who might be sympathetic to her cause, there were none who possessed any true influence.

Returning to my desk after lunch, I found a note from Jackson requesting that I come see him. Probably I would be given my next assignment. But my heart did not leap at the thought of it. Carefully, I climbed the stairs which led to his office on the third tier, rising above the din of the cavernous space, dreading what I would next be asked to do in the service of the firm.

I found him reclining in his chair, turned towards the window. On his credenza, the image of his Labrabull glared at me, its visage again favoring more Pit Bull than Labrador. Were the photo capable of snarling, I was certain that it now would. The picture of Jackson's sports car had been joined by another, from a neighboring country. I seated myself, and Jackson swiveled around to face me. Before saying any word however, he arose and closed the office door. As he again sat down, I speculated about the next compromising assignment that I would be presented with.

"This is your last day at Ashton Tate," Jackson informed me.

I needed a few moments to absorb his words, while, in a calm, rational voice, he methodically explained how I was not fitting in well with the firm. As a result, my immediate termination seemed to be the best course of action. His words fell on me hard, but, to his credit, Jackson was making a concerted effort to lessen the blow. He offered me hope that in the future I would still be able to pursue a successful legal career with so many other countless, unspecified firms. But just not with Ashton Tate.

"But make no mistake," he added, "Ashton Tate is still grateful for your service here."

And, as a sign of this gratitude, the firm was graciously providing me with a generous parting gift, the entire amount of salary that I would have earned had I fully completed my summer internship. To receive this amount I would simply have to sign some standard forms as a formal termination my employment.

"Go see Ms. Nichols," Jackson advised. "She has all of the paperwork."

And with that Jackson extended a hand towards me across his desk. I gathered that I was required to shake this hand, and then, with as little commotion as possible, discretely remove myself from his presence. Were I to grasp the hand, he would mostly likely give me a standard one pump handshake. He would then force an empty smile and turn again towards the window, with the expectation of not ever seeing me again. But, still curious about my dismissal, I did not grasp his hand.

"So, why exactly am I being dismissed?" I asked.

A good attorney normally has an appropriate answer always ready, and Jackson was a good attorney. In response to my question he retracted his hand and assumed a consoling air. He now addressed me as though I were perhaps a dear friend desperately in need of counseling. I stared into his eyes, which had softened, almost to the point of seeming compassionate.

"Well Paul," he let out, "your attendance record here has been dismal. Ms. Nichols has kept track, and more often than not, she's found you coming to work late, very late."

"Other interns come in late, or sometimes not at all," I countered. "Take Bryce Davis for example."

"Bryce Davis is an exception," Jackson said.

"An exception?" I asked. "He's an intern too. How is he an exception?"

"Well, he's different," Jackson admitted. "He's somebody….and you're not."

This was not the discussion that I had hoped to engage in. But regardless, it seemed that Jackson was not going to change his mind.

"I see," I said, nodding into Jackson's gaze.

And with this response, Jackson seemed satisfied that the matter was closed. I arose from my chair, and Jackson extended his hand out to me again, this time with a consoling smile and a wish of good luck. But I did not grasp his hand. I simply made my way to the door.

"Good luck to you too," I said as I left him, his hand still hanging in mid air.

Back on the main level, Ms. Nichols had been expecting me. With characteristic efficiency she escorted me to a conference room, the same one coincidentally in which I, as a first day intern, had been initiated. She began guiding me through the necessary paperwork. In all, there were five documents, in duplicate, which required my signature. As I completed them, Ms. Nichols grouped then into two precise piles. Each separate pile was eventually tucked into its own awaiting manila envelope, one of which she handed to me. Ms. Nichols' sole remaining duty was to then escort me out of Ashton Tate.

"Is there anyone you'd like to say goodbye to?" she asked.

In truth there was no one, save Agnes Cook, that I still wished to see. I would encounter Bryce Davis again in law school in the fall. But Agnes Cook, I would probably never see again. I asked Ms. Nichols to accompany me to her desk.

"Sorry that you're going," she consoled. "I never imagined that this would happen."

"Don't feel bad," I said. "Maybe it's for the best."

I was going to miss her, her leather portfolio, and her business suits which always fit just a bit too snugly. As I made my way through the firm's cavernous space, I tried to think only of her, rather than of the many other Ashton Tate attorneys, as being representative of the legal profession.

Out in the lobby, Ms. Nichols informed the receptionist of the change in my employment status. She then escorted me to the elevator and waited as I stepped inside. As the elevator doors closed before me, I offered her a final nod goodbye. Over her shoulder I caught one final glimpse of the fashion model receptionist and of the abstract painting which hovered behind her, my last image of Ashton Tate. As the elevator doors closed, Ashton Tate's rendering of Lady Justice stared back at me, her scales still firmly tipped to one side.

25.

The next day, a Saturday, I awoke with a troubled mind. I'd spent the night tossing and unsettled, half dreaming, trying to come to terms with the sudden shock of my dismissal. In one particularly troubled dream I found myself playing golf with, of all people, Andrew Jackson. This golfing dream had proceeded along quite pleasantly enough until Jackson managed to sink a hole in one. He then gloated over this fortunate triumph to the point that, enraged, I suddenly whacked him, violently, with a five iron. I laughed as he then doubled over, visibly hurt. But, from out of nowhere, his Labrabull then unexpectedly appeared, growling, nipping at me, and chasing me around the greens bent on revenge.

The entire night had proceeded in this manner, filled with strange dreams, and I arose feeling un-rested, and with my spirits dismally depressed. Oddly, the morning mirror gave no indication of this. The scarlet tinge of my skin had subsided over the past week to now resemble a healthy red glow. For the rest of that morning I sought to reconcile myself to the fact that I was no longer employed at Ashton Tate. I soon realized however that my dismissal was not the true crux of the matter. What would I tell Jenn? That was my real concern. Crystal's video release party was scheduled for that evening, and Jenn and I had planned to attend it together. I could not spoil the mood of that evening with any dismal news.

"*But perhaps this is actually good news*," I thought.

My severance had amounted to all the remaining wages that I would have earned as an intern. So was there really any harm done? What I had been given was the gift of time, the remainder of the summer that I could now spend with Jenn. With this newfound mindset, I banished all thoughts of Ashton Tate, and simply set my sights on the evening's party. For good measure I had also invited Laura, who had recently returned from Moscow. Sheepishly, she'd inquired if she might also bring a guest.

"Sure," I had told her, "my friend Dave won't mind. The more, the merrier, he always says."

Jenn, Laura, and her guest, were scheduled to rendezvous at my apartment that evening at seven. Jenn was the first to arrive. She carried with her a new outfit, still wrapped, and a new hairstyle, also still wrapped in a snug fitting scarf about her head. After a brief greeting, she rushed into my one bedroom to change, while I, already shaved and dressed, waited for Laura. Jenn was still primping when Laura and her friend arrived.

"This is my friend Libor," said Laura. "I met him in Moscow."

Libor offered a gracious smile, and as I reached out my hand I was accosted by a pair of sapphire blue eyes staring at me from beneath a shock of pitch black hair.

"Most happy to meet you," he said with a pronounced Slavic accent.

I liked Libor immediately. He possessed a fond freshness that is no longer found in this country. He also possessed a last name so convoluted that the uninitiated, such as myself, would do best to not attempt it. Laura had met him in the chilly Moscow nightlife. They had become friends, and then more than friends, to the point that he had followed her back to the City of Angels.

"I am in love with America!" he announced. "I feel liberated here."

Life here was enlightened, he maintained, so different from the Soviet system where one man continually exploited another.

"Yes," I agreed, "here it's the exact opposite."

Like me, Libor had once studied the sciences. But, for now, he was employed as a gardener.

"You must come gardening with me," he suggested. "I see from your complexion that you enjoy being outside."

I showed him my hands, also still scarlet from the Eden Ranch.

"Good," he said. "You are not afraid of hard work, and that is good."

But despite Libor's penchant for physical labor, he was actually an aspiring screenwriter, and for this ambition he had certainly come to the right town. He was eagerly anticipating the evening's party, where, with a few choice words, the perfect doors might open for him. Based on his gardening experience, he had already envisioned a plot for a screenplay. He had a short pitch for it, which, in heavily accented English, he was apparently eager to throw at whoever might wish to catch it.

"Here, listen," he said.

"But I'm not a producer," I objected.

"Listen anyway," he insisted.

The screenplay's main character, surprisingly, was a gardener. But this gardener had unexpectedly found himself in the employ of a serial killer. Time after time the employer brings corpses for the gardener to dismember and dispose of in the estate's sizable garden. At first, the gardener complies with this ghoulish practice in order to keep his job. But eventually guilt overwhelms him, and he confronts his employer about the corpses. A struggle ensues and the gardener kills his employer with a set of pruning shears. The gardener has now become a killer himself. But before he can surrender to the authorities, on a cold moonlit night, the corpses buried in the garden suddenly rise up and subsume him too into their well fertilized graves.

Libor fell silent after giving the pitch, awaiting my response. His excitement in the telling of it had left his hands trembling. I too felt a bit unnerved.

"What do you think?" Laura interjected.

Laura maintained that the story was indeed good, and was certain to become a motion picture once the *right* people had found access to it. The only thing lacking, besides the right people, was a good title.

"Why not call it *Rest in Pieces*?" I suggested.

Libor gave my suggestion some brief consideration. But eventually he threw back a condescending look.

"No, this is a serious work," he chided. "Your title is too flippant. I myself was thinking of....*Garden of Ghouls*...."

He emphasized the title, pronouncing it with such eerie drama that it caused both Laura and me to glance about, to insure that no actual ghouls were lurking in any of the nearby shrubbery. Luckily there were none, and, as I looked about, it struck me instead how lovely the evening had become. It was one of those late mid summer evenings where the day's lingering warmth easily mingled with the fresh chill of the approaching night, an evening that seemed pregnant with infinite, unexpected possibilities.

We continued waiting for Jenn, and we chatted aimlessly under the dimming light of an orange tinged sky. But eventually my apartment door opened and, dressed in a flowing taffeta gown and full heels, Jenn at last emerged. Her hair, now uncloaked, fell onto her shoulders in full, streaked tresses. With easy elegance, a short pearl necklace and simple dangle earrings framed her pale green eyes and a luscious pair of cranberry lips. Gone was the image of the young girl from the Eden Ranch, replaced now by the breathtaking vision of a beautiful woman coming into her full glory. In coordinated unison, the three of us fell silent, left suddenly speechless by the angelic vision hovering before us.

"Well, how do I look?" asked Jenn to all of us simultaneously.

Laura and I remained silent. It was only Libor who finally spoke.

"God bless America!" he proclaimed.

The spell of speechlessness remained on me during the drive to the party. Laura and Libor were following in a separate car, so I lacked the benefit of their company to stimulate any conversation. The car's top was up, so as not to muss Jenn's hair. The widows were also up, and so there was not even the sound of wind to fill the silence. The Pacific Ocean sped past on our left, now blanketed by the purple glow of the ensuing twilight. But perhaps it was best that we drove in silence, avoiding any mention of my dismal dismissal, and leaving me free to simply bask in Jenn's alluring glow, radiant as Cinderella's on her way to the ball.

"So how is work?" dropped Jenn, seeking to break the silence. "Did you get a new assignment?"

"Well," I began with some hesitation, "an interesting thing happened yesterday."

And with this introduction, I described how that day had not proceeded as I might have intended. In my defense, I painted Ashton Tate in a somewhat incompetent light, suggesting that the reasons for my dismissal were trivial and unjustified. And for good measure I also painted the entire workings of the firm, and their handling of the Robinson case, with a distinctly demonic tinge.

"But, on the bright side," I suggested, "we'll now have more time to spend together."

Perhaps it was wishful thinking on my part, but I began conjuring all of the possibilities which had now become available to us. I still sought to salvage any hopeful remnants of romance which the summer might have held, and so I suggested that my newly acquired severance could fund any number of alluring getaways. Further west of us, on the deep Pacific, floated the island paradise of Hawaii, and wouldn't it be wonderful if we could take a quick jaunt there?

"Perhaps," said Jenn. "Because I do like you, you know."

I nodded to her, grateful for this shred of hope, and charged by it I then stepped on the accelerator as a newfound electricity surged through me. Dave's party buoyed enticingly ahead of us, and there would be no repeat of the disastrous events of our ill fated star party. By the wave of Dave Richard's magic wand, the drinks would be plentiful, the food exquisite, and the guest list impeccable. It was bound to be a night to remember.

****

Night had fully fallen by the time that we reached the canyon road which led to Dave's place. Many other cars were winding their way up the dark hillside ahead of us, their headlights lining the road like glistening jewels strung onto an enormous necklace. At the crest of the hill, Dave's home, the largest jewel, sparkled with a tremendous light.

"It seems like heaven!" observed Jenn.

Except that in this case heaven also included valet parking. For, when we finally reached Dave's front drive, we were met not by Saint Peter, but by a small staff of valets, who whisked all arriving cars to a separate automotive paradise of their own further up the canyon road. They even took Laura's old car, and we then walked the grounds towards Dave's home. The entire property was extravagantly aglow. I had never attended a video release party, and had not a clue as to what to expect. But from what I could tell, it seemingly involved a tremendous amount of illumination.

Crystal's video was entitled *Bouncing to the Classics*, and we were greeted by the electric strains of a string quartet, piped through unseen loudspeakers, as we entered the home. Dave's vast entry hall had been entirely transformed for the occasion. Larger than life images of Crystal and Jack Engels, precariously posed and displaying the beneficial results of their bouncing routines, draped the walls. A large stage, empty but waiting to be bounced onto, had been assembled and adorned in Rococo style.

We approached the stage to marvel at it. It seemed to recreate a haphazard scene from the French court. There were faux fountains and topiary and ornate benches reminiscent of Versailles. This effect would have been complete except for a few odd stage props - an oversized guillotine and numerous severed heads, hopefully artificial, randomly strewn across the stage.

"This should be an interesting show," observed Laura as we took in the scene.

The party was already well underway behind us. A crowd of guests was firmly planted atop of Dave's blue veined marble floor, spilling past it into the adjoining rooms. Waiters and waitresses, fully costumed in powdered wigs and period attire, dashed about delivering drinks. I gathered that we had been transported into the court of the French Sun

King which, except for the specter of the looming guillotine, seemed to be a very enjoyable place indeed.

"Do you see Dave anywhere?" asked Jenn.

I scanned the room for signs of him, or of Crystal, but none were apparent. A healthy crop of the local film industry sprouted before us, and, as I scanned through the posed faces, there were a few which most anyone might have recognized. The fact that this caliber of celebrity might be found here, at a mere exercise video release party, gave firm tribute to Dave's ever increasing sphere of influence.

"If you see anyone who looks like a film producer, point him out," advised Libor.

"And then what?" I asked.

"And then we'll go talk to him," he said, as though it would be a perfectly natural thing to do.

I liked Libor even more now, and so I scanned the crowd for possible film producers. Dave was a film producer, of sorts, as was Bruce Robinson. But I saw no signs of Robinson either. We made our way deep into the crowd, but in doing so I realized that none of the wait staff was able to reach us.

"Let's go find a drink," I suggested. "Follow me to the bar."

I pushed ahead into the adjoining room. Along the way we brushed by another of the many recognizable faces.

"That was.....you know.... *him*!" remarked Laura, positively awestruck.

"Yes, it was.....*him*!" I added, but unable to recall his name.

Neither could Laura remember the name. But it was indeed *him*. At the bar we tallied how many other notable faces we had recognized, or thought that we had recognized, among the crowd. This led me to tell of the time, coming back from our castle trip, when Jenn herself had been mistaken for a particular film celebrity.

"But you are right!" remarked Libor. "Jenn does resemble *her*!"

Especially on this night, with her hair redone, her face made up, and in the specific light of Dave's home, there was an uncanny resemblance. This resemblance had not gone unnoticed by the many men in the vicinity, whose unrepressed staring caused Jenn to lift her martini glass past her lips, and hide herself behind it. But there could be no denying that Jenn was achingly beautiful. I smiled and reached out to her, gently. As I lowered the glass to below her chin, she lifted her head slightly, and her radiance spilled out again into the rest of the room. I sensed a hush from the surrounding men and drew closer to her, content that, for this one evening at least, I was the one standing closest to her.

Across the room, past the plush couches and mingling guests, I finally spied two familiar faces. Standing before Dave's enormous glass wall of an aquarium, beneath powdered wigs, were the video stars themselves. Crystal, or what was exposed of her, was hidden inside of a heavy billow of full French court attire. A coif of bleached tresses was perched and piled precariously onto her head. Beside her, straining inside a silk frock coat and breeches stood her costar, Jack Engels. They were posed before a group of photographers, apparently giving a media briefing. Driven by curiosity, I motioned that we approach them.

"This video provides a workout for both the body and the soul," Engels declared as we drew closer.

I imagined Engels rehearsing this line many times over so that it would sound spontaneous. But he had delivered it with such unexpected flair that I marveled at how this former Marine had so completely, if not ridiculously, transformed himself. Luckily there were none of his former military buddies in attendance, for certainly they would have doubled over with laughter. I wondered if he, after this evening, could ever go back to such a former occupation, or even function effectively as a bodyguard. With this unexpected transformation, could he ever again make himself threatening?

"*Step aside, or I will be forced to harm both your body, and your soul*," the newly enlightened Engels might be tempted to say, to little effect.

We moved closer to the two stars once their interview had concluded. Crystal attempted a smile on seeing me. But the same could not be gathered from Engels, as he received me with his patented frigid stare. Under the circumstances however he had no choice but to tolerate me, and so I pressed my advantage by inquiring about his costume.

"Who are you supposed to be?" I asked.

"I'm supposed to be Mozart," he volunteered, begrudgingly.

I prodded Crystal for her identity, but she refused to disclose it.

"I won't tell you who I am," she teased. "You'll just have to wait for the show."

"Well I'm going to guess that you're Marie Antoinette. And I hope that your pretty head won't be sliced off!" I joked, thinking of the prop guillotine.

Eventually Crystal and Engels excused themselves for the show, after which Laura then analyzed them from a historical perspective.

"This is ridiculous," she declared. "Mozart was never affiliated with the French court."

"Well, maybe they're in the Austrian court," I suggested.

"No," Laura retorted. "Austria never had any guillotines!"

Laura was right. But she still seemed amused, as anyone might, once they had embraced such a uniquely altered reality. We were in Dave's hands now. This was his world, and he was its master of ceremonies. I scanned the crowd for him once again, especially as Libor was eager to meet a genuine film producer. But Dave was still nowhere to be seen.

"Let's try the veranda," suggested Jenn.

She led us outside and we followed her. I was eager to get away from the many eyes which had hopelessly affixed themselves onto her. But outdoors the situation was little changed. The veranda was also well lit, and as Jenn stepped onto it she was met by similar stares from the other faces gathered there. There was still no sign of Dave. But instead this crowd contained two other faces that I recognized.

"There's Bruce Robinson," I told Jenn. "Let me introduce you."

Robinson appeared more aloof than usual on that particular night. Hovering at the edge of the crowd, he and Bambi Farinelli were keeping a lone vigil. For good measure, a prominent bodyguard stood near, enforcing a finely measured distance to the other guests. This was a new bodyguard. He was not Engels, but an even larger version of Engels. And whereas Engels might instill terror from an icy gaze, this new bodyguard terrorized primarily through sheer mass. Like a menacing wall, he stood between Robinson and everyone else, so much so that, as I approached, I had to forcibly look around him to address Robinson.

"It's you," Robinson said as I peered into view.

I smiled, and extended a hand, reminding him of my name.

"Yes, I know," he said.

The bodyguard had received little indication that I was a welcomed commodity, and so he remained unmoved. As my hand hung desperately in mid air I feared that he would now grasp it and break it off. Luckily, Bambi Farinelli came to my rescue. Unlike Robinson, she seemed genuinely pleased to see me, and greeted me with her characteristic exuberance.

"You're here too!" she exclaimed. "What a surprise!"

"I'm an old college friend of Dave Richards," I informed her.

With Bambi's stamp of approval, the human wall relaxed his stance, and, although Robinson still eyed me coldly, I was now permitted at least temporarily into his protected proximity. I introduced the others in my party, all receiving warm smiles from Bambi, but only cold nods from Robinson. He remained uncomfortably distant, and I wondered if he was perhaps under strict orders from my former employer to do so.

But with Bambi at our disposal, and her so eager to talk to us, it was easy to forget Bruce Robinson. As usual, I found Bambi easy to speak with. Her demeanor, mannerisms, and the slight trace of north shore

Long Island accent, in spite of her elocution lessons, were a comforting familiarity for me. Bambi's fun and fertile nature had lost non of its charm, and in her company I could so easily forget about Jenn, had I to admit it.

That night Bambi Farinelli was dressed, not in her usual pink, but in a bright blue sapphire sequined dress which, with her slightest movement, sent off shimmering sparks into the surrounding shadows. Unthinkingly I had once again found myself wearing my lilac silk suit, which, on this evening, no longer matched Bambi's outfit as it had by chance so many times before.

"Is the one pink suit all that you have?" she observed.

"No, I have two others," I said.

"Poor dear, having only three suits….."

"Well I'm just a struggling law student, you know," I said trying to assuage the pout which had come onto her face.

"A struggling law student, just like Agnes Cook," observed Bambi.

"Yes, just like Agnes Cook. And how is it that you know Agnes Cook?" I asked, surprised to hear the name.

"Oh, I just met her recently."

I wanted to hear more about her meeting Agnes, but it was then that Bruce Robinson stepped out of the shadows. He placed a hand onto Bambi's arm, and nudged her forward.

"The show is about to start," he pronounced. "Let's go inside."

"But we're having such a good time here," Bambi said, throwing him a disappointed look.

"I don't care. You two can talk again later," suggested Robinson.

Robinson's intent was further reinforced by his bodyguard, who had again not too subtly wedged himself between Bambi and the rest of us.

For a few moments Bambi was obscured from view, hidden behind the wall of muscle. But then she reappeared, attached to Robinson as he pulled her away. Both Libor and I watch as she left the veranda, our eyes fixed onto her receding form. Apparently, Libor too had fallen under her buxom spell.

"Venom," he observed as Bambi was led away. "Pure venom."

"Yes," I agreed wistfully. "Pure, sweet venom."

A tentative sound from Laura brought both Libor and myself back into reality. I turned to face Jenn who, absent of Bambi Farinelli's intoxicating presence, once again seemed simply ravishing. I regained my senses, and apologized to Libor that I had not proposed his screenplay to Robinson.

"I'm sorry, but Robinson just seemed very aloof tonight," I told him.

"And he didn't appear to like you very much," observed Jenn.

"Perhaps," I added dryly. "But that feeling's starting to become mutual."

26.

The anticipated show seemed about to begin, and so we flowed with the veranda crowd back into the house. Ahead of us, the stage had been set. Looming in its shadows, several dancers, in period costume, had assumed their positions on either side of the silent guillotine. The foyer's lighting was dimmed, and, as though on cue, every guest fell silent. A fanfare of electric trumpets filled the air as a furtive spotlight then illuminated the foyer's upper landing, where a crowned figure of the Sun King appeared. I had at last found Dave, with his arms reaching out from beneath sable robes, as His Majesty addressed the gathered crowd.

"Guests of my court, welcome!" began the king. "We are gathered here to celebrate that my queen, once a fat trollop, is now one no longer!"

This remark might have been a private joke of sorts, as it sent a smattering of laughter throughout the crowd.

"This horrific incident is now well past," the king continued. "So behold the stage, where this tale of tails will be told!"

And with a regal flourish, Dave directed our attention towards the stage, as it summarily burst into light. Onto it appeared the sobbing figure of Marie Antoinette who, were Crystal to have been a better actress, we would have surmised to have been in the throes of desperate anguish. She sought to convey her desperation with despondent glances cast left, and then right, before finally approaching the awaiting guillotine..

"I must away with myself do," despaired the queen.

The crowd held its collective breath as she exposed her fair neck to the cruel blade. But just as all seemed lost, a muscular Mozart suddenly made a dramatic entrance.

"Fair Antoinette, why doth 'dee despair?" asked Mozart with palms beckoning.

"I must but despair," replied Antoinette, "for I have eaten far too much cake, and the King no longer finds me attractive!"

Mozart seemed touched by her plight. He wiped a nonexistent tear, and in sympathy he offered his hand, beseeching her away from the guillotine.

"Be hopeful, fair Queen," he offered encouragingly, "for I bring music which will benefit both the body, and the soul!"

After Engels had repeated this now familiar phrase, I turned to Laura. My glance caught hers and we both sought to contain our laughter. But as ridiculous as this line had sounded, Engels had delivered it with steadfast confidence and credibility. He possessed an innate stage presence, sorely needed in this case, to bolster Crystal's complete lack of one. Engels then led Crystal onto center stage, and, facing the Queen, he lifted her hand and offered a respectful curtsey. A bit of night *muzik* then filled the air, and the two launched into a slow minuet.

"Do you feel the extra pounds now falling away?" inquired Mozart.

"Sadly sir, I do not!" the Queen lamented.

The Queen then turned her gaze downward, apparently heartbroken. There truly seemed to be no hope for her but the guillotine. But then Mozart stepped forward, and, in a loud voice, proclaimed the needed remedy.

"Then what you need is to be bouncing!" he shouted. "*Bouncing to the Classics*!"

Once Eng-zart had pronounced this edict, the forceful opening strains of Beethoven's ninth symphony filled the room. The stage then dramatically came to life as a dazzling array of colored spotlights darted across it. The background dancers, who had remained as motionless as statues in the Tuileries, suddenly sprang to life with a rapid routine of choreographed steps. Engels then joined them, and with each successive refrain of the ninth symphony, he tore away a piece of his court costume, until all that remained were his many muscles bulging beneath exercise tights and a powdered wig.

The Queen sensed that Mozart had indeed offered her hope after all, and so she too joined the frenzy. She tore off her costume and began bouncing to Beethoven's ninth symphony. I watched Crystal, stripped down to exercise tights, ruffled petticoats, and a large coif of white tresses precariously perched atop her head, as she mirrored Engels' dance steps. But she struggled to keep up with him, and, perhaps it was the lighting, but she seemed even plumper than when I'd last seen her during our sail to Catalina.

"Isn't this is exciting?" exclaimed Jenn as the music grew louder.

I glanced at Jennderella beside me, the expression on her face hinting that she was indeed tremendously enthralled by all this. Behind her now stood the King, who had made his way down the foyer stairway to join us.

"I wrote the show myself," the King informed us, with apparent pride.

I nodded Dave a kind well done, after which, to restore my sanity, I turned again to Laura and we both rolled our eyes heavenward. But Laura and I were in the minority. Most of the other guests seemed to be enjoying the show tremendously, some of them also bouncing along to the music. Beethoven then gave way to Vivaldi, who gave way to Rossini, as performers and guests alike kept on bouncing. Even the guillotine joined in, as its blade, apparently motorized, bounced up and down, reinforcing the claim that everyone's excess pounds were being steadily sliced off.

Somewhere past the trumpet calls of the William Tell Overture however, it became clear that Crystal was having difficulty. She had wrestled with the tall, unruly coif atop her head through most of the routine. But now, as the many bounces began taking their toll, it began to tilt precariously. She strained to keep it upright, but with every successive bounce it continued tilting. Her own hair then began to escape from beneath the headdress, her many red tangles falling squarely into her eyes. It was admirable to watch Crystal coping with the situation as she simultaneously bounced, kept the headdress aloft, and pushed aside her own hair so as to see.

"Are the extra pounds being bounced away, my Queen?" asked Mozart.

"Why yes, they are!" exclaimed the Queen between gulps of heavy breathing.

Engels' routine was proceeding smoothly. Perhaps from his former military training, he bounced precisely in time, executing his steps flawlessly. But Crystal continued to struggle. Her own red curls had draped themselves completely over her eyes and I doubted that she could actually see past them. She was constantly stepping onto the various severed heads that were littered about the entire stage. And were it not for Engels, she would have certainly fallen face forwards over one. In one particularly adroit maneuver he had kept her aloft and had simultaneously kicked the offending head out of her way. Unfortunately, he had kicked it with such force that it flew out clear into the middle of the audience.

The crowd gave out a loud roar at the sight of the severed head flying towards them. Oddly enough, the flying head landed, like a football, squarely into the hands of Bruce Robinson, who then lifted it aloft like a game winning ball. Excitedly the crowd cried out for more, and, not wanting to disappoint them, Engels began launching other heads off the stage. He peppered the crowd with severed heads, one of them kicked with such force that it sailed clear to the back of the room so that Dave Richards himself caught it. He stared at the female head now in his grasp.

"Poor Marie," he quipped to us. "No more cake for her!"

I stared at the head forlornly, saddened to think that she had eaten her last slice. The other recipients of severed heads were holding theirs aloft, and the entire room was now bouncing frenetically, urged on by Engels and his impromptu antics. The onstage routine then reached its climax, and, as the music galloped to a fevered pace, the dancers let out a final frantic burst of steps, and spins, and, of course, bounces. The crowd then burst into pounding applause, as Mozart and Antoinette took their well earned bows.

"Fantastic! What a show!" exclaimed Jenn to Dave's smiling visage.

"Yes, it was," he replied, seemingly confident that it could not have been otherwise.

To seal the moment, a stream of waiters then flowed into the crowd, distributing champagne. One of the goblet laden trays skirted past the stage, and Crystal reached down to it, greedily with both hands. She had not survived the performance as well as Engels. She still gasped for breath, in between which, she then gasped for champagne. Her first goblet of champagne was soon emptied. The second goblet awaited a similar fate, but as she tipped her head back to drink it, the headdress which had teetered atop her head at long last fell off onto the floor, with Crystal seemingly pleased to be rid of it.

"Come, I'll introduce you around," Dave told Jenn. "We'll pretend you're that movie star that you resemble."

Dave pulled her away, and he was about to disappear into the crowd, when Libor called out to him.

"Wait," cried Libor, "do you know of any film producers here tonight?"

"Libor here has a script that he's written," I added as a hasty introduction.

"Sure, there's a few here," said Dave. "What type of script is it?"

On hearing this Libor launched into his prepared pitch. But with the pitch barely started Dave nodded understandingly. He lifted his hand, the one still holding poor Marie's severed head, and pointed to a solitary bearded gentleman across the room.

"That fellow there, Harry Siegel," said Dave. "Just mention my name."

Libor offered his thanks, and, as Dave left us, he looked for a new escort for Marie.

"Here," he said, tossing me the head, "she's all yours."

And with that, Dave and Jenn turned into the crowd. I made to follow them, but Libor tugged at my arm.

"Come," said Libor, "you can be my attorney."

I offered him some resistance, suggesting that he did not need an attorney, and that I actually was not one. But he persisted, and so, along with Laura and Marie in tow, I followed him toward Harry Siegel. Along the way I snatched a glass of champagne as it floated by. I would have preferred some brandy, but I hoped the champagne would provide me enough comfort as I was yet again to suffer through Libor's pitch for *Garden of Ghouls*.

Harry Siegel stood against a far wall. He was alone, but with his trim beard, mustache, and somewhat European features, he seemed perfectly in place with the Austrian mirrors which hung behind him. As Libor's impromptu attorney, I approached him, mentioning Dave's referral as an introduction. Siegel informed us that, yes, he had produced films over the years, some with Dave Richards as a partner, some without. But their partnership had lately dissolved, as Dave pursued other projects. He, on the other hand was still interested in good film premises, and he encouraged Libor to launch into his now well rehearse pitch. Siegel listened, and nodded.

"I like what I'm hearing," he told Libor. "But can I offer a few suggestions?"

Siegel approved of the basic premise of the story, but he implied that, with a few minor adjustments, Libor's script could realize a phenomenally untapped potential. For example, what if the zombies arising out of the garden were all female? And what if they were all, say, naked, with pristine, nubile bodies which the garden had magically preserved, even beyond death? These two minor modifications alone, suggested Siegel, could greatly enhance the appeal of the movie.

"Perhaps," mused Libor. "But this would detract from the fundamental story line."

And there were also other possibilities. What if the zombies did not actually kill the murderous gardener? Such a gruesome ending might possibly make the movie too frightening.

"Yes, but it's a horror movie," Libor reminded him. "It's *supposed* to be frightening."

True, but Siegel hinted at a better ending. Instead, what if the zombies suddenly found themselves attracted to the gardener, say, in a lustful way? Then, rather than killing the poor soul, the female zombies would then simply seduce him into his grave?

"These are simple changes to make," Siegel maintained. "The new ending alone will bring your movie to a more appealing climax, I think."

But still, Libor seemed unconvinced.

"What other films have you produced?" I interjected as Libor fell silent.

"Have you ever heard of *Sinderella*?" Siegel replied. "Dave and I produced that one."

"Oh, I loved that movie as a child!" exclaimed Laura.

"No, not *Cinderella*," corrected Siegel. "*Sinderella*, with an '*S*'. It's a cult classic."

We all nodded understandingly, as I began to wonder what other cult classics Siegel and Dave might have produced.

"I don't think you're the type of producer that we're looking for," suggested Laura.

I nodded in agreement with Laura. But Libor seemed heartbroken.

"I am sorry," he said dejectedly, "but that is not the story I had in mind."

"Sure, I understand," said Siegel, handing him some business cards. "But have your attorney call me if you change your mind."

Siegel then disappeared into the crowd, seemingly in pursuit of someone he had just recognized. Across the hall, on the makeshift stage, the party guests had begun amusing themselves with the prop guillotine. They placed their heads into it, while one of the media photographers obligingly snapped a souvenir photo.

"That looks like fun. Let's go try it," said Laura, pulling at Libor. "Paul, you too."

"No, you two go," I said. "I need to get a drink."

They left, and I stayed behind with Marie, who probably had no interest in visiting the guillotine either. I spied about the room, looking for some trace of Jenn, seemingly now engulfed into the swirl of the party, and nowhere to be seen. But I didn't have the heart to go wading for her amidst the sea of silliness which stretched before me. Onstage, Libor had fitted his head into the guillotine, as Laura made ready to pull on the release cord. On cue, he conjured a frightful expression, which was captured for posterity by the photographer's flash.

My champagne glass was empty, and I made my way to the bar, thinking to refill it instead with some of Dave's best brandy. Except for two other fellows at the bar, all of the stools were empty. I sat myself down and placed Marie beside me on the counter. I spotted a good brandy among the many liquor bottles, and ordered a tumbler full of it.

"And a bloody Mary for my friend," I told the bartender.

The bartender nodded, but Marie did not get her drink, even though she seemed desperately in need of one. The shock of having her head suddenly lopped off had impressed a permanently indignant expression onto her face. As a result, Marie was not really good company. I sat there in silence, nursing my drink, and longing to be somewhere else. Beside me, the two other fellows were absorbed into their own conversation.

"These are certifiable Han Dynasty pieces," I heard one say, "and museum quality, if you know what I mean."

I gathered they were art dealers of sorts, discussing a possible transaction.

"But I'll need some certification that the pieces are authentic," said the other. "That's standard protocol."

"Listen, they're all authentic. Just come by and take a look. You'll see."

Having no conversation of my own, I leaned closer to better take in the one beside me. But as the dealers sensed my presence they shied away, and eventually took their business out of the room. The bartender had also vanished, and I was left completely to Marie's silent company. Across the room, Dave's wall of well tended fish still swam about contentedly. I scanned across the great glass aquarium, looking for Dave's prized fish. But it too was gone.

With my brandy also almost gone, I longed for some outside air and a glimpse of the evening stars. But as I moved to stand up, a hulking shadow suddenly enveloped the room. It was Bruce Robinson's bodyguard, followed not far behind by the bodies he was guarding. Bruce Robinson and Bambi Farinelli then dropped themselves onto a leather couch squarely in my sight. I contemplated joining them, but Robinson's icy stare quickly signaled that I would receive only a frigid welcome.

At this point, I suddenly felt an overwhelming revulsion towards Robinson, and towards everything that was feeding off him. But still, I cast him a steady glance and offered him a reassuring smile. I turned Marie to face him, and gently patted her head to show that I was not lacking in good company.

"Here's another one for you," I said, seemingly to no one in particular.

Robinson did not appear amused by this remark, and, as I downed the last of my drink, the temperature of his stare dropped even lower. I arose from the barstool and, taking Marie with me, I sidled away towards the veranda. I gave Bambi Farinelli a cursory nod in passing. Behind her, Robinson's hulk of a bodyguard watched my every step.

Out on the veranda, the cool evening air was tinged with the scent of ocean mist, and it began to revive me. I felt free and relieved, and glad to be away from the stifling air inside. In the pool, a spontaneous swim party had broken out as about a half dozen guests, scantily clad, splashed noisily. I walked towards the darker confines of Dave's gardens, hoping for a pristine view of the night sky. There I looked up at the sight of my old friends, the stars.

"Look at the stars," I told Marie. "Aren't they beautiful?"

The stars above shone crisp and clear, and I could almost feel their swirling, ceaseless dance through the heavens. I longed that Jenn too might have been beside me enjoying such majesty. But the stars alone offered good enough company, and I now knew that in the long run their's would prove far more reliable than the vague whims of most human hearts.

I felt at ease and at peace, and in need of more brandy. But as I looked up to give the stars a parting glance, the garden suddenly grew darker. I heard a furtive rustling behind me as a shadow suddenly rose up. Then there was a heavy tap on my shoulder, and turning, I caught only the briefest glimpse of a hulking figure before the left side of my face exploded into excruciating pain.

I reeled violently, uncontrollably, only to have another blow land squarely into my stomach. I doubled over, struggling for breath. I fell to my knees as another blow landed squarely on the back of my head. I had come out to the garden to see the stars, and, as my battered body crumpled helplessly onto the ground, I did indeed see them. But this time they were the stars which one sees before going unconscious.

****

When my eyes opened again with the morning's first light, I found myself unable to move. I had lain unnoticed in the garden grounds throughout the entire night, and the cold air had turned all my muscles stiff, almost frozen. Only my abdomen felt noticeably warm, and, as my eyes slowly came into focus, I perceived a large grey mound of feathers squarely encamped there. The mound of feathers also sported a large beak, and eyes, which stared westward into the early morning fog. By my side, I also saw Marie, loyal and unwavering.

I could not move, and I feared that the blow to my skull had left me permanently paralyzed. It was only through the most focused of efforts that I finally brought my muscles slowly back to life. First my fingers, then my hands, then at last my arms moved, much of this to the bemused consternation of the shore bird, apparently a pelican, who could not understand why the soft, warm rock that he was squatting on had suddenly come to life. Pelicans are formidable birds up close, and I did not want to aggravate it. Given my condition, it could probably have gotten the best of me, and I was in no mood for another fight. So

I moved ever so slowly, until at last I sat upright, with the pelican, still camped onto my lap, staring at me.

"You have no idea what a night I've had," I told it.

The bird seemed even further bemused to find that his prized heated rock not only moved, but also spoke. Perhaps the shock of this became too overwhelming, for the creature, without even a farewell glance, spread its substantial wings, and, letting out a loud squawk, flapped off into the distance. I struggled to stand upright. My body was sore and shivering, my throat was raw from the many hours of cold night air, and my head, well, felt as though an anvil had been dropped onto it.

I picked up Marie and stumbled towards the house. The pool party had long disbanded, only a discarded brassiere remained as a token of it. I entered through the veranda. All was empty. Robinson and Bambi Farinelli were gone, and I rested briefly on one of the green leather couches, hoping to get warm. On the far wall, Dave's well tended fish still swam contentedly, while on the opposite wall, more than a few bottles of liquor remained. But I was well beyond their aid.

Like Rip van Winkle, I began to wonder where my friends might have gone. I followed a smattering of voices to the kitchen, where Crystal and a last group of stragglers were having breakfast. Behind a large granite counter, Dave's maid dutifully squeezed juice out of countless oranges, and replenished breakfast pastries onto a large tray. I placed Marie onto the counter, and she gazed, longingly, at the tray of cakes just out of her reach.

"Do you know if *Antwanet* is spelled with a *w*?" Crystal asked me as she noted my presence in the room.

"Or with two *t*'s?" asked the man beside her.

Apparently there was a debate raging over this, but, for my contribution, I only shrugged my shoulders indifferently. Rather, I greedily gulped a glass of juice, which provided no relief, but only scraped my throat as it passed over it.

"There's probably a dictionary in the upstairs library," I suggested.

This was an unforeseen flash of inspiration to which everyone immediately responded. The group arose in unison, and swarmed towards the library. But before Crystal could disappear, I called out to her.

"Is Dave here?" I asked.

"No, he left last night," she said in a straightforward tone. "With your *whore!*"

I could only shake my head in response. Jenn was not my whore, nor was she anyone else's, but I didn't have the strength to argue. I let Crystal leave, and simply asked the maid for a cup of strong coffee. I sat down and sipped it, with only Marie again for company. Crystal's remark should have sparked a flurry of strong emotions inside of me. But in my shattered condition, lingering pain was obscuring any other sensation that I might have possibly wished to feel.

"*Vhimen*," I offered Marie, "who needs them?"

Not until my third cup of coffee did I begin feeling somewhat better, or at least well enough to attempt the drive home. The maid too had vanished, and so before leaving I said my goodbyes only to Marie. It was a lonely trudge up the canyon road to where my car was parked. On reaching it I noticed that both headlights had been smashed out. I shook my head in disgust, wondering what else I might find. But everything else seemed undamaged until, sitting into the driver's seat, I was overwhelmed by the unmistakable smell of urine.

I hardly noticed the drive home, as I spent most of it fighting back a sense of nausea. On reaching my apartment, Jenn's car was nowhere to be seen. I made a straight line for my bed, and collapsed into it. I might have slept for the remainder of the week, had not the phone awoken me later that day, almost at twilight.

"Are you alright?" Libor's voice asked. "We are worried about you. Where did you go last night?"

Uncharacteristically, I told Libor that I was not alright. It was unlike me to burden others with my problems, but suddenly I felt the need to do so. I told Libor of what had happened since he'd last seen me. There was nothing that might be done about any of it of course. But, if nothing else, I felt better just to have told it to someone.

"You should call the police," Libor suggested.

But I already knew how the police would handle the matter, and decided not to waste my time. I also told Libor about everything else, including how I'd lost my internship at Ashton Tate, and how I'd probably also lost Jenn. By the time that I was through, I was on the verge of tears.

"Listen," said Libor trying to be helpful, "come work with me for a while, in the sunshine. It will be good for you."

I said that I would give it some thought. It was a kind offer which, over the course of the ensuing week, became more and more appealing, especially since I had little else to do. I thought further of Jenn and whether I should contact her, knowing that she would probably never call me again. She was gone. But in a strange way I did not miss her. There was no point in my trying to reclaim her, since she had never really been mine to begin with. Slowly I came to accept that, in a silent way, Jenn and I had finally said our goodbyes.

27.

Over the next week I made good on my promise to drive Monica to the airport. With her leaving it seemed that all of the acquaintances I'd knitted over the past year were slowly unraveling. I told Monica nothing of what I'd recently been through, but only wished her well for her new life on the East Coast.

"Your car smells bad," she observed on the way to the airport. "Did you get a dog?"

No, there was no dog. This was not the smell of dogs, but of wolves. And, as I watched Monica's turtle brown eyes disappear into the terminal, I hoped that she would meet chance few of them in New York City, which I knew to be a hard city, much harder than the City of Angels.

Later that same day found me cleaning my apartment, or what little there was of it. In going through my files I chanced across my copy of the Farinelli transcript. I wanted nothing more to do with it, and was about to throw it into the trash, when I thought better of it. I placed the pages into an envelope, with a brief explanation, and mailed them to the District Attorney's office, wanting to never see them again.

Eventually I did call Libor about his offer for work, and I discovered that he was right. The sunshine, fresh air, and hard labor were all good for me. I spent the subsequent weeks helping him cultivate the lawns of various hillside estates. He worked with a small crew of migrant Mexicans, and over the subsequent few weeks I gladly became one of them, even changing my name to the more Spanish sounding *'Pablo'*. We passed each day with almost the same routine – working in the cool morning mist, breaking for lunch, working in the hot afternoon sun, and then sharing a few cold beers. One day, after drinks, Libor suddenly turned contagiously wistful.

"Pablo, see this shovel?" he professed. "One man will use it to plant a tree. Another will hit you over the head with it."

"*Si, Libo*," I concurred. "But such is the way of the world, no?"

I was beginning to sound more like a philosopher than an attorney, and as the start of the fall semester drew closer, my heart began to sink. I was dreading my return to law school. To ease my troubled mind I took a long bike ride along the beach as I used to do. I pedaled the shore path for most of the day, bemused by the thought that, after almost a year in the City of Angels, the path of my life was still as uncertain as it had been when I'd first arrived.

The end of that day found me tired and spent, and seated under a palm tree staring towards the blue Pacific. By then the sun had begun to set, and I watched the sunset's display over the horizon as it transitioned the evening sky from blue to crimson, and finally to a deep indigo. There are many who find epiphanies in the golden sunrise of an early morning. But for me the truest inspiration has always been found in the sight of the stars, as they first appear in the evening sky. There, in the purple twilight, God sends us a daily reminder that, in spite of the trials of our everyday lives, there is also beauty, and peace. For the stars insist on bravely shining, despite the dark energy which is ever working to tear them apart. And in this message one can find purpose, and hope - if one has but the courage to do so.

The next day found me wandering through the university grounds. Students had already begun to appear in preparation for the upcoming semester. One could sense the campus stirring out of its deep summer slumber. Mentally I began to adjust myself to again adopting the monastic schedule that all good students must, come September. Only now I did not nurture the same optimism that had sustained me through the prior year.

Towards the end of that day I found myself on the north end of campus, near the physics building. Its doors were unlocked, and I wandered through it, until finally finding myself in the halls of the astrophysics department. The corridors there were lined with the photographs of famed cosmologists, all unknown to the general public, men who, like myself, had gotten the notion to gaze upwards and marvel at the stars above. I noticed a light shining from an office at the far end of the hallway, and in that office I found a lone rumpled figure, rummaging through a stack of papers.

"Can I help you?" asked the figure as I peered in.

"Perhaps," I responded. "Do you have a minute?"

I knew the figure, or knew of him, as during my undergraduate days I had read many of his publications. I hinted at my familiarity with his work so as to gain his sympathy, and he invited me in. We talked easily. I mentioned my past studies in the field and some of the latest theories that I'd been contemplating. He seemed interested, and actually provided me the long awaited feedback that I'd been trying to solicit from Jonathan. He quickly noted however that my theory was still incomplete, as I had suspected, and that it still required corroboration with the most recent far field observations of the galactic red shift.

For his part, my newly discovered mentor bemoaned about how so few students now seemed interested in astrophysics. These days the pull of the earth was too great, so much so that few cared to lift their eyes above it. As a result he had several available research stipends languishing from a dearth of applicants.

"I could arrange a small stipend for *you*," he suggested, "if you qualified."

This was a generous offer, and, to my surprise, my heart leapt at the thought of it. Were I but to pass the graduate entrance exams, then everything could be easily arranged. To earn the stipend I was also required to assist with undergraduate classes, a trivial matter really, and a light cross to bear. The graduate entrance exams for next spring's semester would be in October, and I left swearing that I would take them. I also promised to continue working on my theory until then, in my spare time.

The new fall semester began with a flurry of activity, as all semesters do. In those first few days there is much scurrying about as students busy themselves with renewing old friendships and adjusting to new routines. I too adjusted to my new schedule, and renewed my old friendships. But I dreaded seeing Bryce Davis again, and luckily, except for one class on legal ethics, our schedules did not overlap much. The ethics class was sufficiently large that I could usually seat myself away from him, although on one occasion I found myself arriving late, with the only available seat being next to his. We exchanged nods and glances as I awaited him yet again proclaiming me to be a fool. But apparently his attitude towards me had softened.

"You know," he only said at length, "you really did pass up a good opportunity."

I nodded a silent response, and we let the matter rest at that. The ensuing semester then transpired as though but a dream. I found myself to be a part of it, but somehow detached from it. By then the Robinson trial had gotten full underway. A jury had been selected, and the actual judicial proceedings had begun. The trial received substantial media coverage of course, and as I followed the daily reports, it seemed as though I were watching a film for which I had already read the script. Barring any new unforeseen evidence, the outcome of the trial had been already guaranteed, I knew, by the screenwriters at Ashton Tate.

****

In October I successfully completed the astrophysics graduate entrance exams, after which, through all of November, my law studies then took on the form of a mere formality. By early December I was already looking forward to spending my Christmas holidays back East when, unexpectedly, the District Attorney's office sequestered me to testify in the Robinson trial.

I surmised that the District Attorney's options had run thin, and calling me as a late witness was either a final act of due diligence, or one of complete desperation. They wanted me to testify about the authenticity of the Farinelli transcript which I, in the hopes of never seeing it again, had sent them. I suspected that my testimony would be irrelevant, but agreed to do so mostly on principles. There were no other bridges with Ashton Tate left for me to burn, but now only charred remains, which I could further submerge into murky waters.

I wore my old woolen suit for my court appearance, hoping that it might impart a tinge of credibility onto my testimony. From my seat on the witness stand, my gaze fell squarely onto Robinson. He was flanked at the defendant's table by both Andrew Jackson and Elliot Reichert. Robinson's stare had not warmed in the least since I'd last seen him. But I now dutifully returned it in kind.

On the stand I was asked to describe my recording of Bambi Farinelli's original testimony, the one which had clearly left Bruce Robinson without an alibi for roughly an hour on the night of the murder. I gave what I thought to be an accurate account. But all testimonies require corroboration, otherwise they are nothing more than hearsay, and unacceptable in a court of law. In this case however, only Bambi Farinelli could have provided such corroboration.

"And is this Ms. Farinelli's signature on the document?" the prosecuting attorney asked me.

"Yes, it is," I affirmed.

"And do you swear to the authenticity of this transcript?" he asked.

"I do swear to it," I said, my eyes fixed precisely onto Robinson.

The prosecutor then had no further questions, and the defense was given license to cross examine. But Jackson declined. Instead he called Bambi Farinelli as a witness. She made her way to the stand with well measured poise, sat down, and took her oath. Then, with a surge of energy, she proceeded to denounce my entire testimony. The correct declaration she maintained was the one prepared by a certain Agnes Cook, and then subsequently submitted into the court records. That was the true account, as she had already testified weeks earlier.

But there was still the matter of Bambi's signature onto my transcript.

"Do you recall signing this other document," Jackson asked her.

"No, I do not recall it," she elocuted. "That is not my signature."

Jackson displayed a copy of each document, and then asked to approach the bench.

"Your Honor," he said, "let the court records show that the signatures on these two documents are clearly *different!*"

From my seat in the gallery, I was not able to see the actual signatures, but I did see that the judge concurred with Jackson's assertion. I surmised that the signatures were indeed different, which only left me to shake my head and smile at the thoroughness of Ashton Tate's handiwork. Jackson then had no further questions for Ms. Farinelli. As she stepped down from the stand, I realized that Bruce Robinson's investment in her acting lessons had been finally justified. Only her words and not her delivery would be recorded in the court transcripts. But she had delivered her lines well, and their effect on the jury had been complete. My own testimony had been invalidated.

I was anticipating that the court would then recess for the day, when one more witness, Agnes Cook, was called to the stand. I was curious as to what further testimony Agnes could possibly provide. But as Jackson proceeded to question her, it became clear that he was leaving nothing to chance. She corroborated Bambi Farinelli's assertions, and proposed that the document which I had produced might possibly have been a forgery.

"And why would Paul Gudsen wish to forge such a document?" inquired Jackson.

"I don't know. Perhaps he was bitter about his dismissal from the firm," Agnes speculated.

"He was dismissed from Ashton Tate?" Jackson asked. "Do you know why?"

"Yes, he was dismissed for poor work habits," said Agnes. "For constant tardiness, to be exact."

"For tardiness?" asked Jackson.

"Yes," Agnes confirmed. "He was always coming to work late, and sometimes not at all."

"And so, do you think that his forged transcript might possibly be an act of revenge for his dismissal?" proposed Jackson.

But with this last question Jackson had stepped far beyond the bounds of proper procedure, and the prosecuting attorney quickly took note.

"Objection, Your Honor! Defense is clearly leading the witness!" the prosecuting attorney shouted. "Not to mention that Mr. Gudsen's motivations are not on trial here. That last question is irrelevant, and should be stricken."

The judge concurred, and he ordered Jackson's last question to be stricken from the record. But the damage had been done, and sufficient implied taint had been smeared onto my personal character that Ashton Tate's victory was complete. My testimony had been discounted, my credibility had been nullified, and, of course, Ashton Tate had prevailed.

I shook my head again, this time in sad disbelief of how the scales of Justice were so easily tipped. But honestly though, I no longer cared about Ashton Tate, or about Andrew Jackson, or about the many webs which he so easily spun. I glanced about the courtroom to see if perhaps Nicole Robinson's visage might be looming somewhere in the gallery, still seeking justice. But she was nowhere to be found, and I suspected that, like me, she too had moved on to the pursuit of better things.

28.

In the ensuing weeks, I sought to put all matters related to the Robinson trial, or to Ashton Tate, or to Jenn, squarely behind me. But, flying back East just a few days before Christmas, I still felt crushed by disappointment. Seemingly, I was now retracing my steps to almost their starting point of the previous year. Of my fifteen months in the City of Angels I had little tangible accomplishments to show for my time spent there. On the morning that I first awoke back in my parents' house, with the winter frost already nestled into the lawns outside my window, the various events of those many months seemed as though nothing more than a vivid dream.

But the cold days of the Eastern winter can produce a healing effect. Through the dormant trees and the grey cloudy days which beckon sleep, nature suggests to us a long sabbatical in which to rest and restore our spirits before the coming spring. Both snow and Christmas were in the air, and they imbued me with a traditional holiday mood which the sun filled days of the West Coast never could. On Christmas Day, as my mother busied herself with the family dinner preparations, my father and I shared a few sips of brandy.

"We're all proud of you for testifying," he said. "You did the right thing."

I was glad to hear of the old man's support, but it was the obtaining of my mother's approval which truly concerned me. She had ever dreamed that our family should include, like the old proverb, a doctor, a lawyer, and an Indian chief. My older brother had gone on to manage the family business, making him the Indian chief, while my sister had brought a doctor into the family by marrying one. This left me as the last missing piece of the puzzle.

After Christmas dinner I watched my father as he gleefully played grandfather to my sister's children. My Indian chief brother had also married, and now he and his squaw, noticeably and happily pregnant, were expecting their first child. His wife seemed the type of woman who could easily produce as many children as one desired, and I had little doubt that my parents' home would be filled with ever more grandchildren as the years progressed. I was starting to feel like the family's black sheep, when my mother approached me. She rested her head onto my shoulder, and wrapped an arm around my waist. Perhaps she had already heard that I would forsake law school for the pull of the stars, for she suddenly spoke with a very resigned tone.

"My poor son," she said wistfully, "my poor wayward son."

She sounded as though I'd been lost to the service of some esoteric priesthood. But I consoled her with the thought that, regardless of my future, I would always be her son, her youngest, unpredictable, and somewhat mischievous little boy.

The next day, with everyone gone, my parents' home suddenly felt so cold and empty that I was overcome with a desire to seek out those familiar acquaintances of my youth. But as most of them had moved on to other towns, and on to other lives, there were none to be found. This part of my youth too began to seem as but a dream.

But a few days remained until my return West, and it occurred to me that I might make contact with Jonathan Schwarzchild before leaving. I reached him through his father's firm, and we made arrangements to meet after work at a bar in lower Manhattan. I remember that it was chill and windy on that particular day, with the dim canyons of the financial district, almost barren at the year's end, offering little warmth as respite. I was already onto my second drink when Jonathan eventually appeared, with a blonde, gum chewing companion in tow. Jonathan had changed greatly since I'd last seen him. He was now clean shaven for one thing, and was dressed in a broad shouldered suit, his hair slicked back and smelling of money.

"Where's Monica?" I asked.

I learned, apparently, that he and Monica were no longer together. She had found the dingy doorways of New York City, and perhaps this new version of Jonathan, not to her particular liking. And so she had gone back to Los Angeles. In her place there was now this new girl, garnered from the firm's secretarial pool. With her seemingly blonde hair piled voluminously atop her head, I was certain that her ears were being kept sufficiently warm on this particular day. But unfortunately for her legs, left exposed from her upper thighs down to her heels by a high cut skirt, they must have been freezing.

"Chamm'd", she said, extending a chilled hand towards me.

By all appearances things were going well for Jonathan. The financial boom had not yet lost any of its potency, and so it was a simple matter for him to merely place phone calls, or receive them, wherein people would then gladly exchange their life savings for whichever dubiously valued shares of corporate stock were recommended them. For performing this arduous service, Jonathan received substantial compensation, sufficient enough that in only three months he had stockpiled the funds necessary for the down payment on a nearby condominium apartment.

"Our firm is always looking for attorneys," he advised. "Just let me know when you're ready."

I informed him that I was no longer in pursuit of a law degree, but, should his firm be in need of an astrophysicist, then I would be more than happy to oblige. He seemed shocked to hear of my changed curricula, but I explained that I no longer had any doubts. There was no future in law, at least not for me. He understood of course. But he also wished me luck, as one might to any gambler about to enter the confines of a notorious casino.

Jonathan and his escort were en route to a party uptown, and before leaving he graciously offered to pay the drink tab. With a flourish he produced a fold of bills, large enough to choke two proverbial horses, from his front pocket. As he peeled off enough money for the tab and a sizable tip, Jonathan explained how he now always enjoyed having at least a thousand dollars handy.

"Aren't you afraid that you might lose that?" I asked.

"He already did, once," explained his date between snaps of gum. "But he just went back to the bank and got more."

Outside, the chill air had grown no less severe, and in the fading light I escorted Jonathan and Michelle, that was her name, to the nearest subway stop, watching as they disappeared into the warmth of an underground tunnel. I had driven my father's car into the city, and as I returned to Long Island I toyed with the notion of finding a joyous party of my own to attend. Back in my home town I stopped into a tavern that I had frequented during the carefree days of my youth, hoping to spot a familiar face. But there were none, and, after two lonely drinks, I returned home, or rather to my parents' home, for my home, it seemed, was no longer here.

****

My parents pleaded that I stay through New Year's Day, but I had already made plans to fly back before then. As for New Year's Eve I suspected that my siblings had cemented their own agendas, with their own friends. This would have left me to serve as my parents' caretaker for that night, a duty which invariably would have involved me waking them in their chairs for the ceremonial midnight toast. Much better I thought if we all simply got a good night's sleep on that particular eve, each of us on our respective coasts, without any feeble attempts at worn pretense.

And so I found myself that New Year's Eve back in the warm and sunny air of the City of Angels. I was in my apartment, doing and thinking nothing in particular when the phone rang. It was Monica, wondering if I had any plans for that evening.

"No," I told her. "I'm free for the rest of the year."

As a result Monica and I found ourselves spending that evening downtown for the so called First Night's celebration. There were street performers, and live music, and throngs of people. As the midnight countdown progressed, we found ourselves pressed together by the sizable crowd. At midnight, when we had no choice but to kiss, I felt warmed inside by the soft glow of Monica's caring brown eyes. I kissed her, and then again, and smiled, thankful that she had called me. There were also fireworks after midnight, and by the time that we'd returned to Monica's new apartment near downtown, it was well past two into the New Year.

"Do you have to leave?" she asked. "It's such a long drive and, it's late, you know."

No, I did not have to leave. It was the first day of the New Year, and there was no reason for either of us to be spending it alone. As we walked to her door I glanced up at the night sky, now clear and brimming with stars. My old friend Orion had resumed his rightful place in the winter sky. As I pointed him out to Monica, she began reciting an innocent nursery rhyme from the days of her youth. And I listened to it, suddenly enraptured by the gentle chords of her voice.

Brilla, brilla estrellita
Un milagro tan bonita

Muy lejana yo te canto
Un diamante en el cielo

Brilla, brilla estrellita
Un milagro, tan bonita

"That's lovely," I said. "How does it translate?"

"Easy," she said. "It goes something like this…."

Shine on, shine on little star
Such a wonder from afar

To you gladly do I cry
Like a diamond in the sky

Shine on, shine on little star
Such a wonder from afar….

Epilogue

As the months of the New Year unfolded I found myself spending more time with Monica. She was easy and enjoyable company, and when we were together it seemed as though hardly anything else really mattered. She was also well familiar with the trials faced by a struggling physicist. And so, as I plunged myself further into my research, I did so with her full support and understanding. Eventually we found ourselves making plans to share a new apartment together.

The small stipend that I received as a teaching assistant was exactly that, small, so much so that I also took a part time job waiting tables for some extra income. Hence, between my studies, my time spent with Monica, and my two jobs, my days became exceptionally filled. I still found time to meet with Laura and Libor on occasion, but as for my other acquaintances, I simply let them naturally wither from purposeful neglect.

Out of morbid curiosity I would search for *Bouncing to the Classics* whenever I chanced into a video store. But, for whatever reason, a copy of it was never to be found, and, of Crystal and Jack Engels, I heard no more. Bruce Robinson of course was a different matter. In February, the trial attorneys finally concluded their closing arguments, and by March, after a longer than expected jury deliberation, Robinson at last received the acquittal which Ashton Tate had promised him.

Although now tinged with notoriety, Robinson did once again occasionally appear in the popular tabloids, usually pictured with a different escort each time. I began to wonder what might have become of Bambi Farinelli, until one day I spotted her image, splashed in pink, on an advertisement hung across the length of a cross-town bus. The advertisement promoted a new energy drink, *Pink Power*, which, it claimed, had been formulated especially for the active woman. I looked for this advertisement whenever a commuter bus chanced by, hoping to discover that perhaps a second version had also been formulated, for use by active pink dogs.

But as for Dave and Jenn, and myself, the distance which grew between us could probably have been measured in light years. While waiting tables one evening I thought that I'd spied them seated across from the area I was working. But by the time I could again glance their way, they were no longer there. I had effectively given up on ever seeing them again when, in the late spring, I received an unexpected call from Jenn. Her father had passed away, and she wondered if I could possibly attend the funeral.

"I think he would have wanted you there," she suggested.

I made the subsequent drive to the Eden Ranch with many mixed emotions. The thought of again seeing Dave Richards and Jenn Devaine filled me with an unexpected anxiety. But I was committed to attending this funeral, and it was only through mental manipulations that I managed to settle my feelings. Instead of thinking of Dave, I thought of Mr. Devaine. It was, after all, his funeral. And rather than thinking of Jenn, I substituted calming thoughts of Monica instead.

The funeral itself was sparsely attended. Besides Jenn, Dave, and myself, there were a few ancient cousins who had made the trek from Nevada, and a few of the local neighbors. But surprisingly, Mr. Devaine's funeral was not attended by Mr. Devaine himself. Instead, at an appointed time, I found myself, along with the rest of the mourning party, standing on the grounds of the Eden Ranch, staring towards the north end of the property. A small prop plane then appeared, and, as it flew across the line of the north ridge, it let out a wisp of dust, presumably Mr. Devaine's ashes, into the warm afternoon air. The wisp of ash assumed the form of a last parting smile, and lingered momentarily, before forever disappearing into the wind.

After a moment of silence we all went inside, where a small buffet had been prepared. I collected a few bits onto a plate and went out to the porch, to where Mr. Devaine and I had once sat. The grounds of the Eden Ranch were beginning to heal from the ravages of last summer's fires. Green shoots now covered large patches once previously red with fire retardant. I stared out at the grounds, so lost in thought that I did not notice that Dave Richards had come out to join me.

"Would make a heck of a golf course, don't you think?" he said, staring out with me.

I imagined how in Dave's mind he had already plotted out the entire project. There would be overnight lodgings up on the ridge, the course itself would spread out before us, and where we now stood, a restaurant and clubhouse. I learned from Dave that Jenn had decided to sell the property, as she really had no interest in it. In fact, with Crystal gone, Jenn and Ariel had moved themselves permanently to Dave's estate.

"After selling this property, she'll be a made woman," observed Dave.

When it was time for goodbyes, I found myself standing uncomfortably before the soon to be made woman. While I struggled for something benign to say, she reached out to me, and we made our truce with a final farewell embrace. Dave for his part offered me a firm handshake, and we made plans to meet again for a future game of squash, although I suspected that we actually never would. Before leaving the Eden Ranch I snuck away a small cutting from the thorn patch which still grew behind the house, with the intent to keep it, irrational I know, as a small reminder of Mr. Devaine, or even, of life itself.

On the return trip I stopped at Monica's apartment, and we spent the night together. The next morning, still the weekend, I returned to my own place and gathered a few books for a ride along the beach. I rode to the Santa Monica pier and stared at the Pacific, still so full of promise and hope. To the south, the shore path wound easily through the lazy beach communities, while to the north the path wound towards the many deep folds of the Malibu hills. I checked my legs, and they felt surprisingly strong that day. And so, drawing a deep breath, I pointed my bike firmly northwards, and made my way into the hills.

THE END

Notes

Notes

Notes

www.ingramcontent.com/pod-product-compliance
Lightning Source LLC
LaVergne TN
LVHW091026080826
845145LV00002B/365

* 9 7 8 0 6 1 5 6 0 5 0 9 8 *